Calexit
-The Anthology-

Collected by JL Curtis

Author's Note: This is a work of fiction. Names, characters, places, and incidents are a product of the author's imagination. Locales and public names are sometimes used for atmospheric purposes. Any resemblance to actual people, living or dead, or to businesses, companies, events, institutions, or locales is completely coincidental.

Published by JLC&A. Available from Amazon.com in Kindle format or soft cover book. Printed by CreateSpace.

Calexit-The Anthology/ JL Curtis. -- 1st ed.
ISBN-13: 978-1978308329
ISBN-10: 1978308329

DEDICATION

To those who put their lives on the line every day, at every level, caring for and protecting their fellow man. Volunteer, paid, active or reserves, every one of them deserves all credit.

ACKNOWLEDGMENTS

Thanks to the usual suspects.

Special thanks to my editor, Stephanie Martin.

Cover art by Tina Garceau.

Table of Contents

Prologue

This collection is from a number of different authors, based on discussions after I published my original novella, The Morning the Earth Shook. We created a very 'loose' working world, if you will, with few parameters that the authors had to adhere to. After that, it was up to the individual authors to write their stories, as they saw them happening.

Editor's Note:
While I tried to keep things as consistent as possible, I deliberately left certain things alone. So we have the Republic of Cali, the State of Cali, the Nation of Cali. All of the names represent one thing: a broken and corrupt state. The stories, which all came in piecemeal, have, perhaps to no surprise, a consistent theme of a struggle for freedom, in whatever form the individual author chose to manifest it. Mr. Curtis did a masterful job in arranging these stories into a flow that create a coherent overall tale and it was my pleasure to be a very small part of this project.

This is the result of that collaboration- May I present Calexit- The Anthology.

A Matter of Honor

J L Curtis

Attention to Orders

October 2022 was off to a good start. Commander Mike James, the token SEAL on 7th Fleet's staff, escorted his petite, still attractive wife Trisha, and son Mike Jr., or 'Mikey', as he was known, through the security gate. Taking them up the brow, and onboard the flagship sitting in Yokosuka harbor, he saluted the watch, asking permission to come aboard. The young Lieutenant JG returned the salute, welcoming them aboard. Turning toward the stern, Mike took them to the Seventh Fleet access, opening the wooden door inset in the watertight door frame, and warning, "Remember, Navy ship. Gotta step *over* the coaming."

Trish glanced around and stuck her tongue out at him, "Yes, dear. You'd think I've never been aboard a ship before." Mikey just shook his head, following his mother through the hatch and making sure it was closed behind him. At seventeen years old, he was as tall as his dad, and had the same wiry build. He was a starter on the basketball team, but knew his career in the sport would be over when he graduated.

Mike pointed up and Trish sighed, "I know, I know, this is why I don't wear dresses on ships, or high heels." Mike admired her still shapely rear end as she started up the steep ladder, noting she was careful to hold on to the handrails, and Mike motioned to Mikey to go next. He went last, and followed them to another watertight door, looking through the porthole before he opened it. Leading them down the passageway, he stopped in the Flag Aide's office, "LT, how far behind is the admiral today?"

Lieutenant Angie Pierce looked up, "He's actually on time. He'll be ready for you as soon as he gets off this phone call," glancing at the multi-timezone clock on the bulkhead, she continued, "It's with Pac Fleet, and it's scheduled for thirty minutes, so if you want to wait in the mess, I'll come get you."

"That works, thanks!" Leading them further down the passageway, he turned down a cross passage, and into the flag mess, automatically going for a cup of coffee, as he waved to the Chief in charge of the mess. Mikey went for a glass of fruit drink, more commonly known as bug juice, and Mike shook his head, 'Really?"

Mikey shrugged, "I like it. It kinda tastes like Gatorade."

Carrying two cups of coffee, he went back to where Trish had sat down, and passed one across to her. The Chief came over, "Need some milk or sugar, Mrs. J?"

Trish smiled up at him, "No thanks, Chief. I've been a Navy wife too many years. Hot, black, and nasty, or not at all. Is Lois going to make the PTA meeting tomorrow night?"

"Yes, ma'am. She's a little worried about taking over as the president, but I keep telling her to just be herself."

LT Pierce opened the door and stuck her head in, "Commander, he's ready for y'all now."

Mike went to pick up the cups, and the Chief said, "Go ahead sir, I got these. And congratulations."

"Thanks, Chief, I think…"

Vice Admiral Larry Mann, Commander, Seventh Fleet, stood up and came around the desk as the lieutenant escorted Mike and his family in, "Mike, Trish, great to see you. Michael, that was a helluva catch and touchdown Thursday night. You saved the game with that one."

Mikey blushed a little, stammering, "Uh, thank you, sir. I was just in the right place, I guess."

The admiral smiled, "You did that with preparation, and keeping your head up and looking for the ball!" He was interrupted by the chief of staff coming in, "Bear, come on in. You remember Trish and Michael?"

Captain Williams smiled, "Of course. Welcome to our humble abode."

The staff photographer's mate came in, camera in hand, and said, "In front of your desk, or the map, Admiral?"

The admiral glanced at the map and said, "Um, let's make it in front of the desk, with the flags in the background." After the photographer's mate got everyone where she wanted them, she stepped back and nodded, and the admiral said, "Lieutenant, if you would…"

LT Pierce handed the admiral two eagle insignia, and he handed one to Trish, as he nodded. The aide picked up the blue binder, "Attention to orders…" She read the promotion order. Then the admiral and Trish, then Trish and Michael mimed pinning on the captain's insignia on Mike, as the photographer snapped pictures.

Over coffee and a piece of cake, delivered by the mess Chief, along with a glass of bug juice for Mikey, the admiral said, "I'm proud of you Mike, below zone, first increment. That's pretty impressive." Nodding at the ribbons and the Trident on his uniform, he continued, "But obviously well deserved. I was half expecting you to show up in BDUs today," turning to Trish he said, "I'm assuming this is your doing?"

Trish laughed, "Khakis I could manage, I'm not sure Mike even has a set of whites here." Everyone laughed, and she said, "I know where *one* set of choker whites are, I think…"

More laughter erupted, and Captain Williams said, "Figures. I don't think I've ever even *seen* Mike in a set of whites, but I've only been here a year."

Mike put his hand over his heart, "I'm wounded, wounded I tell you. The slings and arrows I endure. Bear, if you remember, I actually wore whites to your change of command. Now I know you boat drivers have some memory issues…"

The admiral interrupted, "Before you start slandering aviators, along with boat drivers, I do need to let you know you're going to be on orders next month or so."

All three of the James' looked at the admiral, "You're getting Naval Special Warfare Group One in San Diego. Change of command will be right after the first of the year."

Mike and Trish exchanged glances, with Trish shaking her head slowly. The admiral cocked his head, and Mike finally said, "Captain Holt has some serious medical issues. He's already undergone chemo, and he must have had a reoccurrence. I've known Lee for almost twenty years, and Trish and Beth…"

The aide stuck her head in the door, "Sorry Admiral, Comman… Captain James, there is a secure call for you in Ops. It's from your Joint Task Force folks in the Philippines."

***

January 14th, 2023 dawned clear and reasonably warm, all of 58 degrees. Mikey was already up and out the door for school, riding his bike and promising not to mess up his clothes before Trish picked him up at ten for the change of command. Mike sat in the kitchen of their little blue house on I street, sipping coffee and pondering life and its meaning. Today should have been the happiest day of his life, getting a major command, but it was tinged with sadness. Lee Holt had lost over twenty pounds, and looked like he was 70 years old, but he'd come in most days, filling Mike in on the changes that had been going on for the last two years. Budgets, deployments, manpower, equipment, and the myriad of other issues at the group level had consumed them day in and day out.

Regretfully, Mike knew this was the end of his ability to get in the field with his sailors and earn his trident every day. Now the earning would be done a different, less satisfying way, by protecting his sailors from the vagaries of the elephants in major commands.

The saving grace, if there was one, was Master Chief Operator Jimmy Cameron. He'd taken over as the command master chief a few months earlier, and he and Mike went back almost twenty years. They'd been in the same platoon, then the same team when Mike had been CO of Team One, and master chief had been his team chief. He knew he'd get the straight skinny from him, and the master chief was not a yes man, so he'd keep Mike in check. Finishing his coffee, he got up, "Hon, I'm going to get dressed and go on in. You're going to pick Mikey up at ten, then come straight to the base, right?"

Trish stuck her head around the door, exasperated, "Yes, dear. Just like we have already discussed three times this morning. Honestly Mike, you don't really sound like you want this."

"Oh, I want it. I just wish... Well, I wish it was under better circumstances."

"Beth and I talked last night, she said you being here has helped Lee, given him a second wind. She said he's going to check into Balboa on Monday and start another round of chemo. Oh, have you heard anything about any protests at the gate?"

Mike gave her a quick hug, "No. There are some protests up north at the bases, but I haven't heard of anything down here. We upped the security patrols, both for the compound and for SURFOR[1], but it's been quiet. We had a courtesy call with Admiral Clayborn last week, and we're still at Bravo, with random Charlie days at least once a week. I made sure today was going to be Bravo, with all the visitors we have coming."

***

Captain Holt stood tall in his dress blues at the podium, and read his orders for his retirement, then turned to Mike, "I am ready to be relieved, sir."

Mike, moved his sword out of the way, and stepped up in his place, "I will now read my orders. From Chief of Naval Operations to Captain Michael James, change duty orders 113022. When directed by a reporting senior, detach from standing Navy command element, U.S. 7th Fleet. Report to Rear Admiral Hector Garcia, Naval Special Warfare Command for duty as commander, Naval Special Warfare Group One." Mike stepped back, turned and saluted Captain Lee Holt, "I relieve you, sir." He turned to the senior SEAL in the Navy, Rear Admiral Garcia, and said, "I am reporting for duty, sir."

RADM Garcia saluted and replied, "Very well."

Master Chief Cameron and his flag team took down the command pennant streamer, and it was presented to Captain Holt, as Mike's new command pennant streamer was run up the flag pole. After everyone was seated, Mike gave a few words about continuation of orders, his happiness to be back *home* as he wished Lee the best in his retirement. After the

---

[1] SURface FORces

colors were retired, there was the usual glad handing, congratulations, and a cake and punch for all hands.

Due to Lee's condition, they had decided not to do a formal reception, and Mike was actually thankful for that, as Lee sat under a corner of the sun shade, Beth at his side. Getting Master Chief Cameron's attention, he motioned off to the side, and they walked over to the smoke pit. Jimmy Cameron immediately fired up one of his noxious stogies, and Mike said quietly, "Lee's hurting, but he'll stay here till the last SEAL leaves. I don't want to unnecessarily rush things…"

"I'll handle it. You make the admiral go away, I got the rest. Good on ya for the short speech. I hate long winded assho… officers," he said with a smile.

Mike shook his head, "Dammit, Jimmy…"

Cameron laughed, "Gotcha. I've known you for your entire career. I'm actually proud of you, but don't let that shit go to your head."

"Thank you." Mike turned and walked back to the sun shade and the folks gathered there. RADM Garcia motioned him over, "Captain, we need to have a short meeting. Can we use your secure conference room?"

"Certainly, sir. Who do you want there?"

"You, Captain Ackerman, and Commander Simmons."

Mike looked around and saw the master chief coming, "Master Chief, we need to use the secure conference room."

"On it, sir."

Mike walked over to Trish and Mikey, "Sorry, looks like I have to go to work." Hugging Trish he said, "I'll see you at home later, okay?"

Trish kissed him on the cheek, "Okay. I'll pick up something for dinner."

Mikey said, "Congrats, Dad. I guess I'm proud of you too."

Mike put his hand over his heart, "Be still my heart, my boy actually complimented me!" He smiled and said softly, "Thank you, son. That means a lot. Now y'all get out of here."

RADM Garcia sat at the head of the conference table in the SCIF, watching quietly as Mike came in, "We're good to go, sir."

Leaning forward, the admiral said, "This is… TS… I'm not coming back here, Special Warfare Command will remain in McDill for the foreseeable future, due to the Calexit nonsense. Captain Ackerman, I want you to relocate to Hawaii with Group Three, as soon as possible, and as quietly as possible." Turning to face Mike, he continued, "Captain, I know this is your first day, and I'm dumping a helluva load on you, but I need you to take up the slack for us being gone. You're also not getting Team Five back, they are going to stay in Bremerton."

Mike rocked back in his chair, "So I'll be down to one and seven?"

"And the reserves. We're going to increase Team Seventeen's drill cycle, along with HSC[2] Eighty-Five, since those two drill together all the time."

"Yes, sir."

The admiral looked at Commander Simmons, "Commander, status on your SEAL support boats?"

---

[2] Helicopter Sea Control

CDR Simmons cleared his throat, "Ah, 'bout eighty-six percent avail on a given day, sir. Mostly awaiting parts, no real major issues."

The admiral leaned back in his chair, "Have your supply officer give me a list of your needs before I leave today. I want you one hundred percent up, or as close as you can get. If you've got a boat that is hard down, not repairable in a timely fashion, I want it out at San Clemente, I don't care if you have to tow it out there. And if you do, do it in the middle of the night."

CDR Simmons started to answer, but the admiral cut him off, "Not negotiable."

"Yes, sir."

The admiral sat up, "There's intel that the whole Calexit thing is going left. Apparently Brown is getting ready to open the borders with Mexico, and no immigration policy will be put in place. It will be a totally open border. I don't think that is going to end well. I've also talked with General Ericson at Pendleton, he's going to *loan* you eight up armored Hummers to augment the four you already have. I saw where you've increased the security patrols, but I want you to take it a step further. I want one squad on four hour alert, and one platoon on twelve hour alert, and enough SWCCs and boats to support operations, including Mark Fives. I also want cadre to have armed cover when they are running BUDS classes."

Mike winced, "Admiral, that's a helluva load to add to our ongoing…"

"Understood, but it's not an option. If I had my way, we'd be at Charlie for force protection already, and ready to go to Delta in minutes. I think we're going to be there before long, anyway. I'd also recommend married folks look at getting dependents out of California sooner, rather than later."

Everyone looked at each other in silence for a minute, then Captain Ackerman said, "Is it really looking that bad?"

The admiral scrubbed his face, "Yeah, it's really looking that bad. I'm hoping... Well, I'm hoping it doesn't get to that."

Tensions Rising

Captain James leaned back in his chair at the head of the conference table, and sipped his coffee thoughtfully, "Anybody else?"

As if on cue, the secure phone at his elbow rang, and he looked down at it in surprise, before picking it up, "Group One, Captain James, may I help you? Yes admiral, I'll wait."

People started picking up their notebooks and coffee cups, but Mike said, "Hold on. Let's see what this is about."

The phone finished going through the security routine and he said, "I show you secure, sir. What can I do for you?" Shifting the phone to his other ear, he quickly wrote on the pad at the phone, listening for a couple of minutes before finally saying, "Yes, sir. We'll look at that again. I know the report was sent up through channels." A moment later he replied, "No, sir. It was filed the next morning. They were coming back from San Clemente after weapons training." Another pause, "Yes, sir. We'll open a formal investigation. Thank you for the heads up, sir."

He hung the phone up gently, and rubbed his face with both hands, before looking at the groups around the table, "Well, the Brownies have filed an attempted murder charge against person or persons unknown on Navy warship number seven for attempting to murder innocent fishermen who were attempting to get a disabled boat to shore last Friday evening."

CDR Simmons rolled his eyes, "Oh for fuck's sake… Those assholes attempted to land by the bunkers in the middle of a night training op for the latest BUDS class."

Mike held up a hand, "I know, I know." Glancing at LCDR Villanueva, he continued, "Ramp up the legal side. This will be a full blown investigation. Get with SURFOR and see if you can get a senior officer and senior enlisted craftmasters for the team. Talk to EOD and get one of their weapons guys too. I don't want *any* SEALS or SWCCs[3] involved. Make sure they get copies of all the videos, and set up for them to observe the original, plus interviews."

LCDR Villanueva looked up from his notes, "Got it, sir. I'll get right on that."

Looking at CDR Simmons, he said, "Pull that crew and cadre off rotation, and put seven boat in the shed for now. Make sure the guns are the same ones that were on it that night."

"Yes, sir."

Scrubbing his face again, he said, "Okay, I guess that's it. Back to the salt mines folks." Picking up his coffee cup and notepad, he walked out of the secure conference room and leaned against the master chief's desk. Glancing around to ensure they were alone, he asked, "You getting anything on this shit going on with the Brownshirts and *La Raza*?"

Master Chief Cameron leaned back, "Nothing but rumors that they're tied together at the hip. Can't get any proof, but the Brownies seem to show up just about any time *La Raza* or the illegals throw a pop up riot."

---

[3] Special Warfare Combatant-Craft operators

"You got Dot out, right?"

"Yeah, remember Senior Chief Menendez? Married the little Viet girl?"

"Craftmaster? Wasn't her name Anna or something like that?"

"That's him. He left a couple of weeks ago, heading to Houston. 'Pears her family has shrimp boats down there, so they hauled butt. I sent Dot with them, in my truck, loaded with the important stuff and my guns. Their boy helped with the driving, and she drove on into Stone Mountain the next day. I told her not to plan on coming back. You been able to…"

Mike waved his hand, "No, Trish isn't leaving, and Mikey wants to finish school here. But come June, I'll take them out myself if it comes to that."

"Smart move. What's this about murder charges?"

"That boat crew that ran off the idiots trying to beach down by the bunkers. Apparently there is now a dip protest and they want people arrested and tried for murder, for firing ahead of the boat."

Master Chief Cameron laughed, "I take it you never saw the video then."

"Video?"

"Yeah, one of the cadre filmed the whole thing. If you've got a minute…"

"Shit… Yes, can you put it up in the conference room?"

"Sure." Hopping up, the master chief led the way back into the conference room, went to the computer on the side desk, and brought it up. Hitting the overhead projector control, he turned the volume down, "Gets a tad noisy when the fifty goes off."

Twenty minutes, and a number of reviews and zooms later, Mike was shaking his head, "Unbelievable. Fishermen my ass. The video shows bolt cutters, a cutting torch, and who knows what else. They were either going to rob a bank, or try to crack a bunker. We *should* be giving them at least a letter of commendation. They didn't believe them after the *first* set of warning shots, and the gunner only ate up a few inches of the front of the boat. There wasn't anybody within four or five feet of those rounds."

The master chief laughed, "And did you notice how they left under full power? I think that Brownie had brown stains in his pants, too."

"Probably…"

***

Mike and Trish sat in the stands as the last half of the last basketball game of the year got underway. Coronado versus Chula Vista was usually a pretty good game, and tonight was proving to be no exception. The lead had never been more than two points in either direction. What was unusual was the number of police, Brownshirts, and other LEOs in the gym. The crowd had been separated from the git go, with officers directing people in one door or the other at the start. They had even opened two concessions to keep the crowd apart, and a line of officers stood behind the Coronado bench to keep the Chula Vista fans from hitting or throwing things at them. Mike spent more time watching the crowds than he did the game, even when Mikey got in the game at the end of the third quarter. Coronado was up by four points, and it was starting to get ugly.

He heard Trish gasp, and yanked his attention back to the court, as Mikey went diving after a ball on the sideline and ending up in the Chula Vista crowd. One of the police officers hauled him out, and they saw blood streaming down his chin. Mike started up, but Trish grabbed his arm, "No, sit." Mike sat back down grudgingly, as Mikey walked back to the bench, blood dripping between his fingers. A medic came in from the hall, took one look, and led him out of the gym.

Mike and Trish got up and headed for the exit, brushing by the policeman standing at the door, "That's my son. I want to know what is going on." Outside they found Mikey sitting on a stretcher, tears in his eyes, as another medic looked at his lip. Mike walked up, "That's my son. How bad is it?"

The medic stood up, "He's going to need stitches. It's a puncture, all the way through, just under the lip. Couple of teeth are loose. We can take him to the hospital…"

Mike shook his head, "No, I'll take him to Balboa." Looking down at Mikey he asked, "Where is your stuff?"

Mikey, spitting blood, said, "Locker room."

The team's equipment manager came out of the gym, and asked, "Mikey coming back?"

Trish replied, "No, we're taking him to the hospital. Can you get his clothes for us?"

The equipment manager nodded, "Be right back." Five minutes later, he was back with Mikey's gym bag, just as the medic finished bandaging him up for the trip to the hospital.

Trish thanked him for the bag, and Mike helped him up, thanking the medic. They walked slowly to the car, Mikey wobbling a little bit, and Mike asked, "You dizzy?"

Mikey mumbled, "Somebody kicked me. Kinda dizzy."

Mike and Trish looked at each other, and Trish said, "Mike, leave it. It's not worth it."

An hour, and twenty-two stitches later, Mikey was being examined by the on call neuro doc, who finally said, "Maybe a slight concussion. Pupils are equal and reactive, a little bit of a slow nystagmus, but nothing else. Kid's got a hard head, but I'd watch him for twenty-four hours. If there's any change in the pupils, or the headache gets worse, bring him back in, okay?"

***

Two weeks later, Mikey was finally cleared off all protocols and was allowed to eat something other than soft food. His first request was for Mama Rosa's, down in Harborview. Mike almost vetoed it, due to the problems they were seeing in town, but Trish convinced him it would be okay. They agreed to meet there for lunch, and Mike took civilian clothes in to work with him.

After the morning meetings, Mike finally caught up with the master chief in the smoke pit. "What's the latest on the situation out in town?"

Shifting his cigar, Cameron replied, "Sucks. They are no longer reporting crime statistics, but my contact is saying petty crime is up fifty percent, violent crime is up thirty-five percent, and murders are up at least twelve percent, at least the ones that get reported."

Mike shook his head, "Fuck. We need to get the families out of here. Sooner rather than later."

Cameron shrugged, "As of today, we're down to fifty that haven't done anything with their dependents. Most of them are married to Hispanics, so they're figuring to ride it out."

"Fifty enlisted, or fifty total?"

"Fifty total. You need to get Trish and Michael out. The sooner the better."

Mike shrugged, "Two months. That's all I need. End of May, they are out of here."

"I'm not sure you've got that much time."

"Lemme know if shit blows up, Jimmy."

"I will, you know that."

Mike changed into civvies, and drove down the strand to Harborside, marveling at the tent city that had seemed to spring up along the beaches that were open to the public. Pulling into Mama Rosa's, he saw the bright yellow Karmann Ghia convertible parked squarely in front of the door. With a sigh, he got out and walked toward the restaurant, *Dammit, I know she loves that car, but this isn't the time to be driving it around, especially with the top down. Not here, not now.*

Walking in, Mama Rosa got down from her stool at the cash register and came to the hostess station, giving Mike a hug, "It is so good to see you. I have put you in a quiet place, *Señor*." She led him back to the screened private room, and said, "Enjoy your lunch."

"Thank you, we always do, Mama!"

She cackled a laugh, and walked back to her stool, as a young waitress swooped in with his iced tea, and more chips and salsa. They ordered and enjoyed lunch, with Mikey eating all of the chips in addition to his lunch, Mike asked, "Tired of soft food, huh?"

"I've been starving. And not being able to eat anything spicy is… It's not good Dad."

"And you haven't been able to put any liplocks on Alisa either, have you?"

"Daad!" Mikey blushed, "We don't…"

Trish laughed, and Mikey blushed even more, as Mike said, "I was your age once. Just sayin."

Mikey, knowing he was losing the battle, just ate more chips and salsa, and didn't say another word. After they finished, they walked out and Trish handed Mikey the key to the car, "You can drive home."

Mikey's smile went ear to ear, and he hopped into the driver's seat saying, "Yes!"

Mike gave Trish a hug, and said, "I'll see you later at home."

He started to walk back to his truck, when he heard an anguished, "Dad, it won't start!"

Turning back, he shook his head, *Now what? If it's not one thing, it's another. Gas? Battery? Geez…*

The lights worked, the horn beeped, but the car resolutely refused to start. Trish was on her phone, as Mike continued to try different things, checking the starter solenoid, when a voice, said, "Allow me, *Señor*."

Mike looked up and saw Chuy standing over him, "You did this on purpose, didn't you?"

Chuy laughed, "If only *Señor*, if only I could command cars to break just down from my shop. If I had that power… I would be *rich*!"

Mike got up and shook hands with him, "Hell, Chuy, you ought to be rich off the amount I've spent on this damn bug at your place."

"Ah, but *Señor*, you are only one customer, ten like you, maybe…" Chuy fiddled with various things, and finally said, "I think it's either wiring, or the solenoid and starter both went out simultaneously, which I doubt. I will go get my truck and drag its carcass over to my shop and attempt once again to breathe life into an inanimate object."

Trish smacked Chuy in the arm, "Hey, don't talk like that about my baby. She's been good to me for thirty years."

"Ah, *Señora*, for you, anything. Michael, it is good to see you, and I was sorry to hear about your injury."

Mikey nodded, "Thank you, sir. I'm better now."

Impatiently Mike, said, "Chuy?"

"*Si, Señor.* I will call when she is repaired."

Mike flipped his keys to Mikey, "I'm almost afraid to do this, but let's see if you can get us home. Then I'll go back to work."

Road Trip

Mike and the master chief sat in the monthly schedules meeting, passing notes back and forth as CDR Pierce, the operations officer, and team and platoon OICs[4] hashed out training schedules, operational deployments, and watch rotations. What was unusual was that both Team Seventeen and HSC-85 COs were in the meeting, considering that they were reserve outfits and hadn't been called up. His attention was brought back to the issues as hand as LCDR Villanueva, fourth platoon, interjected, "No, we're ready to go to Guam. It's our turn in that barrel, and we need the jungle workup we'll get doing MIO[5], and cross training with the JTF partners down there. I've got three newbies that definitely need it."

Mike wrote a note and passed it to the master chief, HOW MANY MARRIED IN P-4? The answer came back, TWO- RAMIREZ AND HILTON BOTH LOCAL HISPAN WIVES. NO PROB. That prompted another thought, and he wrote, WHAT ABOUT T-7? THEY ROTATE PLATOONS NEXT WEEK??? Jimmy Cameron shook his head and scribbled, DID YOU NOT READ AM RPT? DEP PLAT CLR, RTN PLAT USE LV TO MV.

Mike cocked his head as he unscrambled Cameron's writing, *Oh yeah, the Team Seven guys all have their dependents out, and the plan is to give the returning platoons enough basket leave to get their*

[4] Officer In Charge
[5] Maritime Interdiction Operations

dependents out of California. Dammit… I need to get Trish and Mikey out… Another fucking month.

"Captain? Any words?" CDR Pierce asked.

Mike thought for a second, "Um, no, not really." Glancing down the table at CDR Gherson, Team Seven's CO, he added, "Need any commendation or award write ups as soon as you can get them in. I'll be going out with Fourth Platoon to Guam Friday. I need to do a handshake tour out there, and want to possibly get to Manila, and talk to the Joint Task Force rep on the embassy staff there. With MIO and CARAT[6] ops coming up, we might need to push a second platoon out to cover all the options."

CDR Gunn, the cadre commanding officer asked, "Captain, you want to pull any cadre to support CARAT this year? We have done that in the past…"

Mike shook his head, "No, I don't want to pull anybody out of cadre right now. Y'all are busy enough with the additional support and security requirements. Speaking of security, I did get a call back on the *incident* where boat seven got involved in stopping that beaching last month. Admiral Clayborn called yesterday afternoon, he had the captain in charge of investigation for SDPD and the sergeant assigned to the case meet with him and the JAG yesterday morning. Apparently the boat the sergeant was shown was *not* the one in the video, and it had some thirty caliber holes in the middle of it. And the icing on the cake was the complainant never said there was a

---

[6] Cooperation Afloat Readiness And Training exercises

Brownshirt on the boat. So our folks are free and clear, and the JAG delivered a pretty strong message about our security forces being fully authorized to take action to protect our assets."

Chuckles around the table, and a thumbs up from CDR Simmons made Mike smile, and he finished with, "Keep doing what you're doing. Let's hope things don't go to shit, but I want everybody ready if it does. That's all I've got."

Master Chief Cameron followed Mike into his office, quietly shutting the door, "What the fuck? Guam? Now?"

Mike held up his hands pleadingly, "I know, I should have given you a heads up, but dammit Jimmy, I *do* need to get out there. I should have gone last month. At least this way, I get a free ride out on the C-17. I don't plan to be gone more than a week, and the XO is up to speed. Besides, I'm counting on you to herd him in the right direction…"

"Dammit Mike, I should be going with you. I can handle stuff here, and I'll keep an eye on Trish and Mikey, but…"

"Sorry. That's all I can say, I'm sorry."

Somewhat mollified, Cameron said, "Well, don't let it happen again."

***

Mike groaned and stretched as the aft ramp on the C-17 started down. Looking over at LCDR Villanueva, he said, "Not one word. Don't say a fucking thing…"

Villanueva grinned, "Me, Captain? Say anything to disparage my commanding officer? How could you possibly think…"

"When you get to be my age, you'll be feeling it too. Trust me."

LCDR Schultz, Platoon Two's commander, strolled up the aft ramp, looking tanned and fit, "Captain, Ramon, glad to see y'all. We've got billeting arranged, and Captain, I got you in the VIP quarters over at the sub base. Got you a truck too. Commander Fischer is coming in from Seventh Fleet on Monday."

Mike nodded, "Sounds good. What have you got laid on for tomorrow?"

"All hands at zero eight, Turnover brief at zero nine hundred for, you, Ramon, and the team chiefs. The SWCCs rolled two weeks ago, so they are good to go, and I've invited their OIC and chief to the brief. It's a down day otherwise, since it's Sunday."

"All your people back?"

"I've got six coming back today, a fire team, and a sniper/spotter team that were on a MIO det. They're due in from the PI at sixteen hundred."

"Okay. I've got a meeting Monday morning with the SUBRON Fifteen commodore to talk about scheduling and getting y'all on and off their boats."

Shultz rolled his eyes, "Good luck with that one Captain. Their schedule is even more fucked up than ours is. Half the time, we're chasing the boats trying to find them to load aboard."

Mike shook his head, saying under his breath, "Oh lovely." Out loud he asked, "Anything on for tonight?"

Shultz smiled, "Sleep. Five hour time difference, plus the flight screws us all up." Fishing in his pocket, he pulled out a truck key and a key card, "Here you go, sir. I'll take care of getting Ramon over to billeting and get his folks in."

The roar of a skid loader blocked any further conversation, and Mike grabbed his bag and briefcase, walked down the forward stair, found the truck, and drove over to the sub base. *Food or sleep... Damn, I'm getting too old for these flights. Fourteen hours in the air, a three hour stop in Hawaii for gas and a new crew, fuck it, shower and bed. I'm done.*

Mike woke up at four in the morning, flipped and flopped for a half hour, and finally got up. Putting on his gym clothes, he headed out for a run, and about two miles into it remembered why he hated Guam. He was sweating like a hog, felt like he was breathing water, and he hurt all over. *Oh well, this is payback for not doing enough exercise at home. Like they say in BUDS, the only easy day was yesterday...* Glancing at his watch, he figured he was on a seven or eight minute pace, and decided to do five miles and call it good.

By six, he was dressed, had handled the morning, well really, the evening emails, and was hungry. Loading the briefcase back up, he picked up his phone and sent a quick text to Trish, UP AND ABOUT. HEADING IN TO WORK. LOVE YOU. Thirty seconds later, she replied, LOVE U TOO. QUIET HERE. MISS YOUR WARM BODY. He smiled as he headed for the truck.

Driving toward the front gate, he saw lights on in the galley, and decided to see if he could eat there, rather than the McDonald's off base. He pulled into the parking lot and walked in, getting in line behind six or eight submarine sailors, some in uniform, some in civilian clothes. He finally got to the head of the line, and said, "I don't have a chow pass, and I'm an officer. Can I pay for a meal?"

The bored Guamanian glanced up, then referred to a printed sheet, "Four seventy-five." He handed her a five, and she gave him a quarter back, "Sign in." He signed in, thinking, *Damn, not a lot of personality in this one. I hope she's not a total bitch to all the sailors.*

He got in line for the omelets, and the young sailor in front of him gave his order to the mess specialist behind the counter. Mike followed him, and thirty minutes later was out of the chow hall, and wondering what to do next. He headed over to the SEAL's compound, found a coffee pot and a computer drop, and worked until it was time for the turnover brief.

***

Four days, a trip to Manila, a side trip to Saipan, and an eight hour out and back on a sub, combined with the lack of sleep, had Mike woozy with fatigue. Walking into the OIC's office, he saw that Villanueva was now behind the desk, indicating the platoons had officially turned over. Schultz was sitting at the side of the desk as they reviewed packout and equipment that needed to go back to San Diego. They popped to attention when they realized he was standing there, with Villanueva said, "Sorry, sir. Didn't see you come in."

"No problem. What's the schedule for the C-17?"

"It's supposed to be here Sunday, we'll load out Sunday afternoon, and launch for San Diego Monday a.m. I saved a seat for you, Captain."

Mike sat down with Villanueva and reviewed the upcoming schedule after the various meetings. He finally leaned back, "I think you can handle it with your platoon, assuming nobody gets hurt. But, if you have issues, I need for you to let me know."

Villanueva nodded, "I will, Captain. I've got no problem calling for help if I need it."

"Okay, I'm going to call it a day."

"Yes, sir. Have a good evening."

Mike came wide awake, wondering what was going on, when he realized his phone was ringing. Fumbling for it, he hit speaker, "'Lo?"

"Mike? It's Jimmy."

A chill ran down Mike's back, "Jimmy, what… What's up?"

"Trish and Mikey aren't answering their phones. And there was a riot down in Harborside this morning."

"What?"

The master chief sighed, "Mike, I've been checking in with them every day at noon, but today, nothing. Trish had said something about getting her car. I'm hoping it's just that the cells are having problems again. Have you gotten any texts or a call?"

Mike sat up, turned on the light, and checked his messages, "No, nothing since last night… Well, early this morning there."

"I'm going to go check your house and the school. I'll call you back in an hour."

"Okay. Let me know, and I'll…" A beeping noise indicating another call got his attention, "Hang on, I'm getting another call." Punching the screen, he inadvertently conferenced the calls together, and said, "Hello?"

The voice on the other end said, "Captain, this is Admiral Clayborn. I need to notify you that we believe your wife and son were swept up in the riot this morning in Harborside. San Diego PD has notified us your burnt out SUV was found down there, but your wife and son are currently missing."

"No!" Mike hissed softly, "Oh God, no…"

"Captain… Mike, we aren't sure what has happened, but I've arranged transportation back to San Diego for you. There is a B-52 leaving Anderson in two hours. You have a seat on it. I'm sorry to be the one to break this news…"

"BUFF, two hours? I'll be on it, sir. Thank you. Oh my God. Not this. No…"

"Is there anything we can do on this end?"

"Just find them, please, sir. I'll be there as soon as I can."

"I'll say a prayer too, Mike." The admiral hung up, and Mike sagged, tears running down his face, moaning.

"Mike, I heard. We'll meet you. I'm still going to go check the house, and reach out to my connections."

"Jimmy, I… Find them please. I don't care how. Just find them!"

"I'll do my best."

"I'm going to go catch the BUFF, I'll call you as soon as I land." Mike hung up, then dialed Villanueva,

"Commander, I've got an emergency at home, I need a ride to Anderson ASAP. I have to catch an airplane at zero six hundred." Villanueva said it would take him fifteen minutes, and Mike hung up. He tried calling both Trish and Mikey's phones, but they both went to voice mail immediately. Looking at the clock, he realized it was four in the morning, and he got up, moving like an automaton as he showered and packed.

Mike was sitting on the bumper of his truck when Villanueva pulled up. He threw his pack in the back, climbed in, and said, "My wife and son are missing, and there was a riot in Harborside this morning. You've got the ball here. If there are issues, get with Master Chief Cameron."

"Yes, sir." Villanueva got him over to Anderson Air Force Base quickly and silently, and pulled into base ops at five in the morning.

Mike grabbed his bag and said, "Thanks." Then turned and walked into base ops. An hour later he'd been to the bathroom, was stuffed into a flight suit, helmet, and oxygen mask and strapped into the Electronic Warfare officer's seat on the upper deck in the B-52.

A click in his helmet was followed by, "Captain James, Colonel Horton, are you ready?"

Mike fumbled for the mic switch, "Yes. As ready as I'll be."

Another click was followed by a chuckle, "Well, we'll do our best. Here we go."

Mike felt the engines spool up, and the airplane started vibrating, then he sensed they were moving slowly. He kept waiting for the airplane to rotate, like an airliner, but he never felt it, suddenly, the vibration lessened, and he heard the pilots doing a checklist. Mike looked around but didn't seen anything other than blank panels staring at him, as the systems were turned off. He squirmed around, trying to get comfortable, but his butt was already getting numb. At some point, he nodded off, and was surprised to feel a tug on his sleeve five hours later, with the navigator standing next to him, shouting, "You need to take a piss, sir? Colonel also wants to know if you want to watch a refueling."

"Piss, yes." Mike yelled, "Where would I go to see refueling?"

"Jump seat." The navigator safed his ejection seat, and helped him unstrap, then pointed him at the honey bucket, "Don't miss!"

Mike nodded, took care of business, and made his way to the jump seat behind the pilots. The copilot mimed plugging a cord in, and pointed to the bulkhead behind Mike's head. He looked around and found a cord, and plugged it in, then heard a pop, and "Hear me?" He nodded.

"Okay, we're gonna plug here in about five minutes. See the 135 out there?" Colonel Horton, pointed out the center windscreen, then bumped the throttles up slightly.

Mike looked and finally found the KC-135 a couple of miles ahead, as the B-52 slowly closed the distance. "Now we're gonna get kinda close, so don't panic. I don't plan on hitting them, as that would screw up both our days, okay?" Mike glanced over and saw the colonel smiling at him, and he tentatively smiled back.

Mike heard a back and forth conversation with the tanker that left him confused, until he realized the tanker was talking the B-52 in. He couldn't help but cringe when the tail of the tanker passed over, seemingly only feet away. He looked up through the overhead hatch and only saw airplane, but when he looked back at the colonel, he seemed to be relaxed and totally at ease. He heard something about passing gas, and fifteen thousand pounds, and saw the pilot with a grease pencil changing numbers on one of the sheets sitting on the center console. He finally remembered that aviators didn't use gallons, they calculated their fuel weight and flows in pounds. He noticed the colonel adding power slowly,holding the airplane in position. A few minutes later, he heard, "Disconnect." And watched the tanker disappear out the top of the windscreen, then the Colonel added power and started climbing the B-52 to a different altitude. Another pop in his headset was followed by, "Okay, we got gas, another five hours and we'll be landing at NAS North Island. Captain, you can stay up here, or go back to your seat, your choice."

Mike looked out the windows one more time, then made a motion that he was going back. He heard the colonel call the navigator as he unplugged, and made his way back to his ejection seat. The nav popped up beside him, helped him strap back in and armed his seat, giving him a thumbs up.

Rampage and Riot

"Captain? Captain? We're descending into San Diego. You awake?"

Mike fumbled for the mic switch again, "Uh, yeah. Awake."

"We'll be on the ground in thirty minutes. There was a message that you will be met."

"Thanks." Mike leaned as far forward as he could, then back, rocking his head side to side, he moaned softly, *Good God, how do these people do this every day? I'd go nuts, and need a new ass after every flight! God, if you'll let me, I want to ask a favor. Please let Trish and Michael be alive. I know that's a lot, but please let them be okay.*

Twenty-five minutes later, there was a thump, screech of tires, and he felt the airplane slow rapidly. Mike felt the airplane swerve off the runway, then slow to a stop, as the navigator climbed up, and started unhooking Mike from the seat. Mike took the helmet off, and the nav said, "Just leave it in the seat. When you're ready, climb on down and I'll have the ladder down for you. We're on the taxiway, they've got a follow-me truck out here to pick you up." Mike nodded and the nav disappeared down the ladder.

Mike stuck his head in the cockpit and yelled, "Thanks, Colonel. Appreciate the ride."

Colonel Horton nodded and replied, "I'll say a prayer."

"Thanks!"

Mike climbed down the boarding ladder to find the navigator at the base of the ladder with his bag and briefcase in hand. He took them and yelled, "Thank you!"

The nav nodded and pointed to the follow-me truck sitting in front of the B-52, gave him a thumbs up, and started climbing back in the airplane. Mike trudged over to the truck, put his bag in the back, and got it, briefcase in his lap. The airman driving it nodded and pulled away then turned across the ramp. Hearing the B-52's engines run up, Mike looked back to see them taxiing to the end of the runway. As they got further away, the airman said, "Sir, you've got folks meeting you at base ops. We'll be there in five minutes."

"Thank you." Mike opened his briefcase and pulled out his cell phone, turning it on. As it booted up, he asked, "What time is it?"

The airman looked at his watch, "Twenty-three thirty, sir."

When the phone came up, Mike immediately checked for messages, and only had one, from Jimmy Cameron. It said, AT BASE OPS. Hoping against hope, he dialed the voicemail, but there were no new messages. Killing that call, he tried first Trish's, then Mikey's phones; they both went to voicemail. They pulled in front of base ops, and Mike said, "Thanks for the ride."

Getting out, he grabbed his bag out of the bed, and started up the stairs. Hearing a roar behind him, he stopped and turned, watching the B-52 rumble into the night, heading out over the Pacific. Looking up, he saw that it was a perfectly clear night, but chilly compared to Guam. *Damn, I didn't give them the flight suit back, I guess I can mail it back, or send it on the next parts run. Oh hell, stop it. Go find out what's happening...* He opened the door and stepped into base ops, seeing Jimmy Cameron leaning against a pillar, he started walking over, and stopped cold when Admiral Clayborn got up.

The admiral walked over, followed by Jimmy, "Mike, I'm sorry to break the news this way, but your wife and son are... gone."

Mike slumped against a pillar, and asked softly, "How?"

"They were killed in the riot yesterday morning in Harborside, on Broadway. Apparently, they had gone to get your wife's car at... Chuy's?"

Mike nodded, "Chuy had it, trying to fix a wiring problem."

"Well, they apparently got trapped down there, and... were killed during the riot. They... Their bodies were recovered this morning out of the remnants of the shop."

"Remnants?"

The admiral ducked his head, "There was a fire. But the folks at Balboa said they were dead before that. There was an autopsy done on both of them... And... Well, they were cremated."

Mike looked up in horror, "Cremated? Before I even had a chance to view the bodies?" His voice went up, "How the fuck could they do that? I don't even get a chance to... View the bodies?"

Jimmy stepped up, "Captain, I made the IDs, and no, you didn't want to see them. Trust me. Remember them as they were."

Mike slumped down, head in his hands, as tears rolled down his face. He halfway heard Jimmy say, "I've got this, Admiral. I'll get the Captain to quarters."

The admiral replied, "Captain James, please take whatever time you need. Again, my apologies for having to deliver the news this way, but I thought it best to do so in person. My condolences."

Mike nodded, and he heard the admiral walk away. Jimmy leaned over, putting his hand on Mike's shoulder, "Come on, Mike. Let's get you back to the base."

Mike reached out for Jimmy's hand and Jimmy pulled him up, Mike wiped his eyes, picked up his bag and briefcase and said, "No, I want to go home."

Jimmy shook his head gently, "No, you don't. Not right now. We're in FP Delta plus. All personnel are on base, and we're at military and dot gov employees only. I moved your stuff into the VIP quarters in the BOQ." Picking up Mike's bags, he motioned toward the door, "Come on, we can handle the rest of the stuff in the morning. You need some private time, and some sleep. How long have you been up?"

Mike thought for a minute, "Dunno, somewhere around… Well, I slept some, shit, I don't know. My watch says seventeen hundred, and I started at oh four hundred." He followed Jimmy out the door, and was surprised to see an up armored Hummer idling at the door. "What's this?"

"Not taking any chances. Admiral Clayborn mandated any units off base be defensible vehicles."

"What was he in?"

"The Marines had him in a convoy, with a bulletproof Tahoe for the admiral and his two guards."

A half hour later, the Hummer pulled through the front gate at Coronado, past sandbags, and a manned machine gun. They pulled up in front of the BOQ, and Mike got slowly out, turning to take his bags, he said, "Thanks Chief Nealan, sorry to drag you out."

Chief Nealan replied, "My pleasure, sir. And my condolences. I'll say a prayer for their souls."

Mike just nodded and walked slowly up to the BOQ. Slipping his key in the door, he dropped his bag and briefcase, and walked into the bathroom. After he'd finished, he flopped his bag up on the bed and started pulling his clothes out. Opening the closet, he was surprised to find his uniforms neatly lined up in the closet, and he opened the drawers, finding underwear, socks and incidentals. His boots, black and brown dress shoes were neatly lined up on the floor, and he remembered that Jimmy said he'd taken care of his clothes. He just shook his head. Stripping down, he took a long shower, and flopped on the bed, finally letting the tears come. He prayed for Trish and Mikey's souls, and vowed revenge against those who'd killed them, if he ever found them.

***

Eight hours later, he woke up, still in the same position, and groaned as he rolled over and sat up. After another shower, he got dressed in multicams, and walked over to the office. Coming in, he looked in and saw Jimmy sitting at his desk, "Master Chief, if you would?" Mike continued down to his office and sat down, unloading his briefcase, and plugging the computer in.

The master chief came in, and Mike said, "Shut the door." He did so, and turned toward Mike, who continued, "I want to go see the scene. I want to go now."

"Mike, are you sure that's smart? There's still a lot of action down there right now."

"This morning. Now. Where's my truck?"

The master chief sighed, "No, you're not going in a truck. You go, it will be in a Hummer."

"Get one. Get one now."

The master chief came to attention, "Yes, sir. I'll have one out front in ten minutes, sir." He opened the door, and disappeared down the hall.

Mike slumped back in his chair, *I shouldn't have done that. Jimmy didn't deserve to have his ass chewed like that. I can't take what happened out on him. I know he feels like shit already. But dammit, I want to see what happened!* Getting up, he went to his safe and pulled his .45 and holster out of the safe. Strapping it on, he walked down the hall and out the front door. Sure enough, Chief Nealan was sitting there with a hummer, M240 in the turret, and Petty Officer Vasquez manning it. The chief nodded and pointed to the passenger's side, and Mike walked around and climbed in. The master chief was sitting in the left passenger's seat, headset and tac vest on, and an M-4 slung between his legs. Petty Officer Camp was sitting behind his seat, similarly attired. He looked closer at Chief Nealan, he too had a headset on, and a pistol on his hip.

The chief said, "Harborside, Chuy's VW repair, right sir?"

Mike nodded, "Please, Chief."

A half hour later, the chief nosed the Hummer against the police tape in front of what remained of Chuy's shop. Petty Officer Camp and the master chief hopped out as Mike pushed open the weighted door, and slid out of the Hummer. He was immediately hit with the burnt pig smell, and immediately knew that more than one person had burned to death here. A SDPD officer stared at them curiously from inside the tape, until Mike started walking toward the shop. The PD officer put up his hand, "Sorry, this is a crime scene, you can't come in here."

Mike stopped at the tape and growled, "Get whoever is in charge over here. Now!"

The PD officer stepped away, and said something into his radio, and moments later, a harried looking investigator came out of the building, "What do you want… Captain?"

"My name is James, my wife and son were killed here. I want to see the scene. And that burnt out VW SUV," pointing to a hulk next to the fence, "Is what my wife was driving."

The investigator scrubbed his face, "James?"

"Trisha Harmon James, age forty-six, Michael Edward James, age seventeen. My wife and my son. They were her to pick up her Karmann Ghia that Chuy was fixing the wiring harness on."

The investigator turned to the PD officer, "Log him in, my approval." Turning back, he said, "Sorry, I shouldn't let you in, but I can only let one person inside the scene. Not your guards."

Mike said, "Master Chief?"

"Copied all, Captain. We'll be right here."

The investigator walked Mike through the scene, telling him six bodies had been found inside the office, including Chuy, Trish, Mikey, and three mechanics. He let Mike walk out back by himself, and Mike saw that all the cars Chuy had been working on were also burned up. Trish's Karmann Ghia was totally destroyed, and about the only way he knew it was hers was he could read the partially burnt plate on the front. He kicked what was left of a screwdriver, and on a whim, picked it up and unscrewed the front plate, sticking it inside his shirt. Walking back out, he thanked the investigator, then retraced his steps, and the PD officer logged him out of the scene.

***

Mama Rosa limped slowly toward the Hummer, as Mike cleared the scene. He stopped as she held out her arms, and Mama Rosa hugged him tightly, saying, "*Señor*, know that these were not my people that did this. What they did… Is not human. Trisha and young Michael did not deserve to die here, for nothing. I would beg you, find those who did this, and punish them." She hugged him fiercely, and whispered, "Kill them for me, *Señor*. Kill them dead!"

He hugged her back, "I will Mama, this I vow, on my honor."

She stepped back, and Mike saw tears in her eyes, as she said, "*Vaya con Dios, Señor*."

Slipping the license plate in the floorboard, he climbed into the Hummer, as Chief Nealan asked, "Back to the compound?"

Mike nodded, and they rode back in silence. Mike walked back into his office, took the license plate and propped it in front of the pictures of Trish and Mikey on his desk. *Tribute or reminder, I'm not sure which at this point. Don't have enough details to know what really happened, and the investigator wasn't a lot of help. The bodies were burned inside the building, but was that where they were killed? At least there isn't any family I have to notify, there was only us…*

Immersing himself in paperwork the rest of the day helped a little bit, and he finally walked down to the beach late in the afternoon. In the distance, he could hear the cadre working a BUDS class in the sand, and watched the Mark V boat patrolling slowly back and forth, as the sun sank toward the horizon, painting the clouds a deep red. Red sky at night, sailor's delight. Red sky in morning, sailor take warning. Why the hell did that suddenly pop into my head? *Am I going completely off my rocker?* He took a deep breath of the salty air, and, with one last look, headed for the BOQ.

The ringing of his phone woke him a little after 0500, and he grabbed it, "James."

"Mike, it's Jimmy, you need to meet me in the SCIF as soon as you can."

"What?"

"Get over here as soon as you can."

Not sure what was going on, Mike jumped through the shower, dressed quickly and carded into the building in twenty minutes. Buzzing the door to the

SCIF, he heard it click, and pushed it open. The master chief stood there, a cup of coffee in hand, "I need to show you a video."

Mike bristled, "You woke my ass up for a video? What the…"

Shoving the coffee at him, the master chief continued, "You need to see this in private. Now. I've got it cued up in the conference room."

Mike walked into the conference room and was surprised, then scared, when the master chief didn't follow him. Steeling himself, he walked over to the computer, and refreshed the screen. It took him a minute to recognize what he was seeing, and it looked like a video of a riot. With trembling fingers, he clicked the mouse over the play button, staring intently at the screen. Suddenly he recognized the front of Chuy's shop, and almost stopped the video, but let it run. He saw Chuy come out, yelling something in Spanish, but he couldn't pick it up. He watched as Chuy was beaten down, then Trish come through the door, going toward Chuy as if to protect him. Someone swung on her, and he saw Mikey come running out, yelling, "Leave my mother alone!"

He watched in horror as a Hispanic female with a baseball bat teed off on Mikey, hitting him in the temple as he reached for Trish. As he collapsed, she took another full swing and hit him in the back of the head, and he saw his son's skull fracture and depress. Trish, bleeding from her face, screamed and turned to crawl to Mikey, as a Hispanic male swung a machete at her, hitting her square in the face. She fell boneless, and Mike knew that was the killing blow. The male grabbed the female and they posed with their feet on the bodies, and both were yelling something at the camera.

Hands came out of the crowd, and the three bodies were picked up and thrown back in the building, and someone off camera threw a lit Molotov cocktail into the building as the camera panned away. Mike watched it a second time, then a third, fixing the faces of the male and female in his mind. If he saw them, well, he'd be in jail for murder, but at this point, he didn't care. Stopping the video, he walked woodenly out of the conference room, the cooling cup of coffee forgotten. "Jimmy, I want screenshots of those two, and I want to know what they said. I want as complete a transcript as you can get."

The master chief nodded, "You'll get it. The reason I called you, is News Eight is going to run the video this morning. I didn't want you blindsided…"

Mike reached out and laid a hand on his shoulder, "Thanks, Jimmy. I'm gonna take a day here. If you need me, I'll be down at the beach."

"Roger that."

Mike dropped his hand and walked blindly out of the SCIF, then out of the building to the beach. His thoughts in a turmoil, he kept coming back to the end of the video, *I'll find them. I will do what Mama Rosa wanted. It's not about revenge, at least I know they went out fighting. Now it's a matter of honor, I will honor Trish and Mikey the only way I know…*

The master chief called the duty office, "I need Vasquez and Ramos in the SCIF in forty-five minutes." Waiting a few seconds, he followed up,

"No, report to me directly, and yes, I know what time it is. Just do it." Hanging the phone up, he poured another cup of coffee and deliberated going to the smoke pit and firing up the first cigar of the day.

An hour and a half later, the two petty officers, Vasquez and Ramos, came out of the conference room, shaken and pale. Ramos handed the master chief four sheets of paper, "Master Chief, this is the best we can do. The audio sucks, but it looks like the guy with the machete is Miguel, and the Indio female with the baseball bat is Esmerelda or Estrella. There was somebody behind the camera giving them directions, but we couldn't pick out enough to say for sure what he was saying. I can't believe they killed, they *murdered* the Captain's wife and son."

Vasquez nodded, clenching and unclenching his fists, "We goin' after them?"

The master chief shifted the unlit cigar to the other side of his mouth, "Not right now. We'll turn this over to the PD and see what they do with it. You sure she was Indio?"

Vasquez said, "Yep, I grew up around them down by Julian. I saw the scene yesterday. That was fuckin' brutal, Master Chief, that was fuckin' animal."

He nodded, "Thank you for doing the translation for me. I'll pass along to the Captain that you helped."

***

Mike sat at the head of the table in the conference room, waiting as the rest of the department heads came in. Glancing occasionally at the papers in his hand, he looked idly around the room, fixing it in his mind. When everyone had filed in, it was standing room only, and he stood up and stepped to the lectern, "Okay folks, we've got a MOVORD. This is direct from Admiral Clayborn. We are going to abandon Coronado and move onboard NAS North Island. We are to secure the spaces and other facilities as well as we can, in the next seventy-two hours."

He waited for the hubbub to die down, and continued, "*Everybody* is moving. We're consolidating down to Pendleton, Miramar, Thirty-Second Street, and North Island. They are all defendable. Coronado isn't. Too much beachfront, and not enough people to patrol or control the perimeters."

"Bullshit!" was heard from the far end of the table, and Mike looked up sharply.

"No, it's not. Logistically, we can't do it with the manning level we are down to. Now what I want to do is…"

Seventy-three hours later, Chief Shell activated the last booby trap on the command building, backed out the front door, carefully locking it and pulling it closed. He made a notation in the book he held, turned around, and saluted Mike, "Captain, the next to last charge is set. This makes one hundred and three emplacements. We are ready to clear the base. Once we do, I will set the final charge at the gate."

Mike came to attention and returned the salute, smiling, "Chief, you and your folks are to be commended for your initiative, your attention to detail, and the fact that you didn't blow yourselves up. Carry on."

An hour later, Mike reported to Admiral Clayborn, "Sir, we have officially completed the evacuation of our Coronado facilities. All of our sailors have been relocated to North Island, and a supplemental watch has been stood up to support the security forces."

The admiral nodded, "Thank you, Mike. I'd like for you to be a member of my direct staff, if you don't have a problem wearing another hat. Something like an executive assistant to me, since you're the senior officer present with ground combat experience, and command level experience."

"No, sir. I don't have a problem with that."

"Welcome aboard, Mike. There is an open office just down the hall."

"Aye-aye, sir."

The rest of Mike James' story is told in the novella, "The Morning the Earth Shook".

Last Plane Out

Bob Poole

Michael Garabaldi and his wife Myra huddled in the corner of the bedroom of their single story house in the south El Monde neighborhood where they lived for the past 25 years. He heard the crash and screaming from the house two doors down, and raucous laughter from the people surrounding the house.

It was a 'Retribution Visit'. Basically a raid/theft given an officious name by the local watch captain, who was also the leader of the "Brownies", the local paramilitary militia that Moonbeam's people started. He slid over to the covered window, moved a corner of the blackout curtain to survey the house, and saw the mob flowing out of the house carrying the belongings of his neighbor into the street, as they hollered and yelled to each other.

Michael wanted to take the baseball bat wrapped in barbed wire that he kept near him, and charge into the mob to save his neighbor, but he knew that to so would mean death to him and his wife, and wouldn't change anything. Michael felt tears of shame course down his cheeks as he stood by and watched as his neighbor's house was ransacked, and pillaged in a way that would have made Attila the Hun proud. All he could do was watch impotently as his neighbor's house was set on fire, as a warning to others not to oppose the edicts of the neighborhood watch captain.

The next morning Michael got ready to go to work. He made himself a small breakfast as the coffee maker spat out the "near coffee substitute", because that was all he could get from the local market. Michael dressed in his work uniform, went back into his bedroom, and gave his sleepy wife a hug as he got ready to leave. He went into the garage, opening the door with the manual release because power was intermittent due to the rolling brownouts. He couldn't leave the car outside when he got home from work--that was risky because, the mob of 'youths', as the media calls them, would steal anything that wasn't nailed down, and trash the rest. The older model, nondescript Ford Focus was vitally necessary for him to keep his job. Riding Public Transit would be dangerous for him, being a white guy in an area that hates whites. He knew a couple of his coworkers had gotten a 'retribution' beating on the Green Line on the way home from the airport.

Michael backed the Focus out of the driveway, shut the car down, got out, closed and locked the car door, and double checked to make sure that the garage was secured. He climbed back into the car, cranked it up and backed out of the driveway. He wasn't allowed to leave it running; that was one of the edicts passed by Moonbeam's people to combat climate change, and Michael knew that some of the neighbors would snitch in a New York minute to the watch captain to curry favor. He surveyed what was left of his neighbor's house as he slowly drove by, headed out of the subdivision, following the secondary roads that would take him to the access road and onto Interstate 10 to go to work.

As he neared the interstate, he saw a roadblock ahead. It was the local "Brownies" running an ID checkpoint. He drove up slowly, grabbed his papers to present to the young unshaven Hispanic man wearing a Brownie uniform. As Michael handed his papers to the guard, the other two guards were walking around the Focus, examining the car. He inwardly nodded as they noticed all the *progressive* causes and Moonbeam for Governor stickers that plastered the car. He'd grabbed them off of EBay real cheap, in a bundle package. He had joked to a coworker after they saw it on his car at work, "Its camouflage, to not get hassled or the car vandalized."

He watched as the guard looked at his paperwork; he could see that the guard couldn't read the ID, but went through the motions. The other guard walked up and asked him, "Where are you headed?"

Michael glanced at him and replied, "Going to work like you are."

The guards laughed as if it was a joke, then one asked, "Where is that at, Señor?"

"I work at the airport for United Airlines. I am a mechanic there." The guards nodded, and as he got his papers back, they motioned him on. As Michael slowly drove the car away, he kept an eye on them in the rear view mirror.

As he drove down Interstate 10, he absently listened to the satellite radio; he had given up on local radio long ago because all they did was praise the 'Cause', and sing the praises of Moonbeam. Michael noticed the lack of traffic on the interstate, and he mused, *Well that is one way to kill the infamous gridlock*, remembering when LA was famous for that. He turned onto Interstate 405, finishing the run to the airport, where he parked in the employee lot and caught the rattle-trap shuttle bus to his work area on the concourse at LAX.

Michael reported to his crew leader for his briefing and work assignments, then headed to his toolbox to get his bag of tools and toolbelt. Climbing into the battered Ford Ranger that served as his maintenance vehicle, he headed to the planes that had landed and required a checkout before they could fly again.

He looked at his list, saw his first plane was parked at the concourse and was already positioned in the Jetway. Michael saw the truck used by the cleaning crews at the rear of the plane and the moving stairs already in place. He parked in the safe area, and headed around the front of the plane. He climbed the ladder to the Jetway, swiped his badge at the door, and headed to the 767 that was his first patient of the day.

Michael stepped in the airplane and noticed the cleaning crew was freshening the airplane up for the next flight, working from the rear to the front. Michael headed to the forward galley, opened a couple of the doors and grabbed the bags of coffee that had been left. Stashing them in one of his cargo pockets of his uniform, he headed to the cockpit to read the log book, and see if the pilot had written anything up. As he read, he was pleased to see that there weren't any crap write-ups, as some of the pilots are wont to do, just to be dicks to the maintenance crews.

He put the log book back on top of the instrument panel, and headed back to the galley to see if there was something that he could scrounge to eat on while he did the check. Michael grabbed some biscotti cookies before he headed back to the Jetway and down to the tarmac to do his check.

Michael walked down the ladder and looked around, noticing how quiet the airport was, he mumbled, "Damn, I remembered when this place was noisy as hell from all the planes taking off and landing." He shook his head, "The economic policies of Moonbeam strike again," he looked around to make sure that he wasn't overheard. In Moonbeam's Cali, snitches abounded.

He muttered to himself, "Jeez these guys must have taken their lessons from the old East German Stasi where one in seven were informers." He walked around the airplane, checking the control surfaces, tires, brakes, and other things that the daily checks called for. He looked around saw the sun and the nice weather that Cali, formerly California, was known for, remembering that was what called him out here, after his hitch in the Army was finished in the early 90's.

Michael finished walking around the airplane and headed back to the Jetway. As he walked back into the cockpit, he saw the pilot had arrived. He recognized him as one the experienced hands that made the pilot and maintenance relationship a pleasure.

The pilot smiled, "Hey, Michael," as he extended his hand.

Michael accepted the handshake, "Hey Dave, you breaking my airplane again?" He chuckled as he shook the pilot's hand.

"You see anything fall off the airplane yet?"

Michael shook his head "Nah, she'll fly, she is a good ship." Dave reached into the cockpit to grab the logbook, and handed it to Michael, who slid open one of the platforms that the flight attendants used, opened the logbook to the proper space, filled in the spaces, and signed off the airworthiness release. Closing the book and handed it back to Dave, who stowed it next to the Jeppesen case in the cockpit.

Dave turned to him, "You still like it here?"

Michael glanced around to make sure that the cleaning crew was not near them to overhear and stated, "I have put in for a transfer to anywhere in the United States to get out of here, but I only have twenty-five years of seniority and that ain't enough, in the bid system. Apparently everyone else wants to get out of the 'workers' paradise'." He shook his head and continued, "California used to be a wonderful place the people, the weather; this place was awesome but Cali is a Third-World craphole. My wife already lost her job. She used to work with one of the financial companies that bailed, due to the pie in the sky edicts from Moonbeam's people coming hard and heavy, in the name of social justice. Now she stays home, and is scared to go out for fear of being targeted by a mob. I am glad that our son, Ryan, is in the Southwest. He's stationed at Fort Hood, he doesn't care for the post, and there is a lot of B.S., but he loves the freedom that Texas has. He's pushing for me and his mom to get out and move there."

Dave nodded, "Take it for what it is worth, you need to get out sooner than later, it will get worse." Michael automatically scanned around to make sure that the cleaners were not close enough to hear them and drop a dime on him. Dave continued, "You know we have our own network, and the headshed has already heard more stuff is coming down from Sacramento, including forcing the company to pay our people in Callors at the official exchange rate."

Michael shook his head, "That crap is worthless, like rubles after the Soviet Union went belly up. What keeps us going with the high rate of inflation is that I get paid in American dollars. If they force me to get script instead, that will kill us." Dave nodded in agreement, as Michael glanced toward the back of the airplane. He could hear the Mexican street music blaring from the aft galley, as the crew pillaged the remaining food and drink items stored there. He knew any company complaint would be worthless, these days; it was the cost of doing business in Cali.

Dave glanced around, and then continued, "I *am* serious, you need to get out sooner, rather than later, I've also heard rumblings that the company may pull out of the Cali routes. The money isn't there like it used to be, we fly in under capacity, and fly out full, people are leaving and after a while the money we get from people leaving will not cover our costs."

Michael nodded in agreement, "Thanks for the info." He shook the pilot's hand, and Dave disappeared into the cockpit to start the preflight checks. As Michael waited for the passengers to clear out, he heard weeping on the Jetway as a man, wife, and their teenage daughter got on the airplane. They were being led by one of the flight attendants who also was weeping a bit. She got them to their seats in first class and gave the girl and the mom a blanket from the overhead bin. Michael knew her as one of the regular attendants that always smiled and chatted with the mechanics.

She walked over to get something to drink, and Michael motioned her over, "What's up, Emily?"

She shook her head, and said in a low voice, "They got pulled out for extra screening by security. Apparently, the mom told security that they were moving out of Cali. They had their stuff stolen, and the daughter was sexually assaulted. Their carryon luggage is gone, it vanished, and nobody will tell them where it is. They might find it if they are willing to wait, but they might miss their flight. Well, the Dad told them, "No, it was okay, they want to get out of Cali real bad."

The flight attendant got some drinks, and smiled sadly at Michael, "I don't want to fly into Cali anymore; I see the same kind of thing every time I fly in and it breaks my heart."
Michael patted her on the shoulder, "You keep doing what you are doing, and we will be alright. You're a good person, Emily."

Emily dabbed her eyes, then gave Michael a hug, picked up the drinks, and headed to the passengers. Michael looked down the aisle and saw that the cleaning crew was disembarking from the rear of the airplane, Michael leaned into the cockpit, waved at Dave, and stepped onto the Jetway, down the stairs to his truck, and headed off to visit the next plane on his list.

After checking several planes, he noticed it was almost lunch time, and he headed to the area at the concourse where the lead's office, conference room and break room were located. The mechanics tended to congregate there to get any updates while they grabbed lunch.

He walked into the break room, pulled out some munchies he had snagged from a galley of a willing Airbus FA, and plopped in front of a computer to do his daily read and signs, or as the crew called it "click and forget". He scanned his company emails, saw a bunch of normal company news, or 'feel good fluff'. Then he saw a small paragraph from the CEO talking about route realignments coming soon. He felt a small ball of fear in the pit of his stomach. He finished wading through his emails, not seeing a response to his bids for anywhere out of Cali. Finishing his small lunch, he stuck his head in the lead's office, "Headed back to work boss."

The lead looked up from his computer, "What, you work? After twenty-five years, you finally decided to give the company some work? What the hell happened? Aliens transmogrify your brain?"

Michael chuckled, "You know me boss, trying to save the airline, one card at a time, one check at a time, and one plane at a time."

The lead choked back laughter, "Jeez that is a lot of bullcrap to dump on your hardworking lead at this time in the day. Now scram before I have you dumping Lav trucks."

Michael smiled as he headed back out to his truck to continue the daily checks queued up on his work tablet.

He got to a Boeing 737 that was next on his list and looked at the brakes and tires, as was his habit, before heading to the stairs to the Jetway. He grumbled as he saw that the front tire and brakes were 'at limits'. He used his work tablet to order replacements from stores, and have them sent to the airplane's location. He quickly did his walk around, went up the Jetway, and went to the cockpit to check the logbook for any other surprises. There weren't any, so he quickly headed down the Jetway to get the stuff to change a tire. Since there was a shortage of people, it meant that he would be changing the tire and brakes by himself. He used his truck to pull the scissor jack out of its cubbyhole, and attached the brake cylinder jig to the back of the jack. He then headed back to the airplane.

He quickly got the jack in position, got his toolbox out of the back of the truck, ran an air hose from the fixture on the wall, and waited for the parts runner to bring the tire and brakes. He pulled out his phone and saw on CNN, the only network that seemed to work in Cali, that Moonbeam was talking about how more economic revenue would be collected, ensuring the great State of Cali would continue to be both a beacon of hope for all peoples of all genders, all races, while making sure that everyone is free from want. Michael shook his head, "Lenin would have approved that speech."

He saw the parts truck drive up with the tire and brakes, and quickly checked to make sure that they matched the part numbers he called for. He quickly jacked the airplane up until the wheel was off the ground, then popped the beauty cap off, and moved it out of the way. He started removing the bolts, spacers, and rings that held the tire on the axle then he wiggled the tire off and moved it away from the airplane. He popped the air valve, heard the nitrogen hissing out, and he started working on the brakes, getting them ready to slide off.

Grabbing the brake cylinder jig, he lifted the brake assembly off the axle, and moved the fixture off to one side. Moving a piece of cardboard so the brake cylinder wouldn't touch the ground, he lowered it until the brake cylinder was flush with the cardboard. Unwrapping the chain from the brake cylinder, he pushed it over to the box that had the new brake assembly. Using the jig to lift the brake assembly out of the box, he pushed it over to the axle, and installed it.

Looking at his watch, he realized that the airplane's ready time was approaching. Michael finished safety wiring the brake assembly, then grabbed the new tire, and wrestled it into place. He finished installing it, and rolled the old tire into the designated location for pickup. He used the jig to grab the old brake assembly and place it in the box next to the old tire.

Michael saw the pilot and copilot starting their walk around, and he waved at them as he grabbed the hydraulic cart to service the plane. He finished the servicing and headed to the cockpit to get the logbook, adding in the tire and brakes change and signed off on the airworthiness release. He overheard both pilots talking about the new tax plan spun by Moonbeam and the fact that it will further drive business away from Cali. He nodded to them as he headed to the stairs and his truck to take some Advil for the muscle pains and ache that he knew were sure to come after his exercise.

Four hours later, after stepping off the shuttlebus, Michael headed slowly to his car. He cranked up the Focus after putting his backpack behind the seat, and headed home. He looked at the gas gauge and grimaced, having to stop at dusk at the local gas station near the house was dicey since the night-life was waking up, hungry for the first prey of the evening. Michael got off I-10 and headed to a gas station near the expressway. It was lit, which was a plus. He parked at a pump, headed inside to pay the attendant for the fuel with Callors, and grab a six-pack of beer from the cooler. He looked at the cooler, and the only selection was Mexican beer. He grimaced and grabbed a six-pack of Bohemia Lager, a Mexican beer with a German flair.

As he told the attendant how much gas he was buying, he asked, "What happened to the other kinds of beer?"

The attendant shrugged, "They don't want to pay the extra taxes to be in this state." Michael showed the attendant the six-pack he was getting and laid it on the counter. The attendant shrugged again, "Well, the distributor told me that the new taxes only go on the Anglo beer."

Michael nodded, "Okay, makes sense, those people don't want to be here in this great state, it is their loss." He paid for the purchase and headed to his car, put the beer in the back, then proceeded to pump his gas. He glanced at the attendant who was looking at him, and Michael was sure getting his tag number to make a report to the local watch captain.

Finally getting home, Michael drove into his neighborhood, and saw that the power was off--the entire neighborhood was dark. He drove down his street, past the blackened shell of his neighbor's house, parked in his driveway. He unlocked the garage door, went to turn on the light, and shook his head, "Oh yeah, no power."

He used the headlights to park in the garage, and closed and locked the door behind him. He reached behind the driver's seat, grabbed the six pack of beer and his backpack that had dinner in it, pulled out two bottles, and quickly put the others in the fridge, so whatever was cold, would stay cold. He got the extra candle out, and lit it from a lighter that they kept in the drawer in the kitchen. Walking into the living room, he saw his wife reading a book in the wingback chair that was a gift from her mom a long time ago. He walked over, handed her a beer, and she smiled as he reached down and kissed her. "I got some dinner."

"Not from the market?"

He took a pull of beer, "Airplane. Who would have ever though that airplane food would have a better variety than what is available in the store?"

Myra smiled that smile that captivated him so many years ago, and he headed to the kitchen to get a couple of plates. Dividing the two meals, compliments of the flight attendant in the first class galley of the 777 that was heading to Tokyo just before he got off work.

As he sat in the recliner, eating and sipping the beer, Myra said, "Power went out a couple of hours ago."

"Well, that means that the power may not be on in the morning, the way things have been going." He got up and checked the batteries that they used to store extra power from the solar panels. He tapped the gauge "Well they are getting a little bit of juice, so the solar panels haven't been completely destroyed by the rock throwing *youths*, whose entertainment in the neighborhood was to break things. "It will keep the fridge going at any rate."

He sat back down in the recliner, nursing his beer and noticed that she was still reading the book by candlelight. "Aren't you concerned about your eyes, reading in the poor light?"

Myra put the book down and said. "I don't mind, the book by James Patterson reminds me of better times."

Michael grimaced slightly at that thought, and he faded out as the Advil kicked in. He dreamt of events several years ago, when the upstart named Donald Trump won the 2016 election, the progressive rage that exploded across California, and the resulting Calexit movement. When people asked him who he voted for, he always commented, "Hillary was the best candidate," and the people who asked him went away satisfied.

Michael rarely gave his personal opinion to anybody. He wasn't, by God, going to tell anybody that he voted for Trump. He saw the rhetoric coming out of Sacramento getting more strident, stirring up the mob, more and more. After the reelection of Donald Trump in 2020, the referendum came down and California seceded from the Union in 2022. There was euphoria in the streets, people dancing with joy that they had stuck it to the hated 'cheeto man'.

Michael had seen the mobs on TV pulling down the American flag where they could find it, burning and defiling the flag in any way possible. He'd ranted at the TV, "You fuckers desecrate the flag that my friends and family are buried under!" He'd thrown his coffee mug at the TV shattering the screen. Myra had jumped up from the couch with surprise; it was rare for him to really lose his temper.

In the following months, the edicts and rulings from Sacramento starting coming fast and furious, with rubberstamping from the legislators. Moonbeam ran Cali with an iron fist, tightening the socialist grip on what was left of the state. Firearms that were already restricted became totally banned, along with ammo. The comment often heard was, "If you want to play with guns, join the Brownshirts, and protect Cali diversity and values from the hated conservatives."

As soon as the firearm ban was announced, Michael immediately sealed and buried his guns and ammo in the back yard, thankful that none of his neighbors knew he was a shooter. Global warming also became a State of Cali priority, and the taxes started going up to support the new laws coming on.

There was a *fairness* tax, where if you had a certain amount of money you had to pay extra for the privilege of having more money because you worked for it. Michael also saw the Brownies start assuming the responsibility for the internal security of Cali. The Brownies reminded him of the Stasi from East Germany, but with the dregs of society in charge.

Michael was startled awake by the sound of tires squealing on the street, and a few thumps on the wall as the local youths drove by playing rap and throwing rocks and bricks at the passing houses. Myra whispered, "At least they didn't break any glass on their drive-by this time." He looked at the wall and was glad that the house was brick. He dozed a bit, woke up, glanced at the time, and saw that it was after 3 AM. He felt a bit of a chill in the air, glanced at his wife, and saw her asleep in her favorite chair. He gently took the book from her lap, slid her bookmark into place, and draped a blanket from the couch over her.

The next morning he made ersatz coffee, the coffee he got from work going into a Tupperware container to be used for barter, especially for things that they couldn't seem to get from the local market. He made a small breakfast for himself and Myra.

With three days off, he dressed in older clothes and headed outside, mainly to look at the house, and see if the rocks last night had done any damage. As he surveyed his property, he noticed the dilapidated look of his house, but it matched the others in the neighborhood. There was a pattern in the youth attacks, if you had a neat well-kept house, for some reason it seemed to attract the mob like a magnet and the house got vandalized.

One of his neighbors, Jorge Ramos, walked up to him, asking, "So what did you think of the Turner house? The one that got raided."

Michael looked at him and inwardly suspected that the guy was a snitch and was trying to trip his neighbors up for extra favors from the Brownies. "Well, it was deserved. The Turners were against the people of Cali, and the enlightened policies of our governor; they deserved whatever they got."

The neighbor made some small talk and headed to his house. Michael looked at the guy's receding back and thought, *You will get yours, you sanctimonious piece of shit, you were the one that narced on the Turners.* Because they had a food plot in their backyard, they had been called 'preppers' and that was enough to call down the wrath of the Brownie mob on them.

Mr. Turner only told a couple of people that he had a garden in the backyard, and one of the people he mentioned it to was Ramos. He was a trusting person, which was his mistake. Michael finished checking out the exterior and the yard, and went inside to find the power was back on. Turning on the news, he saw the live report of rioting and looting at a PX on one of the military bases in San Diego. He was shocked to see the mob tear apart the commissary, and attack anybody that was in the way.

Michael sat with tears in his eyes as he saw the wanton destruction, and watched some of the dependents being brutalized on TV just for the entertainment of the mob. He knew there were going to be deaths, he'd seen that before. Myra walked in, saw the destruction, and murmured, "Oh, my God," as she covered her mouth in horror.

Michael glanced up, "We are going to have to leave soon. I know the military, and they aren't going to stand for the murder of their dependents and soldiers. I saw it in 1989 when the Noriega dignity battalion beat up an Army LT and raped his wife. We went in shortly after that and kicked his ass out."

Myra nodded sadly, "I'm ready to go when you are; there is nothing here for us anymore, and this house has become a prison. Ryan is far away from here, and I thank God for that."

He leaned back and thought for a second, "I can try to get you on a flight, but the ticket prices are very expensive, and legally we have to get approval from the local Brownie commissioner to stamp your travel papers, so you can get through security. If we're lucky, it will only take several months, and I won't be able to go with you. They want one of us to stay here, kinda like a hostage thing to ensure the other's return."

She nodded with tears in her eyes.

After finishing his 'coffee', Michael walked down the street to visit the home of the local watch captain, who was also in charge of the local detachment of Brownies. Michael knocked on the door and the assistant flunky answered the door, saw who it was and spat out "What is it you want, gringo?"

Michael looked at the pimply Hispanic kid, "I would like to see Mr. Moore".

The young man spit next to Michael, "Señor Moore will see you in a few minutes." And slammed the door. Michael knew that the man wasn't busy, but he liked to show his power and have people wait fifteen minutes or more before seeing them. After the fifteen minutes had gone by, the door opened and the same Hispanic kid opened the door and spat, "Gringo, Señor Moore will see you now."

Michael entered and noticed the smell of unwashed bodies. He was escorted to the 'office' Moore had set up, and the first thing Michael noticed was the huge picture of Moonbeam in the same motif that was used for President Obama in the 2008 election, except Moonbeam's had the word 'Equality' on it. He glanced down and saw the very rotund body of the watch captain, wearing the uniform of a Brownie officer that was at least two sizes too small. He looked at Moore's face, noticing the sheen of sweat, and the receding hairline of a man that wasn't aging well.

Moore looked at Michael through porcine eyes, asking, "What do you want?"

Michael, used to the bad manners by this time, said, "I need travel papers for my wife, her sister has taken ill and there is fear that this one may be terminal. Cancer, you see, and she wants to see her sister while she is still able to recognize her. She only has a few months to live."

Moore shook his head, "That is a shame Mr. Garabaldi, I am sorry that your wife's sister has taken ill." The words sounded sincere, but the body language said different. "Where does your wife need to travel to?"

Michael replied. "She needs to go to North Carolina, near Charlotte."

Moore shifted in his seat, "I can get the papers for you but they will take time to process."

Michael grimaced a bit, he knew what was coming as he said, "I would appreciate it if there is some way that you can expedite the process."

The watch captain narrowed his eyes and shrugged, "If you are willing to make a donation to the poor and downtrodden, I might be able to push the paperwork through."

Michael inwardly snorted, wondering *What would be acceptable to help the poor and downtrodden*?

Moore smiled "Well you have a seventy inch TV that you purchased almost a year ago. That would work well to assuage the feelings of the poor of this area."

Michael nodded, resignation on his face, "Okay, I will bring the TV this afternoon."

Moore smiled again, as he opened a desk drawer and pulled out the paperwork, "Go fill this out and bring the paperwork and the TV at the same time."

Michael kept his face deadpan as he took the paperwork, turned around, and nodded to the Hispanic kid who was happy Moore had humiliated one of the few Anglos that still lived in this area. Stepping outside of the house, he drew a breath of untainted air and walked past the charred remains of his neighbor's house back to his house.

Michael closed the door and looked at Myra, "I got your paperwork, but it cost us the big TV".

"How do they know what kind of TV we have, and when we bought it?"

Michael walked over to the coffee maker, got a cup of hazelnut coffee, and sat down at the kitchen table, "Probably one of the neighbors, they might have seen me bring it home and pull it out of the car so I could park. They have this place set up where half of the people spy on the other half for extra food or favors." He picked up a pen and filled out the paperwork, making sure that he included a return date, even though it wouldn't be used.

Michael walked over to the TV, looked apologetically at Myra, and unhooked it. He carried it to the garage, then pocketed the remote, and put the travel paperwork in the other cargo pocket. Picking up the TV again, he carried it down the street feeling the eyes of his neighbors on him every step of the way.

He kept looking around to make sure that one of the roving gangs of '*youths*' didn't jump him to snatch the TV. He made it to Moore's house, knocked on the door, and the same leering Hispanic kid answered. The kid's eyes lit up like Michael remembered his son's eyes would light up at Christmas when he was little.

The kid opened the door, "Come in gringo, you can wait in the hallway while I let Señor Moore know that you're here. " Michael waited for the expected minutes as the smells and sights bombarded him, from the nasty carpet, to the revolutionary posters adorning the walls. It showed the world that Moore was a true believer in the cause.

He knew better. The fat bastard was in it to line his pockets. Why work when you can terrorize people, and get your graft and jollies that way?

The door opened and he was motioned into Moore's office of the. "Ahhh, Mr. Garabaldi... I see that you are well....good, good.....do you have the paperwork, and the offering for the poor?"

Michael nodded, "The TV is on the landing and here is the remote. I hope this goes toward assuaging the poor in our area, and righting the scales of Anglo privilege."

Moore nodded sagely, "Wise words Mr. Garabaldi, I will be glad when the stain of inequality is finally washed away and our society can flourish." He motioned for the paperwork, looked at it, and put it in the inbox. "Thank you for your offering Mr. Garabaldi, you may go." As he motioned his hand imperiously in dismissal.

He walked home in the gathering dusk, and when he saw a glow a couple of streets away, he snorted, *Another Retribution Raid, just an excuse for the thugs and trash to rob and loot under the guise of social justice.* Somehow only the Anglos were ever targeted. It was just one more sign that whites weren't welcome in Cali unless they are a member of the intelligentsia, and were 'down with the cause'.

Michael got home, locked the door, and told his wife, "The paperwork is turned in, but the way it works, it will take months to process."

Myra hugged him and he gathered strength in the physical contact of the only person who really cared about him, the only person with whom he could let his guard down and be himself.

Summer turned into fall and Michael continued the daily grind of working at the airport, and avoiding as much contact as possible away from work with people. He was working a 767, getting it ready for a Hawaii hop, and had just finished servicing the three hydraulic systems, when he saw his pilot friend, Dave, doing his walk around. Michael smiled as Dave broke away from his walk around, "Hey Michael, you putting your nasty fingerprints on my clean bird again?"

Michael chuckled "Of course, I gotta make sure that it matched the fingerprints on your car."

Both laughed, and Dave asked, "How is it going?"

"Well, I put in the paperwork several months ago for Myra to travel to visit her sister. Just waiting for the Cali bureaucracy to decide if she is a flight risk. This stuff takes months unless you have connections, and I don't have any with the local party apparatus."

Dave nodded, "You hear of any job openings in the system?"

Michael kicked a wheel chock, "Still bidding on anything to get out of here."

Dave glanced around the nearly empty flight line, "You noticed that there are fewer airplanes coming in here."

"Yeah, I have noticed the fifty percent drop in our flights coming in, and there are fewer mechanics working the airplanes. People either ain't coming to work, or are starting to leave, or they've found something else. The United Concourse will be a ghost town before long."

"I've heard rumblings from the headshed that they will be diverting more flights away from LAX, and landing them in either LAS, or SEATAC. It's getting difficult to get basic services here; you noticed that we don't fuel here anymore, didn't you?"

Michael nodded, "We heard about bad fuel."

"The company doesn't want lawn darts, bad for the stock you know," Dave replied. Both men chuckled at the gallows humor and Dave continued, "All the planes land with more fuel, meaning we have to land heavy."

"Well, that explains the overweight landings in the log-book." A truck drove to the back of the airplane and the platform raised the box in the back to allow entrance for the cleaning crew.

Dave gestured at the truck, "That is the other problem; the cost of the pillaging by the 'barrio bunch' is starting to effect the bottom line. There is only so much loss the company is willing to eat, before they cut bait."

Michael nodded in agreement, "Well, let me finish the walk around so you can fly your butt out of here." As he was filling out the logbook he saw Emily, one of his favorite flight attendants, who ran up and gave him a hug, "Hey Michael, how is my favorite mechanic?"

He smiled warmly, "Much better, now that I have seen you, my day is complete."

She swatted his arm playfully, "You suck-up, and you are so full of it! If you weren't married I'd take you home with me." Michael smiled at that as she headed down the aisle to go take care of the first class passengers. He finished the logbook and signed off the airworthiness release, then laid the logbook on the glareshield.

As he stepped on the Jetway, he saw the fear, relief, or anger on the faces of the passengers, depending on their particular situations. *Dammit, what is holding up Myra's papers? Did Moore even put them in?* He saw some movement under the concourse, at one of the baggage carts, and headed until he got close enough to see a bunch of what they call the 'barrio bunch' going through the passengers' suitcases looking for valuables.

They saw him and one yelled, "Beat it gringo!"

Michael put his hands up and walked backward until he was out of sight of the group. He then turned around and headed to his truck to get the next job order.

***

As Michael drove home, the lack of traffic confirmed the state was dying, and if they didn't leave soon, they were going to be in real trouble. He stopped at the corner market to pick up some groceries, and parked near the entrance to lessen any chance of getting ambushed carrying the food to the car.

The selection was even sparser than normal, but he grabbed a basket and walked around to see what he could get. He picked up a couple of spuds, then saw the bruising and black marks on them, and put them back. He found a couple of sad looking carrots, and put them in the basket along with some other vegetables. In the meat department, they had the newest poster from PETA with the slogan "Meat is Murder" plastered everywhere, and he looked around for something that looked edible.

He saw a pack of chicken and grabbed it before somebody else did, then headed for the canned food aisle. He looked at the almost empty shelves, and grabbed he could, without being picky about the brands. For some reason, the aisle reminded him of what he saw when he'd gone into East Berlin while he was attached to Field Station Berlin. Even though it was supposed to be the showcase of communist Eastern Europe, the shops didn't really have a lot of food stuffs, mostly tourist things like crystal ware or binoculars.

Michael took his basket to the cashier, who rang it up lackadaisically. When he saw the total, he winced. The price was higher, for a worse selection, of poorer quality that last week, but he had not choice, so he paid for his selections and headed to the car.

He noticed a couple of *youths* looking at him, and he quickly unlocked the car, threw the bag inside, jumped in and locked the door. The *youths* got there seconds too late, and started banging on the car, trying to open the door. One of them pulled out a gun, and pointed it at Michael, who quickly threw the car in reverse, and ducked down.

He bounced over the curb, threw the car into drive, punched the accelerator, and hoped the car held together. The Focus shuddered under the demands, but careened into the street as he glanced at his rear view mirror.

Since he wasn't being pursued, Michael slowed the car down to the speed limit to avoid getting pinched for speeding, while he tried to get his breathing under control. There was no point in calling the cops, because it would be catch and release, with the *deprived and misunderstood youths* coming looking for him.

Michael pulled into his driveway, shut the car off, and took several deep breaths. He didn't want to worry Myra; she already had enough issues with living in this area now. He got out of the car, walked to the mailbox, and saw a packet. He quickly stuck it in his back pocket, and headed to the garage to get the car inside, before too many of the neighbors got nosey.

He pulled the car in, climbed out, and quickly closed the garage door then unloaded the food and brought it inside. He dropped the groceries on the counter and ripped the packet open. It was the travel papers for Myra and he yelled with joy.

Myra came running into the kitchen, "What is the matter?"

He smiled and said, "Your travel papers are here, pack your bag, nothing valuable, the Brownies in security in the airport will just steal them. I will get you a ticket for tomorrow, and I'll get the valuables through security.

"You know we can fly for free, and save the money, right?"

Michael hugged her, "Normally yes, but all the flights are full leaving with paying passengers, and I want you on that plane out of here tomorrow, I don't care what it costs!"

They argued back and forth a bit more but she finally saw his point. He booted up the computer and logged into the company network, finding a ticket that was leaving tomorrow to North Carolina via Dulles. He was smiling for the first time in a long time, as he helped her pack.

In the morning, he opened the door after Myra had put her bag in the trunk and had gotten into the car. He went through the ritual of closing and locking the garage door, and quickly cranked the car, heading for the airport.

Myra looked around, and Michael remembered that she hadn't left home since the riots almost eight months ago. As the car hit the on-ramp to the airport, he said a prayer that there was no Brownie checkpoint this morning. Myra kept looking around at the light traffic on Interstate 10 and they made small talk as the car headed to the airport.

He was really happy for the first time in a long time, something about the presence of his wife always made him feel good. He drove to the departure section of the airport, got out, and popped the trunk. He gave her a kiss and passed her small carry-on bag to her, saying, "I'll meet you on the other side of security.

Don't tell them that you are not coming back. If they ask, just tell them that you are visiting your sick sister and can't wait to come back home because there is no place like Cali."

Myra nodded and Michael smiled and hugged her again, watching as she turned away and walked through the departure doors. Michael drove around to the employee parking lot, got her other bag, went through the turnstiles, and caught the shuttlebus to the United concourse on LAX.

He immediately clocked in, picked up his toolbox and loaded it and the bag into his truck. He headed to the 767 that he knew that his wife would be on. Climbing the stairs to the Jetway, he swiped his badge, and headed to the cockpit. As he flipped through the logbook to see if there were any write-ups, Dave walked into the cockpit, "Hey Michael, how you doing today?"

Michael saw his wife entering the cabin, and with tears in his eyes he replied, "Getting my wife out of here."

Dave saw who he was looking at, and Emily heard his tone of voice. She hugged Michael, "We'll take good care of her, matter of fact she's going to be in first class, somebody will get moved."

Michael walked to his wife, hugged her tightly, and with a catch in his voice smiled "Hey, Sweetie." She smiled and he handed her a bag with her jewelry, gold coins and other valuables that he brought with him. Walking back to the cockpit, he said, "Take good care of her, she is my world."

Dave nodded, "Will do."

Michael was sitting in his truck, doing reports when he saw the Boeing 767 climb off the runway, and the tears flowed freely. If nothing else, Myra was finally free from the prison the State of Cali had become. He watched until the plane disappeared, and whispered a prayer before he went back to completing the reports.

He drove home to an empty house and that didn't bother him anymore. Myra had texted she was at her sister's house, and all was well. He parked the car inside the garage, secured it, walked in, and threw his keys on the counter. Fishing in his backpack, he pulled out a meal that he 'liberated' from an Airbus A330 headed to Beijing. It was ersatz Chinese, but it was better than anything he had in the house.

The next day Michael checked in with his lead, and was told there would be a meeting in ten minutes. Michael shrugged, checked his email, and headed to the meeting. He picked up a cup of coffee, and sat down with the other mechanics, as they bantered back and forth, until the lead showed up.

He had a piece of paper in his hand and a worried look on his face as he said, "I have the letter, but the gist of it is the CEO was pulling the plug on Cali. Basically, they will be shutting down operations in all Cali airports after Christmas. The economic cost is too high, the company is losing money flying the routes, and safety of employees, passengers and equipment is becoming questionable. The company will give everybody until Christmas to find a place in the system."

Michael slumped as the hubbub around him rose and fell, with shouted questions, gripes, moans and groans. He had suspected this was going to happen, due to the low incoming load factors, and the reduction of flights per day in to LAX and Cali in general.

He remembered Dave telling him that the company was reassigning routes for the pilots and FAs. In a daze, he grabbed his work tablet and sat in the truck, he'd put in a bid for Dulles, but hadn't heard anything back, and was beginning to worry that he might just have to make a run for it, and hope to find a job with another airline, if it came to that. The nearly deserted ramp, limited activity, and the blowing trash made the place look like a ghost town.

He turned on the radio, only to hear Moonbeam ranting on the radio about the betrayal of United Airlines leaving the great State of Cali, how they had turned it back on fairness and equality for all, betraying the trust of Cali, in their search for social justice for all. Michael turned off the radio with a snort, "What a load of leftist bullcrap, spinning unicorns, and rainbows for his braindead followers. All while they run Cali into the ground."

Late fall was turning to winter and Michael continued to work the flight line at the airport. He would get cryptic emails from his wife, talking about the treatments that her sister was getting to keep the illusion going that she was there to help her sister out with her illness. He would duly let the watch captain know there were still issues, but Myra hoped to be back by Christmas, that she missed Cali, but her sister was still hanging on. Michael was convinced that the State of Cali was monitoring the internet and emails, so his answers were always about how great things were.

There was one change in mid-December, Michael came home and saw his house was spray-painted with graffiti calling him a traitor to the cause and United Airlines evil for *abandoning* Cali. Michael shook his head and thought to himself, *Screw it, I don't care*. He left it alone, but a couple of nights later several bricks came through his windows with the word "traitor" painted on them. Michael knew that this was directed at him from Moore, the watch captain.

He drove to a local Home Depot, dodging all the illegals looking for work, and giving him the finger as he passed. Michael picked up several sheets of plywood and talked the employees into cutting them in half so he could get them in the car. He did the garage drill, then wrestled the plywood into the back of the garage and used a table saw to cut blanks to cover the broken windows, and the leftovers to go behind the other windows, in case some of them got broken as well.

It was Christmas Eve, and he was checking one of the few 767s that still flew in and out, when his friend Dave came in the cockpit, shedding his overcoat, "So, when you leaving?"

Michael shrugged, "Still waiting for some of the results of the latest bid so I can leave."

Dave shook his head, "I wish the company would make an offer, you are a damn good mechanic, and I would hate to see you get boned."

Michael glanced at him, then back to the whooping and hollering from the aft galley, as the barrio bunch found some good stuff, and started throwing food out the door into the platform truck. He shook his head in disgust, "I am so ready to leave! I'm tired of being treated like I don't belong here, when I have lived here longer than damn near everybody in the neighborhood has, but it don't matter, because they have protected status and I don't."

Dave nodded and put his hand on Michael's arm, drawing him all the way into the cockpit, "Some more gossip from the pilots' underground, You know that United announced their last flight will be on the 31st of December, right?" Michael nodded and Dave continued, "The actual last flight will be on the 27th. There are rumblings from corporate security that Moonbeam is planning on staging a massive protest with the Brownies, shutting down all the Cali airports, and seizing the airplanes on the last day. Security says they will demand reparations for climate damage and other things... Delta and American will be stopping their airplanes at the same time, if not sooner, since none of the carriers want their planes and passengers held hostage."

Michael smiled, "Worst case scenario, I'll ride the jump seat on the last flight."

"I'll hold it for you. I'm scheduled to fly the last seven six flight on the twenty-seventh, that six a.m. departure." Michael smiled in appreciation and waved to Emily as he headed out to continue his routine.

It was December 25th, Christmas day, when Michael drove home and saw his front door open.

With a sinking feeling, he parked his car in the driveway and walked into his living room. Everything he owned in the living room was either covered in paint, feces, or broken. He dropped to his knees and wept as he picked up what was left of the family portraits and other things that made the house a home for his family.

After calming down, he walked into the bathroom to get a towel and saw that somebody had busted the toilet with a sledgehammer, and thrown everything in the tub. He checked every room in the house, and what wasn't stolen, was vandalized.

He turned around and walked outside to open the garage to get the car inside and as he was opening the door he heard, "Merry Christmas, Mr. Gringo," and some raucous laughter from a couple of cars filled with Brownie supporters as they slowly drove by.

Michael keeping his face stoic, just waved back, and said, "*Felez Navidad.*" in return. He parked the car inside and closed the garage door. After closing and bracing the front door he walked into the bedroom, grabbed a rolling suitcase that was still in the closet and threw several pairs of work uniforms and toiletries in the suitcase. He went into the back yard, found the spot where he had buried his pistols, dug them up, cleaned them and loaded them. The revolvers had belonged to his dad and he wasn't going to leave them behind. Michael stashed the pistols in his suitcase with his uniforms and toiletries, and threw it in the back of the car. . Michael opened the door to the garage and backed the car out and left the car running closed and locked the garage door.

As a parting shot, he went into the kitchen and turned on the gas in the oven, figuring the vermin would return and throw Molotov cocktails into the house. He smiled grimly. He wanted to have a surprise for them. He eased the front door shut and drove slowly back toward the Interstate. He waved at the neighbors, whom he was sure were taking notes to notify the watch captain, and he wanted to make sure they knew he'd left before anything blew up.

Michael drove back to work, knowing he was on the cusp of a major life event. He parked the car in the employee parking, and he left the keys in the car, knowing he wasn't returning. He grabbed his suitcase and ever-present backpack, rolling them to the turnstile, after scanning his badge he humped his bags to the bus stop, and caught the shuttle to the United Airlines concourse. Going through the known crew access, Michael spent the next two days working airplanes, logging massive overtime because there weren't but three mechanics available, and sleeping where he could until the morning of the 27th.

He wrestled his suitcase and bags into his truck, and headed to his lead's office, to see him throwing a couple of things into a bag,"You still here?"

Michael shrugged, "Soon."

"I'm out of here," said the lead, "I have a flight to catch, and you need to get out of here today! The company has already shipped most of their airplane parts out of the state in cargo, and whatever is left has been rendered unusable. The company is fixing to fry the computer network so information can't be pulled off it and used against us."

Michael held out his hand, "You are a good man, a good boss, and I hope to see you again." The lead shook his hand and walked out of the door.

Michael headed to the 767 on the concourse. Parking his truck, he climbed up the ladder carrying his small suitcase, walked into the Jetway, and stepped into the forward galley, sliding his bag into the corner. He picked up the logbook, looked to see that everything was good, and signed the airworthiness certificate.

Dave stuck his head out of the cockpit, "I suppose you need a ride. Did you get a slot?"

"If you don't mind, you said you'd save me a seat. I'm going to be working out of Dulles. Seven six maintenance again."

Dave gave him a thumbs-up, and motioned to the jump seat, "It's yours once we push back." Michael stood in the galley as the passengers loaded, fidgeting as the clock in his head counted down. Finally, the cabin door closed, and Michael stepped into the cockpit, pulling the door closed, as Dave and his co-pilot were going through the checklist.

After pushback and engine start, the 767 started rolling down the taxiway as Michael let out the breath he hadn't realized he was holding. The sounds of the cockpit washed over him, as they took the runway and Dave said, "Okay, here we go." He pushed the throttles to full power, released the brakes, and the plane started rolling down the runway.

The copilot called V1, and Michael felt the plane lift off , as Dave and the co-pilot worked through the checklist, the noise as the gears retracting, flaps coming up and the vibrations smoothed out as the plane climbed.

Michael felt tears rolling down his face, a mixture of joy, sadness, and relief as the plane banked left and started climbing to cruising altitude in the early morning sky. To the south, there were a bunch of flashes of lights and a couple of seconds later there was a bit of turbulence.

Dave immediately contacted LAX Departure to get a report, and Michael grabbed the spare headset. The tower told them that there was a lot of military activity in the San Diego area and to come further left to avoid the area. Michael commented to Dave, "Looks like an airstrike, or set of strikes. I recognized the package and the pattern; looks like something blew the crap out of the naval station at San Diego

As the big 767 climbed toward the sun, Michael smiled. He was going to see his wife, live in free America, and start over, like that Lee Greenwood song that was so overplayed during Desert Storm.

Michael hummed the lyrics softly, as the plane headed east.

Carpetbaggers

Cedar Sanderson

Ryan sat at the top of the stairs, and listened hard to the conversation below him. It felt faintly ridiculous - he was, after all, fifteen -- nearly sixteen -- and technically almost an adult, not a toddler to be sitting here while the adults discussed stuff he wasn't supposed to know. But what he did know was that if he went downstairs, the conversation would shift, and they wouldn't be talking about what they were.

It wasn't the political part. He could hardly escape knowing that he was no longer a resident of the Beaver State of Oregon. He was now residing in the bright shiny newness that was Jefferson, a product of the messy split of California from the United States of America. That tear had left ragged edges, like ripping a sheet of paper from a notebook, and the inhabitants of the southern part of what had been Oregon and the northern part of California, had banded together against all others, and formed the territory. It wasn't a state yet. According to his social studies teacher, it just had to be ratified into statehood by Congress. But according to one of the lively conversations that took place below him in the big great room of his parent's ranch house, being a territory meant more independence from the Feds, and that was a good thing. They might vote to pass on statehood.

Ryan wasn't sure where he stood on the issue of independency, to use a word from his mother's favorite movie. In theory, he liked it. He was looking forward to becoming an independent adult, unlike his friend Brynna whose family had stayed behind during Calexit, and who had just found out that driver's licenses were no longer available to minors. She wouldn't be getting hers for two more years, while he would have his in just two months. Cali had decided that kids could get hurt, driving too early, and it was part of the sweeping Nanny Laws they had passed following their leave-taking from the good ol' USA. Ryan had been driving since his feet could reach the pedals while he could see out the windshield, on the ranch. The license was just a formality. He remained indignant on Brynna's behalf, though. She'd been quite vocally unhappy in the group chat they both belonged to when she found out she was going to have to wait. She couldn't get a job, either. Child labor...

But politics was not the central part of the low-voiced and urgent conversation under him. That, he'd have been down there for. No, this was far more disturbing, and he strained to make it all out.

"... the Wilman's place was hit hard." His father's low voice was gravelly, and hard to hear.

His mother's voice was higher, and clearer. "I offered Vi and the girls a place, but they are going up to her aunt's in Portland. There's a hospital there, although she did finally give in and let the SANE nurse collect samples from them at Medford General."

Ryan knew Pat - she purely hated Patty - Wilman. He went to school with her. She was a good kid, not girly at all. He was worried about her; he had texted her earlier and no reply yet.

"It was an *atrocity*." And that voice, cutting through the murmurs, was *Doña* Marguerite. She wasn't formally a *Doña*, but everyone called her that. Ryan thought he understood. She was regal, a real Lady.

She kept talking. "These Brownshirts are a plague on our land. They think they can come in, and take, and the Law matters not at all to them. My great-great-grandfather would have hunted them down and shot them. Or perhaps strung them up on the routes out of town. He did have a flair for the dramatic. He was also a law-abiding man, and would be horrified to see his race represented so." She snorted. "*La Raza*, indeed."

Ryan still felt a little cognitive dissonance - he rolled the word around in his mind, liking how it sounded - at hearing the tiny Hispanic lady talk about the formerly illegal immigrants who now made up the majority of the Cali Border Patrol.

"It's not just the Brownies, although I think Don Miguel would indeed be rolling in his grave. It's the carpetbaggers." His mother was very close to Doña Marguerite, and Ryan thought it was weird both of them referred to a long-dead Mexican-Californian Don like he was still alive and in the room. He guessed that was what came of having a historian for a mother.

The next morning, Ryan seized the opportunity when he was alone with her. "Mom?"

She looked up from the tortilla dough she was kneading like it had done something to her. "What, Ryan? Is this about riding out on the south fence? Because both your father and I have told you that you *cannot* do that one alone already."

Ryan felt a twinge. "I'm not a baby, Mom." He was taller than she was by half a head, and still growing, she said.

"You're always going to be my baby." She looked up at him, her hands stilling and her face softening. "I know you're near a man grown. But we want everyone to be riding in at least pairs, for now."

"That's not what I wanted to ask. What's a carpetbagger?" He grabbed a piece of the dough, and she made like she was going to swat him.

"You haven't heard that before? Oh, your school. Bleah." She sighed, and he could tell she was about to go into the rant he'd heard before.

Ryan held up his hand to stop her. "I know, I know, I'm getting a very watered-down biased view of history and they don't even call it history any more, it's social studies..."

She laughed. "I guess I've said that too many times. A carpetbagger is a term for people who descended on the South after the Civil War. They preyed on folks who had lost everything, and they forced them off their farms, because they'd been on the losing side. They were like a cuckoo's egg."

"What?" Ryan was confused.

"The cuckoo lays their eggs in other bird's nests, and when they hatch, they push the other nestlings or eggs out, until they have the parents feeding them and only them."

"So what does that have to do with carpet bags, and farms?"

She covered the dough so it could rest. "Well, the South had spent a lot of money during the War. They weren't material rich like the North was, so after the war ended, there were a lot of people who were flat broke. It wasn't about slaves - we've discussed that before - it was sheer economic disruption."

"Ok. What does that have to do with Jefferson? And cuckoos?"

She came and sat next to him at the table. "You overheard us last night."

"A little. Not all of it." He was pretty sure he wasn't supposed to have heard any of it.

She sighed sadly. "Jefferson isn't very rich, yet. We're trying to abide by regulations put in place when we split off from the FedGov, but they will be ending soon. We had a three-year restriction on mining and five on logging, for instance. Once we can tap into our own resources, then we'll be able to defend ourselves."

"From the Brownies?" Ryan used the slang term for the Border Patrol, who weren't as upright as their title made them out to be.

"And from people who are coming in, offering pennies on the dollar to buy ranches and farms, and desperate folks are taking them up on it. The cuckoo is pushing them out of their nests. But if the rancher doesn't take the offer..." She shrugged. "Something bad happens."

"Like their house burns down."

"Oh, baby..." She put a hand on his arm. "I'm sorry, but that's the least of it."

Ryan felt like someone was strangling him, his throat was so tight. His eyes started burning. He stared at her hand on his brown arm. He was tanned, but she was paler, and it was a funny contrast. He'd inherited his hair color from her – light brown, until he'd been out in the sun, and then it was white-blonde – but his skin was closer to his father's reddish brown in summer.

"I've got chores to do." He told her roughly, and headed for the door. She didn't follow him. She was a good mom, and gave him space when he needed it. Ryan found that the heavy work of shoveling manure out of stalls was helpful to get his brain off what might have happened to his classmate, and working on other problems. The exercise cleared his mind. He was working on the last stall when his father came and leaned over the stall door.

"Hey, son."

Ryan looked up at the tall man with dark hair and sober gray eyes. "Dad."

"Want to ride south with me?"

"Sure."

Ryan appreciated his father's style. Where his mother would use half a dozen words - and big ones, too - Dad just said enough to get his meaning across. And if you knew him well enough, you could read him from the expression on his face. Ryan knew some of his classmates were convinced his dad was scary. Brian had called him a 'mean mother...' but Ryan had put a stop of that phrase with a well-timed elbow to his friend's gut. Brian had shut up. He knew Ryan's dad wasn't a bad man. At the moment, Ryan could tell his dad was worried. He'd probably heard all about Ryan's talk with mom. A little while later, in the saddle and ambling slowly along the fenceline looking for breaks, that was confirmed.

"You know riding fences isn't just mending, these days."

"I know. We're looking for evidence that the Brownies are traveling through Jefferson up to Oregon." Ryan thought that was baloney, personally. They could just fly into Portland if they wanted.

"Ayup."

"And raiding ranches."

His dad looked at him hard for a minute. They were riding side-by-side. It was clear, open country near the house, they'd get into more broken hills and brush later, then some open patches of Ponderosa pines near the southern end of their range.

"It's not been confirmed," was what he said out loud. But his tone told Ryan that he hadn't been off the mark.

Ryan twisted to look off toward the east, where the Wilman place was. He felt the rifle barrel in its saddle scabbard as a reassuring pressure against his thigh. The old Marlin 30-30 was meant for bears and lions, but it would work fine against two-legged varmints.

"We don't know yet, kid." Now his dad had that soft tone his mom had been using earlier. "The Sheriff is doing everything he can to collect solid evidence he can use. We cain't just go vigilante."

"That would lower us to their level." Ryan was still struggling with that concept. He guessed that you didn't bully a bully. But you darn sure gave him a swift punch, if you wanted him to stop and let the little kids alone.

"Ayup. For now, we ride, and we watch."

They spent the rest of the morning doing just that. Ryan and his dad didn't talk much, except when they saw some sign. They rode within sight of one another, mostly. Sometimes the terrain got them separated for a minute or two. Ryan found that he was tense and nervous, jumping at every movement in the brush.

They had a place they liked to stop for lunch - a long-established camping spot, with a fireplace built out of loose stones. Ryan knew they wouldn't build a fire today, just sit and eat their sandwiches and relax for a bit before getting back to the chore. They were just loosening girths for the horses' comfort when Ryan heard other hooves approaching through the brush. He stiffened and turned toward the sound, and his father caught the motion. The older man held up a hand, signaling for Ryan to stay still and stay quiet.

A voice called out, loud and cheerful. "Halloo, the camp. I'm comin' in."

Ryan and his father relaxed. They knew that voice. A minute later a big man on a horse appeared out of the brush, followed by another man. Ryan's dad walked up to the first man and held out a hand.

"Boll. Good to see you, what brings you out this way?"

"Wa'al, it might be I heard Ms Irina made some gingerbread cookies." The county sheriff dismounted easily. He wasn't exactly graceful, but his movements looked deceptively easy for a man of his size.

"I can spare some." Ryan's dad turned to the second man. "Eddie. Good to see you too. Didn't make you for havin' a sweet tooth."

The smaller man grinned, revealing missing teeth in his narrow face. "I hain't much for sweets. Doc says I got diabeetus."

Ryan hung back, feeling awkward with the unexpected company. He knew them, but with the rifles in saddle scabbards, they must be on serious business and he was still a kid. The sheriff saw him. "Ryan, you have grown up some."

Ryan shrugged, looking down. The sheriff turned to his dad. "I'd say we're just here for the cookies, Dev, but it'd be a lie. We're asking for help, and Irina said we'd find you here."

"Y'know I'll do what I can." Dev gestured at the rough seating around the firepit. "But let's eat while we talk."

Ed climbed off his horse. Ryan thought the old cowboy was the most awkward person he'd seen on land, but throw him on the back of a horse and he could accomplish things that left the boy in awe. Ryan always made sure he was ringside when Eddie was riding at the fair or rodeo.

They nodded at one another now, the man and boy. Boll picked out a broad stump someone had cut and rolled it into place for seating. "Dev, you heard about the Willman's." It wasn't a question, just a starting place.

Ryan's dad, biting into his sandwich, just nodded. Ryan offered Ed a half of his tortilla wrap, but the man just waved it off with a grin.

Boll went on. "We're getting a little more proactive. Shoulda, coulda, woulda," He shrugged, letting his hands fall loosely into his lap. "No money, no manpower. So I'm goin' round asking for volunteers."

Ryan wondered why he hadn't just called. Dad had a cellphone in his pocket.

Dev answered Boll, "I can't give you much time. But..." He pointed at Ryan. "He's a good rider, and a decent tracker."

Ryan jerked upright. Was Dad saying...

Boll nodded. "He's a good kid. Won't leave you shorthanded?"

Ryan's dad shrugged. "Yeah, but needs must."

"When the devil drives." Boll finished the catchphrase Dev used all the time. "Thanks. I'll take care of him."

"You do that." Dev twisted around to face his son. "Ryan, you listen to Boll. And to Ed, here. You do what they say, and you do it prompt."

Ryan nodded. His heart was racing. He was being deputized!

"Dad, will you be okay alone on the fence?" Ryan remembered what his Mom had said.

"I'll be good, son." Dev's face was serious. "Don't call and talk to anyone about this. We're maintaining strict security protocols, and one of those is assuming cell transmissions are being monitored. Got it?"

Ryan noticed his father's speech had changed, from his normal drawl to a crisp, precise tone. Dev kept talking. "Don't even call your mother to let her know you're going off with Boll. When, or if, you get internet access, don't talk about where you are or what you're doing."

Ryan nodded again. He wasn't sure what to say, or if he needed to say anything at all. This was now exciting and scary.

Boll reached over and patted Ryan's shoulder. "You'll be fine, kid. I just need more eyes to look for sign. Lotta these city boys don't know what's up."

"Yessir." Ryan responded. He knew his eyes were probably wide, but he couldn't help himself.

Boll stood up. "I hate to run off."

Dev stood as well and they shook hands again. "You haven't got time for social niceties."

Boll shook his head. "Always freaks me when you drop the country boy act."

Ryan's dad just laughed. Ryan got up and headed to his horse, to cinch up the saddle. His father followed him, and squeezed his shoulder. "Keep your powder dry, son."

Ryan knew what he meant. His very modern rifle didn't need powder, not like the old muskets. But... "I'll be careful, Dad."

Ryan mounted and followed Boll and Eddie out of camp. They rode quickly, but in silence, for about an hour. Boll knew where a gate in the fence was, and took them through it, and then they headed east, and south. Ryan kept an eye on the ground, since he'd been told to look for sign, but he also paid attention to where they were heading. He didn't know this range well, but he'd ridden over it before with his friend Brian.

When they broke out of the brushy and broken ground, Boll waved him to come ride beside him. They'd been single-file on the trail, with no room to come abreast. Ryan obediently nudged his reliable gelding to move. Eddie peeled off and started scouting in an arc.

"How you doin', kid?" Boll asked.

"Doing fine, sir." Ryan looked around. He could see a good distance. "Sir, are we headed to the Fritzes?"

Boll looked approving. "Yep. Let's see, Jimmy's nearer your dad's age than yours. And he's doesn't have kids."

Ryan shook his head. "My friend Brian and I sometimes do a little work for Jim and Diane." The couple were in their late seventies. Jimmy did his best, but running a ranch was not a single-handed job.

"They reported some movement. Jimmy was out riding the range, but when he got in, he could see that three-four men on horses had been near the house."

Ryan nodded. He could see right off why that was a problem. The elderly couple was easy picking for the carpetbaggers if he understood what his mother had explained right. "Sir... what happened at the Willman's?"

Boll's face got still. He looked at Ryan for a long minute. "You're about the age of the older girl."

"Pat's in my class at school."

Boll sighed, a long, slow letting out of breath, and it seemed he deflated as the air went out of him. "Kid. I can't tell you much."

"I've been texting her and she's not answered."

Boll shook her head. "You keep trying. She's been through a lot, and she's likely to be spooky around you when she gets back. If she comes back here. But she'll need friends."

"Is she okay?" Ryan felt a stab of alarm.

"No. She's not. Sorry, kid. She'll live, but this'll be rough on her a long time. Might be all her life. M'sister went through something like it."

Ryan's throat felt tight and hot again. Boll changed the subject. "Here's the plan. We're goin' to try to catch them in the act. We'd really like to be able to prosecute some of these fuc- uh, bad guys."

Ryan didn't tell him he didn't care if he swore. Ryan felt like doing some himself at the moment.

"We'll scout, figure out where they were, and where they're likely to come at the farm from. Then we'll wait on them."

Ryan took a deep breath. "I'd like to wait with you."

"Thought you might. We're glad to have you. Your dad says you're a good shot. But there's to be no shooting until I say, got it? I want some of 'em alive. Doesn't have to be all of 'em."

Ryan thought about Pat, and her riding side by side with him, laughing at some stupid joke, and he felt a burning sensation wash over him. He'd be happy to pull the trigger when the time came, he thought. "Will it just be the three of us?"

Boll shook his head. "Nope. Got a couple of fellers in the house with the old folks. Jimmy has another team covering the East side of the valley. We'll be taking the West.

"Ok." Ryan shifted in the saddle. It wasn't near evening yet. "How long, um, do you think?"

"Might be tonight. Jimmy cut his trip short, but he was supposed to be out through sometime tomorrow. They were talkin' on their cell phones, which is why we think we shouldn't use those."

That was frightening to Ryan. He knew from books and TV that you could track a phone by the GPS, but he'd never thought of people being able to listen in on his calls. "Should I turn mine off?"

Boll shook his head. "Nah, not for now. Later, maybe."

Ed waved up ahead, and both Ryan and Boll kicked their horses into a canter. They reached him in a couple of minutes.

He pointed down. "See?"

Ryan could see it clearly. Several horses and one man, walking. Ryan leaned down, and his gelding followed his cues to walk a little down the trail. "One man wearing boots. I wonder why he's walking?"

"Ah see it." Boll dismounted.

"Probably can't ride." Ed pointed out. He was leaned back in his saddle rolling a smoke. Ryan found it unsettling, but his father had paddled him hard a few years back when he'd mouthed off to Ed about smoking being poison. Ed had just laughed and said he didn't want to live forever, but Dev hadn't been happy about Ryan's lack of respect. Ryan had learned that day that just because his teachers said something was bad, didn't mean he had the right as a kid to tell adults what to do.

"Probably. Those are military boots." Boll frowned and walked along the trail, snapping photos with his cell phone at a few places.

"Milspec don't mean anything." Eddie told Ryan while they waited. "Could be surplus, and all innocent-like."

"Yeah." Ryan didn't get it himself, but his friend Brian loved old combat boots and camo stuff.

"But it might mean somethin'." Eddie mused aloud.

"The military might be involved?" Ryan couldn't quite believe that. His dad was a veteran, and Ryan remembered meeting some of the men Dev had served with. And it seemed like half the men in town, and a few of the women, were vets.

"Naw, not the US military." Eddie tapped the side of his nose. "But they's some that don't like Jefferson."

"Oh." Ryan thought this over. Cali would like to have back those resources his mom had been talking about. He wasn't sure how that connected with the carpetbaggers, but it certainly had to do with the Brownies. He wanted to be sick as he thought about what they might have done to Pat.

Boll rejoined them. He'd overheard Ed, it seemed. "If we can prove we can take care of ourselves, then we can keep them from claiming we're lawless and steppin' in with a military governorship."

That made sense to Ryan. So what they were doing was bigger than just getting the guys who had hurt Pat. And her family.

Boll got back on the big horse he rode. "I think you're right, Ed. One less horse than there should be, so that one's walkin'"

"Slow 'em down." Ed commented.

"That it will. Helps. They're likely to have not gone too far." Boll tipped his hat back a little. "I think we're headed for camp and watching time. They won't move until dusk, earliest."

The three of them rode with more purpose, now that they knew where the men had been. Boll or Eddie had scouted this spot before, Ryan realized. They headed right for it. A little bench under the ridgeline let them tether the horses by a small stream that curved along the side of the hill, undercutting it badly in places. Ryan wouldn't have liked to be here in spring; it would be a muddy mess. But there was a stand of trees that offered concealment for the men as well as the horses, and they could lay up on the ridgeline and see the western slope into the valley where the Fritz place lay. Ryan recalled there was another group over on the other side, but he couldn't see any trace of them.

He couldn't call his mother, and it wasn't dark yet, so he found himself fussing over rocks and twigs in the camp area, making it neat and clean. Eddie shook his head at him, then faded into the trees. Ryan didn't follow. Boll ate a sandwich from his own saddlebag. "No fire, kid. Cold dinner tonight. Tomorrow morning if we can we'll get breakfast from the Flanagan place."

Ryan nodded. Boll jerked his chin upward. "I'm going to go keep an eye on the trail. Come along."

Shortly after, Ryan found himself lying on the ground just at the ridgeline. The sun was down, but there was still blue light at the horizon, fading slowly up to the inky black over their heads. A lone star was out, and Ryan wondered if it were a satellite. Boll, lying beside him with binoculars trained on the trail, shifted his weight. Ryan wondered if he were lying on a rock. Ryan had shoved a few out of his way when he slid over the ridgeline, but he'd missed at least one.

"So, kid." Boll's voice was low, but light. "Whatcha thinking?"

"I was wondering about your name." Ryan blurted. He could feel his cheeks heat when he realized he'd said that out loud.

Boll chuckled quietly. "I'm assumin' you don't mean Black."

"Boll?" Ryan really was curious, and it didn't sound like the Sheriff was mad about it.

"Well, m'given name is Cotton. When I was 'bout your age, I decided Boll was cooler."

"Oh." Ryan digested this. The teasing must have been intense.

"Could be worse." The Sheriff went on in a musing tone. "M'sister's name is Silk."

Ryan silently agreed. It could always be worse. "Um. Why...?" Ryan couldn't figure out how to politely ask an adult if their parents had been nuts. He heard in his tone, as much as saw, the big man's grin as it flashed in the dark. Boll shifted his weight again.

"W'al, Mom was a bonafide hippie. Me'n Silk, we were born in a commune."

Ryan looked toward Boll's face, but it was dark enough he couldn't tell if Boll was pulling his leg.

"Keep your eyes peeled, kid." Boll wriggled back from the edge a bit before getting up. He wouldn't skyline himself, even as dark as it was.

Ryan kept looking into the darkness. He was listening, now, rather than using his eyes. He could faintly hear Boll's footsteps crunching away behind him. He could hear a coyote yipping, and an insane number of crickets and stuff chirping. But no hooves on stone. The tracks they had seen were of shod horses, which would make more noise. He remembered reading that Apaches, the greatest guerilla fighters, only rode ponies with bare hooves. But who would have shod an Apache's horses, anyway?

He heard Boll coming back, and felt a gentle touch on his boot. He slithered back a ways before he felt like he could get up.

"Ed's taking watch. Turn in and sleep, kid."

"Yessir." Ryan yawned, and he could hear Boll chuckling behind him as he headed for his bedroll.

Ryan woke up to Ed shaking his shoulder. He blinked.

"Breakfast." Eddie announced cheerfully. "You one o'those kids that drinks coffee?"

"Um." Ryan sat up and rubbed his eyes. "Mom doesn't like it, but yeah."

Ed laughed and pointed at the thermos. Ryan rolled out of his sleeping bag and shook out his boots before stomping them on. Ed handed him an enameled mug and a sandwich baggie of jerky. "No fire, smoke can be smelt for miles. My own recipe, that" He pointed at the jerky Ryan was now holding.

"Ouch." The metal mug transferred heat way too easy, Ryan decided. "Thought breakfast was going to be at Brian's place?"

"Change of plans. No movement last night. Sending you home for the day."

"Oh." Ryan tried not to feel a pang of disappointment. It didn't work.

"Your mom needs you."

Well, that felt better. Until it hit him that she'd been virtually alone at the house. "Is she okay?"

"She's fine. Just..." Ed tapped his nose again. "Needs a kid, she said."

"A kid?" Ryan echoed, confused.

Ed shrugged. "Anyway, you can ride up to the road and trailer home. Faster. See ya tonight."

Ryan chewed on the jerky slowly. It wouldn't have been his choice for breakfast, but it hit the empty spot in his belly nicely.

"This's really good," he told Eddie, who grinned. He wasn't just being nice, either. The dried meat was very tasty, not so spicy he couldn't taste anything, like some of the homemade stuff he'd tried had been.

It wasn't more than an hour later he was pulling into his home driveway. Sitting in the passenger seat, he watched the countryside roll by and mused on how short this felt compared to the hours of riding the day before. It was very normal and after the tension of hunting men the day before, he felt like he had mental whiplash.

His mother came out on the porch, wiping her hands on a dishtowel, then waving at him. It would have looked right in some Western movie. Ryan waved back, and then helped get his gelding out of the trailer. Holding Salsa's reins, he shook the driver's hand awkwardly. "Thanks, Sam."

"See you tonight." the other replied. He tipped his hat in the direction of Irina, and then climbed back in the truck.

Ryan entered by the kitchen door after he'd put Salsa safely in the corral. He started levering his boots off in the mudroom. "Mom?"

His mother put her head in. "Oh, good. Come in here, please?"
Ryan walked sockfoot into the other room, which was full of people. He looked around, bewildered. His mother was standing at the stove, cooking pancakes from the smell. "Um, hi?"

"Ryan." Dr. Brandt looked up from the table. "This is Letrice."

"Hey?" Ryan waved awkwardly at the slender teen girl sitting at the table. She looked vaguely familiar, but he didn't know from where. There were very few people in town with that velvety black skin. The other people in the room were an older couple, probably her parents as there was a strong resemblance, and a nurse he recognized from the clinic, but didn't remember her name.

"Hi." The girl flicked her fingers. "I'm, um, Space Whale."

Ryan's jaw dropped. He couldn't help it. No wonder she looked familiar. He'd seen her on grainy video chats more than once when the group chat he was part of was feeling social. "Spacey?" his voice cracked at the end of her nickname.

"You said... you said if it got real bad I should come to Jefferson. I, uh, brought my family too."

Ryan stepped forward and hugged his friend. "I was worried about you when you stopped talking in the group chat."

She clung to him for a minute and he could feel her shoulders hitch, like she was trying not to cry. Her short, curly black hair felt soft and he tried not to pet it while he patted her shoulder. He was having sensations he'd rather not, at the moment.

"Not that I'm not glad you're here, but how did you find me?" He asked. Ryan looked over at his mother. "I'm not putting our address out there, Mom, I promise. Not even to the chat."

Letrice shook her head. "No, I played detective. You put a pic of those cool spurs you got in the chat?"

"Yeah?" Ryan sat down at the only empty chair. He was still wondering why the doctor and nurse were there.

"You sorta put the package too close..."

"You hacker!" Ryan laughed. "Okay, I didn't even notice."

Letrice grinned. "Anyway, so we came."

"You're okay?"

"I'm okay. Or I will be, once..." She ducked her head.

The doctor cleared his throat. "We need to get the chips out of them as soon as possible. And now that we know how they found us..."

Letrice's father leaned over the table, holding out his hand. Ryan shook it, feeling weird that this older man should be offering his hand. "Thank you, young man. Letrice wouldn't tell us how she knew where to go. She just kept saying you were like a brother - well, she said you were the chat dad." He looked at his daughter with a bit of a wink. "I don't mind. Not now that I see you."

"Oh, ok." Ryan shrugged. "It's just that I make bad jokes."

"And take care of people." Letrice put in.

"What's this about chips?" Ryan asked.

His mom interrupted the conversation. "Water's boiling. That's the timer."

"Right. It's time." Dr Brandt stood up, and Letrice's dad stood up too. "You first?"

"I gotta set the example." He grinned at his daughter and wife. "If'n the big bad Marine can take it..."

His wife rolled her eyes at him. "Former Marine, Jon, former."

"Honey, they ain't no former Mah-reens." The cocky man followed the doctor out into the other room, where Irina and the nurse had already disappeared to.

Ryan turned his attention to Letrice.

"Chips?" he asked.

"Microchips. They chipped us like dogs!" She threw her hands in the air. "And they can track us anywhere, so if we don't get them out they can track us down and drag us back."

"What?" Ryan didn't believe it. "You're not slaves. They can't just haul you off. Can they?"

Letrice's mother put her hand out and her daughter reached across the table to hold it. "No, we're not slaves. But that chip, it made us feel like they thought they owned us. And Jon really fought hard against it. But we didn't have a choice if we were going to be allowed to work, to have a driver's license, to keep our house..."

Ryan felt his jaw drop again. Before today, he'd thought that was a figure of speech, but today he was learning a lot.

"So now your house is like the Underground Railroad." Letrice bounced a little. "And it's such a cool house! Your mom is the bomb."

"Um. Yeah, she is." Ryan was still trying to wrap his head around the whole microchip thing. "You have a chip, too?"

He didn't think she had a job, and he knew she wasn't old enough for a driver's license.

"Yeah. They said it was a vaccination, but it wasn't. Dad lost his mind." The two women exchanged glances.

"That would make me mad, too." Ryan said. "So you decided to get out of Cali?"

"Yeah." Letrice sighed. "Took a while to persuade mom. Sorry, Mom."

"It's okay, honey. I just didn't see the whole thing crumbling around my ears until what happened to you. I was more concerned with work than politics and such." She patted her daughter's hand.

"So we're here. And your Dr. Brandt said that he had work for dad, already. I guess medics are in short supply."

"Social workers, not so much." Her mother put in drily. "I'll find something."

"And your mom said I could get a job." Letrice sounded super excited, and she was bouncing up and down again. "It's not illegal for kids to work, here!"

"Uh, yeah." Ryan remembered how mad she'd been about the elevation of legal age for work in Cali. "You know, I think I might be able to talk to someone about that."

He was thinking about the Fritzes, alone at their place all day while their son was trying to keep the fences mended and cattle in. "I don't know how much they could pay, but it would be a place to stay."

Jon came back into the room in time to hear that. He was shirtless, and he twisted around to show them the small bandage in the center of his back. "See?"

"My turn, I guess," Letrice's mom stood up.

"A place to stay?" Jon asked, before kissing his wife and swatting her on the butt. "Go, woman!"

"Well, maybe. It's just an idea."

Ryan's Mom came back in carrying a pot of steaming water. "What's your idea?"

"Well, the Fritz's could use some help." Ryan squirmed. He wasn't used to being the center of this much attention.

"That's a good idea." His mother put the pot back on the stove. "Have you eaten?"

"Yes, but I'll take pancakes." Ryan got up and fetched a plate. "Spacey, did you eat?"

"I'm stuffed. Your mom is a great cook."

Irina laughed. "Thanks, Letrice. He really is the dad, isn't he?"

"Oh, yeah. Makes sure we all eat, and do our homework." Both women laughed, and Ryan could feel his ears heating up.

"He's a good kid." Jon had gone somewhere - probably the bathroom, Ryan guessed, and was now fully dressed. "Ryan." He stuck out his hand. "Seriously, man. Thanks."

Ryan took his hand again, balancing his plate in the other. Jon pulled him in and hugged him.

"We woulda come out, anyway, but this..." He let go and waved his hand toward the other room where his wife had just let out a yelp, "this is a lifesaver."

"Um." Ryan wasn't sure what to say.

"We're delighted to help." His mother rescued him. "And I think Ryan's idea for you to stay with the Fritz's for a while, at least, is a good one. We don't know if they were tracking your chips. They - the Brownshirts - have a lot going on at the moment. But for various reasons, there's a team of men doing overwatch at the Fritz place." She nodded at Ryan. "That's where he was last night. He'd still be there if Letty hadn't insisted she'd only talk to him."

Ryan shot his friend a dirty look. She just rolled her eyes at him. Ryan sat and started to eat. Behind him, Jon was talking to his mom. "Could they use a former Marine?"

"I thought you said there was no former?" His daughter smart-mouthed at him.

His response was interrupted by her mother's voice calling for her.

Irina answered serenely, as though nothing had happened. "Yes, I'm sure they can. We're shorthanded out here."

Which is how Ryan found himself guiding Jon back up to the campsite a few hours later. It was past noon, and his mother had insisted on not only packing a lunch, but sending dinner along with them. She and Letrice's mom, who turned out to be named Shanika, "but just call me Nika, honey," had teamed up in the kitchen. Jon had leaned over and stage whispered to Ryan, "Women get upset, they cook. But don't you go makin' 'em sad, boy, then they stop cooking for you and throw pots, instead."

That sally had gotten them banished to the barn by Nika. Letrice, it turned out, had never been on a horse. Ryan told her he'd teach her how to ride, but they didn't have time. He tacked and saddled Salsa, and one of his dad's horses, a big quiet blue roan named Moke, for Jon. Jon, it turned out, had done very little riding.

"They's not a lot a barns in LA, kid." He explained. "I might be better walking."

"Well, maybe. But we might need to move faster than that." Ryan wasn't sure. The veteran was quick on his feet.

"Oh, I won't turn it down. Just warning you."

When Sam pulled in, they were ready to go, and now they were riding back to where Ryan had spent the night. Jon was armed with a shotgun and then Irina had gone to the display over the mantle. She had gently taken one of the pieces hanging there, a 1911

Ryan knew had been carried in WWI by his great-grandfather. Jon looked at the antique semi-automatic pistol Irina had presented him with along with its leather holster. The man had acted like she'd given him the crown jewels. "You sure about this?"

"You look like you know how to take care of it. Not drop it in the dirt. It's loaded." She looked him in the eyes, and he straightened his back.

"Yes, Ma'am. I'll take good care of it. And it's an honor."

Ryan knew it had been his grandfather's gun. He wondered why it was so special. He was carrying his Marlin. He'd decided his competition rifle wasn't the right gun to carry out on the range, and it didn't fit in the scabbard. Re-zeroing the scope would be a witch with a B, and he didn't believe he'd be shooting someone today.

"Hello, the camp." He called out in a low voice when they got near. Eddie stepped out of the brush, and Ryan jumped so hard he almost fell off his horse.

Ed bent over laughing. "You brought backup," He managed when his fit was over.

Jon, grinning, bent over and offered his hand. "That was brilliant, man! I'm Jon Silverman."

"Ed." They shook hands. "You saw me comin'."

"Well, I was trained on ambushes. But I figured the kid could use the lesson."

Ryan gave them both a dirty look. "Ed, he could have shot you."

"Nah." Jon shook his head. "He don't smell like a Brownie."

Ryan tried to figure out if that was a joke, or a racist remark.

"Come on up to the camp." Ed led the way on foot, the geldings ambling behind them. Jon, for all his protestations about riding ability, wasn't bad once he was in the saddle.

"Boll's on watch. How about you relieve him?" Ed suggested once they were dismounted and the horses cared for.

Ryan was glad to leave the company of the men who had been teasing him. He slithered into place next to the big sheriff, who was lying in the shade of a bush.

"Afternoon, Ryan." Boll greeted him. "Mighty quiet up here."

"Yep." Ryan said. He was dealing with that feeling of weird shifting again. From sitting in his own house with his internet friend, to lying on top of a ridge in a scene straight out of an old Western.

"I hear you brought reinforcements." Boll said.

Ryan wondered how he'd heard, since they weren't using cell phones. "Just one, father of my friend. He used to be a Marine."

Boll chuckled, his body shaking. "With a Marine, there's no used-to-be."

"That's what he said." Ryan felt left out of the joke. "And I was thinking that my friend's family could stay with the Fritzes."

"Yep, I heard that. Your mom's taking them over now."

Boll pointed, and when Ryan squinted he could see the thin plume of dust that indicated a vehicle traveling along the long dirt drive. "She must have left not long after we did."

"She said that Letty can handle a gun, but Nika refuses to learn to shoot one." Boll went on.

"I didn't know that." Ryan didn't remember Spacey -- Letty -- ever talking about learning how to shoot. He'd shut up about shooting and hunting after Brynna lost her mind in the chat group over it. So Letty must have learned by example from her crash and burn.

"We all learn things - 'bout ourselves and friends - when crisis comes." Boll opined in his deep voice.

They fell silent for a long time. Ryan was watching a hawk riding the wind up, then dropping back down in precipitous dives. Birds were cool. He wished he could fly like that, it looked like fun. The bird broke off its dive abruptly and pulled up, flying to the side and into the hillside trees.

"Boll." Ryan pointed. "Something spooked a hawk over there."

There was enough brush and trees to conceal what was moving on the ground, but the hawk had been right over it when he thought better of his playtime. Boll trained his binoculars on the area.

"Huh. Didn't think we'd see anything in daylight. They're gettin' bold."

He shifted and pulled a bulky handheld radio out of his cargo pocket. "N1UUX to base, over."

The radio crackled and Ryan recognized Diane Fritz's voice. "Base, we hear you N1UUX, go ahead, over."

"Base, we have eyes on three men. No horses, might not be all the men down there. They're in a tangle, over."

"N1UUX, will repeat back to the office. Base out."

"N1UUX out." Boll clicked off.

"What is that?" Ryan asked.

"Ham radio. Not many of us still bother to keep licenses, but I got bored settin' in the office, started picking up skills. And once in awhile there's a search out past cell tower range."

"You don't think they can hear you?" Ryan asked.

Boll snorted. "We're frequency-hopping, and transmittin' in the clear, but they don't seem to have cued into it yet. It's old school."

"Mom's down there." Ryan said. He wasn't telling the other man, just verbalizing his thoughts.

"I know, kid. We won't let them get anywhere near her."

"What are we going to do?" Ryan asked. He could see the men, now. They were following what looked like a deer path, walking single file. There were more than three of them.

"First, I get in touch with the other camp. Ed's out there, and your friend's probably along with him."

Boll lifted his hand and used small finger motions to show Ryan where he thought Ed and Jon were. "Ed scouted that yesterday, he said it was a good ambush spot."

Boll lifted the radio again. Ryan watched the file of men. There were, unless he'd missed one or two, ten men. No horses in sight. They must have decided they would be able to sneak up better without the horses raise dust. Boll ended his brief conversation and looked at him. "You okay with being here alone?"

"You're going down there?" Ryan looked back at the men. He'd like to be part of the force stopping them. They had hurt Pat. And now they were threatening his mom.

"You're overwatch. I'm leaving my 'nocs with you, and you have that rifle of yours. If you can't make that shot, I'll eat my hat. I know what your momma was." Boll gripped his shoulder. "You'll do, kid."

"When do I know I can shoot?" Ryan felt his stomach cramp at the idea of shooting at the distant men, even while he wanted to put them down like rabid dogs.

"You'll know."

Ryan listened as Boll left, but he didn't look away from the men. With the binoculars, he could make out facial and clothing details. Half the men were in Cali Border Patrol Uniforms, but oddly there were no rank markings on the dark brown shirts that lent them their nickname. Ryan knew it had a double meaning, his Mom had explained that one. He had to wonder who had thought a brown uniform shirt was a good idea, given history.

The hawk circled overhead, also watching the men with suspicion. He wasn't playing his game with the air currents anymore. The day was getting hotter, and it was very quiet up on the lonely ridge.

Ryan set up his rifle the best he could. He didn't have a scope on it, so he wasn't as sure as the sheriff he could make a good shot. He also wasn't sure he wanted to. He did, but he didn't. He waited, and time seemed to slow to a near stand-still. The silence was broken by the snap of a gunshot. The men were directly below his hiding spot, having followed the trail where it curved up through a meadow that was full of sun-bleached grass, leaving them in the open. Boll and the others must have been in that clump of cottonwood by the creek, facing directly at the line of men.

Ryan looked through the binoculars and saw that one man had fallen. One of the ones in the stripped-down uniform. The others were scattering wildly, some headed for the cottonwoods. Two more shots, and two men fell down, the third headed in that direction zigzagged off to Ryan's left. Three down, maybe just injured, but down, and seven more now hiding. Ryan could see that two had simply dropped into the tall grass and were lying still.

He wasn't going to shoot someone who was just lying there. But the man who had zagged away from the ambush was now in the brush, and creeping toward the cottonwoods, keeping the brush between him and the ambushers but in plain sight of Ryan.

Ryan steadied the rifle, feeling the warmth of the metal from the sun, and the silky wood of the antique stock on his cheek as he sighted in on the man's back. He felt sick. But he couldn't let the man sneak up on his team. On his friends. He let out his breath slowly, held it, and squeezed the trigger. The man fell, and only then was Ryan aware of the echoes of the shot ringing in his ears.

One of the men in the grass jumped up and ran. But he was headed back in the direction he'd come from, and Ryan let him go. His hands were shaking. He put the rifle down and picked up the binocs again. No one was moving down there, right at the moment. The men who had been shot were lying still, dead or playing possum. He couldn't tell. One of the men lying in the grass started to move, snake-like, but also headed back in the direction they had come in. After a few minutes of this he got up to a slouch and started to run, bent over. No one fired at him, and he glanced over his shoulder a few times, gradually standing upright and running until he was back in the brush.

Ryan didn't know where five of the men had gone. Four were shot - one by his hand - and one was sitting on the ground on the trail, just his foot in sight. He waited.

Boll appeared out of the cottonwoods, walking straight like he wasn't afraid of anything. He stopped, looked around, and shouted something. Ryan couldn't make out the words, just sounds, from his vantage point. The big man was carrying his pistol by his side, but it was pointing down. He ambled up to the first man and looked down at him, then headed for the next one, calling over his shoulder. Jon and Ed appeared at the edge of the woods, both carrying guns at the ready.

Ryan kept watching while the three men swept the meadow and reached the brushy trail. Ed and Jon were covering Boll, who was still walking like he ruled the world. They reached the sitting man, and Boll hauled him into sight, one beefy hand on the man's uniform collar. He put cuffs on him, and they started walking back toward the men lying down in the meadow. Ryan felt dizzy, and put his face down on his sleeve for a second, then he went back to keeping a watch.

They had two prisoners, now, one of the shot men sitting up was being handcuffed to the one who'd sat down and given up. Ryan could see a movement on the trail back up-valley, and then heard a short volley of shots. The other team must have found the runners who were retreating from the ambush. Ryan relaxed a little. He watched helplessly while Jon and Ed shouldered their guns and picked up the man he'd shot, one under each shoulder, and carried his limp form over to the others. Once Boll had all four in one place, he lifted his radio. Ryan assumed he was talking on it, since he couldn't hear anything. Then Boll looked up, straight at him, and waved his hat.

Ryan got the horses and headed slowly down the hill, leading all of them. He felt really shaky and sick, now. He was half-afraid there would be a man hiding in wait for him, but the woods were quiet until he made his way into the meadow. Boll was standing with the prisoners and bodies, but Jon was lounging in the shade. Ed was nowhere in sight.

"Aha. Good job, Ryan." Boll met him with a clap on the shoulder. "We've got a chopper comin' for this lot. Even if there are other snakes, we've got a headless rattler to wave in their faces and prove we can fight 'em, and show the world who's doin' this to our folks. Now that we've got 'em, I don't plan to lose 'em.'"

"Yeah." It would really suck if this were all for nothing. "Did the other team...?"

"Got 'em all."

Ryan felt the relief wash over him. "So the Fritz place is safe."

Boll nodded. "And others. This one," he pointed at the man who'd sat down on the trail, 'has been singin' like a bird already."

Jon ambled up. "Are we goin' to go check on the ranch?"

Boll nodded. "You two ride on in. Ed and I will wait for the 'chopper."

"We'll wait." Ryan was surprised by how firm his voice came out. He was still shaking internally. "We'll go when it's all done."

Jon nodded at him, but for once didn't crack wise. Boll just smiled. "Reckon that's a good idea, Ryan."

Ryan looked at the cluster of men behind them. "How many dead?"

"Two here, one at the other team's position." Boll reported, then half-turned. "You didn't kill your man, Ryan."

Ryan's knees shook. "I wasn't sure. I broke protocol and didn't aim for his head or chest."

"He'll never walk right again." Jon put in, his voice grim. "Not any more than he'll rape again."

Ryan recoiled. He had been mentally avoiding that word since his vague conversation about Pat with the sheriff.

Jon went on remorselessly. "Put a shot right through the hip and pelvis, came out through his balls."

Boll held up a hand. "He doesn't need the gory details."

Jon looked Ryan in the eyes. "You want to court my daughter, son, you have my permission."

He walked off, and Ryan felt like someone had just clobbered him upside the head with a two-by-four. Boll seemed to be having a choking fit.

"But... I don't want to court anyone!" Ryan finally managed to choke out.

"Now, now, don't tell him that right now." Boll's amusement came out in his voice. "And I wouldn't tell him just yet your momma's a sniper, neither."

"I have no idea what's going on." Ryan decided he'd take the horses to water. It seemed like the best bet.

He was standing in the shade watching them suck up cool drinks when his cell phone vibrated. It startled him. He'd forgotten he'd left it on, and now he checked to see who had texted him. It was Pat. She'd just sent two words, but Ryan felt tears start to fall, much to his inner rage. She'd just said "be okay."

He'd be okay. She'd be okay. They'd all be okay. He swiped at his face, and straightened his shoulders. He wasn't a kid anymore. He could hold a man's place. It would be okay.

Overhead, the thumping of a helicopter's blades came closer and closer.

Night Passage

Tom Rogneby

"'Night, Joe," Jennifer said as she passed her hand under the clinic's reader to clock out. A faint beep and a flash of red light from the appliance let her know that it had recognized the chip in her right hand and that she was officially able to start her vacation.

"'Night, Jen," Joe replied. "Gonna be another hot one tomorrow."

"We're heading to a bed and breakfast in Monterey for a few days," Jen held the door open as she paused to talk with the man. "It'll be cooler on the coast."

She was tall, with long legs and well-muscled arms. Her hair, which one of her college boyfriends had once described as the color of honey in sunshine, ran down the back of her faded gray scrubs in a tight braid.

"At least you'll be away from all this smoke." Joe's teeth stood out against his dark skin as he smiled at the nurse and stepped out to join her on the cement entranceway. "You want me to walk you to your car?"

The smell of wood burning struck Jen as soon as she stepped out of the clinic's air-conditioned comfort. The news feeds had been bursting with reports of wildfires in the Sierras all week, but the government had assured everyone that no damage to homes or businesses was expected.

"Nah, that's all right," Jen said, smiling again. "It's just over there." She nodded at the small, beat-up compact she had parked on the far side of the parking lot. It was the only vehicle left in the lot, since Ramon, who had relieved her for the night shift, had been dropped off by his boyfriend. The harsh light of the LED bar that hung above the entrance reached just far enough out that she could see its dull gray outline against the trees.

"Well, I'll be here if you need me."

"Thanks."

Jen gave the parking lot a good, long look before stepping away from the crumbling patio at the building's entrance. Her car sat in the shadows of tall eucalyptus trees at the far end of the lot, their pungent scent competing with the smoke in the faint, hot breeze. Above it, the skeletons of floodlights, which she had never known to work in the two years she had worked at the clinic, looked down on the cracked asphalt like immense aluminum flowers. Seeing nothing, she fished her phone from her bag.

She tapped "Hi hon. lving work. C U in the AM. Miss U" onto the screen once she had unlocked it with her identity chip and the CalSec emblem had faded to allow her access to the network. She hit send just as she reached her vehicle. The car noticed her presence and unlocked the door for her. It cheerfully chirped at her and helpfully turned on its interior lights. Their dim illumination made her feel better as she looked over her shoulder to see if Joe was still standing at the door to the building. He saw her look and waved.

Jen raised her hand to wave as well, when she heard rushed footsteps coming across the pavement. She turned to see where the noise was coming from just as someone grabbed her from behind and threw her up against the side of her car.

Instinctively, Jennifer threw her elbow back just like her instructor at her "Strong Women of the Future" class had taught her. Pain lanced up her arm as she felt the corner of her elbow impact with something that crunched under its hard bone.

"*Pinche puta!*" a voice squealed as Jen screamed for help. She tried to turn around to confront her attackers, but strong hands forced her head down. Blood bloomed from her forehead as it caught the hard edge of the door. Jen heard voices behind her, then felt hands tearing the thin fabric of her scrubs.

She screamed again, thrashing to get away. Her phone rattled to the pavement beside the car, along with her bag. Her struggles gained her enough freedom to stand upright once again, and she caught sight of the door to the clinic closing as Joe ducked back inside.

Then, someone grabbed her long braid and used it to drag her head back, then shoved her hard against the windshield. She felt the drawstring of her pants scrape along her hips and thighs as they were yanked down, then another blow to her head made the world fuzzy and dark. The last thing she heard before slipping into unconsciousness was the sound of laughter as someone cut the strap of her bra.

***

Jen heard someone's voice as if it were far off and under water. Pain, again fuzzy and far off, crushed in on her from every angle. The blinding light that struck her when she eased her eyes open, however, was insistent and instant. She blinked a few times, which for some reason added to the pain, before her vision cleared and she blearily looked around the small room.

Jen blinked again, trying to get a better picture of where she was. The concrete block wall opposite her was painted a soft gray, with a single maroon stripe running diagonally across it. Harsh sunlight was coming through dusty blinds on a narrow window, some of it reflecting from a mirror above a sink. To one side of her a dingy plastic curtain hung from a long metal rod. On the other side, a small woman wearing a plain brown suit looked down on her with a look of concern. Her pale complexion made her look cadaverous under the cheap light fixtures embedded above the bed. To Jen's somewhat addled mind, it looked like she tried to compensate for it by wearing too much make-up. On the lapel of her jacket, a badge of some kind winked in the light, driving daggers into Jen's eyes every time the woman moved.

"Ms. Bradford-Costa?" the woman said in a sweet, gentle voice.

"Missus," Jen slurred. Her tongue scraped against the roof of her mouth as she tried to speak.

The woman picked up a cup from the small table next to Jen and pressed its straw between her lips. Jen sipped, letting the cool water swirl down her throat. Swallowing was agony, but the feeling of the water in her mouth was heavenly.

"Thanks," Jennifer said tiredly. She slowly pushed her tongue across her dry lips, then withdrew it when she felt stitches prick at its tip.

"Ms. Bradford-Costa?" The woman's voice was reedy and pitched in a way that made Jen want to wince.

"I'm married. It's Mrs. Costa."

The woman's lips quirked up in a faint smile. "My name's Gloria Anderson-Hermosa. I'm an investigator with People Services."

"Where am I? Where's Mark?"

"I understand that he'll be here in a few minutes, but I have to ask you a few questions first."

Jen tried to take a deep breath, but stopped when pain from either side of her torso stabbed at her. "What happened?"

"Well, that's what I'd like to know," the woman said. "Just let me get this down, all right?"

Without waiting for a response, she pulled a tablet from her shoulder bag and waved her hand over it. The tablet chimed and a green light started flashing across its top.

"May I have your identity, please?" she asked sweetly. Again, not waiting for Jen to answer, she brought the tablet down to Jen's hand, causing it to chime again as it recorded her identity code.

"Ah, excellent. Jennifer Lynn Bradford-Costa, born January 24, 1993?" Gloria read as she looked up questioningly at Jennifer. Jen nodded and replied, "Yes."

"Good, now the doctor told me that your co-worker found you and brought you into the clinic…"

"Clinic?" Jen interrupted. "I'm at work?"

"Mister… ah, Hamilton found you in the parking lot and carried you in when he got off shift this morning."

"Hamilton?"

"Joseph Hamilton, the security guard," Gloria explained, trying to continue with the session script that was flashing on her tablet.

"Joe?" An image of the security guard closing the door to the clinic behind him flashed across Jen's mind.

"You're pretty badly beaten up," Gloria patted Jen's hand. "Let's talk about your husband."

"Mark?"

"Ms. Bradford-Costa, I know how hard it is to talk about something so personal, but we know that most violence like this comes from those closest to the victim."

"No!" Jen said forcefully, ignoring the pain that washed across her middle. "It wasn't Mark!"

"An accident, then? Someone hit you with their car?"

"Someone grabbed me. They hit me, and they… they…" Jen let the words fall from her bruised lips, then whispered, "They raped me."

"They?"

"There was more than one of them. I didn't see them, but one of them swore at me in Spanish when I hit him."

Gloria's expression changed from mildly gentle to studiously neutral at Jennifer's words. "Spanish?"

"Yes!" Jen said, her voice becoming hoarse. "Ask Joe. He saw it happen!"

"Mister Hamilton?"

"Yes!"

"So, you're accusing members of an oppressed community of attacking you, and a member of another community of failing to help you, even though he's the one who brought you here for help?" The investigator's lips drew into a thin, red line of waxy lipstick as she considered the woman lying on the gurney next to her.

Their conversation was cut off as the door behind Gloria slid open and Ramon swept into the room. He nodded nervously to the woman in the brown suit, but then smiled radiantly at Jennifer.

"Jen, *querida*! You're awake!" he said in his ever-cheerful tone. He and Jennifer had worked together for her first year at the clinic before Ramon was promoted to supervise the night shift.

"Hey, darlin'!" Jen said tiredly. Her accent came out as she spoke with her friend. "You're still here?"

"Well, somebody's gotta keep this place running while they bandage you up!" He quickly took Jennifer's vitals and noted them on the tablet he carried on a chain attached to his waist. Gloria watched their interaction while she tapped something out on her own computer.

"Now, you relax for a bit," Ramon gently touched her arm with the tips of his soft fingers. "I'll be back when the doctor's done with your discharge paperwork."

Jen nodded painfully as Ramon closed the door behind him. Her neck ached as she turned to face the social worker again.

Gloria regarded her coolly for a moment, then shook her head. "I should have known."

"Known what?" Jen asked. Her throat had dried out, but she could not move her arm to reach for the cup, and the social worker made no move to retrieve it for her.

"Typical." Gloria sniffed dismissively and stepped closer to Jen. "White woman accuses a brown man of attacking her."

Jen tried to swallow, but the feeling of crushed glass at the back of her throat prevented it. "There are cameras everywhere out there!" she croaked. "They'll show you I'm telling the truth!"

Gloria bit her lower lip and shook her head.

"Environmental Services had to disconnect the power to those appliances to conserve energy. There's no record of anything so far from the building," she replied.

"But I…"

The social worker ignored Jennifer. She picked up her tablet and selected something with the tip of her manicured finger.

"It may seem inconvenient to the outsider, but now that I know what you did, it all makes sense," she said in an icy tone. "I've read the doctor's report from last night, and there's nothing about sexual assault in it."

"But…"

"And I've spoken to Mister Hamilton. He says that he found you and brought you here, and he didn't say a word about seeing anyone else in the parking lot last night."

"I…"

"And I've listened to your racist hysterics long enough!" Gloria shouted, slamming her pale hand down on the table next to the gurney. She glared at Jennifer as she raised her tablet to eye level so that she could see both it and Jennifer. "I know what you are!"

Jen could only gape at her in shock as the social worker began to read.

"Jennifer Lynn Bradford-Costa, born January 24, 1993, in Birmingham, Alabama." Gloria worked a derisive twang into her voice as she read those last words.

"Resident of Cali since 1997. Graduate of Cal State Sacramento in 2017, with a bachelor's degree in nursing." She looked up from her pad and gave Jennifer a saccharine smile. "How nice."

Jennifer could only stare at her in silence as the social worker continued.

"Married to Mark Junipero Costa, Cali native from Fresno, in 2019. He works in the Cali Ministry of Technology here in Sacramento. No children." She looked up from the tablet and tilted her head questioningly.

Jennifer nodded slightly, feeling the tendons in her neck protest at the movement.

"No criminal history, although you've been warned by the CHP for speeding a few times. Oh, and there haven't been any serious health issues reported to CalHealth, although there is a note here that you resisted implantation of your identity chip last year."

She looked up and smiled coldly at Jen. "Sounds wonderful. But now we get to who the real Jennifer is, don't we?" Her mouth turned up cruelly as she started reading again. "You didn't take part in the Resistance prior to separation from the United States. In fact, according to this, you actively argued against it, both with your co-workers and on social media."

"I'm not political," Jen protested. "I only…"

"Neither you, nor your husband, have turned in any documents linking you to the government of the United States, even though we know you honeymooned in Japan, so you must have a passport."

"But…"

"You maintain regular contact with counter-progressive elements, both here and in the United States, and have repeatedly expressed a desire to rejoin your parents back in good old Alabama." Again, she forced a derisive twang into the words.

"What does that have to do with me being raped?" Jen cried out. She could feel hot tears running down the side of her face. Gloria ignored her question and looked over the green blinking light of her tablet to glare at Jennifer.

"And now you accuse members of our community of not only sexually assaulting you, but also accuse the oppressed worker who helped you of ignoring your so-called assault!" Gloria hissed as she lay her tablet on the end of the gurney.

"Yes," Jennifer sobbed. Pain stabbed through the center of her head as she screamed the rest of her answer, "They raped me!" More tears streaked her bruised cheeks.

The social workers' lip curled back on her too-white teeth as she shook her head in disgust.

"I see racist scum like you every day, you know that? Interlopers like you, who came here from whatever jerkwater sewer spewed you out, wanting nothing more than to tear down what we've built here."

"I was raped!"

"No!" the social worker spat back, jabbing a long, thin finger at Jennifer's face, "No, you weren't!" She pointed out the window and continued, "You parked at the edge of the parking lot where there would be no video of your so-called 'assault,' ripped your own clothes, and rammed yourself into your own car to make it look like you'd been attacked!"

The accusation brought Jennifer's sobs to a halt as she gaped at the other woman in disbelief. "I know what you're doing, you racist whore!" Gloria shouted. "You've got something against Mister Hamilton, an African American."

"I never…" Jennifer shouted back.

"Good daughter of the South just can't stand to see a darkie in a good job, now can you?" The forced twang in Gloria's words dripped with malice.

"I…"

"Jennifer Bradford-Costa, I am recommending charges under the Crimes Against the Community Act," the social worker said in a formal tone as she brought her tablet closer to her face so that the recording would be clear. "You are advised to not make any further statements until you have spoken with an attorney. A member of law enforcement will be by soon to arrest you and set your identification token for home arrest until you are brought to court."

She pressed a button on the tablet's side, and the blinking green light went out. Jennifer felt herself sag back. She had not even noticed that she had sat up, but now pain pushed her back down on the thin mattress. "I have to say, you did really well on this one," the social worker said as she slipped her computer into her purse and turned toward the door. "You certainly had the doctor fooled for a while. Took two calls from my office to get him to change his report."

She opened the door, then paused. "Cutting your hair off and slicing up your face was a nice touch. I'll have to look to see if you had an accomplice or if you did it to yourself. Where was your husband last night?"

***

Mark helped Jennifer down into one of the wooden chairs at a long table. Next to her, a tired looking woman with what might have been dark hair a decade before rifled through a stack of file folders.

"I'm sorry, *Señora*," the woman said softly as she pulled a thin folder with a red and white sticker from the middle of the pile. "We don't have pads like the People's Advocates do."

Jen gave her a reassuring smile. "You've been wonderful to us." She looked around the room, then turned back to her attorney. "This won't take long, will it?"

"No, no," the woman replied. "You've already signed the agreement, so this is just a formality."

Jennifer nodded tiredly. Ramon had been coming by the house every couple of nights in the weeks since she had come home, and he had helped her to recover a lot of the movement in her shoulder. But all she had for the lingering pain was what Mark could get at the pharmacy, and the constant reminder of that night dragged on her. The bumpy ride across city streets to the courthouse had jostled her about, and the ache in her bones was sapping her energy even before she began the day's business.

"Do we have to do this?" Jennifer asked. "This isn't right."

The woman shook her head sadly. "It's either this, or they convict you of crimes against a downtrodden community. That would be a lot worse."

"Worse?" Jen asked numbly.

"Ten years for each offense, and your husband loses his job and probably goes to prison too." She pointed to the front of the courtroom. "And this way," she sighed, "there's only one camera."

Jennifer shook her head and pursed her lips. She felt Mark put a gentle hand on her shoulder, and reached up to squeeze it.

The door behind them opened, and a man in a dark business suit, followed closely by Gloria Anderson-Hermosa, walked in. The investigator gave Jen an icy stare, while the man, tall, blonde, and tan, gave all three of them a wide smile.

The man reached across Jennifer to shake hands with the woman sitting next to her. "Consuela, it's good to see you again."

"Jeff, thanks for doing this."

"It's always easier for things to go this way."

The door at the front of the room opened, and a large woman wearing a brown and tan uniform, complete with a gun on one rounded hip, walked into the room. She nodded to Jeff, who stepped across the aisle to stand next to Gloria. The court reporter, a small man in an ill-fitting suit, entered behind her. He held a large tablet to each of their hands, moving on to the next after the identity reader flashed their pictures and names across its screen.

Once that was accomplished and the little man had retreated to a desk at the side of the room, the bailiff barked out, "Please, rise!" in a voice that seemed to be forced into a low pitch. At her words, a small woman with dark, curly hair entered the courtroom. Mark helped Jennifer struggle to her feet, while Consuela merely stared straight ahead as she stood stiffly with her hands at her side.

Once Jennifer had straightened to stand next to her attorney, the judge took her seat and nodded. Again, Mark had to help Jennifer down into her seat. The judge glanced at Jeff, who gave her an imperceptible shrug.

With a sigh, the judge tapped the microphone and intoned in a bored voice, "This is Judicial Hearing number 25-721, People's Deputy Tedalla Bainbridge presiding."

She nodded to the tables in front of her. "I have Mr. Brooks and Ms. Anderson-Hermosa here, as well as Ms. Rodriguez-Turner and her client, Jennifer Lynn Bradford-Costa. And you are, sir?"

"Mark Costa, your honor. I'm Jennifer's husband."

"Splendid. All of you understand that you are directed to tell the truth in this hearing, under penalty of incarceration for perjury?"

Everyone at the tables nodded their understanding.

"Good. Well, let's get this business over with. I've looked over the plea agreement Ms. Bradford-Costa and Mr. Brooks signed, and it seems to be in order. I also listened to the recording Ms. Anderson-Hermosa made of her interview with the accused, and I'm glad we're all being spared a trial for such a horrible crime."

She looked up to survey the small group before her. The prosecutor gave her a smile, while Consuela merely nodded her agreement. "Are we ready to do this?" the judge asked.

Brooks stood up and smiled at the camera installed in a console next to the judge. "We are, madam Deputy. The accused has agreed to surrender her license to work as a nurse in the Republic, pay a fine of five thousand Callors, remain under house arrest until she has done five hundred hours of community service at one of the clinics for the indigent here in Sacramento, and has received counseling to help her overcome her racist tendencies."

"I understand that she has finally surrendered her passport from the United States?"

Consuela spoke up. "She has, your Honor, as has her husband."

"Good. Now, Ms. Bradford-Costa, if you will stand and look into the camera there, we can finish this business."

Mark moved to help Jennifer stand, but stopped when the bailiff put one hand on her pistol and waved a chubby finger at him. Mark sank back into his chair, a look of worry on his face. Jennifer suppressed a groan as she stood. She gritted her teeth and straightened as best she could against the brace that dug into her back. Brooks also stood and faced her.

"You admit to faking an attack on your person on the night of June 15, 2025?" he asked in a theatrical tone that carried across the courtroom.

"I do, sir," Jennifer said softly. She could feel her face reddening.

"Speak up!" the judge said sharply. "We need a good recording of your confession for the media."

"I do, sir," Jennifer repeated, this time her voice seeming too loud for the small room.

"You cut your own clothes and hair, then injured yourself to make it appear that a member of our community had attacked you?"

Jennifer took a shuddering breath before answering. "Yes, sir."

"Please describe how you did it."

Consuela stood up. "Is this necessary, madam Deputy? It's all in the plea agreement."

Brooks' smile wavered for a moment. "The people demand a full accounting of her crimes." He motioned toward the camera at the front of the room.

The judge moved her head back and forth a couple times as she mulled it over. "If the people deserve to hear it, then she can tell it." She nodded to Jennifer. "Answer Mr. Brooks' question."

Jennifer closed her eyes for a moment, then recited the words Consuela had put down on the plea agreement form.

"Joe Hamilton and I never got along," she lied, feeling her cheeks turn hot with anger and embarrassment. "Where I come from, people like him know their place, and he shouldn't have had that job. It got to be too much for me, and I couldn't get permission to look for another clinic to work in."

She looked up at the ceiling, feeling hot tears roll down her face once again. "That night, I parked in the dark part of the lot where the cameras don't work. I didn't want there to be video of what I did. I took a knife and cut off my hair, then cut my cheek. I ran at my car a few times to make it look like someone had beat me up, and I cut and tore my clothes."

Brooks shook his head sadly for the camera, then asked. "And you lied to investigators about someone from the Hispanic community attacking you? You lied about being raped?"

Jennifer's breath caught in her throat at his words. She forced herself to nod.

"We need to hear the words," the judge admonished from her bench.

"Yes, I lied," Jennifer said, letting her head fall forward. Her hair, which had started to grow almost long enough to style, fell to either side of her face.

"You admit to racist grudges against the African-American and Hispanic communities?"

"I do"

"Explain them."

Consuela again looked to the judge, but did not stand.

Jennifer paused again to remember the words Consuela had coached her on. After taking another long breath, she recited, "I come from a racist culture, where people who don't look like me are discriminated against. I have let those feelings hurt the people around me my whole life, and for that I beg for forgiveness. I condemn those beliefs now, and I am ashamed of my past and of the United States' racist culture and policies."

"And now?"

"I recognize the evil that resides in my own heart, and with the help of the Republic, I will expose them to the cleansing light of our new nation. I will become a fully functioning part of our new society, and I will forever know the shame of my past." She lifted her head and gave the camera the smile she had practiced for so long in front of the mirror that morning.

Brooks nodded wisely and pressed his lips together with masterfully displayed regret.

"Your Honor, the people are satisfied with this confession."

***

Mark walked wearily into their apartment, then closed the door and threw the dead bolt. He smelled onions cooking in the kitchen, which brought a tired smile to his face as he put his bag and coat on their hooks in the hallway.

Jennifer's hair, which she had taken to dyeing a light brown since she had begun leaving the house to do community service, swayed to the rhythm of her arms as she chopped vegetables for their dinner. The thin, pale line of the scar running from her cheekbone to her upper lip stood out on a face reddened by the heat of the stove.

She jumped as Mark entered the room, almost falling as she tried to swing around toward him. Her husband gave her a sad smile as she slowly put the knife down on the cutting board.

"I'm sorry, sweetie," he said soothingly as he put his arms around her and gave her a hug. "Didn't mean to sneak up on you." Jen suppressed the urge to shrink from his touch. Even now, months later, it was sometimes hard for her to let anyone come close to her, even Mark.

"It's okay. I was just thinking and I didn't hear you come in."

"You alright?"

"Yeah," she said as she pushed her hair back with the back of her hand. "I got a call from that attorney again."

"Hamilton?"

Jennifer nodded. "Joe's suing the clinic for the 'distress' of the whole situation, and I have to go in for a deposition in a couple of weeks."

"I'm sorry, sweetheart. I'll call that guy down at Legal Aid."

Jen only answered with a quick shrug. She pointed to the table, where a salad waited for him. "Start without me. The rest will be ready in a couple minutes. How was work?"

Mark sat down, picked up his fork and tossed his greens around the bowl for a moment. Finally, he looked up and watched as Jennifer scraped the vegetables into the wok and started moving them around with a bamboo spatula.

"I've been moved," he said.

Jennifer looked back toward him. This required her to pick up the pan and turn her entire body. "Moved?"

"Easy there. Don't drop dinner!" Mark said half-jokingly. Jen got around pretty well after several months of Ramon helping her get some movement back in her neck and shoulder, but she still couldn't do some things that others took for granted.

Jennifer turned off the burner and set the pan down. "Well? Moved where?"

"Zhong's decided that it's too much trouble having me in the office after… well, after our problems. Says he keeps getting requests to put someone else into my slot."

"Requests?"

"From… from People Services."

Jen shook her head angrily, but said nothing as she scooped the steaming vegetables into bowls. Picking them up, she walked to the table.

"After word got out that you're married to racist redneck, is that what you mean?" She immediately regretted her words, and the look on Mark's face demonstrated just how much they had stung.

"Baby, I'm sorry," she said softly as she put his bowl in front of him. She put her own bowl down and sat at the chair next to his. "Nobody would blame you for leaving me after the last few months."

Mark reached over and gently hugged his wife. This time, it was easier to not flinch. "For better or worse, remember?"

Jen nodded as she picked up her fork and picked at her own salad. "So, what does this mean for work?"

"They've found me a place in the highway department. I'll be back on desktop support."

"Well, at least you'll be around people more."

"Yeah, but it'll mean more time away from home."

Jen threw down her fork and brought her hands up to scrub at her face. "Which means it'll be even harder for me to get out. Another clinic refused to take me today, and my case worker says that if I don't get more service hours in, they'll revoke my plea agreement."

"What does that mean?"

"Don't know. Consuela isn't taking my calls."

"Can you do anything else to get the hours?"

"The case worker said that nobody will take people like me. I'm pretty sure she wants me gone just to get me off her plate."

"We'll figure something out," Mark said. He reached for her hand, but stopped when he saw her flinch.

"I love you," he said after a moment of searching for better words.

This time it was Jen that reached across the little table and squeezed his hand. "I know, babe," she said. "I love you, too. We'll figure it out."

They both stiffened when they heard the chime of the doorbell. Mark got up and warily approached the door. He peered through the peephole, then looked back over his shoulder.

"It's Ramon," he whispered.

"He and Jimmy are coming over for dinner tomorrow," Jen replied in a hushed voice. "What's he doing here tonight?"

Mark opened the door and peered out at their visitor.

"Let me in," Ramon said. The gentle affectation he normally kept in his voice was gone.

"Ramon, what's going on?"

Ramon hurried in from the chilly evening air and waited until Mark had shut and locked the door. He put his finger up to his lips and motioned toward the tiny kitchen. Soon, all three of them were huddled around their table.

"I was down at the *mercado* getting some coffee and I heard something about you two."

"What?"

"Two of the Brownshirts were talking. Said that the neighborhood council is trying to get you kicked out of your place."

"Can they do that?" Jen asked. Her face had gone white with shock.

"Your landlord's on the council, isn't he?"

Mark thought for a moment, then nodded.

"One of the Brownies said that they didn't want someone like you in the neighborhood." He looked at Jen. "Said that this wasn't a place for a racist Okie to live."

"They can't do that!" Mark erupted, getting up from the table. "We'll get a lawyer!"

Jen looked down at the table, then up into Ramon's eyes. "That's not what frightened you, is it, Ramon?"

Ramon bit his lip, then said. "They said they're going to get a bunch of homeys from downtown and throw you out tonight."

Mark stopped at that. The Brownshirts rarely had to resort to violence anymore, but when they did, it was done to send a brutal, public message.

Jen was the first to speak. "How long do we have?"

"An hour, maybe two. They were just ordering their food when I left."

"What do we do?" Jen asked, looking to her husband. "If I leave the house, they'll send me to prison."

Ramon put his hand up. "Do you have family here?"

Mark shook his head. "My folks died a couple years ago."

"My folks left after Calexit. Went back to Alabama."

Ramon breathed out through his nose. "I know somebody who can get you out, but it's not cheap," he said in a voice not much louder than a whisper.

"Out?" Mark and Jen said together.

"To Nevada, through the mountains."

"Ramon, it's illegal to leave without permission," Mark objected.

"It's illegal to leave the house, too," Jen said flatly. An idea formed in her head. "If we can get to the States, Mom and Dad will help us."

Mark thought for a moment, then nodded. He turned to Ramon and said, "What do we do?"

***

The screen in front of Jiminez flickered once or twice as the breeze made the small camera one of his men had placed in the bush outside Jen and Mark's building wave up and down. The basement room he occupied was otherwise dark and quiet.

"How much longer?" he said quietly, then snorted when he realized that his quarry was a mile away.

"I told him to have them on the road by ten, so pretty soon. They're certainly taking enough crap," the man sitting at the desk to his left said.

Never been kicked out of an apartment in the middle of the night before, Jiminez thought derisively. *Typical rich people*.

They watched as Mark helped Jen into the back of a beat-up minivan, then got into the passenger seat next to Ramon. The ancient motor cranked a few times before catching, and soon it was out of sight of the camera. The screen in front of Jiminez changed to show the view from one of the normal surveillance cameras, which showed Ramon's van making its way down the street.

"You gave him the name for that place over in Rosemont?"

"Yes," Sadana, the woman who sat to his left, replied. "We're pretty sure the old man doesn't know that he's been compromised."

"Good," Jiminez said. "Lucky break, catching that guy's boyfriend in a prostitution sting."

"Lucky, my ass," Sadana said with a chuckle. "We've been trying to get something on him for a month."

***

Ramon drove them across Sacramento using surface streets. He and Mark kept checking their mirrors to see if they were being followed, but Jen just sat and watched the darkness roll by the van's dirty rear window.

She lost count of how many times they turned before Ramon stopped the van and put it in park without shutting off the motor.

"Stay here," he said nervously. "I'll get us in the garage."

Jen strained to look out the front window, but saw only the hazy reflection of a dim yellow light off the dirt on the windshield. She heard something clank in the quiet night air, then Ramon was back in the van.

Without a word, he put the vehicle in gear and eased it forward. Jennifer watched the light bend around the front of the van, then Ramon stopped. The light from the rear window cut off as she heard someone lowering a door.

Immediately, the sliding door next to her opened, revealing a fat man in a dirty tee shirt. In his free hand, he held a long length of pipe. The man peered around the interior of the van, then motioned to Jen.

"Come on," he said in a phlegmy voice. "Get out of there."

Jen unfolded herself from between their suitcases and stepped out with a groan. It took a moment for her eyes to adjust to the gloom, but her nose tickled with the scent of old motor oil and grease.

Mark got out of the passenger door and put a protective arm around his wife. "We're…" he started to say.

"Shut up," the fat man snarled. "Don't need your name, and don't ask mine." Now that Jen was close to him, she could smell alcohol on his breath.

Ramon walked around the front of the van. The man looked at him suspiciously.

"You sure you know Bill?" His words slurred a bit. "Not normal to get folks in like this."

"Bill told me to come here in an emergency," Ramon stammered. He pulled the thin packet of money Mark had given him before they left the apartment and held it out to the white-haired man. "These guys are going to get picked up by the Brownshirts tonight."

The man looked each of them over, then shrugged. He took the envelope and put it in the back pocket of his jeans. "Well, if Bill said its okay, then let's get them downstairs until the truck gets here."

He motioned with the pipe toward a door on the other side of the van. Beyond it was a creaky set of wooden stairs that led down into a concrete block chamber. Several chairs sat around a folding table, while some rusty cans of food peered down on them from shelves bolted to the wall.

"Old bomb shelter," the man explained. He stopped to cough wetly. "Granddad put it in when he built this place."

Ramon cleared his throat. "Can we get their stuff out of my van so I can get out of here?"

The man nodded. Mark and Ramon went back up the stairs and returned a few moments later with their bags.

Ramon set down his load, then hugged Mark and Jen. "Good luck," he said. His voice was tight and pitched higher than normal. "Be careful."

"Thank you," Mark replied. "We'll send something when we can."

"No," the man said. "No contact after this. Brownshirts'll notice and then we're all fucked." After a few more goodbyes, Ramon made his way back up the stairs, followed by the fat man. Jen heard the garage door open, then after a moment, close again. The stairs creaked as the man took a few steps down.

"Stay here 'til somebody comes for ya," he called down the stairway. He turned without waiting for a reply and closed the door behind him. Jen heard the snick of the lock as he closed the door.

"Another adventure?" Mark asked, giving her a reassuring smile.

Jen squeezed his hand, then eased herself down into one of the folding chairs. "Another adventure."

***

Jiminez watched the feed from the surveillance camera up the block from the old service station. The van had been inside for about ten minutes before the door slid back up and it backed out again.

"That the place that guy told us about?" he asked.

"Yes," Sadana replied. She ran a hand through her dark hair to push it back from her face. "Watch when he gets to the corner."

As they watched, Ramon stopped his van at the next intersection and flashed its lights.

"Bingo," Schmidt said.

"Mark that place as Target One," Jiminez ordered, "and pick up the nurse before he gets on the freeway."

"Yes," Sadana said again. "Already on it." Her fingers raced across her keyboard as she sent orders to the teams they had positioned earlier that day.

A moment later, Sadana gave a whoop of satisfaction as text started scrolling in one of the windows on her screen. Jiminez looked at her questioningly.

"It's just like the informant said," she explained. "Two minutes after the van left, somebody posted that Jim and Sally had twins."

Jiminez nodded and cracked a smile. "Good," he said. "Then we know how they're communicating. Tell those dickheads down in Santa Clara to get off their asses. I want to know the real names of everyone who's in that chat room."

***

Jen and Mark sat in the basement for what seemed like a long time. Without their phones, they had no way of knowing how much time passed before they heard the garage door cycle again. A moment later, a thin woman wearing jeans and a flannel shirt carefully made her way down the creaky steps.

"You the ones I'm supposed to pick up?" she asked in a flat tone. Her hair was almost as short as Mark's, and her dark eyes flicked between them suspiciously.

"I guess," Mark replied. "Nobody else's come down here."

"Get your stuff and put it in the back of the truck," the woman said. "No talking until we're out of town."

***

Jiminez watched as an old pick-up pulled out of the garage and headed off into the night. The view on his screen switched between surveillance cameras until the truck passed the last checkpoint in the capitol district.

He looked over at Sadana and snapped, "Did the Chinks come through with that drone or what?"

"It's on station," she said. "I can tell them to follow the truck for us, but we didn't pay for video."

Jiminez swore under his breath. "Fine, tell them to let us know where it is every ten minutes. I want to know every time it stops."

Sadana nodded and typed into the chat window to the operations center at the airbase in Fairfield.

"That chat room lit up a few minutes ago," she said.

"What about?

"Something about nobody knowing that Jimmy and Sally were expecting."

Jiminez frowned at that. "Shit," he spat. "They might waste those two just to protect the network."

"We'll at least get the garage," Schmidt, who sat to his left, said.

"Yeah, better than nothing, I suppose. Let me know what you get from the Chinese. I'm gonna go piss."

***

Jen and Mark lay in the bed of the truck. The woman had given them a small, dim lantern before closing the hard-shell cover like a coffin lid. A dirty foam mattress saved them from the worst of the bumps, but Jen's shoulder and back screamed at her every time she slid against the front of the small compartment.

She must have drifted off, because the next thing they knew, she heard the squeak of gravel on the tire next to her head and felt herself being pulled toward the tailgate. Rocks kicked up by the tires sounded like gunshots against the bottom of the bed after the monotonous hum of pavement underneath them.

"Where are we?" she mumbled.

"Don't know, sweetie," Mark replied sleepily. "The mountains, I guess." They jounced around for a long time, then Jen felt them take several sharp turns. Finally, they came to a halt.

***

"The operator at Travis says they've stopped about twenty miles northwest of Placerville," Sadana said to Jiminez. "They're sending over screen caps in a few, but I've got old imagery that shows a hunting lodge or something near there."

"All right," Jiminez said. "Mark that as Target Two. How far out is Jackson and his team?"
Sadana looked at the tracker on the map in front of her.

"Should be in Placerville in about fifteen minutes," Schmidt replied. "We've kept them back so they wouldn't be spotted."

Jiminez let out a long breath, then nodded. "Good. We'll see what these *pendejos* do, then send Jackson in."

***

Mark and Jen heard and felt the truck's door open, then close quietly. They sat in silence for a long while, then Jen heard someone opening the cover above them. The tailgate opened with a groan, letting in a wave of frigid air, then a bright, white light shone on them.

"Who're you?" a man's voice growled quietly. The speaker's breath created a fog that rolled through the beam of the flashlight.

"I'm Mark Costa," Mark said as he sat up with a hand extended to shield his eyes. "This is Jen."

The yawning muzzle of a shotgun appeared in front of the light. "Wasn't nobody supposed to be coming up here tonight. All we know is that somebody dropped you off at the garage."

"Our friend, Ramon," Jen started to say, "he…"

"Shut up," the voice barked. The gun jerked to the right a few inches, casting long shadows across Jennifer's face. "Get out, both of you."

Mark helped Jen sit up, then they both eased to the rear of the truck and stepped down. Packed snow crunched underneath their feet.

"Get on your knees."

"My wife, she's…" Mark started to say, then stopped when something metallic clicked in the cold darkness behind him.

"Man said to get down, so get down," the woman who had driven them from Sacramento said menacingly. Mark reached over and helped Jen down to her knees.

A third set of hands roughly searched Jen, then Mark. They heard zippers opening from the bed of the truck as someone searched their bags.

"Clean over here," the woman called out.

"They're clean too," the man who had searched them added. His voice was not quite as deep as that of the man holding the gun on them.

"Alright, get 'em up and inside," The first voice ordered. "Get the truck out of here."

Mark stood up, then lifted Jen to her feet. The barrel of a large revolver appeared in the light and motioned them forward. After they got moving, the flashlight turned off with a click, dropping them into inky blackness. Jen stumbled as her feet met the end of a concrete pathway, then she followed it as they made their way up a gentle incline. Behind them, they heard the truck's door slam. A moment later, snow and gravel crunched under its tires as it turned around and drove back down the mountain.

"Get inside," the second male voice said quietly. "Door's open." Mark obeyed. A moment later, a switch clicked, and they were bathed in the light of a table lamp.

They stood in the living room of what looked like someone's weekend cabin. An old couch sat against one wall, while a mounted buck with a wide rack looked down on them from the wall above it. At the far end of the room, a black iron stove sat upon a platform of bricks. Jen could hear the crackle of a fire coming from it, and the heat it put out felt good after the shock of the winter cold outside.

Opposite the couch was a wide desk bearing a computer and a rack of what looked like old stereo equipment. On one side of the desk was a doorway leading to a bathroom, while on the other a set of stairs led up to a loft that overlooked the room. The ceiling soared over their heads, but the steep-pitched roof gave the room a boxed-in feeling.

"Sit," the young voice said from the doorway. Jen looked behind her to see a young man with a dark beard and hair pointing to the couch. Mark and Jen eased down onto the worn sofa, which did its level best to swallow them up in its overstuffed cushions.

The young man said nothing more, but watched them intently. The revolver in his hand wasn't exactly pointed at them, but he made no move to put it away, either. A few minutes later, an older man with a long, gray moustache came through the door. His shotgun was slung over his shoulder, and he carried a large black garbage bag, which he set down on the floor in front of the couch.

"Mark and Jen, huh?" he said in a gruff voice.

"Yeah," Mark replied. "Ramon told us…"

"Never heard of Ramon," the younger man said. The older man gave him a hard look.

"Listen, we're just being careful," the older man explained. "There's a way this is supposed to be done, and this ain't it."

He paused for a moment and looked intently at Jen. "Your hair always been brown?" he asked.

Jen exchanged a look with Mark, then replied, "No. I've been dyeing it."

The man pursed his lips and nodded. This made the ends of his moustache wriggle back and forth as they dangled below his lip. "Thought I'd seen you before. You're that lady that got attacked down in Sacramento a few months ago."

"How?"

"They splashed your confession all over the net. News ran with it for a couple days."

Jen felt her cheeks heat up. "Listen," she said, "I…"

"You got raped by a bunch of guys and they made you say you made it up?"

She looked at the man in shock. "You, you believe me?" she stammered.

"Ma'am," he said, his tone now not quite as harsh, "after the past few years, there's not much about what goes on in Cali that I won't believe."

He nodded to the younger man. "Get on the line and tell folks it's okay." The young man put his revolver in the pocket of his jacket and walked over to the desk. When he touched the computer, a chat window with multi-colored lines of text appeared on the monitor. He started adding comments, which caused a cascade of new conversation in the window.

***

Sadana whooped with glee when she saw the new comments scroll across one of the windows on her screen.

"Got 'em!" she cried out. Jiminez looked up from his own monitor.

"The twins are safe at home and everyone is looking forward to getting some rest," she read from the chat.

"Good," Schmidt said. "Jackson is just getting to Placerville, so once they get the local yokels to block off traffic around the target, they can take it down."

Sadana looked over at Jiminez. "Don't we want to wait for them to get to the next place?"

Jiminez shook his head. "No," he replied. "They're too close to the border. If we wait, they might get across and we won't have her pretty face for the newsies."

"Nah," he said as he leaned back and looked up at the dark ceiling. "We'll bag these guys and get the rest from what we get out of interrogation."

***

Jackson banged on the window of the brown and green SUV parked in front of a gas station in Placerville. The window came down slowly, letting a puff of warm air escape into the night. The man inside wore a brown uniform underneath a warm jacket, and his close-cropped red hair was flecked with streaks of silver.

"You Andrews?" Jackson asked, not waiting for the other man to speak.

"I'm Sheriff Andrews," the other man said suspiciously.

"I'm Tom Jackson from Dee-Ohh-Jay down in Sacramento." He showed the man his credentials and gave him a business card.

"Yeah? Is there a problem?"

"Human trafficking," Jackson said. "We've been tracking them from Sacramento, and they've stopped at some cabin a few miles outside of town."

"Don't get much of that through here," Andrews replied.

"Yeah, these guys are getting fugitives out through the mountains."

"What d'ya need from me?"

"We can take down the house, but we need you for traffic control and that kind of thing."

"I'll have to wake up my guys," Andrews said. "Give me a few."

"No problem. We're getting some coffee and if I don't take a leak soon, I'm gonna need a new pair of pants." Both men smiled at the joke.

"Tell Susanna in there I said to make you my special brew," Andrews said. "That'll wake you up."

"Will do. We're over in that van there." Jackson jerked a thumb over his shoulder. "Give me a shout when you've got your people ready." Without waiting for another reply, he turned and walked back to his van.

Andrews his window back up. He picked up his phone from the console and started dialing his deputies as he watched Jackson make his way across the parking lot to the brightly lit front door of the gas station.

While he dialed with one hand, he opened the laptop on the dash next to him with the other. A couple clicks on the mouse brought up a chat window.

***

Sadana watched as a new message scrolled across the chat window in front of her. "Got something," she said in a bored tone.

"What's up?" Jiminez said.

Sadana read a few more lines of text, then replied, "Says that Juanita went into labor a few hours ago, and it's too soon."

"Who's Juanita?" Haven't heard that one before.

"Not sure. Might actually be a real person. There're a few of those in here. Wait, there's more. Said they're transporting her to the hospital in Indio, and they want everyone to pray."

"Indio's on the other side of LA. Watch for anything going on up here."

"Will do. Don't forget, the chinks will be taking the UAV off station in ten minutes. We only paid for a few hours."

Jiminez swore under his breath. "All right, tell that asshole Jackson when we lose coverage. He'll have to do this the old-fashioned way."

***

The older man motioned toward the sack on the floor in front of him. "Here's your clothes. Mariana'll ditch your bags and the rest before she gets back down in the valley."

"Dad," the younger man said.

"If they were here to take us down, we'd be dead by now," the older man replied. "I'm Luke and that's Ted over there."

"I'm…"

"We already got your names, and I think that's as much as we need to know about each other," Luke said, cutting Mark off.

Mark nodded gravely. "Where do we go from here?"

"First we'll get some food into you and let you rest for a bit. It's about an hour or so to Tahoe on the back roads, so we'll take you across tomorrow night," Luke replied. He took the shotgun off his shoulder and leaned it against the desk. "Border Patrol'll be there to process you, and after that they'll get you to where you need to go."

Jen felt a weight fall from her shoulders as she sensed the mood in the room change. "My mom and dad…"

"Yeah, they'll get you in touch. For now, let's get you comfortable," Luke said as he opened one of the desk's drawers and took out a couple cans of soup.

***

Andrews approached the white and tan van. The sliding door opened before he got close, and several sets of dark eyes glared out at him. He stopped when he saw several guns pointed at him.

"I'm the guy Jackson talked to," he said slowly.

One of the men looked to the back of the van and said, "*Jefe*, somebody's here to see you."

The back door to the van opened and Jackson stepped out. He wore baggy gray fatigues, with a black mesh vest over his chest and back. "DOJ" was emblazoned across the vest in white letters. One hand was on the grip of the short rifle that hung across his chest, while a steaming Styrofoam cup was in the other.

He gestured to the men in the van, who lowered their guns. "Whatcha got?" he said.

"All three of my guys'll be here in a few. You know where this place is?"

Jackson nodded to one of his men, who produced a small tablet and showed it to the sheriff. One window showed a map with a blinking dot on the side of one of the roads winding through the mountains, while the other showed an oddly-colored picture of an a-frame cabin and a couple of outbuildings. Andrews studied it for a moment, then looked up at Jackson.

"Yeah, OK, that's one of the hunting lodges up in the El Dorado. We're in luck."

"Luck?"

"One way in, one way out. We can leave one of my guys to block the road and the rest of us can do perimeter for you."

"Sweet. We should be heading out soon."

Andrews nodded and walked back to his truck just as the first of his deputies pulled into the lot.

***

Luke was helping Mark pull the couch out into a bed when Ted came down from the loft with a couple of pillows and a quilt. He set his load down on the desk, then glanced at the monitor. Luke looked at his son questioningly when Ted cussed at the computer.

"There's police down in Placerville," Ted said, pointing to the chat window. "Arrived about half an hour ago."

"Passing through?"

"Nope. Message is 'transport to Indio.'" This time, it was Luke's turn to cuss. Jen came in from the bathroom just in time to see father and son burst into movement.

"What's going on?" she asked. She moved closer to Mark.

"We're busted," Ted replied as he pulled the desk out from the wall. He jerked a small door behind it open and began pulling out canvas bags.

"One of our lookouts down in Placerville says that there are people on their way up here. We gotta go," Luke explained as he pulled his coat back on and lifted one of the backpacks Ted had pulled from the wall.

"Where?"

"Looks like we're all going to Nevada tonight. You know how to ride a horse?"

Mark nodded, then pointed to the garbage bag that contained their clothes. "Put more on," he said to Jen. "We won't be able to bring it all." Jen looked at him in shock, then flinched when he grabbed her good shoulder and turned her. "Honey, we gotta move."

Jen nodded numbly and fumbled through the tumble of clothing that came from the bag when Mark upended it onto the couch. Soon, she was pulling on another pair of pants and several more sweaters.

Ted pulled the last of the bags from behind the desk, then grabbed the computer and disconnected it from the radio. He opened the back of one of its bigger pieces and pulled something out. The smell of ozone and scorched insulation soon filled the room. "I'll get the horses ready."

"Stay in the barn," Luke ordered. "They might have someone watching. No lights." Ted headed out as

Mark and Jen continued to pull on extra layers of clothing.

***

Schmidt looked over to Jiminez and said, "Jackson's team has support from the locals, and they're moving out. Should be at Target Two in about half an hour or so."

"Good," Jiminez replied. "Is the team in Sacramento ready?"

"Yep," Schmidt replied. "They can take down the garage whenever you're ready."

Jiminez looked at his monitor for a moment, then nodded. "*Via*," he said. "Do it."

***

Willie lay propped up in the corner of his couch. The screen across from him was playing an old Mexican soap opera, but he had passed out hours earlier. An almost empty bottle of cherry vodka lay on the table next to him. Beside it was his phone, which had buzzed insistently several times over the last hour.

Suddenly, the screen and the hallway light both went off, and his phone went silent at the same time. Willie snorted in his sleep, then turned over to get more comfortable.

A heartbeat later, the front door blew in with a bang, and several small cylinders followed the door into the living room. These exploded with loud, sharp roars and flashes of blinding light, which struck Willie just as he lurched up from the couch, the length of pipe in his hand.

His screams of fright and surprise were drowned out by the shouts of several dark-clad figures as they piled in through the doorway. One pointed a stubby weapon at him and depressed the trigger. Two darts arrowed out, embedding themselves in Willie's chest. At that instant, the wires trailing out behind them energized, passing a massive shock through the fat man's abdomen. He stiffened for a moment, unable to breathe, then fell to the floor.

"Clear!" the team leader shouted. Other members of his team quickly searched the house, confirming that Willie was alone. At his feet, Willie was being cuffed as a large hood was pulled over his head. The team leader tapped out a message on his phone as the last of the shouted reports rang through the house. 'Target One secure. One in custody.'

***

Schmidt relayed the message from the takedown team in Sacramento to his boss. At the same time, he exchanged a high-five with Sedana, who had watched the assault via the surveillance camera they had used to track Mark and Jennifer earlier that evening.

"*Bueno*," Jiminez said with a nod of satisfaction. "Tell the interrogators I want a report for the AG in four hours."

***

Mark and Jen followed Luke into the building behind the cabin. It smelled of sweet hay and horse manure. Ted was waiting for them with two large dappled gray horses, which he had already saddled.

"Mark, get behind Ted. I'll take you, Jen," Luke said quietly as he strapped one of the bags he carried to his saddle.

Mark helped Jen onto Luke's horse, then climbed onto the other mount. Jen cringed as she felt Luke's hand go around her waist after he pulled himself up into the saddle, but that was lost as Ted pulled the barn door open and Luke kicked their mount into motion. The first heavy snowflakes were falling just as she heard Ted's horse step across the threshold behind them.

***

Jackson swore as hot coffee sloshed over the side of his cup. "You going for high score, *Juanito*?"

The driver snorted. "These fucking roads," he muttered. "There's a hole every three feet, I swear." The wipers ran across the windshield again, pushing away the wet snow that had started falling a few minutes after they had driven up out of Placerville.

"You know, sometimes I miss Barstow," Jackson said sarcastically.

"Yeah, sandstorms are a real party."

Ahead of them, they saw Andrews' SUV slow, then turn onto a steep-pitched road that seemed to grow out of the mountainside. "Watch it," Jackson said. "He's not slowing down for us. Don't let him get away."

"'Slow down, *Juanito*!'" Juan replied in a squeaky falsetto. "'Speed up, *Juanito*!'"

They followed Andrews as he drove along a series of switchbacks. After a few minutes, Jackson heard someone retch behind him.

"You puke in my van," he growled through clenched teeth, "and I will fucking leave you here." He gave up on his coffee and opened the window so he could throw it down the mountainside.

Damn mud was making me sick, anyway, he thought sourly.

***

Jen shivered as they rode through the storm. Wet snow stuck to her hair, and it dripped down her neck when it melted. The wind cut into her legs and made her hands numb from the cold. She could see nothing in the pitch black, but Luke seemed to know where they were going. They changed direction often, but she felt gravity pulling her back against his chest, so they must have been going up.

The horse lost its footing every so often, and she could hear hooves on rocks behind them when they were behind something that blocked the storm, but other than that, the only sound was the wind moaning around them.

Finally, they slowed to a stop and she felt Luke climb down from the horse. He took her hand and helped her down, then supported her when her legs started to give out from underneath her. "Easy now," he said gently. "We're almost there."

Mark appeared next to her, and she put her arms around him and shivered.

"We'll give the horses a rest here for a bit. The lake's just over that ridge."

"Lake?" Mark whispered.

"Tahoe. Nevada's on the other side."

***

Andrews pulled to the side of the road and got out of his cruiser. Juan pulled the van in next to him.

"That cabin you showed me is about half a mile further on," Andrews said through the window after Jackson lowered it. "We can block the road from here."

"Can't they drive out the other side?"

"It dead ends about two miles past the cabin, and they're not going off road in this." Andrews gestured to the thick snow falling from the dark sky.

Jackson nodded, then opened his door. His men opened the back of the van and stepped out onto the slick gravel.

"All right, leave one of your people here with your truck," he said to Andrews. "You and the rest of your crew can keep the perimeter while we take down the house."

"Yep," Andrews said, then turned to relay the order to the men in the cruiser. One of his deputies got in the driver's seat, while the other two, bundled up in heavy coats and boots, joined him on the side of the road.

"No radios after this," Jackson said sternly, "and no lights. We don't want to warn them."

"You got it," the deputy in the SUV replied. "I'll just make sure nobody comes down the road."

Jackson and his men followed Andrews and the other two deputies up the snow-covered gravel road. Soon, the night swallowed them up. The deputy in the truck swung his vehicle around to block the road, then tipped his seat back and relaxed.

***

"They're leaving the vehicle and getting set up on Target Two," Schmidt reported as he pointed to the screen at the front of the room.

"Tell Jackson I want prisoners, not bodies. And make sure they bag any computers or phones they find."

"Yep," Schmidt replied as he typed the order out on his computer.

After a moment, he turned back to his boss. "No answer from Jackson. Probably no coverage to his phone out there in the boonies."

Jiminez shrugged. "He can do it without us holding his hand."

***

Jackson pulled his night vision goggles down over his eyes once again, then eased up to the small cabin. He heard his men's feet crunching in the snow to either side of him, then almost fell when his foot caught on a rock the snow and darkness had hidden.

When he reached the building, he pointed to Juan, who placed the muzzle of his shotgun against the lock on the front door. A moment later, the door flew back with a roar, then the man next to Jackson threw in a couple flash bang grenades. When their explosions met the echoes of shotgun's report, Jackson and his men ran in through the doorway.

Inside, they found a room with a desk, couch, and a pile of clothes. He heard glass breaking as other men came in through the rear entrance, then shouts of "Clear!" rang through the house as his men checked each room.

"Barn's empty, too!" someone shouted through the shattered back door.

Jackson kicked the couch in frustration. "Call Central and tell them that Target Two is secure, but nobody's home!" he snarled. Juan pulled a phone from his vest and punched a button.

"No signal," he said flatly. "We're too far out."

"Fuck!" Jackson roared. He thought for a moment, then pointed to Juan. "Get your ass down to the van! We had signal there."

Juan nodded and trotted out into the storm. Jackson looked around at his men. "Tear this fucking place apart!" he shouted. "Where's that dickhead from Placerville?"

***

Andrews and one of his deputies were walking up a fresh trail they had found behind the barn. When he heard explosions and shouting from the house, the sheriff figured it was okay to turn his flashlight on and move in closer. He nodded to his deputy, who turned and shuffled back down the trail.

"Who's that?" A voice called from the outbuilding.

"It's Andrews," he replied. He had to shuffle his feet in the snow to make sure he didn't trip.

"I've got the sheriff out here in the barn," the man said into the microphone at his throat. "Want me to send him in?" He listened for a moment, then jerked the muzzle of his gun toward the house.

"Boss wants t'see you," he said. He shined the bright light slung under his weapon out into the woods. "You see anything out there?"

"Nope," Andrews replied as he walked across the barn. "I've got my guys checking to see if they can see anything now."

***

"*Chenga*!" Jiminez shouted at the ceiling. "How the fuck did they get away?"

"Jackson says that one of the outbuildings is a barn, so they might have gotten out on horses," Schmidt replied. He tried hard to not cringe at his boss's tone.

"Get the goddamn Chinese on the line," Jiminez snapped, pointing to Sadana. "I want that drone back."

Sadana chatted back and forth with the Chinese operator at the air base in Fairfield, then set her jaw before swiveling back toward Jiminez. "They say they can't do it. The drone we had before is out for service and we don't have enough credit in our account to get another one."

Jiminez considered throwing his coffee cup at the woman, but instead turned to Schmidt. "Get some helicopters up there and find them!" he shouted. "They can't have gotten far!"

***

Jen and Mark were huddled together under a rough blanket while Luke and Ted took care of the horses. Mark had tried to help, but after a few fumbled attempts at getting a saddle off in the dim, red light of a flashlight, Ted had gently suggested he take care of his wife.

"Almost there, sweetheart," Mark said quietly. "Just gotta get across the lake."

Ted watched grimly as his father set the horses loose. They had fed them as much as they would take and rubbed them down so they wouldn't get cold from the sweat under their saddles, but that was all they could do for them.

"Hope somebody takes them in."

Luke nodded. "There're folks who'll be on the lookout for them," he replied. "If they find them, they'll take care of 'em."

He turned to their charges. "Time to get going again if we want to be across the lake by dawn." They loaded their things on their backs and trudged into the snow. It was slow going, but the lights of the border crossing to their right kept getting brighter as they climbed the last ridge. Finally, just when Jen's legs threatened to go out from underneath her, they crested a hill and saw the lake below them.

"Praise Jesus," Luke whispered. His words came out in a ragged stream of vapor, and in the first dim light of dawn, Jen could see steam rising from the black ski cap he wore.

They half walked, half slid down the hill toward the shore. At the bottom of the hill, they rushed across a wide road, with Ted watching both directions as Luke and Mark helped Jen run to the woods on the other side.

A few minutes later, they reached the edge of the trees and looked across the lake. The water looked calm, but a thin coat of ice ringed the shore.

Mark opened his mouth to speak, but Luke shook his head and pointed away from the lights to the south. The little group made their way along the shoreline until they came to a clutch of floating docks that pointed out into the dark water. Across a narrow drive from the docks were several small buildings with garage doors.

Luke took a long moment to look about for anyone else up so early, then casually walked toward one of the buildings. Ted waited a moment to see if there was any reaction to his father's presence, then tapped Mark and Jen on the shoulder before following. By the time they had caught up with Luke, he had the side door to the building open and had stepped inside.

They found him standing in front of a metal cabinet and pulling out several items and a gas can. Next to him, a boat and trailer sat under a tarp.

"Here," he said quietly, "put these on." He handed out flat, green vests to each of them. At a questioning look from Mark, he explained. "Life vest. The wind's going to come up when the sun comes up, and we'll have to run if we're spotted."

"Can we get across? The sun'll be up soon."

"We'll be as quiet as we can, but we took longer to get here than I hoped."

Jen looked dubiously at the thin material before pulling it over her head with her good arm.

"It's self-inflating," Ted explained as he helped her fasten the vest's straps. "You go down a few feet, then it'll fill up with gas and bring you back up."

"Used to wear them in fishing tournaments," Luke said has he tightened his own straps. "Hope they still work."

Mark helped Ted uncover the boat while Jen and Luke opened the garage doors at the front of the building.

"This is gonna suck without the truck," Ted muttered as he pulled a pair of wheel chocks out from under the tires. Mark hurried to the other side and pulled out the other set.

"Ramp's only a couple hundred yards up the road," Luke replied. "Jen, you get up and sit in the back of the boat. That'll help us lift the front."

Mark boosted Jen up into the fishing boat, then joined Luke and Ted at the trailer's tongue. Luke nodded to Ted, who tilted the trailer back a few inches, then the older man removed the cotter pin for the leg that held the front of the boat up and folded it up.

Mark grabbed the trailer and all three of them strained at it until it creeped forward. Once it started moving, they guided it out of the shed and turned it down the street toward the boat ramp.

***

"Nothing?" Jiminez demanded. "Four hours and all you've got to show for it is one helicopter that wouldn't start after it got refueled and two crews that are threatening to call Human Resources over flight hours?" He paced at the front of the room and glared at his subordinates.

"The snow covered up any tracks," Schmidt replied nervously.

"What about IR?" Jiminez spat back. "We paid a buttload of money for that Chinese crap!"

"The repair crew at Tahoe said that one of the birds' scope never worked, and the other quit after the first hour," Sadana said, not looking up from her monitor.

Jiminez opened his mouth to shout, then stopped and took a long, slow breath, "So, I've got to go to the Attorney General and tell them that in exchange for a couple million Callors, all I've got is a fat gringo who's going to take days to interrogate once he sobers up and a *chengada maricon* who doesn't know shit," he said calmly through clenched teeth. "Is that it?"

Schmidt and Sedana didn't say anything, although Sadana's cheeks flushed at the sound of Jiminez's slur.

"Anything on that chat room? Any idea on where they might be heading?"

"It went quiet after we hit the garage," Sedana replied. "Everything's gone quiet."

Again, Jiminez closed his eyes and blew his breath out between clenched teeth. "Where are the choppers now?"

"The one that can still fly is fueling up at Tahoe. Jackson and one of his guys are on it," Schmidt replied.

"Fine." Jiminez looked up at the clock. "The AG's driver is supposed to call me when he picks them up in an hour. I want something to report by then, got it?"

"Yes, sir," Sedana and Schmidt said in unison.

***

Ted cussed as he tried to loosen the straps holding the boat to the trailer. The nylon was stiff from the cold, and the boat had shifted a fraction of an inch when they had dropped one of the wheels in a shallow pothole on the way down the street.

"Just cut the damned things," Luke growled. He and Mark were straining to balance the boat at the top of the ramp. "We're never going to use them again, anyway."

Luke pulled out his knife and sawed through the tough material. When the last strap was hanging loose and frayed below the trailer, he trotted up to the front and helped the other men guide the boat down the ice-slick ramp.

"Tell me you put the plugs in," he said with a sarcastic grin at his father. "This thing'd make a crappy submarine."

"Yep," Luke said through bared teeth. His left foot went out from underneath him, but he recovered without losing his grip on the trailer. "Did that before we left the shack."

The trailer's wheels crunched through the thin ice that sat at the bottom of the ramp, then the boat floated free as the men let go of the trailer. It was a wide craft, made from silvery-gray fiberglass and aluminum. The three men clambered aboard and Mark dutifully took a seat next to Jen when Luke pointed to it.

Ted picked up the gas can and poured its contents into a tank at the back of the boat while Luke unfolded a small motor at the front.

"Batteries probably aren't charged for shit," Ted grumbled. "That trawler isn't going to get us far."

"Get the big motor ready," Luke said as he pushed the trawling motor over the side with a quiet splash. "We'll need it if we're spotted."

He unfolded a chair at the front of the boat and sat down. Using a foot pedal, he used the small electric motor to push them away from the shore and toward the steadily brightening sky on the other side of the lake.

***

Jackson watched as the small airport on the Cali side of the border crossing dropped away beneath them. They had stayed on the ground long enough to use the restroom and report their status to Sacramento. His joy at being able to relieve himself after too much coffee and too much time in the cramped seat of a helicopter was ruined when his status call had devolved into observations on his incompetence and questionable intelligence and heritage.

He keyed the microphone on the headset the copilot had given him and pointed to the north. "Sacramento says to try looking at the logging roads over there," he said curtly.

"Yep, heading that way already," the pilot replied in a flat tone. Jackson glared at the back of her head, then looked over at Juan. His subordinate looked as tired as he felt, but was still scanning the terrain to the right of the chopper.

It's cold as fuck out there, Juan thought. He shivered as he shifted in his seat. *Not exactly toasty in this damn thing.*

He looked across the lake into Nevada and noticed several white and green trucks parked on the far shore.

"Looks like they're expecting someone," he said into his headset. He pointed toward the trucks.

Jackson turned to look, then something on the surface of the lake caught his eye.

***

Mark watched as the insect-like shape of the helicopter drew nearer. He was letting his breath out as it seemed to pass in front of them without changing its course, but then his heart sank when he saw it bank and come around to pass behind them.

He raised his hand to point, but Luke and Ted were already reacting.

"Get that motor going!" Luke shouted, all hope of a quiet crossing gone.

Ted twisted the key in the console, and they listened as the engine cranked. It coughed once, twice, then caught. The motor roared as Ted pushed the throttle as far forward as he could, and the nose of the boat bounced as it hit the small waves the morning wind was kicking up on the surface of the lake.

Jen felt herself rise up from her seat, and both she and Mark clung to the stiff upholstery. Underneath them, they could feel the vibration of the motor as it propelled them across the lake.

***

With a cry like a hound sighting a fox, Jackson pointed at the boat as it left a wide wake in the water beneath them.

"That's them! That's them!" he shouted excitedly.

The pilot maneuvered her craft to cut in front of the boat, but merely flew over the top of it on her first try. Jackson watched as the boat rocked in the turbulence of the helicopter's passing, but it kept on its course across the lake.

"Run them down!" he shouted into his headset as he hauled back on the charging handle of his carbine and clawed at the handle to his door. Juan copied his movements on his side of the chopper.

***

Ted heard the helicopter coming around for another pass and hauled the boat's wheel over to try to angle away from it. Jen screamed as shots rang out from the aircraft, cutting a line of splashes across the water in front of the boat before several bullets smacked into the hull just forward of where Luke sat.

"We're OK," Ted shouted, more for himself than for his passengers. His father had climbed down from the platform at the bow, and Mark pulled Jen down to join him on the floor of the boat. The helicopter roared in front of them again, the pilot trying to slow to a hover so that they would have to either turn away from shore or ram into the aircraft.

***

"They've reached the border!" The copilot said over the intercom.

The scream of the helicopter's slipstream garbled the message in Jackson's ear, so he leaned back into the chopper and screamed "What?"

"They're in American waters!" The co-pilot said firmly. "We have to break off!"

"Fuck that!" Jackson shouted back. "Sink that fucking thing and we'll pick up the survivors!"

The co-pilot turned to confront his passenger, then stopped when he saw the agent's finger on the trigger of his carbine.

"You got me, fucker?" Jackson snarled across the intercom.

"I got you," the co-pilot said. He turned back to his controls.

***

Gus Patterson sprinted up the hallway of the Border Patrol command post in Stateline, Nevada. He normally supervised the monotonous night shift, but he had been greeted by the region commander and several suits who had flown up from Las Vegas. He and every other agent that usually just manned the ill-used border crossing on the edge of town had been put out to patrol the lake shore all night. The suits had ensconced themselves in the post's conference room, while the commander had spent the evening in the radio room.

The commander, a tall, lean Texan named Davis was now bent over the desk next to the dispatcher, listening as calls came in.

"Chopper's coming back around. I think I hear gun shots," a voice on the radio reported.

"Which side of the lake are they on?" Davis asked. The dispatcher relayed the question, then waited for the reply.

One of the suits was right behind Patterson. "Is that them?" he said breathlessly.

"Well, if it's not, then the Cali's have some outstanding Fish and Wildlife enforcement going on," Davis said drily.

"Outpost Seven says that they're about half a mile out from shore."

"That's Hernandez and Chung up by Zephyr Cove," Patterson said. "That's on our side of the border."

"Well, then," Davis said, "maybe we should remind them of that." Patterson thought he caught a glint in the older man's eye as he turned to the dispatcher. "Put me on the guard freq."

Ted cursed into the wind as the helicopter dropped until its skids were a few feet over the water, then maneuvered to get in front of him. The boat skipped across the surface once more as it hit the aircraft's wake again.

Jen screamed as she was thrown up into the air, then bounced against the seat at the back of the boat. Ted reached for her, taking his hand off the wheel to do it, then the boat hit another wave, throwing her up and over the side of the boat.

The frigid water struck her as if she had leaped onto concrete from the top of a building, sending her tumbling across the surface for a heartbeat before she sank beneath the waves. A moment later, something tightened around her neck, and she felt herself being dragged back up.

Jen bobbed to the surface, the orange skin of her life vest scratching at her neck and cheeks. The air was filled with the roar of motors and she felt the wind beat against her.

***

Juan whooped as he saw the form of one of the fugitives tumble into the water, then pop back up. He sighted along the barrel of his gun and let off another stream of bullets at the boat as it turned around to pick up the orange blob bobbing in the waves. Unlike Jackson, who had brought along his personal carbine for the search, Juan had grabbed one of the old belt fed guns from the back of the van. Jackson had complained about its bulk in the close confines of the helicopter, but now he cheered as Juan braced himself against the frame of the small door and pulled the trigger again.

He walked a line of tracers into the path of the boat, then watched as they bisected it lengthwise. Immediately, a black plume of smoke erupted from the rear of the small craft and its nose came down as it slowed to a stop a few yards from the person in the water.

"Get us down there!" Jackson screamed excitedly.

***

Ted cried out in pain as splinters from the fiberglass and plywood making up the boat lanced through his jeans and into his calf. Mark, who had been running to the front of the boat to help Luke grab Jen and pull her back aboard, pulled himself up shakily just as the engine died. He looked around for something to throw to his wife as he heard the helicopter come closer.

Luke was pawing at one of the canvas cases, trying to open it with hands made stiff from the cold and wind. He had it half open and was tugging at the rifle inside when another burst of gunfire stitched across the bow of the boat next to him. He and Mark threw themselves to the deck.

***

The pilot was banking around to hover above the small boat, now riding lower in the water, when the radio squawked in her ear.

ATTENTION CALI AIRCRAFT OVER LAKE TAHOE. THIS IS THE UNITED STATES BORDER PATROL. YOU ARE VIOLATING UNITED STATES AIRSPACE AND FIRING ON A VESSEL IN OUR WATERS. CEASE FIRE IMMEDIATELY AND RETURN TO YOUR SIDE OF THE BORDER OR YOU WILL BE FIRED ON. OVER!"

Jackson turned to the pilot when he heard the message over his headset and screamed, "Just get me down there!" He put his hand on the butt of his pistol.

The pilot opened her mouth to reply, when the co-pilot shouted, "Look out!"

A stream of tracers from the shore came at them in a long, slow rope that missed by only a few yards. Again, the guard frequency sounded in their headsets.

CALI HELICOPTER OVER LAKE TAHOE, I SAY AGAIN, CEASE FIRE AND RETURN TO YOUR SIDE OF THE BORDER. WE DON'T MISS TWICE. OVER.

The pilot looked over at the man next to her, then hauled back on her controls. Jackson opened his mouth to shout at her, then thought better of it. Setting his jaw, he pulled himself back into his seat and slammed the door closed.

"Get us back on the ground," he growled as Juan shut his own door. Both men cursed as the helicopter banked to the west and crossed back into Cali.

***

Jen was too numb to grasp the rope Mark threw to her, but she was able to hug it tightly enough that it didn't slip through her arms as he dragged her back to the boat. It took both her husband and Luke to haul her out of the water and onto the torn green carpet of the deck, but soon she was huddled under several blankets as she watched Luke tromp down on the control pedal for the trawling motor.

"Main motor's shot!" Ted shouted from his perch on the stern.

"We've got enough juice to keep us from drifting back across the line," Luke replied. Now that the helicopter was gone and the big outboard was quiet, he could almost talk in a normal tone.

Mark pointed to the tree lined shore. "Somebody's coming out!" he shouted.

"That'll be the Border Patrol," Luke said. "First time I've seen one of their boats in sunlight." He chuckled at that.

A moment later, a large green and white boat pulled alongside them. A young man stood in its bow, manning a machine gun with a long barrel that he kept trained on the far shore. A tall man in brown trousers and a heavy green coat stood on the back deck. After Luke had tied his boat off with the line one of the crewmen threw to him, he helped Mark and Jen across to the large vessel.

"Mr. and Mrs. Costa?" The tall man drawled in a loud voice after he had helped the two of them up onto the deck.

"Yes," Mark said. He tried to pull himself straight, but the boat rocked as small waves hit it broadside.

"Welcome to the United States!" the tall man shouted over the wind, a glint in his bright blue eyes. "Welcome home!"

Roll, Colorado, Roll!

Alma TC Boykin

Andrew "Andy" McDavitt giggled as he studied the lines of code on the two screens. "This is too easy," he whispered. No one left a dam's spillway-gate controls just hanging out for gosh and everyone to find. But there it was.

Or was it? Andy frowned and ran a hand over the bottom of his beard. Dominic said that two gates would let the river run again, one on the north and one in the south. The code activated emergency flow control systems, but were the right ones? He didn't want to send the river where it had never gone before. Andy hunted around among the scraps of paper for a mostly empty one, found a pen, and made note of what he'd found. He'd triple-check with Dominic. They had to wait a little longer anyway, since the spring flows were only just now starting. Andy smiled, hands behind his neck and stretched in his chair, looking at the lines of code and imagining what the Colorado's estuary would look like next year, after the flows had been restored. It would be very good.

He backed out of the water authority's files, still wondering how anyone could be so foolish, and if they really were. Nah, this was Cali, and the Bay Area Water Authority he was looking at. They were that foolish. What about LA's Metropolitan Water Department, the famous Metropolitan Water District of Southern California, a.k.a., the MWD? Andy stretched again, then began typing.

***

Dominic Exposito struggled to look at least politely interested and mildly understanding as the witch from the Cali National Water Board kept talking. "All treaties and compacts signed with the United States and Mexico concerning water are still valid," she repeated for the twelfth—thirteenth?—time. "Arizona has a duty to continue storing water for the people of Cali and Mexico, especially the new farming communities in the Imperial Valley. *Los Hermanos de la Tierra* are concentrating on sustainable, community-centered agriculture as they reclaim the land both for themselves and for the natural environment." She blathered about the LHdT for another minute or so, then blinked. "Moonbeam is concerned about rumors he has heard concerning restoration releases that will interfere with irrigation and municipal demand."

Kira Nguyn, district supervisor for the Bureau of Reclamation, gave Dominic a poke as she said, "I'll let our hydrologist explain, Ms. Villanueva."

Dominic straightened up and toggled his microphone on, shifting the camera his direction in the process. He didn't bother with a greeting, since she'd bite his head off for the crime of being a pale male from Wyoming and a former Cali resident. He'd gotten out just before the chipping started. But, his sister and her family had not been so fortunate.

"Per the Colorado River Environmental Management Plan of 2004, updated in 2020 and 2025, a seasonal flood simulation release is scheduled for late May or early June. We are not publicizing the date because of the white-water rafters, as you know" She probably didn't but that was her problem. "It is the semi-annual release, in order to move sediment and rebuild the proper riparian habitat within the Grand Canyon. Smaller releases downstream will precede it, because of this year's snow pack and the predicted run-off. We do not want a repeat of 1983."

She glowered. "Remind me. What did you foul up that time?"

"Snow pack of greater than three hundred percent of yearly average, combined with rapid warming and an unusually wet May led to emergency released from all the main-stem dams on the Colorado as well as at Imperial and several other irrigation diversion structures. Even so Hoover Dam suffered some damage." Hell, for several hours they thought they might lose Hoover and everything downstream with it! The river would win, sooner or later, and it had almost been sooner. The old photos still gave him the willies.

"Don't interfere with the irrigation flows at Imperial or the municipal diversions, do you understand? If you do, Cali will consider it a breach of international law and possibly a declaration of war, as will Mexico. The reclamation farms will get their water, as will the rest of the country." She didn't say "or else," but she didn't have to.

District Supervisor Nguyn took over. "We quite understand the Cali Water Board's concerns, and have taken them into consideration, Ms. Villanueva. Flows from the upstream Colorado River basin will not be interrupted."

"They'd better not be. Villanueva out." The logo of the Cali Water Board replaced her on the screen.

Mrs. Nguyn turned off the Bureau's end of the call and stood. She ran one hand through her grey-frosted black hair and gathered print-outs with the other. "So, straight scoop. How high will the water get, Dominic?"

The others around the conference station leaned forward. Rick and Lupe had a bet going, that much Dominic knew for certain, and he suspected a few others did too. "As high as eighty-three, I can tell you that much. Maybe higher if this rainfall continues. El Niño has been very good to us this year, a little too good for the engineers' peace of mind." Since the white-board was full with a large "Do NOT erase" note on it, he flipped over one of the print-outs of the proposed meeting order, pulled a freebie pen out of his shirt pocket, tested it on a corner of the page, and sketched a curve with flat ends. "This is your normal water year. These are your municipal and irrigation minimum flows," he pointed to the flat bits. "The peak in May-June is the average release when the Bureau releases environmental restoration water if there's enough melt to do so without endangering late-season irrigation flows."

Everyone nodded and a few looked bored. "This is this year, or is what the Colorado really wants to do to us this year, with the help of the Gila and Green and a few other friends." He drew a second curve, with a much higher and wider peak. "This is what we, meaning the hydrology and dam-management people, hope will happen. We've got three-and-a-half times average snowpack at least, since we don't know what exactly the depths are across the Cali border, and it is still raining and snowing." He drew a saw-tooth, with a very sharp initial peak and steeper decline below the first two curves. "This is what the people downstream don't want, and what the dam managers sure as hell don't want."

"As I recall, no one engineered the big boys for over-the-top flows," Pat "the Ranger," the Wildlife Department liaison said, running a finger under his nose.

"Or to operate with the spillways ripped out and new side-channels created." Dominic straightened up. "Ms. Villanueva and the Cali Water Board want option one. We will probably have to go with option two, and start releases a little early just so we don't overload the diversion dams."

Domingo "Frio" Gavrijlla made a rude sound. "Those of us in the Central Arizona Project appreciate your concern. Even though we're not taking much this year."

"What, no surfing the irrigation canals?" Rick teased, nudging the dour liaison from Arizona's largest irrigation operation. Frio had relatives on the Cali side of the line, some of them decent people, or so Dominic seemed to recall.

"We're already fishing for whales. I swear someone called and reported seeing a shark on one of the Gila-River cross-overs last week, and they sounded sober." He gathered his own papers and straightened them with a frustrated tap on the table. "It may be too wet for the cotton this year, and we've lost some of the produce already. One more year like the last two and I'm going to stop thinking that radio preacher with the giant boat is crazy."

"You and me both," Dominic said. "It's like the 1920s all over again, in terms of hydrology."

Kira Nguyn asked, honest puzzlement on her face, "So everyone gets their full allocation?"

Frio nodded. "Everyone, upper basin and lower basin. Top off the reservoirs, shower for an hour or until the hot water runs out, grow rice in Utah, whatever floats your boat."

The others groaned or rolled their eyes. Nguyn winced. "Right. On that note, the conference is over. Go get some work done."

Dominic and Frio managed not to snort at someone from the federal government encouraging productivity. On the other hand, when the Bureau fouled up or goofed off, people tended to die in headline-making ways.

That evening Dominic's house phone rang. The caller ID showed it as a call from a very fancy hotel in Singapore, and Dominic shook his head. What was Greenie up to now? "I'll get it, dear," he told Carla. "I think it's Raj calling about the conference paper."

"OK." She stopped washing dishes for a moment, head turned toward the living room as he headed for his 'office.' Carla leaned back, trying to peer around the door. "Tony, Maria, what are you doing?" When no answer followed, she asked, "Dear could you check on them? It's too quiet in there."

Dominic detoured through the living room. Both kids were working on coloring books and not attempting to color each other. He waved and kept going to the modified walk-in closet that held his tiny home work-space. He caught the phone just before the machine did. "Runningwater Hydrologic Services, how may I help you?"

"Mr. Waters, this is Mr. Babbage. I need confirmation on some locations for our irrigation and reclamation contract."

Dominic's heart rate surged as he heard the hacker McDavitt on the line, but at least he was maintaining some semblance of security. He made himself take a deep breath, sit down at the desk, and get out a small write-erase board and marker, along with a book listing all the facilities with information about them. "Certainly. Just to confirm, this is the Calexico program contract?"

"Yes, it is."

"Thank you." He rotated in his seat so he could see the wall map with all the dams and take-offs on the Colorado and its main tributaries. "Go ahead with the locations, please."

'Mr. Babbage' recited a set of lat-long coordinates. Dominic noted them down, then thumbed through the book's reverse-location index to find what was where. The first one was the Imperial diversion structure. The second was a smaller upstream diversion. "I have a third one, but it might not be as suitable." Dominic heard doubt in the hacker's voice, and wondered what he meant.

"Let's see what it is and we can decide. It may impinge in at least one of these."

Dominic's eyes bulged when he saw the third set of coordinates. Parker Dam? Babbage had found a way into the diversion controllers at Parker Dam? They couldn't— That was supposed to have been firewalled so tightly even Old Scratch couldn't get in or out. "I'm afraid the third location's not really suitable for the irrigation idea, since it is already taken by a main-stream dam and most of the surrounding terrain is quite rugged. Or is this the possible salt-remediation site that we've discussed?" In plain English, was this really what Babbage had in mind? Because if they could open it as a flood flow came through, it might take out the two downstream diversions on its own. It would also take out Yuba City and a lot of other things as well. But if it hurt Cali, or more importantly, the LHdT, he'd take the chance. And Yuba City was two-thirds empty already.

"Yes, it is the possible salt-remediation site." Dominic heard relief and excitement both in Babbage's voice.

"It certainly would have more effect there than downstream, assuming your client was not concerned with re-concentration due to evaporation."

"Hmm. I'll ask him. But the other two would be feasible?"

"Certainly. You will have to confirm water availability, of course. I believe Kewitt, Richards, and Crocker now has international water lawyers on staff who are certified for the U.S. and Cali both." That firm probably did, since money was involved.

The voice at the other end calmed down. "Very good. Thank you, and I will call back when I have more details as to exactly what my client has in mind."

"Certainly, and thank you for calling. I'd rather sort things out now than in the field."

"I quite agree, Mr. Waters. The less ground-truthing required, the happier I'll be."

After he terminated the call, Andy stood up, stretched left and right, and twisted at the middle. Something went pop and that nasty catch he'd had since the climbing accident let go. "Aahh. Much better." Even though he worked for the Bureau, Waters wasn't a bad guy.

Andy knew Waters wasn't his contact's name, but it was safer to use at least two layers of falsification. The feebs had infested EarthFirst! because people got careless, and he really did not want his plan for restoring the Colorado River estuary ruined by some fool who thought they knew rivers from rivets. Underestimating the Cali Water Board's computer and other security people probably wasn't too smart, but shit. They'd let the MWD have full access to everything, including operational files? Really? Andy glanced at the clock and checked once more that the wireless was turned off and the computers powered down.

The landlady had been whining about electricity costs again. She ought to have put in a wind turbine and solar when it was still easy. The engineering part of his mind reminded Andy about what happened when solar panels burned, like that massive apartment fire just before the Calexit. He laced his sneakers, pulled his satchel over his shoulder and wrestled his town-bike quietly down the stairs. The air felt drier than it had for the past few weeks, so maybe they were getting to the end of the spring rains. His boss complained that she was starting to feel moldy. Hey, if Mother Nature wanted to mess with humans, that was her privilege.

As he rode through the neighborhood and past the park entrance, Andy wondered if Waters really worried about the state of the Colorado's delta the way he said he did? Probably not. They'd met, no, collided was the word, at a conference in Pima that Andy and his allies from Natives United and Gila Free! had protested. Andy'd been waving a sign and chanting "Free the waters, free the waters." One of the hydrologists had come over, read some of their literature, and had started laughing.

"This is so out of date!" He'd guffawed. "You need to keep up with the science if you don't want to look any more foolish than you already do."

That had stung, and Butterfly had snarled, "So what should we be reading?" The man had rattled off a list of titles, wrapping up with, "Or just go to the library and look up 'Hydrology Today'." Andy had. Given how many big, nasty water projects used computer controls, it made sense to study them along with his real classes. One of the girls had broken up with him over it, but she'd been more of a purist. Andy slowed for a stop-light, wishing the city would see reason and make the big rigs stay outside the residential areas, especially this time of evening.

What had happened to her, Evangeline it was? She'd been from San Diego. Had she joined the Brownshirt Brigade? No, he started pedaling again. She'd have gone to that environmental action youth group. Those bastards in Sacramento should have listened to their environmental people instead of screwing them over. Land before People, that had been the slogan they used to get the votes for secession. He'd show them what it really meant, if he could, even if it was four years later.

That night, Dominic stood on his back porch, watching the stars. If the houses would disappear, he could have also seen the San Francisco peaks north of Flagstaff. Monica, his sister, had loved the mountains. Now she and three of her and Lawrence's children were dead, and poor Bobby still had nightmares about his and his father's escape through the Sierras. Lawrence had done everything he could, but the monsters had secretly chipped Monica and the newborn when she had her C-section, and had tracked them when the family tried to escape. Monica— Dominic closed his eyes.

The monsters had televised her murder as a warning. He had not been able to call their mother before she saw it, and she died of heart failure not long after. Lawrence had almost managed to save Mary as well, but a bullet aimed at him missed, ricocheted, and hit her. She died before they could reach Reno.

Dominic didn't want to kill innocent people. But there were no innocents in Cali, not any more.

Certainly not in the government, or with the *Hermanos de la Tierra*. They'd killed his niece and nephew, working them to death in the Imperial Valley farms.

If Babbage was right, the Cali government would pay for those murders, for his nephew's nightmares, for his brother-in-law's unending pain and guilt. "Never, ever piss off the engineer," Dominic whispered to the stars.

***

Chinmalis glared at Eloi. He gave her that lazy grin that meant someone was going to die, painfully, if he didn't get his way. "They don't work, they don't eat, that's tribal law. You don't survive in this environment without everyone working for the good of the group. You know what the Ancestors said."

Chinmalis wondered for a fraction of an instant if the Ancestors had really forced pregnant women to work in the poisoned fields, but forced the thought from her mind. "Is there another rotation available until the three deliver?" Rosa would probably go into labor that night, the *curandera* said. The other two weren't as important, since they weren't citizens of the tribe, but labor was labor and they worked hard, trying to earn their places.

"No. They work the north field, and the *Chiles Verdes* work along the river." Where he could watch the younger woman 'volunteers' and quickly pull one from the line if he wanted her, Chinmalis knew, but didn't dare say. No one criticized Eloi. He was connected to the Old Blood on both family sides, plus he had the political connections that let *Los Hermanos de la Tierra* take over so much land and water. "Any other questions, *mi hija*?"

"No, *compadre*, none."

He picked up a carved jadite cylinder off the desk and rolled it between his hands. "Do the verdes up north have any idea where their organic food comes from?"

"No. Or if they do, they probably pat themselves on the back for being so enlightened and supportive of minority agriculture." She knew the sneering and condescension too well. Two thirds of the leaders of Cali had that same tone when they talked about reclaiming the land and returning it to those who deserved it. Moonbeam never had made good on his promises. And the Chinese, the ones who wanted even more food and to run the farms themselves? Even worse and just as damned racist as the *Yanquis*.

Eloi chuckled, low in the back of his throat, a predator's sound. He stood, and Chinmalis backed out of the way, letting him go first out of the office. The air conditioners whirred. Chinmalis preferred to keep the building warmer, but Eloi had overruled her, as always. And he had a point in mid-summer, when the computers needed to be protected, but today when it was seventy degrees outside? She followed him down the hall. He turned right, going to his secondary office. She continued past to the main door, nodding to the muscular *Hermano* on security duty sketching at the desk as she left. He looked up from his drawing but didn't say anything. She preferred him to the one who always leered at her.

Chinmalis winced a little as she stepped out of the shade of the broad patio around the *Projecto de Imperio* offices. The sun shone for the first time in a week, at least, and the white gravel and sand around the building gleamed. She put on her dark glasses and after some hesitation decided to go check on Rosa. The labor manager tied a bandana over her tight-braided hair, then a helmet and gloves. She climbed onto her little electric four-wheeler, started the motor, and headed north and east.

The track led through brown and white desert, brown with native plants and dirt, white where salt crystals clumped in drifts and small piles. The gringos had poisoned the land, abusing it and bringing the salt to the surface, then dumping chemicals onto their imported plants and destroying the great inland lake they called the Salton Sea. Some of the books claimed that it had been made by accident, but Chinmalish knew better. The river had carved the lake before the gringos locked the river away. Now only a tiny fraction of the waters that should fill the lake were permitted to trickle into the giant valley.

Chinmalish took her time, looking at the plants and stopping once to inspect one of the *ak-chen* gardens. The plants looked too wet, as if they had been gorging on too much water. The desert garden was meant for dry years, normal years. She considered moving some of the rocks to allow better drainage, then changed her mind. They needed to see how it worked, or did not work, in wet years. They knew how it worked in dry, at least farther east, in the *Di'neh* lands. Chinmalish made notes on her little data-pad and continued out to the north field.

Salt glittered on the edges of the huge expanse of leafy green. Stooped figures in floppy sun-hats and faded denim worked between the rows of strawberries and other produce, gathering the crops. The land was not as sick here as it was closer to the Salton Sea, but breathing the dust for too long, well… If the greedy *tontos* had not attempted to avoid doing their proper duties as citizens of Cali, then they deserved a lesson in earning their living. Most of the women and children had been caught trying to evade border patrols and sneak out, or had hidden their children to avoid being chipped. Except for Rosa.

Chinmalish parked the four-wheeler and plugged it into the solar charger, then walked to where *Tío* Moctezuma stood, cradling a shotgun in his arms as he watched the workers.

"The little one is starting to moan and claims she's in labor," he nodded to a skinny figure at the far end of the row, one of the *gringas*. "I told her to shut up and keep working. Women of the People don't whine."

"True." The little one was under a double sentence, for attempting to leave without a departure visa and for hiding her military dependent status. Chinmalish didn't really care if she and the child died or lived. "Rosa?"

"Over there. I told her to stop and sit when she needed to." *Tío* 'Zuma shook his head a little. "Nice girl, too bad she was stupid."

"*Sí.*" Rosa had gotten pregnant but wouldn't say if the man was of *la raza pura* or a *gringo* or something else. She'd told Eloi it was none of his business. And so she was here. She tried hard, all the work bosses agreed. "Any trouble?"

"No. All quiet."

Chinmalish didn't expect any trouble so soon after an execution, but she'd been surprised. People could be so stupid. Came from living too easy, she'd decided. People like her, who grew up with the rats and with *gringos* and slant-eyes sneering at them, they grew up hard and smart. "*Bueno*." She unplugged the four-wheeler, drove it to one of the filled produce trailers, and hitched it up. No point in wasting a trip.

She heard a commotion, and looked to see three of the other *gringos* rushing back to where the little skinny *chica* had been standing.

Boom! The shotgun thundered. "Keep working!" *Tío* 'Zuma ordered. "Or the next barrel is yours."

Chinmalish started down the road. She didn't need to know.

***

That month went fast, Dominic sighed as he looked at the calendar and the hydrographs. The water's going even faster.

"Are we going to lose Glen Canyon and Hoover?" Rick pointed to the numbers, showing the flows coming in from Colorado, New Mexico, and Wyoming.

"Not Glen Canyon," Dominic assured everyone packed into the conference room. "Smith and Begay told me they have permission to start additional releases tomorrow. Hoover's open already, and Parker should open soon to lower Lake Havasu. I am told," he gave District Supervisor Nguyn a tired look. She'd given someone his direct phone number. "Told that the Imperial Diversion and other Cali diversions are opening. I was also informed that we are attempting to destroy this year's crops by water-logging them." Controlling the rain was far, far above his pay grade.

"Wait." Frio Gavrijlla uncrossed his arms and leaned onto the table between Lupe and Ranger Pat. He picked up a laser pointer and circled the current estimated flows at Parker Dam. "Estimated? Should be open? I thought they were up and running per protocols."

Kira Nguyn winced and rubbed her chin. "Remember the trouble they had just after Cali declared its independence? The flood flows and the lightning strike that took out the power station there?"

"Ah, vaguely."

"Cali refused to allow Bureau techs from Arizona or anywhere else in the U.S. into the facility. Ran them off a gunpoint and said we were trying to sabotage the system and divert the power to the U.S."

Frio facepalmed. "Oh sh— yeah. The Battle of Lake Havasu. Sorry."

"Ten lashes with a wet noodle for not remembering," Nguyn chuckled, then sobered. "We hope they got things repaired. We know they got the power reconnected, outgoing power, but as far as if the emergency spillway gates, the primary spillway gates, and other things still work? No idea."

Rick coughed. "There's also the little landslide problem after that earthquake two years ago. Kicked loose a bunch of sediment not too far from where the

Cali side mates with the bedrock. And we don't know about the foundations, if anything moved down there."

"Does brown water, clear water work for high arch dams?" Frio asked with a wink.

"It does, sort of," Dominic answered. "If you see brown water from the bottom, be nervous. If you see brown water pouring over the top, you should have started running a few hours ago."

Kira Nguyn clapped her hands together, bringing the meeting back onto target. "Dominic, what's our worst case scenario?"

He moved to the next slide, showing the chewed-out remains of Hoover's emergency spillways from 1983. "This, but as high as the dam is tall. Absolute worst case is if one of the main-stem dams were to be overtopped. That's not going to happen with the ones on U.S. soil if everything continues to function the way it is now. But if Glen Canyon were to go, then we'll lose everything downstream." Should he say something? Possibly, just in case. "I'm worried about Parker. We don't know what the real-time flows are, we don't know if everything's been repaired and tested, and we don't know if the landslide and earthquake opened weaknesses in the flank of the dam and the grout curtain on the Cali side. If it were to have a problem, which I hope it does not," he crossed his fingers under the desk. "If it has a problem, it could possibly take out Imperial and the other downstream diversions."

"We've already ordered evacuations of Yuba City and a few other places downstream of Parker, just based on projected emergency releases per the current protocols," Frio said, nodding. "And we've closed the intakes on the Central Arizona Project. Lord knows we don't need any extra water at the moment."

Supervisor Nguyn nodded, looked at the slide again, then pinched the bridge of her nose. "That's what's coming. Dominic, ride herd on this, so to speak, please. Everyone else, we'll touch base again at the usual time or if something changes."

"Same bat time, same bat station," Ranger Pat muttered under his breath, triggering giggles from Lupe.

"Careful, you'll show your age," Dominic kidded him.

Pat stood, looming as much as a broomstick could loom. "I happen to be an aficionado of classic television, sir, not old."

Frio rolled his eyes and Rick grinned, then launched into, "Return with us now to the thrilling days of yesteryear—" as Dominic hummed the appropriate music.

"Hey! It's not my fault the last person to use that computer left the speakers turned all the way up!" Pat protested, rolling his papers into a tube and swatting Rick.

"Back to work," Nguyn ordered, looking up at the ceiling and imploring her deity for patience.

Four days later, Dominic stared at the numbers scrolling up his computer screen, shaking his head. Five hundred thousand cubic feet per second (c f/s)? Good Lord have mercy. The nightly news was full of dramatic pictures of the enormous white sprays of water coming from Glen Canyon and Hoover as they released water as quickly as was safe.

And Lake Havasu was rising. Frio had shown him photos taken from a recon drone, and the gates appeared open, no more than would be standard for this time of year. "I don't like that," Frio had stated. "That's a lot of water running through the turbines."

"That makes two of us. I really hope they know what they are doing, or that they are going to open the emergency spillways." Dominic had leaned forward. "Can you zoom in here?" he pointed to the eastern side of the dam. "Something looks odd." Frio tinkered with the image, then leaned back as Dominic peered at the screen. "Yeeessss. There, by the end of the turbine house," he pointed to the rectangular concrete structure that angled southwest from the western side of the dam. "It looks turbulent, bubbling, and not where it is supposed to bubble, I don't think. And why are the roads closed?" He straightened up. "I wonder if they are worried about undermining right in that area, if the quake shifted an unknown fault?"

Frio shook his head, then ran a hand through his short hair. "No idea, but we've finished evacuating everyone we can on our side downstream. It won't take much to overtop it, will it?"

Parker looked odd compared to Hoover and Glen Canyon, set lower in the water and hiding most of its mass within sediment under the lakes. Dark brown, rugged rock on both sides showed why the cleft had been perfect for a dam. No cars moved on the switch-backs on the California side, or drove across the dam. Well, the road had been closed since Cali's departure, so that was not new. The additional pale grey superstructure above the roadway reminded Dominic of a crown, almost white against the dark blue of Lake Havasu and the downstream river, and the brown-red rocks on the opposite side of the lake. The water always looked too high against the dam, even at low water.

Dominic had shrugged. "Not much more, but they don't have the gates fully open yet." They should have, but this was Cali, after all. What did the government care if people downstream drowned so long as Sacramento, LA, and the Bay got their power, electrical and otherwise?

Now Dominic wondered if Mr. Babbage had gotten his message. If he had, then he probably had something to do with the odd numbers and the stopped flow at Parker. If not, then Cali's lack of repairs were about to bite them, hard. Concrete high-arch dams could take a lot, they had to. But the water would win, possibly in thousands of years, perhaps overnight if something geologically *exciting* happened. As the Chinese had rediscovered the hard way. Was that why the Chinese liked Cali so much? Neither one cared if their people all died so long as the Party and the military, or Brownshirts, got what they wanted? Dominic filed the thought away and returned to what he was supposed to be doing. Floods came, and floods went, and he needed to run those numbers for the next restoration release, based on the new data.

***

Just after noon the next day, Andy McDavitt cracked his knuckles. Started typing, and slipped in

through the back door he'd found in the MWD's
security net. They'd managed to get one of the gates at
Parker, but his blocking code held steady on the other
motors. He shook his head again and sipped his mid-
day pick-me-up. They'd had access to Imperial as well
because of the tunnel and canals stealing water from
the Colorado and sending it to the Bay and LA. He'd
been alternating using the Bay Area Water Authority
and MWD, just in case someone wised up and started
looking at either one.

Thus far, he'd only found another hacker, probably
a bored Russian. Andy wondered idly if the MWD
even had computer security, then shrugged. Not his
problem after today. Today, June seventh, the wild
river would run once more. He smiled and typed
command codes, then waited, one eye on the feed from
the security camera at Parker, the other on the code
screen. One minute passed, and nothing happened,
other than a bird flapping past the lens.

Parker wasn't opening. Andy glanced from the
camera display to the code screen again. What was
going on? He'd entered the commands and everything
looked good, so why wasn't the blasted thing opening?
He gulped some of the high-test coffee and started
entering the command again.

A light on second-order river-system display that
he'd rigged caught his eye, and he turned to see what
was going on. He tapped the alert light. A message
flashed up, brilliant red. "Emergency spillway
activation. Evacuate downstream communities." It was
Cooledge, downstream of Parker on the Gila. Ooh,
double whammy!

Alma TC Boykin/Roll Colorado Roll/ 208

He glanced back to the video feed and saw water starting to jet out of the emergency spillway, and the power tubes. "Oops," he whispered, grinning "patience, Andy, patience." He erased the half-entered command and backed out of that file. Two down, one to go.

He opened Imperial and locked it open. Then he left a present for the Brownies in the Imperial Valley, bypassing the flood-alert systems and silencing the auto-broadcast warning system "This one's from Mr. Waters. He says eff you." He closed his eyes, imagining the water racing through the valleys, bursting out of the dams and canals, and rejoining as it danced into its true delta. He'd been re-reading that chapter in Aldo Leopold's book. It would be so beautiful, oh, so beautiful, water free of man's chains.

Dominic was in his office, watching the water-levels when he heard voices rising in the hallway. "What is it?"

"We don't know, but the guys at Imperial can't close anything. It's like someone welded the gates open."

"Well, remind them to go to manual."

"That's the problem. The Calis wouldn't let us maintain anything after they seized the diversions and dams. Apparently they didn't know how, or didn't have enough people, and their computers have gone tit's—er, belly-up."

They killed off everyone who knew their ass from a flood-gauge, Dominic snarled inside his head. *Like Monica and her kids and the poor souls with them. And Mom.*

Kira Nguyn's voice, much closer, said, "Have they been able to evacuate the Arizona side?"

"Oh yeah, moved the last people out a week ago because of worries about Parker. The repairs after the last big water didn't look so good," Rick replied, stepping into view. He tapped on Dominic's doorframe. "You have any monitoring real-time readouts from between Parker and Imperial?"

"The ones that are about to wash away? Yes."

"Patch them into the conference room and set it up so we can talk to Denver and DC as well, please. It looks as if Parker Dam is going, and Imperial's having some kind of trouble already."

Dominic acted confused. "I thought they reported normal yesterday?"

"They did."

"Huh."

As he patched the data through to the main conference room, Dominic let himself imagine the chaos unfolding as the Colorado's waters began pouring through the dams and canals. The tunnel and diversion to the coastal cities, and the All-American Canal, were not meant to take this kind of flow. Thousands, if not hundreds of thousands of gallons of water at tens of thousands c-f/s poured through them, overtopping the canals, racing across the desert lands, seeking the old channels, looking for a place to go. He idly wondered how high the Salton Sea would get this time, or if the river would take the primary channel, and punch south to the Mexican delta. He hoped most of it would go south. After drowning every single *Hermano de la Tierra* in the Imperial Valley.

He heard yelps as he got close to the conference room. "That's not supposed to happen!"

"You see it, I see it, it ain't CGI. Blessed Mary, Mother of God be with everyone downstream."

A quieter voice—Frio—said, "Yes. Yes. I don't know, ma'am, but if it does back up the Gila, it will flood so badly that we'll probably have cacti running for high ground. Yes, ma'am, I'd do that." Dominic found Frio in the hall on the phone. Frio covered the phone, "Governor De La Cruz," he mouthed. "Yes, exactly, ma'am. Yes. I will. Yes, ma'am."

Dominic stepped into the conference room, saw the main screen, and whistled. "That's not supposed to happen."

The eastern flank of Parker Dam seemed to be tearing out. The brown rocks on the Arizona side had disappeared under water. It overflowed the shoulder of the dam, and a chunk of stone ripped free of the hillside and crashed into the river downstream of the dam with an almighty splash. "And here I was worried about the western bank."

"What western bank?" Kira Nguyn pointed. "It seems to be coming from between the turbine house and the main dam. The army's trying to get a drone up for a look, but I don't think there's much left of Parker Dam resort." White spray and foam surged and bubbled. "It overtopped even though the gates opened."

Vengeance is mine sayeth the engineer, Dominic thought, snarling. *That's what you get for murdering my family*. "The gauges have not been reading properly for at least six months, ma'am, so I don't know what the flow is."

"It was seventy thousand c-f/s on the Gila," Frio said. "Crest is probably going to be over a hundred thousand, unless the Colorado gets there first and backs the Gila up."

Dominic tipped his head to the side and ran some numbers. "If the Imperial Diversion stays open, that will take some of the pressure off downstream, for a while, unless the river decides to take advantage of the lack of maintenance."

"Wow! I'm glad that's not Hoover," Lupe exclaimed, skidding into the room. "Is it? No, Hoover doesn't have that superstructure. Parker?"

"Parker," Nguyn confirmed. They heard a chime and saw the incoming message alert. Everyone moved and sat as the screen split and the President and Greg Lemmons, head of the Bureau of Reclamation, appeared. Dominic watched another chunk of rock tumble into the foam. If the water was traveling at twenty miles an hour, then what just passed over Parker should reach the Imperial Diversion within eight hours. Yuma, Arizona had another two hours after that, maybe.

"What's going on, Mr. Lemmons?" the President demanded.

"Ms. Nguyn?" Dominic heard the sound of a buck passing rapidly from DC to Denver and thence to Flagstaff. Judging by the expressions around the table, he wasn't the only one.

"Parker Dam on the lower Colorado River has been overtopped and it appears that the water is chewing out rock from the sides of the dam. Downstream towns on the Arizona side have already been evacuated because of the anticipated flood releases, sir, but this could destroy all the downstream water diversions and dams. Suggest planning to evacuate Yuma, Arizona if possible."

Both the President's and the Bureau Director's eyes bulged. "Yuma? How many people is that?"

"A hundred-thousand people or so, sir," Nguyn said, reading from a pad Frio held up just off camera. "The river might divert completely into California as it did in the early Twentieth Century, but more likely it will split. The Gila in Arizona is already flooding."

"I know, I just signed the disaster declarations," the President snapped. "What's worst case?"

"Worst case, sir, is Parker dam is ripped out. That would drain Lake Havasu and cut off Cali's water pipeline as well as their power from the dam. The flooding will also damage the Imperial Dam downstream and the All-American Canal, so there goes the irrigation in the Imperial Valley and more water for LA and San Diego."

"Lemmons, what's our responsibilities if that happens?"

The Director took a deep breath, blinked a few times, then exhaled with a bit of a whistle. "The Bureau is responsible for the maintenance of the dams, sir. But Cali has not allowed us to maintain them, and fired upon our technicians the last time they attempted to inspect Parker. We cannot get to Imperial or the All-American because they are inside Cali. The contracts for the dams and the Colorado River Compact as a whole is only for states within the United States, and it was not renegotiated with Cali." He paused his recitation to breathe.

"And, so what?" the President churned the air with one hand. "Cut to the chase."

"There's not a damn thing, pardon my pun, we can do until the river level drops. That will be as long as a month, depending on the weather. Then we see what Arizona needs, and if the CAP waters are still accessible."

"The CAP?"

"Central Arizona Project, sir, Arizona's canals and pipelines from the Colorado River."
The president blinked, then leaned over to the side as someone whispered and handed him a piece of paper. He read it and snorted. "As if I don't have enough trouble. It seems that President Moonbeam is accusing us of sabotaging the irrigation works in the Imperial Valley and deliberately releasing water to flood his new 'farms'." He shook his head. "The Brownshirts prison camps, I should say.

"So there's nothing we can do until the water goes down, and we had nothing to do with the water coming up?"

Bureau Director Lemmons nodded, as did Ms. Nguyn. She said, "That is correct Mr. President, Mr. Lemmons. The very high snowpack and rainfall of the past three years caused the flooding. We had to release water from upstream, and Cali did not, or was not able, to release enough water from Parker to prevent the dam from overtopping and erosion happening."

Frio's phone chirped and he got up and ducked out of the room. He came back in a few seconds, scribbled on the note pad and held it up. Nguyn read it and nodded. "Mr. President, Mr. Lemmons, Governor De La Cruz has just issued orders for the full evacuation of Yuma and other towns along the Colorado River and the lower Gila. The National Guard will be moving out to assist the local authorities."

"How long do they have?"

Dominic held up both hands, fingers spread, and mouthed "Ten."

"Ten hours is the estimate, Mr. President. We do not have good water speed data yet, sir."

The president took of his glasses and rubbed the bridge of his nose. "Of course this would happen right now." He put his glasses back on. "Thanks. Keep me advised if it gets any worse, or once you know the status of the dams."

"Will do, sir," Mr. Lemmons promised. The president's face disappeared and the Bureau Director's expanded to fill half the screen. "OK, how bad is worst-case bad?"

Ms. Nguyn read off the notepads Frio and Dominic had slid across the table to her. "We lose all controls on the Colorado downstream of Hoover Dam. Lake Havasu is gone, the Imperial Canal and water diversion for Cali are all gone. The water diversions for the Central Arizona Project are badly damaged and will need a lot of repair. A quarter of Cali's remaining electrical power is gone. The river either returns immediately to its delta in Mexico, or fills a lot of the Salton Sea and Imperial Valley before turning south again. And several hundred thousand people in Arizona and Cali drown. We don't know how many on the Mexican side might be lost, sir."

She lowered the notepads. "Apparently, per the phone calls we have gotten, the Calis are unable to close the diversions at Imperial Dam and the All-American is already over-full from the high releases. And the water tunnel that supplies LA has been damaged and flows are being interrupted."

"And they are blaming us," Lemmons stated.

"Yes, sir."

"Are all our people accounted for?"

Lupe nodded vigorously and gave the thumbs-up. "Yes, sir, they are." She glanced over at Frio and he nodded as well. "So are the CAP folks."

"Thank God for small miracles." Lemmons ran a hand over his beard. "Right. We watch, see, and get ready for complaints about the lack of fishing at Lake Havasu and the bathtub ring in the canyon."

"And the stench from the mud," Ranger Rick murmured, very quietly. Dominic's nose recoiled at the prospect. All that anaerobic activity, the sulphur alone would drive away anything with a sense of smell.

"Yes, sir," Nguyn replied. Dominic frowned. The flow at Parker seemed to be increasing, if that was possible, at least judging by the amount of spray. Part of the column-and-lintel-like superstructure tipped. Everyone sat up, eyes glued on the dam side of the screen. It tipped a little more.

"Oh shit," Dominic heard and realized that it was him.

Mr. Lemmons stared as well, shaking his head. "God save the people downstream," he whispered.

Muted "Amens" came from the observers in Flagstaff.

"I've seen enough. Keep me updated if anything changes. Lemmons out." His screen went black and the dam filled the main screen once more.

"Ten hours?" Frio asked.

Dominic nodded. "Ten. I'm assuming Imperial will slow it a little."

"Assuming. Eight hours then. 'Scuze me," Kira Nguyn waved her permission and he creaked up from his chair and left, dialing the phone as he did.

She looked at the screen again. An incoming call chirped, and Ms. Villanueva of the CWB appeared, face flushed, all but spitting fire. Before Nguyn could speak, Villanueva thundered, "What the fuck do you bastards think you are doing? Stop the upstream releases at once and open diversions! You're going to kill us!"

Nguyn muted the pick-up in the conference room. "No one say a word unless I tell you to, understood?" Everyone nodded. She unmuted. "Right now, Ms. Viallanueva, we are watching part of Parker Dam give way. One of the sides appears to be ripping out."

"That's impossible. We've maintained the dams, no thanks to you. And we need techs now at Imperial. The President has authorized a one-time entry for ten of your people to come in and get the gates closed."

She muted the send again. "Can we do that? Close the gates?"

"I don't know, ma'am, but we do not have override access or remote capabilities, or so I heard as of a few weeks ago from IT," Dominic replied.

Lupe nodded. "We do not. And we do not have any personnel we can send at this time."

"Damn it, answer me, what the fuck did you do to my dams?" Villanueva's face grew redder, and Dominic thought he could see the vein on her temple throbbing. She had rage tears in her eyes as she pounded the desk. "You're going to destroy everything *Los Hermanos de la Tierra* have struggled for, you fucking *gringos*!"

Nguyn unmuted the microphone. "We do not have the people to send to Imperial. We are not permitted to send technical staff across the border without authorization from the U.S. president. And we had nothing to do with the high flow—"

"Bullshit!" Thump. "You opened the upstream dams. You're deliberately flooding the Imperial Valley so people will starve to death. This is an act of war."

Nguyn went red, then white. "No, Ms. Villanueva. This is an act of nature, the Colorado River doing what rivers do. They flood when there is a lot of rain and snowmelt. That is what rivers do," she repeated, hands at her sides, voice calm. Dominic wondered if she were going to reach into the screen and slap Ms. Villanueva.

"Fine. What you won't give, we'll take. The Army of Cali will bring those technicians back to us. You'll see. This is a declaration of war by the United States on Cali." The image disappeared.

Silence filled the meeting room. "Can they even do that?" Lupe asked.

Ranger Pat shook his head. "Not with that river in the way."

"Still. Lupe," Nguyn said, "Warn people. I'll pass the word up-channel. The rest of you, we have things to do before the media arrive."

Groans and sighs arose, before they scattered out. Dominic went to his office, closed his door and smiled. Ten hours until the waters reached the Imperial Valley. Ten hours. "But let judgement roll down like waters," he smiled as he quoted from the King James Bible, Amos 5:24.

Chinmalis nodded once as Eloi shouted orders. "You and you, get the prisoners moving. You, chase the work-camp crews out of the barracks. Point them west."

"What about the ones in the infirmary and cells?" someone dared to ask.

"Screw them. They need to drown anyway. It is the will of *Tlalac*." He snarled, started to turn, and they heard gun-shots, screams and yells, and a chant of "USA USA!"

What? That was impossible. "Get them!" Shotguns thundered, people screamed, and she saw a flash of light on a metal something as a man brought a hoe down on one of the guards, chopping his face. "Get their guns!"

Eloi raced into the night, Chinmalis close behind. He jumped on her four-wheeler and started off. She cursed, looked around, found a three-wheeler. She climbed on and started it. It acted sluggish. The power had been off and on all day, so that explained it she thought. A figure loomed up in the headlights and she dodged, almost tipping over. She looked back and saw a skinny, pale female waving a shotgun, death in her eyes. Not bad for a *gringa*, Chinmalis allowed, then turned her attention back to the road and following the headlights ahead of her. She and Eloi had to get to the next post, to get reinforcements.

Over the rumble and hiss of the tires she heard a sound, a low burbling. She looked left and right and saw nothing but darkness and stars. The crescent moon wouldn't rise for a few more hours. A coyote, the four-footed kind, darted across the road and she slowed. Three more coyotes, some rabbits, and *paisanos*, roadrunners, darted or jumped through the light, all racing north. What was going on? The burbling and hissing from the darkness grew louder, and the lights ahead of her slowed, then stopped. She heard Eloi starting to curse, then he turned the four-wheeler around.

"Flood water, damn it. Someone must have fucked up with the canal. We'll have to go south, to the high road."

Before they could move, knee-deep water surrounded them. Chinmalis turned off the motor. She did not want to be electrocuted. They could just sit out the surge, and she lifted her feet onto the saddle. The machine shifted, the water slapped higher, and Eloi swore, then tried to drive off. The motor revved once and stopped with a loud splash.

"Help me! Bitch, help me, I can't sw—" He screamed, then gurgled. The water pushing against the three-wheeler slammed harder, cold, very cold, cold like the stars overhead. The three-wheeler shifted, shifted again. Before Chinmalis could do anything, cold black water grabbed her, sweeping her off the three-wheeler and tumbling her, filling her lungs as she tried to call for help, then smashing her down, down, into the depths of an arroyo before continuing on its way to the sea.

The next morning Andy looked at the aerial images Mr. Waters had sent him from the American's drones and satellite. He smiled. The river had erased the farms of the Imperial Obscenity and was racing through Mexico, once more in its proper path. Brown and blue covered the basin, and brown and blue stretched down, from Pilot Point toward the old delta. Andy smiled serenely.

The river had gone home.

Final Flight

Bert Opperman

He heard the *boom*. Turned on his tablet and checked the cameras. Yep, they'd gotten past the trees he'd laid across the road and had moved far enough to hit the first trip wire. The bridge timbers were still raining down as splinters across the vehicles. He'd now made the opening move. He sure hoped his son would get back soon so they could get out of here before these assholes called for help and that help arrived. He could handle these amateurs, he thought, but if professionals showed up, he was outgunned and likely out-equipped. He pulled out his cell phone and texted his son: *Hurry!*

***

"Well, shit"

The alarm was loud and piercing and it got his attention from fifty feet away. It was the computer attached to his wireless surveillance network system telling him that someone was coming up his driveway. Then his phone went off as the alarm was retransmitted via his Wi-Fi. He heard his tablet warbling in the living room as well. He cancelled the alarm and opened that window on his monitor.

He'd been sorta waiting for them to arrive for weeks now, but he'd been hoping that it would have taken a bit longer.

He lived at the end of an eighteen-mile long dead end road outside of Panamint City, a ghost town since the 1940s: a gate, and then two blind turns and a gravel two-track through the trees. It was a fairly primitive road. If you knew the road and had a decent vehicle, it would take you over an hour to get to the house. If you didn't, it could take four, if you didn't get stuck. No one not from around the area could know that there was anything at the end of the lane. He'd been careful with his light discipline after sundown and he'd kept the noise to a minimum. People local to the area knew he lived here, but he'd been trying to make 'em think he wasn't at home anymore. He'd set his telltales carefully, and his surveillance cameras had detected movement and set the alarm. He watched the convoy struggle through the deep pea gravel that made up the road as they tried to get up the hill.

The vehicles were a mismatched pair of 4wd trucks driven by amateurs and a trio of 6 x 6 trucks that had Army or National Guard markings, also driven by folks unfamiliar with the vehicles. He'd fixed up the land here in a very remote part of the mountains on purpose. He'd planned on the road being difficult for nearly anyone to traverse. In fact, he'd built the road to make entry to his home difficult. He had left signs that made it look like it was an abandoned mining claim.

If they'd only have given him another week, hell, three days, he'd have been done and gone. All his supplies would have been buried for safekeeping and later retrieval or loaded aboard the old Beaver airplane and he'd have been on his way over the border to Arizona.

His wives and kids were already at Jim's. He'd flown them out two weeks earlier, knowing that this was coming, if not as soon as it had. All he'd needed was to gather the last of his possessions and either safely hide 'em, or load 'em out on the plane. He and his oldest son Jack were planning on taking one last load and saying goodbye to the last neighbor over the hill to the east and leaving, maybe for good, but at least for a long time. Jack had a map for the neighbors, the Martin's, showing some of Daniel's survival food caches so they'd have something to eat if things turned bad…and permission to "steal" the solar setup and batteries and anything else left at the house once they were gone. But Jack wasn't back yet….

Oh, well, gotta take it as it comes.

He waited, watching as the first truck struggled up the hill, rutting the road for the next truck, and the one after that. Wrong gear, set for 4wd-low, it spun the tires and sprayed gravel back into the faces of the men waiting as it climbed. The second pickup was close enough that he could see in the monitor as gravel sprayed across its windshield and cracked it. Idiots, he thought. City folk.

Two hours, he thought to himself. I've got two hours tops, if I don't delay 'em.

He called Jack, but the cell phone reception in the mountains was spotty, and so he got no answer. He chose to write a long text message, telling him what was happening and for him to hurry for the plane. He then called his neighbors, but again, got no answer. He sent them a text, warning them as to what was coming and wishing them luck. Text messages seemed to go through even when voice calls wouldn't.

With that, he turned and began his preparations.

He had plenty of dynamite, and some of it was already placed. He just needed to arm it, and then he'd have more time yet. With a bit of creativity, he could keep this going until daylight tomorrow, if he had to.

With that, he fired up the Arctic Cat four-wheeler and moved it over to the shed. This was gonna be fun...

***

As he worked, he mused: *It had all begun, he supposed, with the "Sanctuary Cities" movement, or maybe even before that. But then the California Senate declared that anyone currently living in the State who had a California ID (and the State had weakened the ID requirements for Driver's licenses and ID's years before, so that essentially meant anyone) was now a citizen of the State of California. This entitled everyone to State Benefits: Free Health Care insurance, Welfare, Food Stamps, etc.*

The State soon had a budget problem (They had been running a deficit for YEARS, but this legislation increased that deficit to unbelievable proportions). Then they raised taxes, both corporate taxes, and individual income taxes. This led, of course, to businesses leaving, upping unemployment from already high levels to intolerable ones. Soon, they raised the State income taxes on Individuals to 40%.

Wealthy individuals left, taking more jobs and wealth with them. Then not- so wealthy individuals began leaving with their assets too... To counter this, the State enacted a 20% tax on all interstate transfers of money out of the state. Which just increased the levels of people selling assets and moving them out of state. Lots of people sold their real estate, converted that electronic money into physical dollars, and moved the resulting cash out of the state in the trunks of their cars or in suitcases.

The election of 2022 caused a great deal of uproar. All year long, there had been calls for California to secede from the Union, and the northern Californian counties wanted to secede from "California". The "State of Jefferson" was formed in that election in a ballot initiative that the State opposed, but which went on the ballot in the northern counties regardless, with nearly 100% of the citizens of the northern fifty-one counties choosing to leave the state of California in that ballot initiative. Another initiative was for California to leave the Union, which passed in the balance of the state at nearly 80%.

The lines were drawn. The Southern half of California became "Cali" and the northern half became "Jefferson"—they had subsequently applied to become part of the U.S., but had not yet been accepted. The elections were also significant in that for the first time, the legislature of the new Cali was dominated by socialists and Latinos.

In addition, since the election, there was a big push from the whole "Reconquista" movement, and it was growing in power every time he listened to the radio or looked on the internet. He expected that soon whites would be second class citizens. He didn't know what was gonna happen to the Chinese and other Asians. There was some ugly talk because whites and Asians held much of the land and businesses....

In the meantime, because almost no one had a job and incomes were low, and there was no tax money to be had, the State chose to enact, via legislature, a Basic Living Stipend.... BLS, it was called. This gave everyone a basic living income. Each and every person in the state with an income of less than $60,000 got a cash card, which could be used like a Debit Card to purchase anything they wished. It was, essentially, a free $25,000 yearly... "Fairness" was the mantra used to justify the program. "Everyone needs an income they can live off of". Of course, this electronic benefit was also taxed, creating two economies. One, above the table, where everyone paid taxes on the electronic transactions, and another, underground, cash based economy, wherein no one paid any taxes. Since a lot of people still worked, many were paid cash instead, and no one reported those transactions so they could continue to "qualify" for the BLS, and no taxes were paid on half or more of their income.

***

He'd heard via the grapevine and the Internet that the "Counselors" (thugs, really) were moving into his area, so he'd stashed his wife and kids at Jim's, and then gone back for a few more loads. He'd flown back and forth once every three days or so for the past two weeks, carrying his art, his guns, his stamp collection and his bullion and jewelry. He'd also buried about five tons of ammo and explosives, and most of his long-term food and other preps, in hastily made bunkers made of visquene and tarps buried at the top of the hill so they'd be able to drain….in the hope that he'd be able to come back for them later. They were individually packaged in sealed containers, so they would likely be okay…..as long as no one found 'em.

But today, he had some other tasks to do first. He was waiting for his son Jack to return from checking in on the neighbors over the hill. He was supposed to be back before dark.

He prepped the plane. Gas, oil, drained the water, and checked the tire pressures. Made sure everything was lashed down. Threw in a few more items until he was just above gross takeoff weight. It was gonna be a cool couple of days, so he'd be okay, even at this altitude. But what he didn't take today he wasn't ever likely to come back for….

Turning on his tablet, he watched, via his surveillance systems, the progress of the vehicles. They had both pickups and one of the big trucks up the hill, and had deployed a couple of chains so the first big truck could pull the other 6x6's up. He figured another two hours if he didn't slow 'em down.

***

The State's deficits increased yearly, to the point where the Federal government began trying to do something about it, as Cali's deficits were beginning to severely affect the buying power of the dollar, already weakened by years of Federal "Quantitative Easing". No other country wanted to buy the dollar, and many international transactions that had once been done in dollars were now starting to be transacted in Euros, Chinese Yuan, and Rupees. Cali (California) was bringing the rest of the country down with it, using the Dollar to drag the other forty-nine states into poverty. The U.S. threatened to change their paper money, and to restrict the State and their banks from using the dollar if they didn't stop the deficits.

Soon, the economy crashed. There <u>was</u> no Cali economy. The state couldn't pay its bills, the Federal Government restricted the transfer of dollars to and from Cali banks, and then changed the face of the bills issued by the Bureau of Engraving and Printing in all other states to try and stop the increasing devaluation of the dollar by the State of Cali. All "old" bills were given an amnesty for conversion to "new" style bills in the other 49 states and soon the "old" bills not exchanged at banks were effectively worthless except to collectors. Fairly quickly, the only "old" bills in use were used in Cali, and the other 49 states no longer honored the old bills as currency. Cali, of course, continued to use the "old" bills as there was no Bureau in the state. They stamped "Cali" over the face of the bills as a temporary expedient, but there were still old style US dollars in circulation for a while. "Old" dollars began to be supplanted by "Callors" which were, theoretically, worth a "dollar" once the State found a way to set up a Bureau of Engraving and Printing to produce them... In reality, they were exchanged for less, generally about $0.75. For a while, both bills circulated, but the banks were only giving out "Callors", and when they received a *dollar, they kept it. It was expected that soon, the dollar would not exist in circulation in the State of Cali.*

Meanwhile, the State was hemorrhaging people and wealth. It was estimated that over thirty billion dollars left the state going east and north in ninety days. People were taking "old" dollars (and, when they had to, Callors), and were buying gold, silver, other precious metals, jewelry, and other items of value and transporting them out of the state, just to get their wealth to where it could be safe. People sold homes and property for less than half the price it had been worth just six months before. Industry (what was left of it) in the state had had enough as well. Production facilities just packed up and left when possible, or closed the doors and left their facilities sitting when it wasn't practical to move. This increased the unemployment levels and decreased the tax revenues. Soon "official" unemployment was at 70%.

Then the farmers were both taxed and forced to raise their wages. At first it had been $15/hour, but the United Farm Workers demanded and got that amount raised to $30/hour, then to $42/hour. In addition, the courts removed any protections to the historical water rights of the farmlands, and instead demanded that the farms pay the State for the right to use river and groundwater for irrigation. The following year, they raised the price of the water cost to double what it had been before. Many farms simply ceased operation. Further, the State set pricing for produce, beef and pork. Often this price was below the cost to produce it, *much less transport it. Lots of farmers went broke trying to feed people.*

The Cali Government soon acted to "fix" things. They declared all abandoned and "unproductive" facilities, manufacturing plants, and farms to be the property of the State and appointed managers to make them productive and employ people. Sadly, no one who knew how to operate those plants was left. Nor were any Farm managers. Appointees tried, but since they were mostly political appointees who knew little about the farms (and city folk as well) , they failed. No one wanted to buy anything the plants had made, and no one outside of the state (and few inside the state either) was willing to sell the State any materials with which to make any products. Further, the "Callor" had no value to anyone outside of the State, so the State couldn't buy anything anyway.

*In addition, there was rationing of gasoline and diesel. There was some oil production near Hollywood and LA and to the east, but not enough to feed the voracious Cali appetite for travel in the state. In addition, there wasn't much refining capacity… those **terribly polluting** refineries had been chased out, for the most part, years ago. And no one was willing to sell any oil or refined petroleum to the State 'cause their money was essentially worthless outside of the state borders. Gasoline, diesel and other petroleum products went for incredible prices. People began smuggling propane and gasoline and diesel over the border when they could.*

Of course, since 2025, he'd begun moving his family and their items of wealth to Arizona. He'd had a lot of stuff. Tons of things that he'd have to now abandon. At first he'd used a pickup and a trailer, but the "customs" folks on the Cali side of the border had begun confiscating a lot of things, so he'd been making trips in his plane to stash smaller items and things that didn't weigh too much at his friend Jim's farm in Arizona. The bigger items, or the heavier ones, he would simply have to hide and write off.....Maybe he could come back later to get 'em, but for now, they were a write off.

But he'd run out of time.

***

Just then, his phone rang. It was Jack whispering. "Dad, listen up! There are folks at the Martin's right now taking whatever they want, Mr. Martin has been arrested, and I just barely got out. I'm in a tree right now to get some bars on my phone, and they are looking for me. I got your text just a few minutes ago. I think they are coming for our place too, so get ready. As soon as I can I'll be on the trail and back at the house. Figure three hours. I'm out. Love you dad. I'm turning off the phone now for quiet."

And the phone went "click" and the call was terminated.

Proud of his son for not wasting time, and yet worried about him, he smiled and got to work.

He took a chainsaw and put it in the Arctic Cat 4 x4. Adding some wire and case of dynamite and some other supplies, he set out for the bridge.

***

The only bright spots in the economy were the seaports and the military bases. These were booming economies, but everything else was failing. Wages were too high, productivity was low, no one wanted (or needed) to work. The BLS had destroyed the incentive to work, and even if an individual chose to work, the State took over half of his earnings. Crime rose, inflation climbed higher and higher.

The seaports were losing traffic as the business moved to Washington and Oregon. There were other ports on the Pacific Coast, and those gave less hassle to the shippers and lower taxes. Cali enacted a tariff for every container that was offloaded at their ports and then raised it (and again, and yet again) in order to raise income which just led to another decrease in traffic each time as shippers moved to other, less expensive ports. Soon the shipyards were idle, and the formerly booming ports were at a standstill. Rail yards and railroads shut down as their traffic became lower and lower Railroads moved their rolling stock across the border for "maintenance" to get it out of the state. Truckers and trucking firms simply drove off with one last container and never returned.

With no way to pay for food, and no way to pay for energy (the environmentalists had driven nearly all the electrical generating plants out of the state years ago) and with little food being produced in the state, and no way to move it, the situation became dire. Blackouts were commonplace, (daily blackouts and power rationing became the norm) and with little food, stores were empty, local produce sellers had to have armed security. People began growing gardens for produce in their backyards, and many planted fruit trees for the same reason...if they had a backyard. Chicken coops in their garages or in the backyard all hidden behind high fences. Soon, people became hungry and restless. Since there was no way to pay enough for police and fire protection, cities became terrible places. People starving and rationing....and riots were often unanswered by police, as there were few police left, most having found other professions that paid more (like private security) that could enable a man or woman to support a family. The same thing happened to other public services like natural gas, electric, water and trash collection. They needed armed security to even do their basic functions. The only place to live well was in the country, in the mountains.

The (special) elections of 2025 elected still more socialists, with their promises to "fix" things. They'd taken the time immediately after the 2022 elections to legislate the ban of all firearms that were capable of holding more than one round, except for special permits for ranchers and such. Even then, they'd limited the calibers to less than .30, and there were no firearms that were legal for ANYONE that held more than three rounds. Pistols were verboten, except for Agents of the State. No semi-automatic rifles. All were purchased by the State at a price determined by the legislators (not the owners) and melted down. If a person chose not to voluntarily turn in a firearm or firearms, then they were tracked by the registration papers and arrested by the State and jailed for one year per gun. There had been two amnesties, then the State got serious. As of July 4 2025, there were essentially no guns in the hands of the people. They *were at the mercy of (and, of course, under the "protection" of) the State of California.*

He'd heard that they had begun sending teams out under the guidance of State employed "Counselors" to confiscate food and other "surplus" items from wealthy estates and rural farms and retreats; pretty much anyone who appeared to be well-to-do and/or not starving. This included cars and valuables (and whatever else the "Counselors" thought they needed to take). From the rumors, these were just thugs with a State issued ID badge and an armed crew who simply took whatever they could, and resistance usually didn't end well. He'd also heard that the State had chosen to confiscate the federal military installations, especially the ports in LA and San Diego. He wondered how that was gonna work. What about all the Marines and Sailors and their dependents and all that equipment? He doubted that the U.S. military was gonna just stand there and let their families be arrested and their possessions be taken.

***

Shaking himself out of his reverie, he crossed the bridge and found the trees he had in mind. Firing the saw, he cut first one, then another, then another to make a barricade that none of the trucks could cross. Then he cut several others to fall across the first trees, making sure their branches tangled. It would take time to bypass, and there wasn't an easy way around, although it was possible.

He then went to the bridge. With a heavy heart, he wired three sets of two sticks each, ensuring that when he was ready he could drop that bridge. He'd built it himself, and he hated the idea of destroying it. But needs must. Dropping the bridge would slow 'em down. The only ford was about a mile or so upstream, and it would take some scouting to find it. The river wasn't too wide, but the soft bottom wouldn't make crossing on either side of the bridge easy, if it was even possible. There were rocks under the mud, but again, it'd slow 'em down. If this had been a rainier year, it would have made a formidable barrier….as it was, it was just a muddy stream, but it would slow the trucks down. .

Looking at his tablet, he saw that they had all three big trucks up the hill, and were apparently taking a break before moving farther. Looked to be about forty-five minutes until they got to the trees. He set a trip wire about a hundred feet past the trees, just enough that the vehicles would be safe when the bridge blew. He connected his wires from the bridge charges to a detonator attached to the trip wires. Then set another trip wire fifty feet from the first just to be sure. He also ran a set to the tree-line, so he could manually set it off if he had to.

***

He was finishing his wiring of the dynamite to the second trip wire when his phone rang.

"Hello?"

"Mr. Daniels?"

"Yes."

"My name is Diego Riviera. I am a Counselor for the State of Cali. Are you at home right now?"

"Yes. Why?"

"My team is here, ready to inspect your property for surplus items that can be used by the State." "We should be there within an hour."

Now isn't a good time for me…can you come tomorrow?

"No, Mr. Daniels, today is the day we have scheduled for you."

"Really, today isn't good. Tomorrow would be better."

"I really must insist, Mr. Daniels. I have the authority to come whenever I wish, and today is your scheduled day. Please, meet us at your gate. Again, we should be there in an hour or so."

"Uh, okay."

"See you then, Mr. Daniels. Goodbye."

He remotely set his gate to locked, and made sure via his tablet and the camera that it was down.

***

He'd put the solar powered cameras in place several years ago, mostly to watch for folks entering his property to steal things. They were wireless, reporting to an antenna at the peak of the roof of his house. Each one had motion sensors in place to turn them on and set an alarm at the house. Now he was glad that he had, as they gave him a great advantage over the Counselor and his team. He could watch them in real-time as they made their way along the road. And the road was, really, the only way in to or out of his property. It had been expensive, but he'd done the work himself and the silver from a fairly rich vein had paid for it, along with a pocket of gold he'd found. He'd also set them to be WiFi repeaters, so he had

WiFi nearly anywhere within 500 meters along the road. Made it easy to keep in touch with his family and to surveil the cameras with a tablet, or even his phone when he wanted to.

***

He finished with his wiring, strung a thousand feet or so out more or less parallel with the road… then he moved up the road about a thousand feet and looked into the culvert there. More dynamite and some gasoline just for show into the twenty-four-inch culvert, just about in the center. The culvert spanned a ditch that was about two feet wide and about three feet deep. It wouldn't stop a decent driver with a 4WD vehicle, but he suspected that these folks weren't decent drivers. Besides, the gasoline would make for an impressive fireball, and he hoped it would make the men in the trucks cautious about proceeding. He set up another trip wire and moved on.

Then to another culvert about two thousand feet past the first one, this one a pair of sixteen-inch tubes, with two sticks each and some gasoline and a propane tank to make things interesting. Then he strung another thousand feet of wire, this time into the brush and up to a path that was passable by the Arctic Cat but not by the trucks. The stream wasn't much here, but it spread out and made the ground soft. A good driver could get past on either side, but he figured these folks might get stuck. The road wouldn't be damaged badly by the charge, but he figured they'd go wide of the road, and he hoped they'd get mired.

He needed to buy time and to slow 'em down. He figured he could do that without killing anyone. But he'd deal with that if he had to. If they got to the house and the runway, they might arrest him. They might confiscate his plane. He was willing lose everything else, but his freedom, his son's safety, and their means of escape….no. He had to buy time until his son returned and they could fly. He wanted to text again, but Jack had said that he was turning the phone off, and he'd already sent the info he had and he'd be here when he got here.

His tablet showed him via the surveillance video that the "Counselor" and his team were starting up the trail again. Best to finish and get ready.

At the bend, he already had holes in the cliff face, easy to push a stick in and the wires were already there too. He'd spent enough time planning for such a scenario, and now he was glad he had. No need for flammables here, the boom oughta get their attention and they'd either have to detour about three miles or climb over the rubble. He set this set of charges with a radio detonator. He only had four, but figured this was a good place to use one. He could bring the face down in front of them or on them, whichever he chose. He made sure via his tablet the camera here was working so he'd have a view of them when they got to the bend at the cliff.

He connected up and moved on.

How far am I gonna take this? He wondered? Will I kill if I have to, to get away?

Yes, he decided. My freedom, and my son's, are worth it. These thugs may get my stuff but I am flying out of here tonight, one way or another.

Three hours. Maybe four. Figure five to be safe. They'd be flying out of here in a few hours if all went well. If he could keep the "Counselor's" team away for that amount of time. His son's report on Don Martin's arrest made it plain that they weren't gonna play nice.

And if the "Counselor" and his team didn't get the message by the time they got to the first culvert… Well, he had lots of dynamite and terrain to play for time. Lots of ammo too, if it came to that.

He pulled out his cell phone and called Diego Riviera back.

"Yes?"

"Mr. Riviera?"

"Yes? Is this Mr. Daniels?"

"Yes. Listen. I can't meet with you today. It would be better for all of us if you just turned around and came back tomorrow. Please."

"No sir, today is your scheduled day. I really must insist. My men and I should be there in about an hour. Does your driveway get any better?"

"No, sorry, Mr. Riviera, it doesn't. It's actually the State road, if you aren't to the gate yet, and they don't keep it up anymore. I don't use it much. I don't leave my land often. And when I do, I have a jeep that can travel on it. I am sorry. Please, can we reschedule?"

"No."

"As you wish then. So be it."

Shit.

***

The land had been his father's and his grandfather's before that. His granddad had bought it cheap in the early 70's when the nearest town (Panamint City) had been nearly a ghost town, the town having died when the silver had played out and the mines closed. He'd made it a farm, and had rebuilt the house to modern standards. It had been something special, both to his father, and now to him. He'd made it very comfortable, with a significant solar power and battery setup for amenities like a small AC unit that dehumidified the air (he hated refrigerated air, but the drier air in the summer was nice) and an electrically powered well, plus lights and satellite internet. There had been the possibility of having rural electric installed, but by the time it became available, he really didn't need it. He had two small streams he'd dammed up for (mostly) year-round irrigation, and micro-hydro power off the dams, and enough of everything else that he was more or less self-sufficient. Neither he nor most of his neighbors had been affected by the events that the Cali Government had allowed to happen in the largest towns and cities. He'd had enough food and energy to not really notice the turmoil going 'round the rest of the state. Far enough away that no one came around to steal, he'd had no issues.

***

All righty then, back to the plane:

It was an old DeHaviland Beaver DHC-2, modified by AirTech in Canada with the more powerful 600 HP engine and an in-cabin fuel tank for extra range. It could, if he could stay awake, take him all the way to Jim's farm in one pass. All he had to do was get his son and get airborne.

He'd taken the precaution of painting the tops of the wings and the top and sides of the fuselage in mottled brown colors, as he was hoping not to be spotted from the air in his trips. He fully expected to have to hide this time, as he doubted Diego Riviera was going to be happy with him. Modern forward-looking infrared could see him at night, but he was surprisingly hard to spot on a hot summer day even with FLIR unless one knew exactly where to look. He had all the tanks full so he should have about 740 miles of flying, maybe a bit less if he had to stay low to avoid detection in the mountains.

Time to prepare the plane for a rapid departure:

He pushed the old Beaver out of the hangar, carefully positioning it in front. He chocked the wheels and checked the oil. Even though he'd checked the avgas earlier, he checked the tanks and then opened the sumps to check for water.

Running the checklist from memory: He set the magnetos for 'OFF' and went to the front of the plane. Pulled the prop through five complete revolutions (10 blades) by hand to make sure there was no oil in the lower cylinders. Setting the parking brake, he set the throttle for 'IDLE' set the prop RPM to 'HIGH', set the mixture for 'CUTOFF' set the fuel pump to 'OFF', the carburetor heat to 'OFF', the flaps for 'UP' and the elevator trim to 'TAKEOFF', set the fuel tank selector to the middle tank. He reached down and worked the wobble pump until he had 5 psi showing on the gauge, then turned on the battery switch.

He opened the throttle about 3/8 of an inch, checked the propeller speed lever again, set the mixture for 'RICH', checked the carb heat was set to 'ON' turned on the fuel boost pump, and confirmed the magneto switch was set to 'OFF'. He pumped the prime lever five times.

Pressed the starter. The prop turned over eight blades, and he turned the mageneto switch to 'BOTH', the engine fired twice and died again. Pressing the starter again, the prop turned over four more times, and then the engine caught and ran with a plume of smoke from the exhaust.

He pulled the mixture closed just a bit, and the engine smoothed out and the cloud of smoke decreased. He pulled the throttle closed just a little and set the alternator switch to 'ON'. Turned off the boost pump. Checked the magnetos.

He had good oil pressure, the alternator gauge showed a charge, and all his instruments showed that they were working. His radios lit up and he set the radio for Guard frequency. He made SURE that the strobes were off and his transponder was disabled by pulling those breakers.

He 'stirred the pot' to make sure his flight surfaces were free and unrestricted and waited for the engine to warm up.

As the engine warmed and the oil temp gauge began to move off the peg, he made sure that the cargo was tied down and his auxiliary fuel tank was still full.

Fifteen minutes later, the oil temp was in the green, and he shut the plane down.

He waited for his son. And checked his tablet for the progress of Diego Riviera and his men. They were nearly to the bridge.

He waited.

***

When the bridge blew, he heard it, even from three miles away. They were making good time (or had been, anyway). He'd just been setting his tablet to let him look at the camera that showed the bridge, and now he opened the window on the tablet and watched the pieces of wood and bridge timbers and decking rain down on the trucks. He was glad he'd set the second trip wire, as they were stopped now, at a point well past the first wire. The first must have failed.

He'd just committed himself. No turning back now. Of course, he had been committed, really, once he'd set his first stick and wired it. But now, it was real.

His phone rang. He looked at the number. Diego Riviera.

He debated for a second pushing it off to voice mail, but decided to answer it instead.

"Hello?"

"Mr. Daniels?"

"Yes."

"What the fuck was that? The bridge exploded! You could have killed me and my men!"

"Sorry, Mr. Riviera, I did ask you to wait until tomorrow. You refused. Please, no one is hurt yet, turn around and come back later."

"You asshole, you could have killed us! What the fuck are you doing?! You've crossed a line you can't back away from now. When I get there, you are gonna be under arrest."

"Please, Mr. Riviera, I set that off well away from your trucks so that no one would be hurt. You really should turn around. Tomorrow will be a better day for all of us."

The phone made a noise and he couldn't hear anything. He looked at his phone and realized that Diego had hung up on him.

He smiled.

***

He'd been mining the more or less played out mine for the past fifteen years, just enough that he'd been able to make a few dollars selling his silver to a company once or twice a year to pay his expenses. More importantly, that had allowed him to buy and possess explosives. He'd had to be certified and to get all of his licenses…But he had 'em, and he had his dynamite. No one knew exactly, however, how much he'd used and how much he'd stored. His paperwork always accounted for his "use" and he'd never stored his excess dynamite where it could be found in an inspection. It sure was handy having that now.

***

He turned to his tablet to see what was happening. Sure enough, Diego had his men out walking across the streambed, looking for more explosives. Watching them, he again thought that they were city folks, as their actions showed that they didn't know what they were doing. Diego was talking on the phone, animatedly waving his arm and apparently shouting at someone on the other end.

As he watched, one of the smaller pickups began moving across the creek to the left of the ruined bridge. It made it all the way across. The stream was muddy, but with rocks underneath it was slippery, but not impassable. Then one of the big trucks did the same, taking a slightly different path. Slowly, each vehicle moved across the creek. Forty minutes later, they were all across.

He could only watch as they formed up and began to move forward again. But this time, they had a man walking in front of the trucks, looking down at the ground, looking for triggers. Again, though, their inexperience showed. If he'd set mines, or pressure triggers, they'd likely have missed them. Lucky for them, he hadn't.

So far, they'd been delayed about forty-five minutes. Time to move.

Daniels fired up the 'Cat and moved out. He wanted to get to the wires he'd left for the next culvert, but he had a stop to make first.

He drove quickly to the pond, and stopped at the spillway and pulled out ALL of the level boards. He'd never done that. He'd never had all of the boards out since he had built the pond nine years ago. They dammed up the stream enough to give him a decent ½ acre pond that stored up enough water to keep his fruit trees alive even during the dry summer months and gave him some of his off-grid electric through the micro-hydro generator. Now he was dumping all the water out to run downstream. He wasn't ever gonna get to harvest the fruit anyway, and tomorrow he'd be either gone or arrested, so no need for power from the micro-hydro generator either….

***

He went down the path, still watching them in the tablet as they proceeded slowly down the road at the pace of the man looking for booby-traps. About twenty minutes later, that individual found the one at the two-foot culvert. They all stopped and looked, and talked. Waved their arms. Then, showing that Diego Riviera wasn't stupid, they turned the vehicles and went right this time. Looking at the ground, they moved to the edge of the stream and tried to find a way across. The man driving the truck that Riviera was riding in pulled it to the edge of the stream and slowly drove down into the water and then, gunning it, up the other side. He almost got stuck, but climbed the edge and, leaving huge ruts, got back onto firm ground. He waved and gestured, and one of the 6 x 6 trucks tried. That vehicle was more capable, and he made it across, tearing more dirt and mud from the edge of the stream bank. One by one, the others started across.

***

While they were crossing, he parked the 'Cat about a thousand yards from where he'd left his wires and sprinted over to find the ends of the wires.

Attaching the firing device, he moved to good cover and waited.

And waited. And waited some more....Watching on the tablet, he saw that the last of the three 6 x 6's was having a hard time. The other vehicles had torn up the edge and it was fairly slippery with mud and the truck just couldn't climb the edge. As he watched, the others got a chain and hooked one of the trucks already past the streambank to the bumper of the stuck one.

Good, more delays.

He texted his son again. ETA?

The answer came back before the truck was on solid ground. "Hour, maybe more."

Shit.

The truck on firm ground pulled the last one up the bank.

The trucks reassembled on the road and began moving once again.

He dialed.

"Yes, what do you want?"

"Mr. Riviera. By now you know I am serious. And capable. Stop where you are. Just stop. Wait until tomorrow. Tomorrow, you can have free rein, tomorrow you can enter freely and take what you want. But not today. Just stop. No one needs to get hurt. Just stop. Turn around and wait for tomorrow."

"Fuck you. I got lots more men coming. You are under arrest and will be tried for interfering with a Counselor. Lots more when I can think of charges. Give up NOW, sir."

"I can't and won't. You are on my ground, on my land, and I don't want to hurt anyone. Just stop."

The phone again went dead.

He looked at it for a moment. Then sighed. So be it.

***

He watched as they approached. Once again, a man out front. Looking down. Looking for tripwires and whatever else might be out of the ordinary. Only this time, there wasn't a tripwire for him to find. The trucks were bunched up, one of the 6 x 6's in front and the rest close on its bumper. Clearly, the Counselor was letting someone else take the risk. Interesting.

He watched them approach the culvert, clearly expecting another ambush as they got closer to the stream. Let 'em. There were no tripwires to find, this time. The water from the pond had done its work, making sure that the flats on either side of the stream, normally at this time of the year only 6 inches across and about that deep, were soaked and muddy and impassable on both sides of the culvert. He just hoped the flood hadn't affected his charges or washed away the wires as it rushed through the culverts.

He debated when. First truck? Last truck? Middle truck? Yep, the middle. He didn't want to kill anyone, but he *had* to stop them. Did he really want to blow up a truck full of men? Men who were likely only following Diego Riviera so they could give their wives and children a decent life in the economy that Cali had become. Where no one had enough to eat, or enough electricity or enough water anymore   Did he really want to cross a line and kill these men? So far, he hadn't and if he could not get out of the state today it might save him. If he killed these men, he would surely be incarcerated….if they caught him. But dammit, he needed his freedom. His son needed his freedom too.

He waited, watching carefully through the monocular, the firing device in his left hand, his right braced on a tree trunk as they approached the culvert. They were spaced a bit farther apart as they came, about 2 lengths between each vehicle. In the lead was a pickup, then the 3 6 x 6's, then the truck that had carried Diego Riviera last time he'd seen him, all led by the poor point man walking quickly, but looking for wires or other triggers.

He waited as the convoy approached the culvert. Waited, thinking furiously. Did he want to do this? Did he want to cross another line? Was he gonna kill these men? Or should he wait for Diego's vehicle. How would they react if their leader was dead? Was Diego even in the last pickup? Or had he moved to a different vehicle?

He made his choice.

***

As the vehicles came to the culvert, he squeezed the safety in his fist and his index finger pulled the trigger hard three times. The charge blew, and destroyed the culverts just before the trucks got there, leaving a five-foot wide trench in the road that was deep enough that even the 6 x 6 wouldn't be able to traverse it. The pickup in the lead stopped, hard, almost standing on its front tires: two men in the bed hit the back of the cab, hard, one flipping over to slide down the windshield and onto the hood, but the 6 x 6 behind it didn't stop in time, and the larger truck rammed the smaller one, pushing it forward and into the hole in the road., where it fell, mostly sideways to the road, into the trench and on its side. The following two 6 x 6's hit the first one from behind and then Riviera's truck nearly hit them. Everything came to halt and the men in the trucks unassed them and spread out, well back from the vehicles.

He picked up the phone. Dialed.

"Diego?" He said, when Riviera answered.

"Yes, what now?"

"I could just as easily have killed a truck or two and the men inside. I didn't. Stop here, while you can. Come back tomorrow, you can take whatever you want then."

"Fuck you, Daniels."

"Okay, Diego: Watch the second truck."

"What?"

"Just watch."

With that, he put the phone down, watched the wind for a moment, picked up his rifle. Four-hundred twenty yards, more or less. Wind slightly from the left.

He worked the bolt and chambered a round. Used his hat as a rest. It wasn't perfect, but he was improvising here. He looked carefully through the scope, making sure the cab was empty. No time for a mistake…not right now. He aimed for the center of the side window. No time for scope adjustments, either. Have to do it "Kentucky". His rifle wasn't on the "approved" list. Nor was it known to the State….until now, that is.

Daniels aimed three feet high and four inches to the right. Gently cradled the trigger with the pad of his index finger. Applied 2. 4 pounds of pressure slowly. The rifle bucked against his shoulder as the sear broke and the firing pin fell on the primer, sending the 168-grain boat-tailed jacketed bullet on its way at 2695 feet-per-second.

About a third of a second later, he saw the driver's side window of the first 6 x 6 explode into shards and fall into the driver's seat. He was lucky, and the bullet passed clean though the cab and broke the passenger's side as well.

It really wasn't that hard, 400 plus yards, he mused to himself. The window was about 16 x 22 inches, and all he had to do was hit it to break the glass, but it oughta get their attention.

He picked up the phone:

"Diego? Mr. Riviera?"

"Yes, asshole, what do you want?"

"You saw the window? Both of them? That could have been any of your men as well. Five-hundred yards away, my friend. I could have used that shot to kill any one of your men. Or even you. I didn't. I picked a truck without anyone in it. I *chose* not to kill anyone. *Yet*….

I'm serious, Diego. Be smart …Stop for today. I don't want to hurt you or your men. But I am serious. Just stop. Go away. Next time I won't be so nice. There are other explosives here, and I know this country like my tongue knows my teeth. I can kill you from up close, or farther away. I can blow you up or shoot you dead: either way, you'll never see me.

Listen. To. Me: Just stop today."

With that, he disconnected the call and ran back to the Arctic Cat and drove back to the house.

***

When he got back to the house, he checked his tablet again. They had tried to pull the pickup from the ditch where it had fallen with a 6x6, but had given up as the pulling had damaged the truck and torn off a wheel. They had also tried to drive the other pickup across the now soaked and muddy flat on the downstream side of where the culvert had been, but had only mired the truck deeply.

He'd created the hour he needed. Probably more. Likely a day's worth or more until the mud in the streambed dried. Maybe longer. They could hike to the house, but he didn't think they would. Not since he'd showed 'em he could shoot and that he had a rifle to respect.

He called his son, but no answer. So he texted him: "Go directly to the plane. Acknowledge". Then he fired up the plane and warmed it again for ten minutes, making sure it would be ready when he needed it, then shut it down again. It had been less than ninety minutes from the time he warmed it up to now.

He heard the helicopter before he saw it. It gave him enough time to push the Beaver back into the hanger and cover the nose with a tarp though. Man, he was getting out of shape. That plane was hard to move, even with the tow-bar hooked to the four-wheeler. Rushing to drape a tarp over the nose had him out of breath.

The helicopter came over the trees, low and fast. He hid under the fuselage, holding still. Seeing one man not moving was hard from the air. Especially when the aircraft was moving fast. It made a high-speed pass over the house and barn, then banked and made another going back the way it had come. Then it turned and went towards Riviera and his men.

Shit. He hadn't expected that.

Just then, his son burst through the trees, running for the hangar. Daniels whipped the tarp off of the nose and opened the door and climbed into the cockpit. No time for safety now, he turned on the battery, hit the primer lever once, and pushed the starter. The engine whined, turned over six blades, he turned the mags on, the engine coughed twice, and started for a few seconds, then died.

"No, you bitch, not now sweetie." he said to the Beaver as he went through the start sequence again.

The engine coughed, spit white smoke, and then fired, running rough until he tweaked the mixture. He advanced the throttle, and released the parking brake. His son ran to the door and opened it and climbed in.

"Dad! I…"

"No time! Belt in." Daniels said, as he advanced the throttle and taxied way too fast to the end of his dirt strip. "Wait 'til we're in the air"

He lined up, set the flaps to "takeoff" verified the rudder and elevator trim, and turned on the booster pump. Setting the prop to HIGH RPM, and not waiting, he advanced the throttle to ¾. As he accelerated he turned on the pitot heat and the carb heat, and watched his manifold pressure go to thirty-six inches. The airplane ran down the bumpy airstrip. He looked to see the flag so he knew his wind, and, as the speed passed forty knots, he lifted the tail off the ground with a little forward yoke. He felt the controls come alive and, watching his airspeed, held the plane on the runway to well past sixty-five mph, normal takeoff speed. At seventy-five, he released the yoke and the plane flew. He stayed in ground effect for a few seconds longer, gaining speed, until he had no choice and then climbed over the trees that were coming up fast at the end of his rough airstrip. For a moment, he let the feeling of exhilaration sweep over him, as it did on every takeoff. He was flying. Every takeoff was like the first time.

Staying low, he flew more or less west, downhill, and trimmed the plane and did his checks. His center of gravity was okay, if not good, and his engine gauges were all where he expected them to be. As he broke five-hundred feet, he set the flaps for 'CLIMB', turned off the booster, and set the prop for 2000. He pulled back the throttle to twenty-eight inches of manifold pressure and trimmed for an airspeed of eighty knots. Set the rear tank to burn off first so he'd have a better CG later.

***

He itched to turn the plane and look at what was happening with Riviera, but wanted to get as far away as fast as possible. So he flew, straight and level, downhill to stay as low as possible to hide in the terrain instead.

Soon enough, his radio came to life.

"Daniels! Was that you in that plane?"

He didn't answer.

"Got a helicopter now, we're gonna get you, asshole."

He chose not to respond. Let Diego stew.

***

Then his phone rang. Since he had the Beaver trimmed out and it was, essentially, flying itself right now, he looked. Sure enough, Riviera.

"Yes?" He answered.

"Ah, I hear that it was you in the plane. Land immediately." He could hear some chatter in Spanish in the background, but couldn't make it out

"No. You can take whatever you want, Riviera, I'm leaving. For good."

"I'll have the chopper force you down."

"If he can find me."

With that, he terminated the call.

"Look for the chopper, Jack. Tell me when you see it, and where."

With that, he turned to his flying. Low and as fast as the old Beaver would go, he continued more or less west at 1500 feet AGL. He normally cruised at between 110 and 125 knots for fuel consumption, but today he was at 155 and wishing he had more. He was dangerously close to max speed, and the air was turbulent, making the ride rough and everything shake.

"I see him! Low, almost behind us, climbing to the north." his son said.

He looked down and back, picking out the Bell Jet Ranger and chuckled, "Him, we can outrun…Relax a bit, but keep looking"

With that, he slid the Beaver behind a ridge, and went down to 500 feet above the ground.

He slid down the mountain, hiding in ridges whenever he could. Soon though, he saw another plane, obviously looking.

Shit, shit, shit.

He kept to the draws and as low behind ridges as he could, warping a path east and south as terrain forced him to. He had to get past the "old" state line (now a national border) to be safe, and when he got close, he had to make sure that the U.S. Border Patrol knew he was coming. The other trips he had made he'd gone over low and slow and (generally) at dusk, and simply hadn't bothered. But this time, with pursuit, he intended to make sure they knew he was coming.

If he made it.

He just kept flying.

***

While they flew, his son gave him the story, all in a rush:

"I went over to the Martins, like we talked about. Wanted to see 'em one more time, and to say goodbye to Ms. Martin and Joe. It's only four miles by the high path, and I can do that easy. Just after I got there, was having a drink of water with Mr. Martin and Joe in the barn, when three big trucks busted down his gate and pulled up to a stop. Mr. Martin pushed us into the barn and told us to go out the back, so we started to. But then the men knocked him down with their rifle butts and kicked him and Joe ran to help his Dad and they knocked him down too. I hid and watched and they handcuffed 'em both and slapped 'em around. Then they went into the house and pulled Ms. Martin and Dawn out and pushed them to the ground too, even though they were women. They weren't very nice. I wanted to do something, but I figured if I even tried they'd handcuff me and beat me up too. So I stayed hidden. I remember what you told me about going off half-cocked, so I didn't. I mean, there wasn't anything I could DO!

They went into the house and started pulling all sorts of stuff out and putting it in the trucks. Stuff like their good Grandfather clock and a bunch of their silver and Ms. Martin's jewelry and such. I thought they were only supposed to take food!

Then they started taking all of their food from their pantry closet and they even made Mr. Martin and Joe help. Mr. Martin didn't want to, but they smacked him around until he did. They filled up one truck and part of another. They didn't leave hardly anything! Then they talked and let Mr. Martin and Mrs. Martin and Joe and Dawn get a drink from the outside faucet. *They* drank Cokes from the fridge in the house. They were coming for the barn and I hightailed it out the back but one of 'em saw me and they all took off after me. I ran as fast as I could and got onto the trail from their house to ours. I hid in the brush and they went past me. That is when I turned on the phone to call you and warn you but I had no bars and couldn't. So I remembered what you taught me and climbed a tree, you know the big pine by the bend near the stream? The really tall one? Yeah, I was up high in that and hidden and had a signal and was gonna call you and then your text came through and I called you and you answered and I told you what happened and then they were coming back so I shut off the phone and waited until they went past and then climbed down and hightailed it towards home. I had to hide twice more, they had a guy who was pretty good tracker so I had to leave a false trail and even took off my boots to leave less prints. That broke the trail for him, so I moved as fast as I could and then I got your text to go to the plane but I was moving so fast I couldn't answer you. Then I heard the plane so I put my boots back on and ran as fast as I could and you know the rest."

He paused to take a breath and Daniels said gently. "Good thinking, son. You did exactly right. There wasn't anything you could do for the Martins, and you came home when you could. Maybe we can help the Martins later, after we get on the ground."

***

Daniels turned his attention back to flying. While he flew, he told Jack the story from the minute the alarm went off. Until Jack, relaxing and winding down from his stress, fell asleep

His other trips, he'd gone south, then east, passing north of Kingman to get to Jim's ranch. The border patrol hadn't been spending too much time looking for, or doing anything about private airplanes until a week or so ago.

He was planning on going to Sun Valley airport in Fort Mohave, if he could. He knew people there, and if the Border Patrol would let him, he could spend the night and refuel. But he had to get there first.

He had one hundred twenty miles or so to the new border, then another thirty or so to the airport *if* he didn't have to detour too much for terrain. He'd never flown this low along this route until today. He'd be at the airport in a bit over an hour at these speeds, unless the US Border Patrol made him land sooner. Or he was forced down by whoever was looking for him under Riviera's orders.

He passed the time, gently following between ridges, staying as low in the valleys as possible, going as south as he could, trying to get south of Death Valley. Each mile farther made him feel more confident. An hour into the flight, he was south of the valley and moving well west. He was approaching the border. About twenty miles to go.

***

He saw it, the chopper. It was travelling south, higher than he was. He chopped the throttle, slowing to nearly stall speed to hide against the terrain below. The chopper passed slowly in front of him, left to right. He could see the occupants in the door were carrying what appeared to be rifles in their arms, and it wasn't the helicopter that had originally tried to catch him. It was a goddamn Gazelle, which was significantly faster than he was.

Just then, the stall burble alerted him to the fact that he was slightly overloaded, even though he'd been burning fuel for two hundred miles. He gently applied a bit of power and lowered the nose to get out of stall. Twelve miles to go. At this speed, ten minutes.

At about six miles to go, the chopper returned, flying up from behind him and to his left. He firewalled the throttle. His airspeed increased to one-hundred fifty-five knots, the needle hovering on the never exceed line.

He heard the shots, and the chopper moved to fly in front of him. The pilot was good, He was pacing the Beaver at a slight angle so the men could still point their rifles at him. He could see a muzzle flash or two, but the planes were separated by at least 2000 feet, so there was no way those men were gonna hit him from a moving helicopter at that range. Still, they were a threat. So far, they hadn't hit him. Yet. He slowed. The Gazelle pulled ahead, then began reducing its speed.

He set the radio for Guard…121.5.

"U.S. Border Patrol U.S. Border Patrol….in the vicinity of Laughlin or Sun Valley. I am leaving Cali. I am a fixed wing Beaver approximately six miles from the border heading east. I am being pursued by a helicopter with Cali state marking. Please reply."

He tried three times, with no reply, then switched to 243.0 mhz on his handheld radio. Same message.

A reply came back almost immediately, "Aircraft calling border patrol on guard frequency, what are your intentions? Over."

"I intend to cross into the U.S."

"Please return to 121.5. We will inform appropriate Border Patrol personnel."

With that, he dove, again, pushing the airframe to one-hundred sixty knots. The shudder was bad, and he wasn't sure the wings could take it.

His dive had thrown the chopper off, and it had to dive to follow him. He knew it was faster than him, so he simply dove for the deck. He was below 3500 feet and above one-hundred sixty knots-well into never exceed speed.

As the helicopter turned to chase him in the dive, he waited, then pulled back on the yoke, feeling the g-forces as the plane zoomed upward. He was SURE he was overstressing the wings, but now was the time to do so if there ever was a time to do it. He climbed to over 6000 feet and the chopper pilot wasn't fast enough, he overshot on his dive, and the Beaver was well above him. As the helicopter flared in an attempt to stay with him, he converted altitude to airspeed, diving, then zoom climbing again until he felt the stall buffet in the yoke. Leveling off, he checked his engine gauges. His cylinder head temp was a bit high, his oil temp was a LOT high, but neither was in the red. Just then his radio came to life.

"Beaver entering U.S. airspace. Please reply."

"Go." he said into the mic.

"You are being pursued?"

"Yes."

"Are you a refugee?"

"Yes, I am fleeing Cali."

"You may enter U.S. airspace. Be warned that you will follow all course and altitude instruction, or be shot down. You will land as specified, and be subject to Customs searches, and possible detainment."

"Agreed."

"State your name and the names of you passengers as well as their ages." He complied, and heard, "Continue on course until further instructed, Mr. Daniels"

With that, the radio went silent again.

Just then, he saw the pursuing chopper fall in next to him about a thousand feet to the left. His radio squawked, this time with another, familiar voice.

"Hello, Mr. Daniels. Do you recognize my voice?"

"Yes, Mr. Riviera. What do you want?"

"You will turn around immediately, and follow OUR course and landing instructions. Or be shot down. Your choice."

Daniels looked at his GPS. Three miles. Fuckit.

He dove the plane, rolling hard TOWARDS the helicopter pacing him and just a bit lower. The pilot of the Gazelle instinctively rolled away and dumped the nose, honoring the threat the old Beaver posed. One man got off a few shots towards him, but the Gazelle was moving in all three axes and none came near him. As the chopper veered away, the men inside had to grab for balance, and he saw at least one rifle spin away from the chopper.

He banked hard the other way, and dove again, dropping from 6500 feet to 4000 feet in just seconds. His airspeed was again at "Never Exceed" speed and the air drummed over the wings and fuselage. He pulled back on the throttle and pointed east as he dropped. He knew there was no way he could keep this up and outrun the Gazelle.

"Cali helicopter, the is the U.S. border patrol. You are about to pass over the border. You DO NOT have permission to enter U.S. airspace. Please acknowledge."

Daniels looked up to see the strobes of TWO Blackhawks with the distinctive black paint and yellow stripe of the CBP about a mile in front of him.

The helicopter with Diego Riviera pulled up and turned to the south, running perpendicular to the course it had been on when following Daniels.

"Thank you, Cali." came over the Guard channel. "Unless you want to claim asylum too?"

The Gazelle continued on a path perpendicular to the Beaver, paralleling the border and away from the Beaver.

"Didn't think so" came the amused transmission from the Border Patrol

"Cali Beaver, please follow us to Bullhead airport in Laughlin. Airport identifier is IFP Do you know the way?"

"Not really, I was aiming for Sun Valley."

"Steer 098 magnetic. The airport is on 123.9 for tower, please follow instructions. When you land, there will be a Follow Me car, please follow instructions and *stay in your aircraft*. Do you copy?"

"123.9, Follow Me, stay in aircraft. Roger."

"Welcome to the USA, sir."

With that, the Blackhawks split up, one staying behind him and the other breaking to the north.

His escort chopper stayed with him until he got his instructions and began his final. Then it broke off to orbit.

He received his instructions from IFP tower, and landed safely. As he taxied to the end of the runway, his Follow Me car appeared, and he followed it to a parking space far away from other aircraft. He followed the radioed instructions to shut down his engine and wait.

Soon three police cars appeared. Armed men got out. A man in CBP uniform came up to the plane and gestured him out of the aircraft. As Daniel's feet touched the ground, the CBP officer put out his hand.

"I am Captain John Carstairs. I bet you have an interesting story. You'll have to tell us about it. For now, welcome to the United States of America."

Freedom's Ride

L.B. Johnson

"Have you got any matches?" - Lord of the Flies - Chapter 2

The mountains northwest of Lake Tahoe are quiet. Her more conservative neighbors fled before the "vote", something she would have done, had she only recently moved to the area.

But her family lived in this state for generations, her dad farming the rich soil down in the Valley like his father before him. The death of Lisa's parents— her father from a farming accident and her mother from cancer several years later left Lisa with just enough money to buy this cabin, and land perched up against a national forest after she had left college. Moving some money into savings from her inheritance, she had restored it to a simple rustic charm by putting a kitchen in the former one-room living area, and adding on a bedroom, den, and bath.

She found it, nothing much more than a hunting cabin at the time, for sale, when she was up here. It was just north of Meadowvale and was her uncle's hunting cabin. Her dad and Uncle Bud had taught her to hunt as a young teen. Her family was hard working, but her dad accepted no handouts, so there were lean years where harvesting a deer meant meat on an otherwise empty table. With all the regulations in California: permits, limited areas of hunting and paperwork--having to fill out a harvest report even if you didn't USE your permit and go hunting, hunting was done out of necessity, not for sport.

In college working on her Veterinary Technician associate's degree, she did the seemingly obligatory stint as a vegetarian, failing miserably one hungry night when she jokingly realized she was about ready to take hostages at an In and Out Burger. At the time, her mom was needing some meat on the table, and she came up here to see if she could get a deer that season, her uncle driving up from his place a few miles down to help get it to the butcher if she was successful.

Sitting in her comfortable warm home tonight she still remembers walking in her uncle's cabin for the first time by herself on her first solitary hunt.

The interior had been shadowed and bare, the only furniture visible when she first walked in, a dust covered chair crouching in the corner as if afraid of the light.

The hunting cabin had been closed up for almost a year. It was a long drive up here but worth it. She would rather have driven for hours then head to the nearest "Squatters' Rights RV campground" where the closest thing to wildlife was the married couple in the next spot that drank too much tequila and had a fight.

When she found the light switch, she saw there was more inside, a couple of couches, covered by a tarp, a small table and 2 more chairs, a sink, though there was no running water, a small refrigerator and some cooking supplies and a supply of bottled drinking water that her uncle left here for her. She enjoyed tent camping, but since she was by herself, this was much better. Putting up a tent on her own entailed cursing and usually bloodletting unless it involves a Pop-Up tent (oh good, tent Viagra). She would go with the cabin any time when she was on her own.

For it was just going to be herself this weekend, friends off with friends or family, doing other things. There was plenty to do as she lifted her firearm from its case, the glint of silver easing the gnawing stillness of the lonely room.

She cleaned up, swept and dusted as best she could, preparing stew and biscuits in a cast iron skillet to tide her over for the next couple of nights, some nut butter sandwiches and apple slices to have in her pack for lunches at the blind. Later days will hold a dinner table set with game, turkeys bewitched to a dark gold, venison succulent with the juice of life, the laughter of friends. Now is not the time for the feasting but for the gathering.

There was no TV, there was no radio. After putting some fresh toilet paper in the outhouse, she sat in the still quiet, thinking back to the city, right now bustling, growing and dying, buildings lined with amber windows that only hint at their human secrecy to the observer in the streets. People rushing to and fro, the casual innuendo of work relationships, fleeting obligations, names forgotten quickly at tedious meetings. Above, the communal wafer of the

*moon shined brightly, surviving the directionless pull
that is the city for some.*

*Soon she was settled in the cabin, far away from
the city, the blind out far away in the woods, her
footsteps back out just a memory for anyone watching.
Before it was even 9 pm, she was snuggled down in
her sleeping bag as comfortable as she could be.*

*In the morning, she could feel the chill in the air as
she had a cup of coffee with her bacon and eggs, over
a small campfire, her breath competing with its steam.
There's a cold front coming in, and despite the
forecast, she knows there is a chance of not just hard
rain, but thunderstorms. She could imagine the clouds
gathering up like an angry crowd even as the
moonlight bloomed in the trees like a faint blue flame.
It would be light soon, time to get out in the blind and
hope the storm would pass her by.*

*It was a long hike out. She had not meant to head
out this far away from the cabin, initially planning on
using the blind within shouting distance of shelter, but
sometimes you make that decision, one that every
adventurer takes, try that new cave, explore that new
trail, put up that blind out where you saw the giant
scrape. Let the cowards ponder other things back in
the safety of the jeep; it's time to blaze a trail that will
either be heartbreak or the profoundly sublime. Acting
on intuition and trusting your gut, you risk a new
adventure or a fourteen-point rack.*

And possibly a thorough, cold soaking.

*The storm was not supposed to be severe. The ones
that affect you deeply never are. First, there was
nothing but a congealed sky, the blue turning to dark-*

the color of cold and constant night. From the next ridge line came a rumble, or maybe that was her stomach, breakfast had been some time ago. But she didn't wish to get into the pack for the real provisions, as the sky had just spit in her face, a challenge she wasn't in the mood to take on.

The animals sensed it before she had, the forest going silent. The only whitetail she had seen all day was there and gone in a blink of an eye. In just the instant before he saw her, all the light in the sky remaining gathered on him, then he disappeared into shadow. He was there, and then he was only a specter of hide and hair. Then nothing but longing, followed by a clap of thunder that echoed somewhere deep inside.

She should have gone back, but she didn't want to. She only had two days to hunt. She didn't want to pack up the cabin and head back to the city. For at least one weekend each year, the woods here were hers, brief moments of time away from the drudgery of pavement and obligations. Time away from loss and explanations and time in tiny rooms that don't allow her to breathe.

It's not easy sitting still in the deer blind, listening only to the hearts whispered confidences, conversing silently with your own regrets. But if you were patient and completely still, there in the distance you may hear it. Not the birds nor the brook, but the soft crunch of leaves, scarcely a sound yet, almost sound anticipated, yet to reach the ear. There it was again, drifting into your hearing, then ebbing away again, sound dying softly on a trail that's leading away from you. It's gone.

She told herself it was a three legged, one eyed, scrawny button buck not worthy of the shot, while down inside she had a mental picture of tines with a spread of two and a half feet and a form that blots out all sound that you will make.

She knew there were deer here; creatures living shadowy in the limbo from which time began, moving around and away from time, away from you. Their forms moved right around her, as her heart sounded out that beat of time, going too fast. If only she could see with the eyes that all hunters have. She knew they were close, moving in and out of the sun's glare, flirting with her with grunts and snorts, hot air from soft muzzles, challenging her to the dual that only one of them will win.

There's nothing else like it; that unforgettable sense of openness. The profound and brooding woods, that lives quietly in her in the city as she bustled around between school and part time job at a dog groomer, the look of the hunter in her eyes behind the thick glasses, not visible to those around her, the fire hidden deep inside. Then later, the hot and wet and cold and warm hands on skin, peeling off clothing, fresh flannel, hot stew, warm coffee, renewal.

So, she stayed out longer than she should and getting caught in a cloudburst was her cover charge. It wasn't a dangerous storm; even she knew well not to head out into the tall trees during one of those. It was a small storm, but small is relative when it takes just one lightning strike to light up your world.

Any thunderstorm out in the open is dangerous, so she found shelter as best she could, avoiding the tallest trees, with lightning cracking within a few miles. The poncho is quickly pulled out of the pack and donned, another to cover her rifle and gear. She settled down to wait, rivulets of water running down her face, thoughts retreating like the tide, exposing a bare landscape of fire and blood, rock, and water.

She thought of her first whitetail hunt, taught the craft by those that loved her, passing down a tradition of survival and preparedness. She field-dressed the animal with coaching but no hands on assistance, there in the fading light, her bloody hands consecrating to them that which was, by God's will and man's patience, accepted as a gift. She grew up that day, in more ways the one, having learned and watched and waited, until she was ready to handle her firearm, ready to use it as a responsible steward of the land, looking at the deer on the ground, the first precious blood she had been worthy to take. Sacrifice with grace, for which we are thankful and repentant.

The rainfall soon snubbed that recollection, memories growing quiet in the tears of the heavens. It would be a brief outburst so she stayed still, and quiet, there under a tree whose leaves were torn fabric against the rain. Given the weather she was thankful she had taken shelter away from the tree stand; semi-squatted on the ground on a tarp under the smallest trees she could find, as far away from the tall trees as possible.

From above a growing patch of blue and in the retreating army of cloud, a brief, violent crack. Was that lightning or a black powder rifle there up in the hills? There was no telling, but the sound broke an awkward pause in the day, and the landscape breathed again. A bird twittered, and from below her, squirrels argued politics as the dome of perfect blue settled back over the earth, the breeze gentle and uninterrupted by moisture. She smiled, and quietly got back up in her blind, slumped back against the tree with the posture of survivors at the end of a crisis. The storm had passed.

She pulled her firearm out from where it had been kept dry, for no amount of fire or rain could challenge what was stored in a hunter's ghostly heart, and her firearm had seen her through both, with neither pity nor scorn for the travails. We waited, the Winchester and she, and waited some more, hoping that with the clearing of the air, man's smell washed from the area, a few deer would roust themselves out before dark.

All things come to he who waits. And she.

For there, as the sun started to yawn and dip in the sky, a buck passed by. He was young, still with much life ahead of him. Not a fat doe, but a youth, a skinny forest hooligan, tempting fate by being out past his curfew. She raised her weapon. The squirrels paused, and for yet another moment that day, the forest missed a breath, her hands coming up, shivering stopped, only blood and desire and life pulsing in her ear, her own breath waiting, trembling, held in as her finger drew back.

And she gently released it, the little buck bolting off into the shadows. She was hunting alone. If she had taken the shot she'd get a little bit of additional venison to add to the freezer but there was a good chance with the location combined with the onset of dark, that she would not be able to get him dressed and out of there before all light was gone.

We all take paths that seem exciting at the time, as we travel the wilderness of a heart, of a landscape. Everything is as it seems to be, you're not mindful of the dangers. Yet sometimes, the sky clears, you look carefully at where you're at, and realize the wisest thing to do is to walk away, clean and with as little blood as possible.

They say that the waters of the Lord can wash away sins, that mountain water cleanses the earth. But what of weakness and regret? What of that one moment of pity for that we are about to diminish, there in that cracking moment when something ceases to live. That moment there between speed and splendor and the casting off of a shell casing. Her family had lived off of the land, and as such, by need or necessity, she had taken life to feed them. Yet that night at the hunting cabin by herself could not, for reasons beyond the logical ones.

The rain was letting off to thin drops that trailed like dew upon her brow, but it was almost pitch dark before the trail led her back to the cabin, with thoughts of warmth and food, refreshing tonic to her brain, the smell of kerosene and leather bringing heat to parts of her too long cold. She peeled off her damp clothes, a strand of long red hair plastered to her breast like warriors paint, hands gathering wood and tinder into flame, fingers still damp with glistening drops.

Another crack of thunder split the night, and somewhere tonight, blood, hot and dense, bringing both pleasure and pain, would soak into the ground, starting the cycle of life again. From the woods, a cry of an animal lingered long on the air, leaving on the breeze the thin echo of regret. Tonight, a small whitetail lives another day, as does she.

She poured a glass of whisky from the bottle she knew her uncle had hidden away and raised a quiet toast to the night.

It's hard to believe that's been almost 10 years ago and now she lives here in that little log home.

She hadn't continued her work as a Veterinary Technician when she moved up to the cabin full-time, not wanting to make the commute into town in the winter's deep snow. Grooming some of the locals' pets in what used to be a shop off the horse barn that had room for some deep sinks and boarding a few horses covered her basic expenses and insurance, the small cabin, and used truck being paid for. She still has a small fireproof box safely hidden inside that held a few thousand U.S. dollars, essential if she needs to make a break for Nevada.

But for now, she has game in the forest, and a bit of a garden hidden away by her horse's barn. She has enough grains, sugar, and salt for a couple of years, provisions her grandmother had taught her were vital no matter how rich your lifestyle seemed to be.

Her stores will be crucial, for according to the local radio station, before it went off the air, within just a couple of weeks locals had broken into the

Meadowvale grocers, looting its contents, leaving just the shattered shell of a once proud family-owned store.

***

Her only close neighbors, a young couple, usually kept just enough food for a week, venturing into town for munchies when the mood struck. She had tried to be cordial when she moved in, even going over one night to their house right by the main road, with cable and all the other fineries of living closer to town to let them know the coyotes were coming in a lot closer in the cold and letting them know that they might want to keep their appetizer sized dogs close by them rather than just letting them out to roam the open back yard.

The neighbor looked at Lisa and said, "It's okay, we have an invisible fence." Lisa couldn't even BEGIN to explain the flaws in that reasoning to them. Good luck getting that collar on Mr. Mountain Lion. The world is not a safe and happy place, something some people find when they least expect it.

They were one of the first in the area to abandon this new "utopia" to flee down to the cities.

Look back into history, cities disappear, countries realign. Whole societies grind to a halt, the precise cause of death uncertain. The stars somehow align overhead by political alliance, high priests of nuclear ability, climate, and promise. All running like fault lines underneath what appears to be placid landscape. Disturbances ignored by the media as larger things erupt and spew black, cumulative movements unseen. The sheep graze placidly while the Tectonic plates of divergent cultures and religion, rub, shifting, jockeying for power until one day something gives way. A city will vanish, a state, perhaps an entire way of life lost as easily as a set of car keys.

We believe that because we've always been the dominant political and economic power on this planet that it will always be so. Legions nod in affirmation to change and power shifts, believing that because it always has been, it always will be. For so many years we lived as a nation on credit, buying with plastic, borrowing on faith. Her grandparents paid cash for everything, not expecting their government or their neighbor to bail them out, and as such, they survived the Great Depression. Her mom and dad had the same mindset. If it was broken they fixed it. If they worked hard to earn it, they took care of it.

Lisa's family owned their own land and measured everything by soil and water and sweat; not stopping and whining if the tractor broke or the mule died. They themselves were raised by a generation of men that went to war, leaving their legacy to a generation of strong women who would tend to it until their return. To their children, they passed on something you could hold in your hand, not press into an ATM machine.

As a young girl, she loved the old John Wayne movies her parents had recorded. She could never forget the climactic moment in one film where the grizzled old marshal confronts the four villains and calls out: "I mean to kill you or see you hanged at Judge Parker's convenience. Which will it be?"

"Bold talk for a one-eyed fat man," their leader sneers.

Then Duke cries, "Fill your hand, you son of a bitch!" and, reins in his courage, rushing at them while firing both guns. Those four outlaws did not provide a threat at the next sunset.

When did her homeland change so? The west Lisa grew up in is now more socialized and urban, more of the citizens pining for things they cannot afford while looking to others to fix their problems. Where she grew up, gardens were tended and food canned, and when threatened by others the wagons were circled and folks cared for themselves, providing for their own, from the land and their hard work.

Her Dad was a third-generation farmer, her mom coming to the San Joaquin Valley as a young bride, and she often told her daughter that she learned fast. There were stories of spring snowstorms thawing into mucky puddles from which a season of new life came. There would be drought and there would be searing heat. Sometimes the crops were abundant, other times not so much. There were a few years that in addition to tending to the almond trees and other growing things, Dad worked as a telephone lineman, just to keep a roof over their heads.

It was not an easy life, especially when sometimes Mom and she were left during the day to do everything themselves. To do otherwise would have left the place in ashes, abandoned, another failed dream. Duty and honor weren't archaic promises; they were words she was raised to live on, no matter how bad things got. Being so small, the idea of 'too big to fail' never made sense.

You saw it there in those last days of California as part of the nation, in the eyes at the feed store, you see it in the determined step of those buying supplies and learning the use them. You saw it in the questions of the many that may have been in the minority with this whole secession idea but were not willing to leave the land where they had lived their entire life. People that are beginning to understand that we have a right to be heard, not silenced because the majority disagreed with us.

Because we're NOT too big to fail and this Calexit thing has a big *fail* written all over it. She thinks of the movie War of the World's wherein the monolithic war machines of Mars were felled by something as simple as a sneeze.

She *is* intensely proud of being an American. She refused to say *was* proud of being an American, the being and cadence of a life of freedom, to work, to arm oneself, to defend and expand that which you personally worked for. Influenced by a bygone era of good guys and bad guys, it is part of who she was, defining both fury and faith.

Because in coming days she is afraid she will find what she is made of.

She's been out here on her own for two months now. There is still electricity and she hopes it continues through the looming winter. From the distance, she has heard at least one car, but no one has attempted her rough dirt track up the hillside into the forest; it is almost impossible to see from the road now. Even when she first moved here, with empty cabins near that might invite a break-in; she laid out tree limbs and such to partially block the narrow path that behind the trees widened to the long dirt road to her home. It was easy enough to clear out when she had a dog grooming client expected but reduced the chances of a home break in. Now she has no clients and she has let the undergrowth take over, but she still had room to get out in an emergency.

She was afraid to take her truck onto the main road into town, which was miles away, after one late night telephone conversation with her neighbor John who lived about a mile down the mountain from her. He was in his sixties, divorced, his grown kids living near Sacramento.

He had told her, "Lisa – don't take your truck out on the road. My kids told me they are taking vehicles from the middle and upper classes, and giving them to the poor, redistributing them for those that are joining the militia."

"Militia?" was all she could stammer.

"The Militia is preventing people from leaving except with what they can carry and they have to walk out. It's been reported that some people were shot when they tried to drive over the border."

She was stunned, not believing such things were happening. She'd heard gunshots from a great distance, but she convinced herself that was a neighbor who had hunkered down out hunting for food.

Today she's going to take her horse, Taxi, out east of her property. She lives high up on a ridge, where there are just two other homes, both long empty and for sale, as people abandoned the state. She is on the east side and if she keeps to the trails east of her home, it will take her in deep forest that eventually leads to an unnamed valley that goes down to the Nevada State line, a couple dozen miles away. It was rough, rugged country, but she was familiar with many of the trails, regularly taking the horse out on the trail rides they both love.

In keeping with what her distant neighbor told her, she didn't take the horse along the trail that paralleled the road into town, and then up to the lake, she stayed back a few yards into the tree line. Needing a short break and a drink she tethered Taxi to a tree and got down to clear a limb that they had maneuvered around last time, but needed to be cleared from the trail. She thought for a moment she heard a car door but figured it was her imagination as she had not seen anyone on this road in weeks.

As she bent down to pick up the limb, a bullet whizzed over her head.

"He's back there!" is all she heard as she took off running. She tripped, falling and breaking open the skin on the palm of her hand on a sharp rock. It wasn't terribly deep but it is painful, and she bites her tongue to keep from crying out as she stumbles the last few feet to her horse.

Lisa wasn't sure what "he" they were referring to, but with her long red hair under a baseball cap and clothing that would never land her on the cover of Cosmo Magazine on her tall frame, she figured the bullet was addressed to her.

She has two advantages – back in the trees, the sun's rays are disoriented and dim. Although it pours down a leaden heat on the landscape, the light wavers and it will take whoever had fired the shot a minute or two to adjust to it. That should give her about one hundred yards. If they have a four-wheeler, she is toast, but they are likely were on foot, with the trail not being suited for a vehicle.

Other shots fly behind her, not as close now, as she deliberately heads away from her home. She hears another car door slam from the road and some shouting as she headed high up the next ridgeline.

She was far enough away from her home when that first shot rang out that it was unlikely they would find it on a search for her, but she needs to find her way back miles further away from the road. There are creeks with water for Taxi, and she has some protein bars, some tarp and rope, and a knife in her backpack should she need to spend the night outdoors before making her way home. Once she could no longer hear anyone else, she removed her bra and wound it around her bloody palm to help staunch the blood flow after washing it out with a bit of her bottled water and some iodine she keeps in her pack.

She thanks the Lord for the warning phone call from her neighbor. Without it, she would have likely come in direct contact with whoever fired upon her. Looters? Militia? She didn't know. Above her, the crests of the peaks were shrouded in cloud, lying motionless upon the land as if an obstacle to her path. She rides deep up into the mist and finds a place to hide for the remainder of the day.

***

She's been three days back at home and there have been no further signs of any humans near the little mountain on which her home is perched. She went to call her neighbor and let him know what happened to find the line dead, likely cut up near the road. She had a ham radio. She wasn't too skilled in its use but she could manage the basics. It was one of those things her dad had taught her. She realized he had probably wanted a son as well as a daughter, but in lacking one, he taught her all of those tasks he would have taught a male offspring. She knew how to hunt, to fish, to put up a tent, to build a fire, and to talk on the ham radio

She had a transceiver, a power supply (for now), an antenna, an antenna tuner, and a microphone. She'd already set up her distant neighbor, from whom she purchased hay for Taxi, as a QSO (contact). She never really made other contacts further away, but she knows if she talked to John down the hill he'd clue her in on what he had heard was happening from his children who lived in the city.

Unlike many of her old friends, she can't play a video game to any sort of level, but she understands from her dad's lessons how most things "work" and can make simple repairs to things with multiple moving parts. She hopes she never has to give herself an appendectomy with a sharp pen and a bottle of Knob Creek, but she can tend to a wound and do the basics to keep things running around here.

She realizes if she was on one of those "Survivor-style" shows, she'd lose, but not from not having the skills to survive, but mainly because she's not a big fan of most other people, and the games involved in interacting with them in such settings. She's glad now, that what little socializing she's done has been with her boyfriend and his family down in the Valley. Her grooming customers already likely having left Meadowvale for civilization, there is probably no one other than her hay supplier, a good Christian man, who knows she is out here alone.

For now, she's hunkering down, hoping that one day she wakes up to reliable utilities and a stream of tourists heading up to the big lake northeast of her. Until then, she will be ready as she can be, not sitting there waiting for her human savior or a handout, hands hanging pale and useless. Sometimes when you are left with nothing you still have your will for the hope to grab on to.

She doesn't understand why so many of her neighbors were willing to sacrifice their personal liberty for that illusion of safety that comes from living under the authority of some higher power? Even as the Highest Power of all has conveyed these words to man – "God helps those who help themselves".

With a loaf of bread baking in the solar oven out in the clearing in front of the house, she curls up with a book. She's glad she has a well-stocked bookshelf, as with the power becoming occasionally intermittent, and her TV having gone Tango Uniform as her dad liked to say, there wasn't a lot to do. The books were like gold in the hand, comfortable and secure.

With the books are those things that remind her why she chose to live her life the way she does now. There's a flag and a small cross, ceremonial shapes of mortality, reminders that some choices are everlasting. There's a tail from a whitetail, taken in a hunt, food for a winter's table. There's some spent brass that either guarded or honored a life, a piece of old uniform fabric and the scents of sandalwood and gunpowder and freedom that soak into her skin and bones like ink, to stay with her to the end of days.

Being prepared is harder work than remorse, a lesson that, as individuals, is easier to learn than as a nation.

She sits down to have a nightcap, carefully rationing out her supply of whisky, knowing she is unlikely to find more. She was glad when there was first the noise of a "scotch shortage" back in 2016 that she filled up the gun safe not just with her hunting rifles, pocket pistol, and revolver, but as many bottles of single malt as she could afford. She didn't even want to think of how many dog butts she had to clean or how many stalls she had to muck out to pay for them.

But she was determined to at least get quality stuff. If the SHTF, as it appears it has, she didn't want to be drinking from a bottle of Nasty McLand or something.

She thinks back to college when she and her roommates made some horrible concoctions of soda and some cheap American whiskey that smelled like an uncapped magic marker and tasted of sharp heat, the taste equivalent of pulling a hot cast iron pan off of the stove with your bare hand. A slight shudder ran through her.

It's not just the thought of the taste that made her react this way, it's a reminder that a year ago, she would be sharing this drink with her boyfriend of the last two years, a man she met when she boarded Taxi her horse down in the Valley before one forecasted brutal snowstorm. He didn't have a ham radio, not sharing her love for such things, and gently teased her for prepping, assured that the land of milk and honey was just around the corner. Her cell phone had never really worked well up here and there had not been the sound of a car coming up the mountain in quite a while. She had no idea if he was alive or dead but she couldn't risk leaving her property to make the drive down, only to have her vehicle "redistributed" to someone without a source of income other than the taxpayers. She knew he loved her, but he also had a disabled mother to care for and she knew he would not abandon his mom to come to her.

Outside, somewhere far in the distance, coyotes howl. She looks out into the darkness, into the ancient and inscrutable face of the night, seeing nothing, knowing that doesn't mean that nothing is out there. The light fades, the wind is brisk, the flow of the outside lights, small incandescent intervals of safety around the house, challenge anyone to come near.

Before first light in the morning, she would make one last trip down the mountain with her truck. It was a risk, but she had to load up this winter's hay from her neighbor, exchanging it for a little cash, some bread, garden vegetables, and a bottle or two of her whisky. She doesn't think anyone with ill intentions will be out at 4 a.m. and she knows the road well enough to drive it under full moonlight, with no headlights.

The Calis still swarming out of the Valley, trying to flee what is left of California are always a threat:

raping, robbing and sometimes killing, desperate for food or supplies, if the stories she has heard through her neighbor are to be believed. She's only seen Militia, not looters, but she can't be too careful. But she has to keep her horse well fed. For if she must, she will attempt to ride through the thick forest to Nevada, hoping she is not spotted and shot on sight by the militia.

Her revolver on her hip and a rifle lying on the bench seat of her old truck, she idles down the long trail to the road. Stopping to assess if there was anyone in the area, she moves the brush away from the entrance to the road, which is really no more than a trail at that point, barely big enough for a vehicle to pass. Putting everything back in place she travels down the hill to the equally hidden entrance to John's house, moving slowly and quietly, so she can quickly abandon the truck on foot if there is an oncoming vehicle.

Her heart is pounding as she looks ahead to the road and then to the sky, stars flying upwards between ancient trees in a black sky. She sees them as brilliant staccato points in the sky that change to a wet sheet. She doesn't realize she is crying as she makes her way down the hill.

As she pulls off the road, replacing the decoy brush and debris that guards John's trail, she hears the sound of a vehicle.

Turning off the engine, she crouches down, just enough light now to see the road, but not so much that she would be seen here deep in the trees. It's a large flatbed truck. On the back are barricades, lots of them, headed east.

They glide by, thankfully not seeing her, probably half asleep themselves. But she realizes the reason for the barriers. They're blocking the roads that lead eventually into Nevada, not just the main ones. That explains the lack of cars and the one bicyclist she thought she saw. You can't really build a "Wall" in the mountains in what is left of California, but if you block the roads, 99% of the populace will not get through, the trek being too long over rough terrain for a hiker.

When all is quiet, she waits another fifteen minutes and the fires the truck up and heads up the hill to John's barn. He greets her with a silent wave and draws her into the house.

"You need to stay here until dark," he said. "I heard the vehicles, it won't be safe to go back home until tonight after they have set things up and gone back to the Valley."

She agrees, knowing Taxi is safe in the barn with enough food and water for a day or two. She doesn't risk leaving him in the meadow when she is gone due to the dangers from mountain lions.

She enjoyed John's company, if only for a few hours. She's in her own little world right now, this limbo between the Calis to her west and the lure of freedom, or death if she heads to the east. She's the swing of the hammer, the trajectory of the bullet, the frame of a window. Most days she works until long after dark, tossing the moon back like a shot of scotch, stopping only to get a small clean glass from the cupboard, last call.

Certainly, it's easier to let others do the work, to just sit back and wait for help, wait for that handout, and wait for that check you did not work to earn. But she can look in the mirror and see the space and the solitude and its rewards, the broken nails and occasional scrape a sign of progress. It's the only way she can live, the entitlement mindset, to her, being like that of an animal, drawn to a baited trap from a wide-open field, the instincts that would recognize a trap now dulled, not even comprehending it is doomed, and no longer afraid, for it was no longer free.

If you rely solely on others to feed you, to protect you and to sustain you, to prop you up and pat you on the back when you fail, you've not just made them your judge you've made them your jailer. Even worse, it's a jail term without end, for it's done with the sanction of your own conscious.

When darkness fell, her neighbor John insisted that he ride shotgun with her the mile home to her place. He said he could hike back. She didn't ask him where he got the AR15 with the holographic scope, but with him being a former Marine, she knew he could use it.

They made it back without seeing anyone, and he helped her get the hay in the barn before she sent him home with some frozen venison stew and a hug. She was once again glad she had not bought a house on the main highway that crosses the hills to her north. It is likely the only reason she had not been discovered.

She runs her bath by candlelight, in the near darkness inside her home. Even though there is not an occupied house, other than John's, for miles she doesn't want the light of her place visible from any distance. Her well is still supplying water, as she prays for a good snowfall this winter to build up the water supply. Drought is what she fears most, not simply because of the supply of well water but because of the fire danger. She has lived here long enough to see flames from the forest licking the forest only 10 miles away. She fled as the C130's began their runs overhead. Now, if there is a fire, there will be no planes. She's not seen a plane of any kind fly over in months, though one night, in total darkness, she swore she heard the sound of a very small plane struggling in the thin air above heading east in the blackness, someone risking controlled flight in the darkness to escape the life in Cali as it exists today.

She opens the wrapper of one her few remaining bars of soap, the brand her mother used, and the smell is as she always remembered. It's like the smell of Crayons. Not what she'd call a pretty smell, but such a familiar and a comforting one. That brand of soap was all they ever had as a child, that and the thick, gritty powdered soap for washing hands after shop and yard work. This plain white bar is what she had washed her face with for most of her life. But she can also well remember how it tastes, for once when she said a cuss word, her mom washed out her mouth with it. It did NOT taste good.

As she finishes her bath, carefully drying her hair and checking her robe for the small handgun that resided there in the pocket, she thought a lot about that world she grew up in, and the one outside of her window now. You can say all you want about what youth of her generation are exposed to, violent video games, bloodshed, sex and violence on TV. But she truly believed that as children, the moral imperatives that initially form in us are in response to parenting, not society or entertainment. That's probably why her mom home-schooled her, back when it was still legal. That was why Lisa knew that there would be dire consequences if she tried to drop an anvil on her cousin's head or blew up the garage with Acme Dynamite like Wile E. Coyote tried to do to the Roadrunner every Saturday morning.

She realized she was just a child back then, but she knew something that those that threaten her now don't - that there is a moral code to this world and that the world as well, did not revolve around our every need and happiness. It was how her parents were raised, and how she was raised. Her parents clothed her, loved her, praised her, and punished her, not without thought and not with an unwarranted decree, but in a manner firm enough it definitely got her attention.

She tested those boundaries when she was a child, because that's what children do, finding that with those boundaries came accountability. One soon learns that a tantrum in Safeway will not get you that toy by the check stand; it will get you a quick and silent removal to the car and home to think about it in your room, without any toys. One learns that if one lies to a parent, that certain things we enjoy are not a right, they're earned by responsibility. One learns that if one tries to jump off the garage roof with a makeshift airfoil, the ground will smite thee only a little less than Dad will. One often, much later, learns that if you carelessly play with what one holds dear, there are consequences for more than just yourself, lessons that stay long after the aftermath.

Now, she thought, most kids are given access to most anything good and bad that the TV and the Internet have to offer, at the earliest of ages, not as a lesson in choice, but as a way of entertainment for parents often absent. Through expectation or demand, children are given possessions so freely that neither the object nor the givers have value to them, and, if acting out in their attempts to cajole or control, their actions are forgiven before forgiveness had been even ventured or earned.

As an only child, she was not insulated from the world and its capabilities for harm. She understood the rudimentary principles of physics, ballistics, and stupidity. Current events were discussed, war, poverty, and mans' evil against other men, but only when old enough to grasp and apply those lessons. She had been given books that would be banned today for being politically incorrect. She had toys that could cause second-degree burns. She had chemistry sets that could actually blow things up. She learned how to safely handle certain firearms and respect the trust of their use, their purpose, which was not to impose our will or to take something we had not earned, but to provide and protect.

But her parents were careful not to give her access to things from which she could obtain knowledge for which she did not yet have the wisdom nor demonstrated the reasoning. Remember Jack and

Roger from Lord of the Flies? Imagine them with Wireless connectivity, Mom's credit card, and free shipping. There are no laws that will prevent what a mind unbound by honor, ethics or the value of others can destroy when their own worth is predicated on unlimited attention and no accountability. And certainly, there are no laws which will sway the actions of a mind caught by madness, who act not with the rational thought of the outcome, but as a man, out of his mind with a gangrene poisoned hand, thirsts for an ax that with its downward stroke will somehow make him whole.

When such evil, be it driven by mental defect, jihad, or ego strikes, it does so at the very lie of safety that are the laws that control behavior, that control our tools, our very actions, for evil knows no such laws. When they strike, there is little left but the invoked ghosts of ones we can never avenge and the media-heralded name of one who should be unnamed, forgotten, buried in an unmarked grave in burnt, damned ground. Then comes the cry that yet another law above and beyond the ones they already broke by their actions.

She gently pats the small firearm in her pocket. It's illegal, one of the many things, it seems, that's called illegal here in Cali anymore. Breaking the law is not in her blood, but without it, her blood could be spilled.

From the beginning of time, there have been laws; there have been tools that can be used as weapons, including firearms. There has been good and evil. There have been two distinct and competing impulses that exist among humans, one, the instinct to live by the law, to act peacefully except in matters of self-defense, to follow moral commands for the good of the group; and the other, the instinct to gratify one's immediate desires without adherence to any such law or moral code, using violence, not as a means of protection, but to simply to obtain supremacy over others or force one's will on someone without defense.

How did that all change, she thinks, to where we are in a world where everyone expects something for free, laws and the Constitution are whims, and those in power do anything they can to stay there, even if it means blood continues to flow in the street? How did we get to a point where greed and self-entitlement broke this once proud land away from our country, which she STILL believes is HER country, with a savage force that would put any earthquake to shame?

She steps outside to lock the gate. It's only one additional thing between the forest and her door, but she sleeps better knowing it is locked, not fear of the four-legged creatures but of the two-legged ones. When she first moved here she replaced the pin tumblers on her gate, grooming station and supply shed with magnetic and combination to make them less easy to "lock-bump" and break in.

***

A hundred yards away, there is a moonlit lane between pine trees and stone. There in the shadows, only steps away, a long shadow shifts. She stops, sensing movement, sensing darkness within the dark, in the woods past her clothesline. Her hand moves to her firearm, poised to use it if needed. It is only a fox, easing back through the trees; a shadow, a form that slides like light through a picket fence, slanting sideways, and then disappears under cover. Her hand eases away from her weapon, but she backs away, towards the candlelight, towards home and sleep.

She walks quietly back towards the house. She goes a different time each day, knowing that predators rely on patterns. There in the distance, a couple of coyotes, trotting along the edge of the meadow, through snow that clutched at their empty bellies, heads cocked, eyes forward, using instinct, tooth and sinew to find that one small morsel there breathing under the snow, trying to hide for its life, a small shivering rabbit, wishing as desperately not to be eaten alive as the coyote desperately wishes to consume. The coyote stops to look at her in the stark moonlight, with what looks to be a smile on his face, not one of welcome but of mockery; the smile of a predator. He watches as she moves on down the road towards her door, round in the chamber, ready if needed.

She walks back towards the house when from the edge of the woods comes motion and sound, a blurred commotion, a high pitched, soft pleading scream that breaks the lie of safety. She looks towards the trees and sees something darting quickly, a dark shape, too small to be human, too quick for her to catch a good glimpse. There, in the ditch, a small white form, a jagged tear in its furry throat, rabbity legs twitching in the remembrance of life.

As she bolts the door behind her for the night, the abandon and innocent glee that was childhood remain forever lodged in her mind, just as do those lessons, even the painful ones. She puts her hands up to her nose and smells the faint, clean scent of soap, something so plain and simple, much like what once stood for truth. Today, she is no longer trusted with either a weapon or a voice but the Calis can't take her honorable heart. What guides her to maintain that honor is not a law, it is not the dictate of a ruling body, and it is bound to her by the honor of the past and the examples of her upbringing.

She moves into the house, ears listening to anything unusual, eyes looking for anything out of order, a habit that is not fear but caution, locking the door behind her, prepared and aware. Outside, the snow blankets the ground with a soft innocence, hiding more than the ground but the very risks of the wild that play out in the night, beyond her sight.

She looks outside one last time to make sure she is alone, the evening air cooling her blood, the field empty and quiet, except for the steady sound of a small wounded animal, a ceaseless and unemphatic cry into the wind.

Winter is firmly here, so far mild, for which she and her wood supply are grateful, should the power go out permanently. She thanks the Lord every day for having the presence of mind when she bought the place to install a wood stove and store a couple of years' worth of wood in the shed behind the house that wasn't being used. It is an easy walk with a wheelbarrow there and back, and she had built a crude fence on each side of the path, so if she had to fetch more wood in the middle of the night, she had a little something between her and any animals that might be roaming her property as well as a blockage to someone wanting to "help themselves" to her firewood. If the power goes out, she'll just run the stove at night, sleeping during the day so that the smoke is not seen from a distance. She hoped it would last her a while.

Still, she plans to use no more than she needs to, climbing the ladder into the open storage loft she has in her bedroom area, the warmer air rising and keeping that spot more comfortable than her own bed right now. Taxi the horse used to spend winters down at her boyfriends, and she prays he doesn't freeze out in his stall this winter, even with some extra insulation intended for a future enclosed porch that she carefully installed around his stall.

She figured she would go out one last time to see if she could harvest a small whitetail, something small enough that she could get it hauled out on the horse, but providing 40 or so pounds of meat that she could store in one of the outer buildings that were freezing, now that the bears would be in hibernation. She still has enough fuel for her camp stove and if there was a day with enough sun the solar oven might still work. She'd actually made a pie in it to celebrate surviving her first three months on her own.

 She wasn't too keen on leaving tracks so she waited until it was still cold but the light snow had melted. Although she had always lived here year-round, the summer dwellers made their way back to the cities with the first snowfall, so this time of year she rarely ran across someone on the higher elevation trails. Still, she always carried a firearm, for she knew that you never alone in the wilderness, in spite of a solitary step. Several people have told her they have seen, while hunting, a large shadow, merging along the edge of vision. They would raise up their arms to appear bigger and shout LOUDLY just in case, and the shadows blend and disappeared. Bear? Bobcat? Who knows?

Even as quiet as it is, she keeps her guard up as she and Taxi make their way uphill. Not all predators are four-legged.

Even with the threats, she still loved being out here. So much of the country envisioned the California of old as simply L.A. and San Diego and San Francisco, vast cities teeming with people when, in addition to the farmland, California had vast beautiful mountains. She wasn't the only citizen who eschewed city life for something remote and wild and as free as you could get in a state that loved to regulate.

Give her a spot for just herself or perhaps a friend, days sliding into the sunset, marked by little more than the sum of breaths taken freely. It was hard to tell one day from another. Mornings would creep in on the breath of small creatures watching from the trees, days spent in reading or hiking, nights simply lying out like one single point of a compass star, feet pointed towards her future, pointing true. She didn't move quickly when she woke, looking at the morning sun with the mild inscrutability of animals awakening, functioning outside of a watch, having left time lying upon the slow and imponderable shore on which her life is moored.

She remembers coming up to her uncle's hunting cabin once with her best friend from high school. She thinks back to that night, the telling of stories in front of the fire, trying to scare one another, as off in the distant the stars flared against a background of ebony velvet. They sipped a can of cheap beer (being young and knowing no better) and talked into the wee hours. Adulthood was looming, both of them soon off to college, both of them still naive to the ways of the world and of men, but both aware of the redemptive power of the woods. They looked to see if they could see the Northern Lights. This far south it was highly unlikely, but it never stopped them, sharing stories and dreams, not realizing how far the years would take them from this place.

For now, she needed to get her mind back on what she was doing – she had an entire solitary winter to daydream by herself.

Taxi's ears suddenly went back and he came to a stop.

"What is it, boy?" she says as the horse refuses to go forward. She doesn't see anything up ahead, urging him forward. The horse is in *park* and that's where he is going to stay.

She senses, rather than feels, coldness at the very base of her spine, a sense, somehow, that she is being watched. There is no sound, no steady growl or rustle or movement upon which her mind will tell her to hurry along. Yet, she knew it is there; the murmur of threat, the panting whispers of predators unseen.

Then she sees it, up ahead on the trail a couple of hundred yards. It is a bear. Did she manage to find the only bear with insomnia in the Sierras? It wouldn't have cubs this time of year, that was one good thing, but it still was a danger.

The bear spotted her. It was a very young bear, lighter brown in color but most likely black bear species as brown bears have not been seen in this area in years. The thought flashed through her mind for just a moment whether the new Cali flag still had a Grizzly on it or they'd traded it out for a unicorn. As the bear huffed, that thought fled her head.

She had her deer rifle with her, but from this distance, she'd need more than that to go up against a bear and he'd be on her by the time she wrangled with the sling and got a sight picture for a round that would only piss it off more. Where's a nice 12-gauge Express Magnum loaded with slugs when a girl needs one?

She raises her arms as high as she can and shouts, waving her arms. Bears usually don't want to deal with humans if they don't have to, and if they aren't startled. The bear wasn't likely very hungry either and with her talking to Taxi as she rode, likely had heard her from a long distance. It stood, sniffing the air, and giving a challenging huff.

She slowly backed the horse up, continuing to try and look as big as possible. She had an adequate distance between them when the bear gave a small bluff charge, then stopped. She continued backing up waving her arms high over her head and shouting until they rounded a bend, out of sight of the bear. She and Taxi then took off, the bear losing interest once they are out of sight. Still, she keeps the horse going as fast as is safe for the trail until they are back home. She is not sure how she rode home as she was literally stiff with fear, listening to the minute seeping of hot blood through veins constricted, as everything was going to the muscles, fight or flight. She thinks Taxi just got them there, her being just along for the ride.

It looks like winter was going to be a lot of canned soup and beans, but she was grateful neither she nor her horse was any the worse for wear.

She had chosen safety over the gathering of game today. It was something that made her think back to the day in which she went on her first deer hunt. She remembered it not so much for the action but for what was passed on. What her father and uncle taught her that day was more than the taking of game. They taught her when to shoot and when not to- that the taking of a life was not something be done lightly, no matter how hungry you were. They taught her what was worthy, and what should be left alone. She learned when the woods were a safe haven, and, with a rumble of thunder, when the woods were a place to leave. She learned not just the rules of the hunt, there in the dark, heavy dew of an April morning, while they squatted, knees crying, underneath a turkey roost. She learned about life, and how precious it is and how quickly lost. She learned without speaking. She learned just by watching. She learned not just when to act, but when to just walk away and let it go. She learned that with freedom comes responsibility, with wrong decisions, comes death, if not in the flesh, then of the spirit.

As she got the horse watered and fed, with a warm blanket draped over him, giving him some precious oats as a thank you, she realized that this seemingly sturdy body, that serves her subtlety and so well, is only so much meat, and her thoughts and life history would only be a night's sustenance to some creature of the woods. . . or to fate.

As the snows gave way to rain, she thinks hard about what the upcoming winter would bring. She has enough to eat, and enough wood to keep her place livable if the power went out, if one liked living while wearing a parka in the house. But one fall, one accident, one encounter with tooth and claw might be a game changer.

There had been no signs of life in a while, no cars on the road, though in September she swore when she was gathering kindling within a glimpse of the road she saw a guy dressed in dark clothing on a bicycle with a backpack, riding around the mountain before it starts the drop into the next state.

The light is all but gone as she heads back towards the house as if the night had slipped up behind her, her back exposed to the creep of time, so enmeshed by the dimming of the approaching darkness that she scarcely heard its whisper. The moon is out, the shadows diminishing to its curve until even the shadows are drenched in black. There at the edge of her property is a young whitetail. For a moment, there is no movement, the deer's still form barely visible, its outline growing weightless and faint; the night itself mesmerizing her with its own primal inertia. As the little deer turns to leave, she thinks that with the coming spring, it too may be her time to slip away from here.

***

As she enters her home and lights a candle, water trails off the tin roof, the sound of it ebbing and flowing, lapping at the corner of her thoughts. Let there be a time and a place, she prays, where she can have this, and the company of friends, without sacrificing her freedoms and her safety.

As best as she could figure it was Christmas Day. She'd been marking days off on her calendar. She had thought about getting a little tree from the forest and decorating it with her Mom's old decorations but she couldn't take a risk of a fall out in the deep snow. The winter still was fairly mild, given the elevation, little in the way of snowpack but there was enough to fall and end up frozen to death. It's as if the entire area, after previous winters of deep snow was collectively thumbing its nose at Al Gore and his friends in Cali.

Unlike the summer, where the light has a weary quality to it, like a backwater pool of light lying low, winter's light is crisp, clean, illuminating everything so clearly. Even with sunglasses on as she goes to bring in some firewood after feeding and watering the horse the vivid noise of sunlight's dance plays on her eyes as she walks, causing her to blink

She can't honestly imagine living some place where it never snowed. She wouldn't enjoy living where, at Christmas, you can't tromp out into the snow and cut down your tree instead of buying one, limp and smelling of French fries from the McDonalds next to the tree lot.

Tonight, there was just one small branch that she cuts a safe distance from the house, with a couple bulbs on it and a little star. It sort of looks like the Charlie Brown Christmas tree but the subtle scent of it in the air was enough for her today.

She picks up the phone. Nothing, no signal. She hadn't expected anything new but there is a part of her that always thinks "they're going to fix the mess, get the infrastructure going, life will be back to normal".

A silent phone reminds her of what a lie that is.

Cell phone coverage in this area was always bad, but until her landline phone quit, she tried calling all the numbers in her directory. There weren't many. Her uncle, who was in an assisted living center in Chico, her boyfriend, her best friend from college, her minister who lived down in the Valley. No one picked up. At first, there would be an answering machine or recorded message on a cell phone to which she'd leave a message

"It's Lisa – I'm at the cabin and I'm OK. Please let me know you are OK too. I love you."

"This message is for Mr. Anderson in room 211. Please tell him his niece Lisa is safe."

"It's Lisa, Julie – please call me, it's the landline number, I got rid of the cell."

"It's Lisa Anderson, Pastor – please let me know everyone is OK."

There were no return calls.

After a while, there were no answering machine or voicemail messages either.

Today, it would just be herself. She really wishes one of her loved ones or friends were here with her to celebrate this day.

She isn't seeking company or the distraction of noise. She is seeking something familiar from which she can measure the happiness of the past, even if she could not recapture it. It wouldn't be gifts, or money or a party, but simply the gathering of promise and hope and faith, that true gift of love without reservation that makes all other things look puny in comparison. But as she put on a cassette of some Christmas hymns in the ancient cassette player she found out in the old shop, it came to her. Whether she is sitting alone or surrounded by others, when she hears the strains of a Christmas hymn, the warmth of that gift came back to her.

To the west, she sees no lights. She's never been able to really see any of the cities, being on the backside of the mountain, but on clear nights, there would almost be a small glow from the West. Tonight, it is as dark as sin, as she gently holds the tiny Jesus from her mom's antique nativity scene in her hand, as the tears flow.

The first day of spring and it was 82 degrees. The sun dips towards the water, its glow, burnished breath upon her skin. The sky is so clear, the soft trailing puffs of clouds, spun air gathered around the tops of the trees like cotton candy. Lisa loves this time of day, somewhere between the first cool breeze that blows against the back of her neck like a lover's kiss, and the first stinging bite of the mosquitoes, marking their territory in blood, driving her in. Outside her home, cicadas will soon strike up the band, off in the distance, replacing the sound of lawnmowers that she only remembers now in her mind with the comfort of familiarity.

She hopes the mild winter and the hot Spring isn't a portent of another scorching summer, with lots of work to be done outside, hot brutal work, everything you touch, burning, sapping strength faster than she would have thought possible.

She never had air conditioning, being in the shadow of ancient trees with a nice evening breeze, but that's a moot point as the power's been out a while. At first, she thought it was just a line down after March's windstorm but it appears the grid itself has failed. Fortunately, there's a manual pump from the original settlers of this place for the well so she can still get water from the ground for drinking and the garden and she still has about 100 gallons stored in the barn in large plastic containers each with a few drops of bleach in them. But with little snowpack this last winter there's no guarantee there will be enough well water by mid-summer. Tending to the garden for food means many hours out in the open air, sun beating down as she catalogs each and every burning piece of earth in which she will pray something takes root. That's not something that she can do without adequate water. But she is thankful she didn't knock down the outhouse that was here when she first moved in, used as the last owners fixed the fire damage and made the home at least somewhat livable as a hunting shack.

There's no escaping that kind of heat. The sun rests atop an inverted tureen of hollow, muted air. Even as she grooms Taxi the horse, talking to him as she performs that little ritual, her words fade slowly and knowingly until they are lost in the murmur of shimmering heat as she puts her tools aside and gives in to windless defeat.

Finishing up, there isn't enough water; it seems, to cool her down. Both she and her horse drink down what water they have in reach, gulping down the liquid without taste or even cold until they finish it, the drops on her lips already dancing like water on a skillet as she headed back to the house.

There's a creek a short ride away. Tonight, when it cools down, she will ride down there for a dip, and make a decision. She misses being able to go canoeing on the water, but can't risk being seen, not knowing who yet lingers on her mountain and what their intentions would be. She does remember the last time she dared it. There had been a few thundershowers; just enough to raise up the water level above the level of her spirits. She grabbed the canoe and stepped into the stream the water yanking at the edge of that last bit of fear and hesitation, pulling her down, water fast and huge and furious. Once she picked up the paddle, there would be no going back, she had to be there, to see if for only a few minutes she was free or die trying, water in a place that's inside of us, water in a place that's somehow holy.

As she stepped into the canoe that day she held her breath and in the silence that followed, so did the water, tremendous and patient and waiting for her to make up her mind. And she hit the water with solemn abandon, simply in recognition of the life left in her, the air rushing from her lungs, supple muscles gathered into the forward motion of arms, and head and heart.

When she was done, she hid the canoe in the brush and hiked back home. She wonders if she will ever return to this land and if so, would the canoe still be there?

Tonight would be one last dip in the creek. Her work for the day is almost done and it is time to break free of it, the heat and the solidity of it weighing down even our sleep if we let it.

***

Even before she gets to the still waters of her evening she has made her decision. Last winter was exceptionally mild, and this summer looks to be a scorcher. If there is a fire of any size she would be trapped. The first summer after secession, there were no vacationers returning to the cabins within earshot and a short trail ride. Her neighbor John has gone silent and she dared not risk a drive to his home. In their last conversation, his voice had changed as if he had heard something he knew to be true, but would never be ready to believe. She didn't know if he was dead, Mother Mature being somewhat unforgiving of error in the woods, or if he had headed down into the Valley, risking it just to see if indeed life had returned to some semblance of normalcy, his grown children safe somewhere.

There's cloud cover coming in from the ocean, the temperature should drop for at least a couple of days. If she stays, there's plenty of grass in the meadow for Taxi but there would be nothing for winter. It's not just that her horse is family to her, her only companion throughout this last year but he's her only escape.

There's no way she can hike over the Nevada border, even though she's in better shape now than when she finished school.

She's going to make a run for it, or trot, if you will

Perhaps it's the heat outside that makes her bold, perhaps it's the heat within her. It's always the first jump into the unknown that is the hardest, that hesitant leap upward propelled by desire and only held back by the gravity of restraint. Once you are past that feeling of helpless weightlessness as you stop off into space, it gets easier. For life waits. It waits to come to you in the heat of the day, secret and swift, wearing air and water and blood and need that flow away like a garment revealing all that you knew. If you close your eyes to it you will see, drifting until the water grows tepid and the sound of future Cicadas is all that remains.

She's going to escape to the America she remembers, and hopes it will take her in. For it waits. It waits in the heated movement that is not the wind. It waits in a rush of roaring water; in a patient pool in the evening, where the hurts of the past are left lying upon a drifting and imponderable shore, washed clean in the heat of a yellow afternoon.

She figures if she stays away from the main road, she can make it in three to four days, and assuming no run-in with bears or Militia, she can pack out what she needs to survive as well as the cash she will need to find her new life.

Perhaps she'll ride out to find that everything she feared down in Cali did not come to be, that after the initial violence and upheaval, it settled into a self-sufficient land, where the citizens had what they wished for and she's been hiding in fear all for nothing.

In her heart, she is doubtful; the breakdown in the grid, the silence on the radio waves speaking volumes.

As she mentally makes a list of what she needs to pack up, she pauses for a moment, among the trees. She's reinforced in the smallness of her form next to their trunks, smiling as the branches separate her from the chatter of the world that echoes outside the woods. There is comfort in these trees, old and strong, even if scarred, their roots sunk deep into the ground becoming one with it, taking nourishment from it with a gravity of purpose we poor ground dwellers wouldn't understand.

The seasons are changing and a small sting of warm rain against her face tells her it's time to get going. The rain wakes her from her thoughts, a pinprick of fluid, each lance full of the promise of its remission, here one moment, then gone, like the tears of a child. One moment, there is the rumble of thunder, water released from above, then it's gone, fleeing southward on the wind, leaving behind only spent confetti of moisture on pale limbs that gather and drip into puddles that reflect the sky that only moments before had imprisoned them.

Leaning against the trees, sun glinting off of those small drops of water that cling to ancient wood, the secret whisper of the wind invisible to her and silent, asks of her - would we find the beauty in anything if we lived forever? Would the gems of thoughts and feelings and desire be so precious if we knew they would always be on our shelf? Or would they fall to the earth, trickling through our hands like water, evaporating on the cold ground, because we thought our hold on them was eternal?

She readies her home as if she is coming back to it. She realizes the improbability of that. She doesn't think Cali will suddenly go "sorry, we made a mistake can we rejoin the team?" She still can't believe Congress even bought off on the secession in the first place but for the incessant bleeding of money from federal coffers to a state that was being abandoned by industry as well as many of its legal citizens at a breakneck pace as it slid into bankruptcy.

So many memories here, she thinks as she grins at the antique "explosives" sign on the horse stall, the "Bee Happy" sign one of the local beekeepers gave her.

With dried food and water for the trip, not a lot but enough to keep her moving, her rifle, her revolver close by and her supplies in saddle bags, it was time to go.

She had some forest service maps from when she first moved here and had plotted out the trails she knew by heart out to an area that was going to be more "there be dragons".

There was a chance she could end up at a dead end, forced to get down to the road which could signal her doom. Once she was on Nevada soil, she'd bury the rifle. Getting shot or arrested by a Nevada native or LEO was not how she wanted to say "hi – can I stay here?"

***

She saddles up Taxi and with a wave, heads east using trails that parallel the road but at a safe distance, keeping out of the most difficult of terrain, but not within eye or earshot of the road. She wonders how it all got to this point. She should be enjoying life like most young people her age, not riding out from all she loves like some contestant in the "Hunger Games." But she knows that if she doesn't do something to save herself, no one else is going to help her.

In just a couple of generations, it seems the entire concept of being accountable to oneself has been undermined, ridiculed even. Self-reliance, the learning of skills that extend beyond a paycheck or a computer screen is treated as some archaic riposte of foolishness, unnecessary symbols of bygone days. Those that practice such skills are often perceived, not as practical or frugal, but as paranoid survivalists who should be viewed with fear and monitored by others.

If you're afraid to fail, you'll never try. If you give up, you just go back. The decision to hunker down and live off of her own work and efforts when Calexit happened may have been a foolish one and there has been more than one time when she has stood in tears in her empty meadow softly saying "why?" as the words catch in her teeth and tear. But she didn't give up even as she may have wept a tear of frustration as she discovered that often immitigable discrepancy between will and capabilities.

She figured she had to travel over forty miles. A horse in good condition could do that in a day in easier terrain. But Taxi had been mostly shuttered in the barn or munching grass in a meadow. She basically had a "couch potato" horse. That was going to mean it would likely take three days to travel that distance. There was a direct, and much shorter way, but the last few miles of it were in totally open country and she'd have to cross a fairly large high highway, likely covered with Militia. The longer way kept her in tree cover until she was much closer to the border.

She had ridden about five hours, stopping to relieve herself in the bushes and let Taxi drink from a small stream when she heard a noise. It was coming down from the trailhead, and it sounded bigger than a coyote or feral dog. Taxi heard it too and stopped, likely remembering the bear incident.

The sound continued towards her as she struggled to make out what it was, with a strained, listening attention. If it was Militia, and more than one of them, she was done, as she would likely take a bullet before she could get the second shot off. Better that than to be wounded, and then raped and left to die, things she'd heard from her neighbor had happened down in the cities when families tried to escape.

From the trees, a flock of birds took to the sky with a loud cry as a man came into view. He was wearing jeans and a flannel shirt, not the garb of any organized group but Lisa threw herself into the posture of a lunging fencer, aiming the revolver at his chest.

He slowly drew a small knife, holding it out to her, and gave her a grin saying "Miss, I think you won."

"What are you doing out here?" she says as he lowers the knife, stepping back from her slowly as she had done when she met the bear.

"I live in a small cabin up on the next ridge line. I was hunting for mushrooms as I'm getting low on meat and haven't seen much game in the last couple of weeks. I mean you no harm, but if you have any extra food it would be appreciated."

She looked into his eyes as a sailor might look at the sea, a watchful gaze that tries to see into what could be friend or adversary, making a decision on which a life depends as to the force and direction of nature's thrust if it chooses to attack.

She lowers her revolver and reaches into her saddle bag for a handful of protein bars.

She looks at the man and says, "I have very little but I will share what I have. I'm going to toss them to the side of the trail, please step off the trail and let me pass before you pick them up. If you don't, please remember I have a firearm."

"Thank you." he says with eyes that were twenty years older than his form, as she carefully walks Taxi past him as she continues up the trail.

***

That night, as she lay in her sleeping bag, her food supplies high up in a tree downwind of her camp and Taxi happily munching on some fresh grass, she realizes how close she came to shooting him. She prays he is okay as she realizes how much she has missed seeing other people. She is normally happier alone. She had found few people in her life that can be content with time alone like she does, most preferring the excitement of crowds, the adulation of the unknown, look at me, watch me, head towards the lights and the noise. That was not for her. She can't find peace in that, though it haunts the edges of it, as if it almost knows what it is like, but can't give in to it. The peace isn't just the silence, it's not the trees or the animals or the water. It's all the senses wrapped up in one as she breathes it in deep from the musty confines of a sleeping bag as she lies under the stars. That smell that has a color to her, almost green, not the longing green of envy or the gray-green of aromatic herbs, but the green of clarity, a smell that makes her weak for childhood, when every morning came with this sense of freedom and purity.

She is ready now to find others like herself, and hope they will offer her a welcome.

A day and a half later, she's within a few miles of what she believes is the Nevada border, there is still one road nearby that she will get closer to than she wishes as she travels those last miles, but in the early morning dim light, she knew she would continue. Stars still glinted overhead as the sun rose ahead of her.

She is going to continue heading downhill and east to American soil or die trying. California was her home but her roots are rooted deep in the freedom of American soil and one way or another, she would return to it.

By mid-morning on day three, she was in the high desert, few trees to shield her, making sure she stayed well away from the road. At one point, she came to a rough barbed wire fence, one built for cattle, of which she saw none in sight. Having no other option, she got her ax and chopped out an opening big enough for them to pass through. In the far distance was a small house. As she approached it a young man, a teen really, looked at her, probably surprised to see an attractive but very dirty redhead on a horse in his yard, even as he had a shotgun at his side.

"Miss?" he said.

Lisa replied, "Where am I?"

He said, "You are a mile from Hot Springs, Nevada. Reno's just over the hills there." Looking at her with eyes full of concern, not of fear he said, "You're not the first person to escape Cali this way; if you need transportation into town my dad is the Sheriff and he will take you someplace safe. I'll take care of your horse until you know what you want to do. Welcome back to the United States Miss." She could do nothing but cry. She should have been lost in wonderment, but like people in fairy tales where everything seems to work out in the end (unless you are the witch) she was too exhausted to be astonished.

She simply got off of her horse, laid down her weapons on the ground and hugged him, looking at their family truck in the driveway as Cinderella probably looked at that pumpkin coach, never doubting that it was real.

The Farm

Eaton Rapids Joe

Prologue

Moonbeam signed a sweeping set of legislation into law on his first day of office.

He spearheaded the drive for a new form of government for Cali in the latest election and was rewarded by a 65% margin of victory over his closest rival. Support was largest in urban centers and in affluent suburban areas. Support from rural areas was tepid at best.

The key points of the new platform included completely decoupling from the United States economy, rapidly transitioning to a "sustainable, low-carbon" economy and providing "justice for the oppressed". Lastly, but most importantly, was setting up a new parliamentary government.

Pursuant to those points, Cali issued its own currency, the 'Callor' which was initially pegged at 1.35 dollars-to-the-Callor.

Wages were frozen so every worker received a 35% pay raise. Universal Basic Income was granted to all residents who were willing to submit fingerprints, retina scans, a DNA sample and accept an RFID implant. All bank accounts and assets were reduced by 26% to transition existing dollars to Callors.

Other actions included a tax on the surface area of all roofs commensurate with the income tax that would be collected if they were covered with solar panels with the power feeding back into the grid at retail rates.

To boost employment and to save the environment, all synthetic herbicides and pesticides were banned. The think-tanks at UC Davis calculated that hand weeding and manual methods of pest control would provide employment for more than six million workers.

Military bases were leased to the Chinese for a five-year period after which they would be absorbed by Cali. The rent was paid in an undisclosed amount of gold, which Cali used to buy access to Colorado River water for the duration. Environmentalists calculated that the solar panels on roofs would provide enough electricity to desalinate the equivalent amount of water in five years.

What could go wrong?

Five years later...

Chapter One

Chad looked up from the post hole he was digging as the sound of footsteps approached him. Some things never change in farming. There are never enough fence posts, gates, hoses, or hours in the day.

It was Miguel. He was not surprised. Miguel was the oldest *student* in his crew of ten. Cali mandated twenty-six years of compulsory education. Starting at age sixteen, academic underperformers (problem students), were shunted into work crews to *educate* them.

As a farmer, Chad was forced to take twelve *students* every growing season. He was allowed to return two of them. Chad had spent four years in the military and was familiar with all of the games.. He quickly figured out which two were likeliest to give him problems and wasted no time getting them off his farm. The sooner they were gone, the sooner everybody else settled down and got to business.

***

Miguel had elected himself as crew-boss, and nobody had contested it. Miguel was almost twenty-six and was about to age-out of the system.

Six of the crew were male and four were female. All of the females had hormonal implants to prevent pregnancy.

Miguel led off, "You aren't feeding us enough."

Chad put down the post driver. "I am feeding you exactly what the book says I must feed you."

Miguel said, "I talked to Ricky who was on your crew last year. He said you fed them more than the book said."

Chad sighed. This came up every year. "I can feed you more if you work more. If you work by 'the book' I will feed you by 'the book'. Last year Ricky's crew worked when the temperature was above 75 degrees. More work, more food."

Cali upgraded the original RFID tags to include biometric tracking information. Bona-Brown passed laws that prevented farmers from working "students" when the temperature was above 75 degrees Fahrenheit. In central Cali, that was most of the daylight hours during the summer.

The chips would beep if the wearer's heart rate went above 120 bpm and the temperature was above 75 degrees. If the wearer said "Play," the chip shut down. If the wearer said "Work," then a crew of law enforcement personnel would come on the run.

Miguel thought about that for a minute: the temperature was 85, but it was a dry heat. The boss was working in it. He was working steadily, but not quickly. Word among the students who had been at the farm before was that Chad took care of his people. On the flip side, he was ruthless to those who fucked with him.

Miguel said, "I ain't promising anything, but what needs to be done?"

"I need a row of fence posts driven from here to that pine tree," Chad said, pointing to a tree sixty feet away. "The fence posts need to be six feet apart and they need to be driven in at least two feet." "Then I need a circle of fence posts driven here," pointing at the scratches in the dirt, "so it looks like the number 6. You can cheat a little bit on the depth of the posts at the top of the six, but the posts in the circle absolutely have to be two feet deep…or more."

Miguel looked around. It was the oddest thing he had ever seen. The boss wanted a sixty-foot run of fence in the middle of nowhere. It started nowhere and ended nowhere.

"When does it have to be done?" Miguel asked.

"I need it done by August first, but sooner is better." Chad said.

"Whadda we get if we do this?" Miguel asked.

"I ain't promising anything," Chad said, "but I wouldn't be surprised if there were some eggs to go with the oatmeal at breakfast a couple of mornings next week."

Miguel looked up at the sun. "You got any problem with us getting started after six in the evening, when it is a little cooler?"

Chad said, "It is yours to manage. I only want to be here to make sure it is done to my satisfaction and to get to know the crew."

One of the other changes since Calexit had been the loss of automation. Izzo Farms used to have 160 acres of producing citrus trees. Twelve years ago Chad had an attachment on the three point hitch that would have driven six-foot Mesquite poles two feet into the ground in less than two minutes. It was not like that anymore.

Calexit had been devastating to the market for premium fruits. Facing bankruptcy, Izzo Farms grubbed out the fruit trees and sold them a chipper for "sustainable energy". Then they converted their acreage to a potato-wheat-cabbage-hay-hay rotation. The potato-wheat-cabbage portion of the rotation was two full calendar years. The two years of hay were necessary to return fertility to the soil and to break the disease pest cycle.

The timing of the change had been lucky. Cali had fifty-five million citizens and quickly learned that foreign exchange markets are not impressed by governments with socialist leanings. The Callor slide from 1C-to-$1.35, to parity, and then then to 4C-to-dollar. With that devaluing of its currency, Cali was hard pressed to feed herself.

It took a couple of evenings for the crew to beat the fence posts in, but finally the strange shaped run of fence was put in to Chad's satisfaction. Chad brought work gloves for the crew the first evening because the youngest ones never had them. Half the crew was Latin and chatted away among themselves the whole time. Chad had never thought it was important to let the students know he was a fluent speaker of Spanish… Listening to the conversation, he agreed that Mardi, his wife, was indeed a fine looking woman.

***

Chad, Mardi, Miguel, and Bonita sat on the front porch of the house. It was 6:00 pm, and the temperatures were still above 90.

Before Calexit, Chad and Mardi would have been inside, where it was air conditioned.

After Calexit, the power from the mandatory, roof-top solar panels was shunted to the energy collection farms in the Bay area, the sprawling barrios of greater Los Angeles-San Diego and the government compounds of Sacramento. The cyber industry of the Bay area was the main source of hard currency for Cali and got the lion's share of energy to run the computers (and air conditioners) while the barrios were always on the verge of exploding into open warfare due to the lack of both. All that said, there was enough power leftover to make ice for their tea.

Bonita and Miguel were not a *couple*, per se. Bonita was the lead female even though she was only 20 years old. The four rocked and fanned, as they planned the next day's activities.

"Looks like another hot one." Mardi said. Mardi ran the administrative side of the farm. Chad freely admitted that he had the better end of the deal. The paperwork had been a burden before Calexit. Under the watchful eye of the eco-terrorists inhabiting Sacramento, it had turned into a 12-hour-a-day job.

Miguel said, "The young ones are getting restless. They are playing grab-ass and getting into fights. It is even too hot to work off-the-clock." Miguel used the term from before the RFID chip days. "We all miss the extra calories and protein."

Chad said, "Well… There is something we can do but it is not exactly by-the-book. I don't mind trying it out with a couple of people who can keep their mouths shut."

Both Bonita and Miguel perked up. Miguel said, "It is my job as lead to check things out. What do you have in mind?"

Bonita said, "Count me in, too. I need to be sure it is good for the girls."

Chad said, "Wait here. I'll be right back."

A minute later he came back out onto the porch. He was carrying a gun. "Before you get excited, you need to know that this is a perfectly legal pellet gun. You pump it up like this." He demonstrated. "You put in a pellet like this. And then…" he pointed it out into the dry yard, "you shoot it like this."

A puff of dust erupted in front of a starling pecking at the ground thirty yards way. The bird squawked and took flight. "Every starling has about as much edible meat on it as a hotdog. Every sparrow is about a half hotdog. They aren't hard to hunt. The hard thing is shooting enough of them to make a meal."

Chad handed the pellet gun to Miguel. "See if you can hit the fence post over there." Miguel pumped it up ten times the way he had seen Chad do it. He loaded a pellet. Aimed. Fired and missed.

"Let me try." Bonita said. She pumped it ten times. She loaded a pellet. She used the railing of the porch for a steady rest. She let out half a breath and eased back on the trigger. The pinging sound of a metallic impact came back.

Chad said, "As you both can see, it is not a race to see how fast you can squeeze the trigger. And shooting is something that women can do as well as men."

Miguel asked, "Why is using this to hunt birds not exactly by-the-book?"

Chad answered, "Two reasons. One is that we need to apply for a permit to control any pests. It takes a month for Sacramento to grant permission and these birds will be a hundred miles away by then. The other reason is that these are lead pellets. Lead is a prohibited substance in Cali and it is a felony to possess it in any form."

Miguel said, "It is going to take me forever to get enough birds to eat."

Mardi smirked. She knew what was coming.

Chad said, "Thing is… I got two of these pellet guns. I figured I would let the girls use one and the boys use the other. As soon as you have ten birds between the two teams we will cook them up and add them to dinner. The way I see it, eating meat regularly tends to make people forget about the fine print that don't matter."

Bonita made a point of asking Mardi for tips on hunting the birds. Mardi coached her. She told Bonita about bait and cover. She told her about decoys and fields of fire. Bonita passed this wisdom to her girl team, they soundly beat the boys in the number of birds they brought to the table, at least the first few times. But the boys watched the girls and they learned so the competition became more evenly matched after that.

Chapter Two

"Do it over." Chad said.

Miguel said, "You have got to be kidding me! We just picked the bugs off of 3,000 feet of potatoes."

"Do it over." Chad said.

Miguel stared at him.

Chad said, "Step over here so we can talk about it." They quietly walked away from the work crew.

Once they were fifty yards away from the crew Miguel exclaimed, "Are you nuts! We just finished those rows."

Chad said, "Your crew was sloppy. You were sloppy. I walked those rows. There are still plants with bugs. You can't miss them. They are orange. There are bugs on the ground. Those bugs will just crawl back up on the potatoes and lay more eggs."

Chad pointed, "The bugs on the ground mean that your crew was sloppy handling the tarps. You are supposed to drag the tarps down the row. The crew shakes the plants. When there are a lot of bugs on the tarps your crew is supposed to *pour* the bugs off the tarp and into the buckets. Then you put the covers on the buckets. Lather. Rinse. Repeat."

Chad continued, "People will perform to your expectation. The way to communicate what you <u>expect</u> is by what you <u>inspect</u>. I inspected the rows you claimed to have de-bugged. They do not meet my expectations. Do them over. Tell your crew that I directed you to inspect each row when they think they are done. Call me when you are sure they will pass my inspection." With that, Chad walked off.

Four hours later Chad walked the rows with Miguel. As he walked, Chad explained "We are not allowed to use chemicals. Sacramento tells us how many pounds of potatoes we must ship each year. That number is higher than what I shipped when I was allowed to use chemical fertilizers and synthetic pesticides."

"Missing any bugs leaves breeding stock for the next generation."

"The other thing you have to consider is what we do with the bugs. Some farms squish them and use them for fertilizer. We do something different."

"Did you ever wonder where those eggs you eat at breakfast come from? They come from ducks. Do you know what ducks are? They are machines that turn bugs into eggs. Those potato bugs become duck food."

"But why should I have to inspect my people's work? It is like I don't trust them." Miguel asked.

"You are looking at it the wrong way." Chad said. "How did you feel when I inspected the rows and they were good? You know that I am a tough inspector." Miguel thought for a minute. "I guess I felt like I beat you...that I beat the game."

Chad asked, "Was that a good feeling?"

Miguel said, "Well, yeah."

Chad continued, "So how do you think the crew feels when they tell you they finished a row and are ready to have you inspect it…and you cannot find any bugs?"

Miguel said, "Like they did a good job. Maybe a little bit proud."

"Damned straight they feel that way." Chad said, "They know it is not your idea. They know that I directed you to do that, so they not only beat your expectations, they beat mine."

"And tomorrow morning there will be three eggs at breakfast for everybody who wants them. More bugs means more eggs. Not from me, but from the ducks."

"Sacramento is sending the welfare people to check out our operation, and we have a problem." Mardi said at dinner later that evening.

"Why's that?" asked Chad.

"The crew weighs too much. I bet they have all gained at least ten pounds since they started." Mardi said. "You know that is going to raise a bunch of questions, starting with the government assuming that we are hording food."

Indeed, that was a problem.

***

Chad had the crew knock off work an hour before dark the following evening. He had something he wanted to show them. "I am going to teach you the fine art of tight-lining for bullheads tonight. Not only that, but I am going to teach you how to make fish traps." Chad told the group. "The aqueduct between here and East Orosi is filled with small fish and crayfish we are going to catch a bunch of them."

Chad showed the crew how to make fish traps from old bicycle wheels, PVC conduit and poultry netting. He cautioned, "These traps are illegal but they catch tons of fish…we just need to bait them with bird guts and road kill. The other thing I am going to do is to teach you to catch fish with a line-and-hook so you have a cover story for all of the fish you trap."

"You need to take turns doing this at night. Everybody knows bullheads bite best at night." Chad said. "I am willing to let the two who go fishing sleep in a little bit but the rest of the crew needs to pick up the slack because we need to catch a butt-load of fish in the next week."

For the first time, Houa Yang piped up, "Count me in."

Early on, Chad had asked Miguel what Houa's story was.

Miguel said, "Houa used to go to some place called Cal Poly but they threw him out."

Chad asked, "Do you know why they threw him out? He is twenty-four and this is his first summer of farm work."

Miguel said, "He told me that the school got tired of his shit and threw him out."

That had Chad puzzled. You did not stay on the academic track until you were twenty-four if you were a trouble maker. "Exactly what did he say?"

Miguel said, "You know how those college kids like to use fancy words. He said, 'The school rejected my feces.'"

Chad, mulling it over, said, "Feces, feces, feces... thesis? Twenty-four at Cal Poly and he was probably working on his Ph.D... And they dumped him because they did not like his thesis." Chad decided he needed to keep a closer eye on Houa. He was quiet but he was probably just being cautious and was scoping out his new environment.

A couple of nights later Houa and Brigid, who hailed from Marin county, brought in a load of twenty pounds of assorted fish in the wee hours of the morning. Chad got up to help them process the fish.

That gave him time to talk to him.

"Houa" Chad said, "I heard you used to be a student at Cal Poly. Is that true?"

"Yup. Sure enough boss." Houa replied.

"How did you get in?" Chad asked. "I thought Moonbeam signed an Executive Order that every school had to have a student population that reflected the demographics of Cali."

Houa said, "Well, boss, there was a way around that. Do you remember when Moonbean signed the Executive Order allowing three adults to join in matrimony?"

"Yes." said Chad. "I just thought that was some kind of big-city weirdness."

"Actually, the Asian community was pushing for that law." Houa said. "The point was buried in the tail-feathers of the order. All members of the family were allowed to claim the national origins of all members of the marriage. My mom and dad married a Latina woman. Not only am I Hmong, I am legally a Mexi-Calian and received a priority slot for Cal Poly."

Chad just shook his head. Just when you thought it could not get any weirder...

"Hey boss," Houa said after they finished processing the last of the fish, "what do you want me to do with the offal?"

Chad said, "Where would YOU put the offal if you were trying to hide the fact that you were catching and eating these fish?"

"Well, fish guts stink so I would put it east of the houses. In the heat of the day, when it would stink the worst the thermals would rise...so I would make sure it were at a higher elevation than the ranch. I would want it in a gully so buzzards would not home in on the…and so you would not see it if coyotes tore into it."

"Why do you ask?" Houa concluded.

"The really smart people from Sacramento, the ones who have caused this mess, are coming here in a week or two for a spot check. There is going to be a problem because you are eating too well. We need to give them a plausible reason for the weight gain of all of the students." Chad said.

"If they don't get a believable reason then they will roll this farm into the collective and the crew with it. Mardi and I will either be put into prison or given the Universal Basic Income and placed into the barrio."

"What do you need to have us do boss?"

"When they ask you what you have been eating, let it slip that members of the crew have been fishing in the aqueduct. If they push…and they might, take them out to where you have been "hiding" the fish guts. With any luck, the stink will convince them that they don't need to do any more investigation.

He made a huge, elaborate wink. "Consider it done, boss. And what do you want us to do with all of this fish?"

"Houa, I think you should have a party. Invite your buddies from the other farms around here. Eat until you puke. Nothing like generating some supporting evidence. I will pony up the kettles and LP burners." Chad said.

Chapter Three

Original Email

To: Magdalene Izzo
Izzo Farms of East Orosi
Head of Records
From: Lois Gale-Leinhart-Diaz
The Cali Department of Education
Agent, Enforcement Division
Date: June 27, 2031

Mz Izzo:
Routine audit of your records indicates multiple
discrepancies and probable non-compliance issues.
Interviews of previous students entrusted to your care
resulted in findings. Based on those findings, The Cali
Department of Education filed multiple grievances on
behalf of those students.
Full disclosure of all records that may pertain to
students hosted since 2021 are required.
Certified records demanded pursuant to Cali
"Education Opportunity Law" 2021-3.1415.9265
Fines will be levied if copies are not delivered in ten
business days.
The Cali Department of Education
Agent-in-Charge
Lois Gale-Leinhart-Diaz
****

Email reply, history redacted

To: Lois Gale-Leinhart-Diaz
The Cali Department of Education
Agent, Enforcement Division

From: Magdalene Izzo
    Izzo Farms of East Orosi
    Head of Records
Date: June 27, 2031

Full copies of mandatory compliance databases respectfully attached. These are the same files we submit every tax year.

Best regards,

-Mardi
****

Email reply, history redacted

To: Magdalene Izzo
    Izzo Farms of East Orosi
    Head of Records
From: Lois Gale-Leinhart-Diaz
    The Cali Department of Education
    Agent, Enforcement Division
Date: June 30, 2031

Mz Izzo:
Routine audit of your records indicates multiple discrepancies and probable non-compliance issues. We already have the files you emailed. We need <u>certified</u> copies. Further, this letter is officially notifying you that we demand ALL records, including emails, related to students hosted by you from 2021 to the present.

*Fines will be levied in nine business days if
compliance is not satisfactory.
The Cali Department of Education
Agent-in-Charge
Lois Gale-Leinhart-Diaz*
****

Email reply, history redacted

*To: Lois Gale-Leinhart-Diaz
    The Cali Department of Education
    Agent, Enforcement Division
From: Magdalene Izzo
    Izzo Farms of East Orosi
    Head of Records
Date: June 30, 2031*

*Per guidelines established by University of California-
Davis, automated software was installed on our
business computer to automatically delete records in
accordance with U-of-C-Davis record retention
guidelines.
You have all of the records that are available to us.
Best regards,
-Mardi*
****

Email reply, history redacted

*To: Magdalene Izzo
    Izzo Farms of East Orosi
    Head of Records
From: Lois Gale-Leinhart-Diaz
    The Cali Department of Education*

Agent, Enforcement Division
Date: July 1, 2031

Mz Izzo:
Your file has been marked as "Hostile and non-cooperative." Cali "Justice for All" Code 2022-1.4142.1356 is activated.
All computational devices (computers, laptops, tablets, smartphones, etc.) are subpoenaed and will be collected by bonded subcontractors at our convenience.
Withholding devices is a class one felony.
You have eight business day to comply with the records request before fines are levied.
The Cali Department of Education
Agent-in-Charge
Lois Gale-Leinhart-Diaz
****

Email, History redacted

To: Lois Gale-Leinhart-Diaz
    The Cali Department of Education
    Agent, Enforcement Division
From: Magdalene Izzo
    Izzo Farms of East Orosi
    Head of Records
Date: July 1, 2031

Your email dated July 1, 2031 explains the presence of the subcontractors who showed up June 30 and presented us with court orders demanding our computing devices.

All devices were handed over in compliance with the order.

To save you a little bit of time, our farm suffered a massive electrical storm with multiple, direct lightning strikes in 2028 that destroyed all electrical devices. The devices collected by the subcontractors were purchased new at that time and they contain no data from before then.

Also, since you collected all devices we are not able to comply with your demand for any records nor are we able to comply with Cali "Education Opportunity Law" 2021-3.1415.9265 record requirements regarding "Continuity of Records".

What do you want me to do?

Best regards,

-Mardi

****

Email, History redacted

To: Lois Gale-Leinhart-Diaz
The Cali Department of Education
Agent, Enforcement Division
From: Magdalene Izzo
Izzo Farms of East Orosi
Head of Records
Date: July 2, 2031

Hello!

*We are approaching the July 4 Holiday weekend
(Summer Solstice, celebrated) and I need to know what
you want us to do to comply with your requirements.
Best regards,
-Mardi*
****

Email reply, history redacted
*To: Magdalene Izzo
    Izzo Farms of East Orosi
    Head of Records
From: Lois Gale-Leinhart-Diaz
    The Cali Department of Education
    Agent, Enforcement Division
Date: July 7, 2031*

*Mz Izzo:
The tenor of your communications and your continued
intransigence has been duly noted in your file.
In light of your confession that you have no intention
of complying with Cali "Education Opportunity Law"
2021-3.1415.9265, a court order has been issued
mandating your presence in Sacramento the week of
July 14, 2031 for administrative hearings and
sentencing.
The Cali Department of Education
Agent-in-Charge
Lois Gale-Leinhart-Diaz*

Chapter Four

The air conditioning was a problem for Mardi. She
was wearing her yellow sundress and on the farm they

no longer had AC so the now-unfamiliar feeling of conditioned air made her feel like she was sitting in a freezer. You cannot take much luggage when your ride to the bus station is on the back of an ancient Suzuki dirt bike so she didn't have a sweater or warmer clothing. Chad had borrowed the Suzuki from their neighbor and had to return it, so she rode behind him as he navigated the cratered roads into Visalia.

The waiting room in the Cali Department of Education, Enforcement Division had a sign that read, "The wheels of justice turn slowly, but grind exceedingly fine." The staff of the Enforcement Division lived by that motto. Mardi logged into the kiosk at 7:45 am on Monday and sat with the huddled masses of supplicants all day Monday…and Tuesday…and Wednesday. Her name was finally called on Thursday at 10:30 am.

Mardi sat on the plain, vinyl covered chair across the table from the fabled Lois Gale-Leinhart-Diaz and her enforcer Terry Branch.

Lois was a fleshy woman--the buttons on her clothes creaked and strained like a wooden sailing vessel being driven by a storm. She shopped at the most exclusive, vanity boutiques. Even though her dress label said that she was a size fourteen (going on sixteen), the same dress from any other shop would have a twenty-two on the label.

Her face was florid, giving evidence to a penchant for, and access to, ample amounts of well marbled beef, sour cream and multiple carafes of chardonnay.

A slightly sour smell exuded from her in spite of the heroic efforts of the air conditioning.

Terry, the enforcer, was wearing a three-piece suit. Terry was pushing sixty and pushing it hard. He fancied himself a lady's man and sported a big, bushy mustache. He radiated bullshit and belligerence and was given to over-arching statements. Lois found him a useful idiot.

Lois started out by placing a document on the table. She said, "This document was generated from the content of your emails. I know you have been away from your home for many days and I am sure you are eager to get back. You can be on your way back home if you sign this document."

Mardi started to read the document.

Lois, thinking of lunch, said, "There is no reason to read it. It is exactly like I said. Just sign it."

Mardi looked up. "I don't see how a half-dozen short emails can take up twenty pages of text. I want to read it to see what got added."

Mardi's eyes returned to the document. She read, slowly.

Mardi started reading out loud.

"Do you have to do that?" Terry said. "It's irritating."

Mardi said, "Kind of irritates me, too." And continued reading…

"Potential penalties for stated crimes include fines, incarceration, cede title of property to proxy of the Agent's choosing, servitude even punishable by death…"

"Nope. I am not signing." Mardi said. "I'm just a simple Polish girl from Cheboygan, Michigan but you don't need a law degree to see this is a raw deal."

"What can you tell me about these supposed violations you are accusing our operation of?" Mardi asked.

Lois glowered. The early, and long, lunch she had been looking forward to had been delayed.

"The violations are almost too many to number." Lois said. "A repeated violation is the frequent shortage of WIFI signal. As you know The Cali Department of Education takes the education of our youth very seriously and you agreed to provide educational opportunities (including WIFI) when you took the students."

"For one thing," Mardi responded, "We did not 'take' the students. You forced us to provide room and board for twelve of them."

"For another thing, I am pretty familiar with the Education Handbook. I do not remember seeing anything about a WIFI requirement. What page is it on?" Mardi concluded.

Lois looked over at Terry. He fiddled with his tablet, cleared his throat and said, "That requirement is on page 783."

Mardi looked confused. "But the Handbook is only 450 pages long. How can the requirement be on page 783?"

Lois smirked. "The Department of Education has panels of experts who meet. They interpret the rules and break them down into observable actions. They publish those interpretations as series of addendums to the Handbook. Clearly, this is in one of those addendums."

Mardi said, "But you don't publish them?"

Lois said, "They are available through the Freedom of Information Act."

"How would I know to ask for them?" Mardi asked.

"That is not my problem." Lois responded. "We are documenting your non-compliances in this meeting and it is beyond the scope of why we are here to re-engineer the Department's policies. So, back to the WIFI outages."

"When did these outages occur?" Mardi asked.

"Most notably during the summer of 2026. Every student from summer, 2026 testified that there were extended WIFI outages."

"Testified…what did you do, threaten these kids with jail unless they came up with some dirt on us?" Mardi was starting to get pissed.

"Terry, enter into the record that Mz Izzo is hostile and uncooperative. Mz Izzo, for your information, the students were sworn in and depositions were recorded. It is standard process." Lois said, looking more reptilian by the minute.

Mardi realized that Lois intended to make her angry and lose control. Mardi took a half minute to compose herself…a quick Hail Mary and Prayer to St Augustine helped.

"2026 is the year the valley the electrical storms. As I told you in the emails, all our electronics were fried. That included the router. We were not the only ones. Most people had to wait for over a month to get a new router." Mardi said.

Lois said, "We are not here to listen to excuses. We are here to verify noncompliance."

Mardi asked, "When was the addendum that includes page 783 published? I could see the Department publishing something like that after the fact."

Terry looked it up. "It was published in 2026 so it applies to that summer."

Mardi asked, "What month in 2026? Summer is half way through the year."

Terry's face flushed. "November." He had seen that it was November before he had stated that "so it applies to that summer" and had been caught.

The "interview" was being recorded on video and he hated to leave evidence that he was sloppy.

Lois tried a slightly different tack. "I am not conceding that the requirement did not apply to the summer of 2026. That is for the panel of experts to decide. It does, clearly, apply to the time period between November 2026 and the present, and there are multiple WIFI failures during that period. What is your response, Mz Izzo?"

"We don't control the electrical power on our farm." Mardi replied. "As you know, the Cali Power Board installed smart electrical distribution panels in every building in Cali. During periods of peak power draw our domestic circuits shut down and that includes the WIFI."

Shivering in the AC, Mardi knew where that power had gone.

"If The Cali Department of Education, Enforcement Division has issues with WIFI uptime then they should take it up with The Cali Power Board."

Lois said, "For the video record, Mz Izzo is being a smarmy, smart-ass."

***

Late that afternoon, Lois said, "The most serious charges are that you failed to meet your production quotas for several years running. You did not just miss them, you missed them by a mile."

Mardi asked, "What are the years in question?"

Terry Branch answered, "Notably the years 2026 and 2027. You delivered less than 10% of your quota."

Mardi, "I don't see why this is a concern of The Cali Department of Education, Enforcement Division. We squared this with the The Cali Department of Food Security while it was happening."

Lois said, "You are not asking the questions here. I am. We are establishing a pattern of flouting official Cali authority. That would make your acceptance of these students fraudulent and verify that you were putting the moral development of these students at risk. These are very serious charges."

Mardi said, "There was no water in the aqueduct in 2026 and 2027. You cannot grow potatoes and cabbage in a desert without water."

Lois said, "It is not documented that there was no water in the aqueduct. Do you care to substantiate that?" Gale-Leinhart-Diaz was hoping to catch Mardi in more falsehoods.

Mardi said, "We had three years of low snow-pack in the western Sierras. The water has to come from somewhere. They shut down the water from the Colorado River. We might have been able to tap into that, but there was no water from there, either."

Lois said, "That did not matter. We had desalinization plants up and running."

"We had some desalinization plants running." Mardi said "Enough to feed water to the fifty million people in San Diego/LA. Another thing the bright boys over looked was the fact that you cannot reverse the flow in an open aqueduct. You cannot pump water 400 feet uphill using infrastructure designed for gravity flow."

"There was no water in the aqueduct until 2028 when we renegotiated the leasing of the military bases to the Chinese." Mardi said.

Lois looked at the wall clock. "For the video record, it is now 5:30 pm. Mz Magdalene Izzo, Izzo Farms of East Orosi, Head of Records is directed to return at 10:15 tomorrow morning for preliminary sentencing."

***

Email

To: Erica Holder-Washington
The Cali Department of Education
Executive Director, Enforcement Division
From: Lucinda Yang-Gomez
The Cali Department of Food Security
Director, Central Valley
Date: July 17, 2031   9:15 pm

Call off your attack dog. Do not prosecute Izzo Farms of East Orosio.
Izzo Farms is in the top two percent of farms for compliance-to-quota.

Cali is on the brink of food riots. This next harvest is critical. Izzo Farms is one of the first operations to harvest and unrest in the agriculture sector will disrupt the entire 2031 harvest. We cannot afford to have any food rot in the field.
Calorie availability has fallen to 1800 Calories per person-day. Contracts with China for grain delivery are on hold pending verification of sufficient collateral.
Repeat. Do not prosecute. Do not harass. Return all electronic devices.
Confirmation of receipt, understanding and compliance with this email is required per authorities granted by PM Bona-Brown.
Copying, forwarding or otherwise replicating this email is forbidden. This email will auto-delete twenty-four hours from when it is opened.
Have a nice day
Yang-Gomez

The trouble with coyotes and raccoons is that they think they are smart when they are merely crafty. They start thinking they are the apex predator when in fact they are in the middle of the food chain.

Lois Gale-Leinhart-Diaz was, at heart, a coyote.

At 10:00 am she slid a card across the table to Terry Branch. It said, "Turn off the video recorder."

Terry stood up, stretched and nonchalantly placed his hands in his pockets as he walked over to the corner with the video recorder. He was tall enough to reach up and press the on/off button. The bright green LED slowly faded.

Lois exploded. "This is complete and utter bullshit! Fucking 'Ivory Tower' executive director has no fucking idea how the world works."

Terry asked, "What's going on?" He had never seen his boss loser her cool like this.

"Fucking Executive Director of Enforcement just told me to let the Izzo bitch off the hook." Lois spat. "Those people on the top floor have no idea how hard my job is. The only thing that makes it doable is to put the fear of God in the rabble's heart. You get something on these people, you put your boot on their throat and you never let up. The only thing they respect is power and the only way to prove you have power is to use it."

Lois sat quietly for a minute. "Terry, we are going off the reservation on this one. She will never notice that the green light is off. We are doing this to protect the Department, to protect the fucking cunt who sits in the Executive Director's office. Just follow my lead…and leave the fucking video recorder off." Terry just nodded.

Ten minutes later Mardi walked into the office. She suspected that she was the first appointment of the day and she had been left in the waiting room to "show her how unimportant she was". She was correct.

Lois started, "We have decided to grant you clemency. You are on probation for the next five years. You will be subjected to random audits and spot checks. You may not leave Tulare County without our advance permission and we require two weeks-notice to process your out-of-county travel request. You may leave."

Mardi asked, "When will you release our computers and other devices?"

Lois gave a causal wave of her hand. "I believe that you can collect them from the evidence room on Monday or you can wait until we mail them to you."

Mardi asked, "And when would they be mailed?"

Lois said, "Probably before the end of the month. That is not in my silo."

Lois said, "You have five minutes to exit the property or I will have you charged with loitering. You may leave know. Have a great day." Lois said it with a sugary-sweet voice and a brittle smile, leaving no doubt that Izzo's troubles were just beginning.

After Mardi left, Lois told Terry to turn the video camera back on.

The possibility that the power switch was a dummy and that high definition recordings of the event had been permanently stored in server farms in Cupertino, Mountain View and a dooms-day, continuity-of-government site in Grass Valley, Cali never occurred to them. Nor did the fact that the key word fields of those recordings were automatically populated by the "resource scheduling" software, the voice recognition software and the voice-to-text software.

Those recordings were accessible to all officials, Executive Director and higher.

Chapter Five

Mardi and Chad leaned back in their chairs on the front porch. Their feet were on the rail. A small libation of Cali Whiskey and Branch Water was at hand.

"Thanks for picking me up in Visalia. I did not know if you would make it in time." Mardi said.

"Ya, no sweat." Chad said. "That's what we do. At least Juan had a Burley cart, otherwise bringing home the computers would have been a real chore."

As it was, the Suzuki dirt bike had not been the friendliest of towing vehicles. It was a racing bike with a very narrow power band and stiff-as-hell springs. Two passengers went a long way to softening the ride, but two passengers raised the center of gravity. Lack of attention by the driver could result in the bike pulling a wheelie that would pitch both people off the back end of the bike….even in second gear. Pulling a trailer only exacerbated the bike wanting to go ass-over-teakettle.

"So how was it that you were able to get the computers before Monday?" Chad asked. "You got me curious."

Mardi said, "I ran into a custodian mopping in the cafeteria. I asked him where the evidence room was. I wanted to scout it out before I made a decision. He told me it was in the basement, something I would have figured out if I had taken the time to think about it. So, I went down to the basement."

"And then…" Chad prompted. Like many guys he liked the shorter version of the story.

"Well, one of the guys in the evidence room noticed my Detroit Tigers ball cap. Turns out he is a HUGE fan of an old show called Magnum P.I. He wanted to know what it would take to buy it."

"I told him that if he liked it that much I would just GIVE it to him. After all, to me it is only a hat."

"After that, it was like I was his favorite niece. It was like I had made his month."

"Not only did they redeem our 'evidence', they gave me some of the backstory on Mz Lois Gale-Lienhart-Diaz."

"It seems like Mz Lois used to be just Mz Lois Gale-Lienhart. Gale is an ambitious woman and she bullied her partner into bringing a Latina woman into the marriage to gain extra EEO points. That would be Mz Diaz."

"Gale was never a pleasant person. In fact, the guys in the evidence room were eager to help me if it would twist her nose. Like I said, she had never been a pleasant person to work with but her personality definitely went into the ditch when her first spouse decided he liked sharing a bed with a sweet-talking, compliant, Latina hottie rather than a frumpy, menopausal, harpy. "

"Seems like she would have just taken Mr Lienhart to court, divorced him and cleaned him out. You know how the courts in Cali are." Chad observed.

"That is what I thought, too." Mardi resumed her story. "But if a three-way marriage dissolves, the vast majority of the assets will follow the most 'oppressed' member, in this case, the young Latina. Game, set and match…Lois Gale-Lienhart-Diaz is screwed and tattooed."

"Damn!" Chad said.

"Yup." Mardi agreed. "And after they logged out our computers, they loaned me a tote and arranged a ride to the bus station. It all happened real fast."

"About that tote," Chad said, "how do we get it back to them?"

"Easy-peasy." Said Mardi. "It is Department of Education property. Just drop it off at any Elementary school and it will find its way back."

"All in all, I think we got lucky." Chad said.

"I am not so sure. I think I made an enemy for life. I got that vibe that this woman is making it a personal mission to destroy us." Mardi said.

"Wow. I have never heard you be that negative. I never took you to be a drama queen." Chad said.

"You weren't there. She makes me think of the witches in Macbeth or a fat spider at the center of a web. It is as if her ego is a black hole and it warps the time and space around her. She has the aura of evil." Mardi mused.

"If I were in her shoes I would bide my time until harvest. That is when we are the most distracted and are really working the kids. My gut feeling is that we better be at the top of our game when the potatoes start coming out of the ground." Mardi said.

Chapter Six

"Look. You have to clip the fence to the posts in five spots. Yes, I know everybody else uses three clips. But here, you gotta use five and most of them need to be near the bottom." Chad told the crew.

It was early August and shortly before the first potatoes were to be harvested. Izzo Farms had a contract with Cali to deliver 40,000 pounds of potatoes, for forty days in a row. The truck would show up at the farm and the work crew was to carry out, and load the semi with four hundred, 100-pound bags of potatoes in less than an hour.

Miguel said, "Boss, this is the weirdest damned thing in the world! Why are we making a fence out here in the middle of nowhere? I just don't understand."

Chad pulled off his gloves and slapped them against his thighs, driving dust into the air. "Okay. You guys have been with me all summer, right? You must have noticed that a lot of people do me favors, favors I don't pay for. Right?"

Most of the work crew were nodding their heads "yes".

"This is how I return those favors. The central valley is cursed with a plague of feral hogs. Folks can't shoot them because all the guns have been confiscated and it takes a month to get a permit to control any varmint. This slope is covered with Jeffrey pine and oak trees. This is the first place in the valley where the acorns ripen. Every hog within fifty miles comes here starting in mid-August."

"We are making an industrial sized, Figure '6' hog trap."

"People will do things for five pounds of pork loin that they would not do for a thousand Callors.

"But don't worry. There will be plenty of pork for us to eat. The thing is, we got a good thing going here, and just one person blabbing can spoil it. By the way, every 'student' who ever worked here gets a little package of pork each year. That is just the way I roll."

Miguel asked, "You know, I never figured out why you get a new crew every year. It seems like it would be way more efficient to keep the same crew year after year. I know you spent a lot of time training us in how you wanted us to do things."

Chad nodded in agreement. "That is how it started out. We got to keep the same crew year after year. But then about three years after Calexit there were some rural uprisings. The people at the Department of Education decided that the students and the farmers were working together too well. The people who make policy decided that it was better to have the farms be less efficient as long as the people they were supervising remained off-balance and easier to manage."

"Things are going to get real busy over the next three months. First, we will be harvesting potatoes, and then we will harvest the cabbage. We will have some long days but we will feast like kings."

***

Ken said, "I am real sorry, Chad. But I am not picking up your potatoes today. Some chick named Lois and a tool named Terry showed up at the motor pool and stirred up a bunch of shit. They flashed their badges and kicked me off my own damned truck. They brought a couple of big-city thugs to drive the truck. Like I said, Chad, I am real sorry but it looks like they plan to fuck you over, big time."

Chad spoke into his phone. "Hey, no sweat. You can only do what you can do. Tell me, how did that dry rub work with the pork loin?"

"Damn, Chad. That was the best damned meat I ever ate. You were right. Slow cooking it at low heat over a tray wet down with a can of beer is the bomb. Gotta tell ya, my wife loved it too. And when mama is happy, everybody is happy."

"Hey dude," Chad said, "I gotta thank you for the heads up. I will let you know if I need anything special. 'Preciate the help."

***

The semi pulled into the loop that ran alongside the shipping shed. A nattily dressed man with a bushy mustache got out of the passenger side. He walked over to Chad and handed him a document.

"My name is Branch. I am from the Department of Education and I am auditing your compliance to your production quotas."

"Isn't that somebody else's sandbox?" Chad asked.

"The moral character of our education vendors, that would be you, is of the highest concern to the Cali Department of Education. We are trying to raise good citizens. That means that we need to weed out people who use fraud and sleight-of-hand to meet their quotas."

"I am not disputing you, but how do you intend to audit my operation?" Chad asked, secretly amused.

"I intend to personally weigh every bag of potatoes loaded onto this truck. Furthermore, I intend to audit the contents of random bags to ensure that you are not shipping dirt, rocks or rotten produce." Terry Branch said.

"What the hell! Weighing every bag will take hours." Chad objected.

"Time is not a concern when justice is at stake." Terry beckoned to one of the goons in the cab. The goon got out and unloaded an ancient, balance beam scale from the trailer.

"You have to be shitting me. You cannot weigh stuff with that. It will take forever!" Now Chad was exasperated.

"This scale is the one that the Department of Education made available to me. It is certified to NIST 2025. The thing about balance beam scales is that they are as reliable as gravity. This is what we have. And this is what we are going to use." Branch said.

It took Terry Branch two minutes to weigh each bag of potatoes. He weighed them to the nearest ounce.

He demanded that one in every three bags be opened and spread upon the ground for inspection.

It took thirteen hours to load the potatoes instead of the fifteen minutes it took when they used the fork truck to move the potatoes into the truck on pallets. It tied up most of the crew for the same time period, causing them to miss the time in the field to pick potatoes for tomorrow's quota. Mardi demanded a copy of Terry's weights. She was allowed to photocopy the raw data.

Later than night, Mardi opined, "Well, we are in deep shit now. We have twenty-five thousand pounds of potatoes in the shed and we are on the hook to deliver forty thousand pounds tomorrow. Branch really screwed us, and our crew. What do you think we should do?"

Chad said, "It is like poker. You play the hand you have, no matter how crappy, and you wait for somebody else to blink."

"It looks to me like we only need one or two of the crew to load if they are going to weigh each bag. I think we send most of the crew out to the fields at first light to harvest the potatoes for the day-after-tomorrow. Maybe we move the first five thousand pounds to puff-up what is there."

"Yeah, but that still leaves us ten thousand pounds short for tomorrow." Mardi (who had always been good at math) exclaimed.

Chad said, "That is why we count on miracles."

He pulled out his phone. "Ken. You were right. They are out to monkey-hammer us."

"Yeah, I could tell by the way they were putting their heads together they weren't planning anything good." Ken said. "Man, let me know if there is anything I can do to help. I hate those assholes on principle. The fact that dicking with you screws up twenty other farmers who count on me for transportation doesn't bother them a bit."

"Well, now that you mention it, there is something you can do. Do you still have that old flat-bed?" Chad asked.

"I sure do." Ken said.

"How many pounds of potatoes do you think it can carry if they are in bags?" Chad said.

"Oh, hell." Ken said. "Probably about ten thousand pounds. It used to be a wrecker, back when everybody had cars.

"Ten thousand pounds! Good deal." Chad replied, "I want two things from you. I want you to unlock the gate at the southeast corner of the warehouse. The other thing I want you to do is to park your flatbed on the corner of Idaho and Ione streets with the keys tucked above the sun visor."

"Whaddya plan on doing, buddy?" Ken asked.

"Nope, I can't tell you. A lot of times it is better to be stupid than to know too much." Chad said.

"Well, if you are thinking of doing what I think you are planning on doing, you are going to have to keep an eye out for Walkers." Ken said.

"Oh hell, Walkers up here? The skinny ones?" Chad asked.

"You know I get around pretty good because I am a trucker. I started seeing them around Visalia about three months ago. They are just really skinny people walking around looking for food to eat. I asked some of the long-distance guys I know and they have been seeing them around Los Angeles for a year, and now they're moving north." Ken told Chad.

"Most of them are like rabbits. They shuffle away if you say "boo" at them. But a few of them downright dangerous. I've seen a few of them around here, now." Ken continued, "If I was doing some extracurricular activities and it involved stuff that was edible, I'd be keeping somebody around with a baseball bat, just in case."

Calling the crew together, Chad said, "I am going to ask for a favor. I expect that most of you will say, 'No thank-you.' That's okay. I know that I am asking for a hell of a favor."

After dark, I need to go into town and steal a hundred bags of our own potatoes out of the warehouse. We got screwed by the system today. They intend to screw us even worse tomorrow and the day after. I, for one, intend to fight back. I cannot, by myself, carry one hundred bags of potatoes a hundred yards tonight. I tell you, humbly, that I need your help."

"No pressure. It is an all-volunteer thing…knowing that what I propose we do is considered a crime by the laws of man."

Miguel raised his hand.

Houa raised his hand.

Then Belladonna and Biff. Belladonna said, "I may not be able to keep up with the guys, step-for-step. But every bag of potatoes I carry out is one that you guys don't need to.

Chad raised both of his hands and waved them. "That is enough. I don't know how many nights we are going to have to do this so I don't want to burn you out."

That night, one hundred bags of potatoes were carried out of the warehouse by five shadowy figures. Undoubtedly, some of the locals saw them but nobody thought it was important enough to report them to the outsiders who had shown up to rub Chad's nose in the dirt.

The five took turns holding the baseball bat while the other four humped bags of potatoes.

The next day, more than 40,000 pounds of potatoes were loaded onto the semi. Every bag that was audited contained sound potatoes. And once again it took thirteen hours to load the semi.

The two crew members helping load the truck took little cat-naps while Branch weighed each bag of potatoes. Branch thought they must be having pleasant dreams since they were all smiling beatific smiles as they dozed.

Chapter Seven

Email
To: Erica Holder-Washington
 The Cali Department of Education
 Executive Director, Enforcement Division
From: Denice Delarosa
 The Cali Department of Food Security
 Executive Director, Domestic Production
Date: August 19, 2031 9:15 pm
Topic: Food Security, Emergency Order dated June 15

You fucking moron:
What part of "Do not prosecute. Do not harass, did you not understand?!"
In her own words, your apparatchik Lois Gale-Lienhart-Diaz is off the reservation and, motivated by a personal vendetta, is hell-bent on derailing the only effort that might, maybe, prevent food riots this winter.

There is no collateral that was not pledged during the 2026-27 crisis. The Chinese will not ship us grain. You, by virtue of chain-of-command, are responsible for a ten percent deterioration in the 2029 harvest season due to your "loose cannon" interfering with our logistics resources.

Per the Food Security, Emergency Order dated June 15 which grants me broad, emergency powers; I require that you view the first three minutes of the video at the following LINK.

After viewing the video you will fire Gale-Lienhart-Diaz. Then you will file a statewide BOLO, Arrest with prejudice orders.

I expect a return email in fifteen fucking minutes acknowledging receipt and understanding of this email and a timetable for the actions outlined there-in.

Have a nice day

-Denice Delarosa

***

"Hey Honey. This is LaShawnda." Mz Lienhart told Lois.

"I don't know what you did but you sure pissed off some important people."

-pause-

"How pissed off?"

"I can't be sure. But I can tell you this: Before today I never saw an arrest warrant with *arrest with prejudice* as the leading line."

"I don't know if you have a place to lie low, but you sure as hell can't come back to Sacramento."

-pause-

"Of course it had to be Terry Branch throwing you under the bus. Nobody else has enough on you."

-pause-

"Look, you gotta wait this out. It sounds like they are going to smack you around some. Sure, they would have believed you before they would believe an idiot like Terry. You know that's why everybody calls him a "Bakersfield Bullshitter"…but Terry already ratted on you and they believe him <u>now</u>. You gotta find some place that is out of sight and let things calm down."

-pause-

"Palm Springs? You have family in Palm Springs? That could work. Maybe you can slip into Mexico or Arizona from there."

-pause-

"Oh, you are already half way there? That is a bit of good luck. You probably ought to ditch the car. They have trackers in them you know. Can you hitch a ride to Palm Springs?"

-pause-

"Yes, I know you are very resourceful."

"Write me when you settle down, where ever you end up going."

Entire conversation, both sides, recorded and subsequently transcribed by voice-to-text and permanently stored in the server farms for posterity.

***

Mardi and Chad looked up when they heard the sound of knocking on the door.

Most folks around here "Yoo-Hooed" from outside, especially during the summer. Folks kept their windows open to catch a breeze.

"I wonder who that is." Mardi said.

"I guess I'll go see." Chad replied.

The sound of the knocking became more insistent as Chad walked to the door.

Opening the door, he saw a stout woman who was grossly overdressed for the high 80's of the early evening.

"What may I do for you?" Chad politely asked her.

"It's not 'what you <u>can</u> do for me'. You are going to do what I tell you to do." The woman corrected him in a command voice.

Chad was taken aback. The woman's rudeness clearly identified her as being from the Big City. It was equally clear that she was a fish out of water. She was wearing what city people call "sensible shoes" with her severely tailored, houndstooth patterned suit. Shoes that are called "sensible" in the big city look pretty stupid on people walking on gravel and rutted roads. Chad could not see where she had parked, but it was clearly more than a quarter mile away. Whoever his visitor was, walking was not her favorite mode of transportation.

Mardi hearing the voices walked up behind Chad. "Oh. It is you."

Then Mardi said, "Chad, allow me the pleasure of introducing you to Lois Gale-Lienhart-Diaz. She is the woman who is overseeing our probation with The Cali Department of Education."

Mardi rarely stooped to sarcasm, so Chad knew that Mardi had been deeply hurt by this woman.

"Please step in." Chad told the woman.

The woman was looking around as she entered. Apparently she found the interior slightly more to her taste than she had found the sun-blasted exterior as her face lost a little bit of the sucking-on-a-sour-lemon look.

Picking the most comfortable looking chair, she sat down without being invited.

She resumed her conversation by announcing, "You are going to give me a ride to Palm Springs."

Chad said, "You obviously have us confused with somebody else. Palm Springs is more than three hundred miles away and we don't have a car."

"Look, let's get one thing straight. I have you guys by the balls. I am not asking for your opinions. I am *telling* you what you are going to do." Lois said.

Chad looked over at Mardi and saw she was about to lose it. This woman obviously had a flair for getting underneath people's skin.

"Honey. It's okay. I will make it happen." Chad said to Mardi. "I need to go over and get Fast Eddie's motorcycle." He looked over at Lois and said, "I know that they send Cali workers into the field with chits for one hundred gallons of gasoline. I need all one hundred of them because the motorcycle does not burn air."

Lois said, "I am not giving you any gasoline rations."

Chad said, "Then how do you expect to get where we are going?"

Lois said, "I will pay as we go."

Chad said, "Well, Ma'am, that might seem like a good idea here in this room, but things are falling apart out there. What do you think all them country boys at the gas station are going to think when they see you reaching into that fanny pack for gas chits? Do you think they are going to say, "I love Cali and let's give this dear lady a discount." or do you think they are going to say, "Good God! I bet she has a thousand chits in that purse. I am going to charge five chits to the gallon."?"

"Besides, I have to give Fast Eddie something for the use of his motorcycle. It is the only game in town and he does not have to loan it to me." Chad said.

Lois looked into her fanny pack and said, "I only have seventy left. I have been driving that car for a month."

Chad said, "It will have to do." Took the chits and left the house by the back door.

Chad was thinking that he had seen people like Lois before. The technique of getting people off balance and to keep pushing them so they could not regain their balance is a very old technique. In fact, compared to his gold standard for that behavior, she was the rankest of amateurs. There was not a single Drill Instructor at Parris Island who could not have torn Lois to shreds. The techniques he had perfected in the military to manage overbearing NCOs would be more than adequate for handling Lois.

Chapter Eight

"I am not going to ride that thing!" were the first words out of Lois's mouth when she saw the old Suzuki dirt bike.

Chad grinned. "The way I see it, you have two choices. Ride or walk." He was starting to enjoy this. Lois was now the one who was off balance.

"Where is my helmet?" Lois demanded.

"You don't get one. There is only one helmet and I get it because I am driving." Chad said.

"I get a helmet because I am paying." Lois retorted.

"You don't get it, do you? What happens if the driver catches a bumblebee when going fifty miles an hour? Instant road pizza is what happens. To both of us." Chad said. "I get the helmet."

"If it gets too windy, just press your face against my back. I promise I won't think you are flirty." Chad said.

Mardi laughed. She LOVED seeing Lois uncomfortable. Lois might think she was in charge but she was clearly out of her element.

Chad said, "We gotta get rolling. It is going to get dark soon."

He revved up the bike and slllooowwwly feathered out the clutch to get the temperamental bike rolling.

At Lois's insistence, they kept off the freeway and traveled along backroads. Lois also had them ride around the larger towns. This is something that Chad loved to do but rarely had a chance. He was stunned to see dozens of people aimlessly walking along the roads.

He stopped at a convenience store and confirmed that he was seeing the Walkers that Ken had been telling him about. They were shambling along looking for anything that was edible, even almost edible, to stuff into their stomachs.

Chad shook his head. He devoutly believed that the Cali's Central Valley was the most fertile land on earth if given a little bit of water and TLC. And here were people starving to death right in the middle of it.

Chad coasted the bike to a stop between Richgrove and Quality. "This is where we part ways. You have to get off."

Lois said, "What the hell are you talking about. I directed you to take me to Palm Springs!"

"Well, Ma'am, I was served notice that I cannot leave Tulare County unless I give The Cali Department of Education two weeks advanced notice of my intention." Chad said.

"That does not apply any more. Now take me to Palm Springs." Lois insisted.

"Does that mean you are not voluntarily getting off this bike?" Chad asked.

"Damned straight, that is exactly what it means." Lois responded hotly. She hated it when 'little people' thought they could play games.

"I want to be really sure. Is that your final answer?" Chad queried.

"It is." Lois replied. "Now step on it!"

Mentally, Chad thought, I kind of thought she would say something like that.

He straightened his arms and locked his elbows. He straightened his back and sat tall in the seat. He nailed the gas and dumped the clutch when the tachometer needle blew by 8500 RPM.

The first time a bike comes over on top of you, your stomach sinks while your testicles rise. If you have not been coached, and many who have, you gasp in surprise. Hitting the ground with your back while inhaling is guaranteed to paralyze your diaphragm and make breathing impossible for three or four minutes.

Chad was exhaling as he kicked the bike away from him. The bike was light and Lois, Chad and the bike were no longer in contact with the ground.

Chad landed on his back. Well, actually, he landed on Lois who was an honest 230 pounds of polyester and body fat.

Lois landed on her back. She whacked the back of her head and simultaneously lost one of her contacts.

Chad rolled off Lois who was completely incapacitated.

"According to the regulations in The Department of Cali Board of Education Handbook, I am duty bound to report mishaps to my local authorities. Since I am on probation, I have no discretion in this matter. You will have to excuse me while I go back to Orosi." Chad said.

Chad righted his bike, started it, and cautiously motored through the Walkers back the way he had come.

***

The Walkers saw that the rider of the motorcycle had left luggage beside the road. It gets cold at night in the Central Valley due to the clear skies. It feels even colder when you have no calories to shiver away.

They started ambling toward the large bundle of clothing beside the road.

As they got closer, they saw it was a woman. Blood was spurting from her (impressively) broken nose.

In time, Lois noticed the ring of spectators watching her. "What is the matter with you fucktards? Don't you see I need a doctor? Call me a cab. What is the matter with you morons, can't you hear?" Lois was skating the thin ice at the edge of hysteria.

The spectators watched without commenting.

One of the people watching was a young Hispanic woman. Really, little more than a girl. Unfortunately, the girl reminded Lois of her second wife, Mz Diaz.

Given a target for her abuse, Lois doubled down.

"Hey, Consuela, you fucking cunt. Why aren't you helping me out…after all I have done for you."

Still no response from the spectators. Starving people don't process information quickly. They stood there. Silent. Motionless. Standing like sentinels in the lengthening shadows and rising mist of the late evening.

"I hate fucking spics." Lois spat. "Don't you know who I am? I am an agent with *The. Cali. Department. Of. Education*!"

No response, although the number of spectators was increasing.

"I can take your babies away from you." Lois shrieked.

No response.

"If I want to, *I can eat your babies* and there is not anything you can do about it because I am fucking untouchable!" Lois screamed.

Some men are sheep. Some men are wolves. Both sheep and wolves are social animals.

When a troublesome ewe endangers the flock, the flock shuns her and forces her to the outside edges where she becomes vulnerable to predation.

Wolves deal with their problem members directly. They tear out the throat of the wolf that endangers the pack.

The spectators around Lois were mostly sheep. But a few were wolves.

Lois had stepped over the line for the last time.

They rolled the body off the road into the channel. One of the more experienced men covered it with rushes to deter the vultures and delay discovery. They did not need to worry about the vultures. They were feasting on the first of the Walkers to die, as they were wont, out in the open.

Eventually, her bones were found but hers were just one skeleton among millions.

The spectators shared the seven thousand Callors and the three hundred gas ration tickets they found in her fanny pack. That boost was enough to allow some of them, a very few of them, to survive the crisis. The skinny, young Hispanic woman took the hounds tooth jacket back home to her mother.

Epilogue

Chad limped back home at 9:00 the next morning. He had slept in Fast Eddie's barn to provide the others with "plausible deniability".

Miguel and the crew assumed that Chad was limping because he had just ridden six hundred miles on a dirt bike. They were impressed. He was elevated to *El Patrón* because very few men could do that in twelve hours and then put in a full day's work the next day.

Mardi had her doubts. She had seen the bruises on Chad's backside but she did not ask about them. She figured Chad would tell her what happened when he was ready.

The BOLO on Lois Gale-Lienhart-Diaz was updated to an APB, and updated again to the top ten wanted list, as an enemy of the state, but rumor had it she'd escaped to Mexico, based on a blurry photograph that showed an older woman in a hounds tooth jacket crossing the border a month after the APB had been put out.

By Hook and Crook

Lawdog

The waitress -- excuse me, waitperson -- winks at me as she catches me admiring the view down her top, then waves a finger in amused admonishment before swaying off through the tables. And the view from behind was every bit as pleasant.

When it comes down to biology versus socialism, never bet against Mother Nature, folks. She cheats. Something that the fundamentalist idiots running the People's Democratic Republic of Cali still haven't quite managed to figure out, bless their little hearts. I take a sip of the allegedly-caffeinated, chicory-flavored dishwater, before turning my gaze to the pasty little guy sitting across from me, who's currently picking his locally-sourced ciabatta tofurkey roll into a little pile of crumbs next to the *papas' fritas* and the tomato-vinegar reduction.

"Relax, Fred," I say, sipping at the cup of despair and regret I'm probably going to wind up paying way too much for, "The key to conspiring is to not look like you're conspiring. Relax. Eat a french fry."

He blanches, "You can't call them french …" He stops, takes a deep breath, then snatches a no-gluten, no-fat, no-sodium, no-GMO, no-taste, Fair-Trade, Locally-Sourced fry off the plate and bites furiously at it. I wouldn't have believed you could make fried potatoes disgusting, but when your Food Code occupies six feet of a library shelf, it can be done.

Ten years after California formally left the Union to form their Own Little Country Based On (insert random bits of Leftist propaganda here), and things have gone every bit as well as anyone with a lick of sense -- or a degree in history -- would have told you. It's a Third World pest-hole.

Which brings me to why I'm in a no-name hole-in-the-wall cafeteria, sitting at a much repurposed card table across from an arch-typical software engineer, drinking what passes for coffee in Cali these days.

"I want out," he says, grabbing another Inclusivity Fry and demolishing it in two savage bites -- I'm a little worried about his fingers -- "I want a fucking steak that came off of a fucking cow; and I want to cook that steak outside on my own goddamned grill; I want to put 50 bucks of real fucking gasoline in my car, and drive anywhere I fucking please whenever I fucking please; and I want to run my air-conditioner all goddamned day, and keep the house at 65 goddamned degrees because I can, god damn it!"

Okie-dokie. I make shushing motions with my hands, but he seems to have run out of steam. He squidges a fry through the puddle of tomato-based Misery Sauce on the plate and stares at it, tiredly, "I want my kids to learn science, instead of feely handwavium. I want my son to be a boy, and do boy things. I want my little girl to be a little girl, and stop being angry and scared all the time." he blinks at the fry, drops it on the plate. "Four of us. I'll pay whatever …" I raise my hand, smiling at him.

"We've got this, Fred. So. Here's what we're going to do ...'"

Ten minutes after a visibly-relieved Fred has left, I hand the waitress five 200-denomination scrip notes that the Cali government laughably calls Callors for the bill; then catch her eye before slipping a folded twenty-dollar U.S. note into her hand. Her eyes get big -- although I'm not sure if that's because tipping is against the law, or because it's technically unlawful to possess American money -- the note vanishes, I wink at her, touch my hat brim, and slip out the side door.

Two weeks later, and the alarm doesn't go off. Looks like we drew the short-straw in another "random" rolling brown-out. Sigh. Luckily I've been lying awake for the last two hours, as I always do before an op -- excuse me, job. I'd make some snarky comment about how the rich areas never come up on the very-touted computerized randomly-generated schedule for power outages, but it's hot, and I've got things to do.

Quick shower, and I'm waiting in line at the *dispensería*, chatting amiably with my fellow sufferers. The tech, a cute little Anglo girl, looks at my card, and frowns at me, "You get four ounces. For your asthma."

"Yes, ma'am," I smile, happily, just another happy customer.

"You're smoking four ounces. Of medical marijuana. A week. For your asthma."

Socialized medicine is expensive. Marijuana is cheap. And since most folks in Cali believe that marijuana is a miracle cure for everything from hamster clap to Mongolian rabies to brain cancer (and if I were a cynical man I'd point out that stoned people don't complain… right up until they're eating their salads from the roots up), the Cali Government has crunched some numbers, and you can get a medical marijuana scrip for just about anything.

However, not everything. She glances at her supervisor, a large, gruff Hispanic female, and unconsciously clenches her fists. I slide my Cali ID card across the counter. There's a twenty-dollar U.S. bill paper-clipped to the back, and she glances up quickly when she sees it. I smile, gently, "I've got a really bad case of asthma. It's okay, miss."

She takes the ID, and murmurs, reflexively, "Don't call me 'miss', Citizen ..." she looks at the ID for a long minute, "... Athelstan King." A quick blink, and she looks at me again.

Whoops. I might have found a History Major. She slides the ID back across the counter. The bill has disappeared.

"Sign here, please."

I smile, scribble some nonsense on the form, take my quarter baggie, touch my hat-brim, and scoot.

Fred has a tiny little bungalow on the outskirts of San Jose, I've been parked down the street watching his house for the last four hours. Nothing trips my professional paranoia, but I've a professional dislike for Brownshirts.

It's not that Cali doesn't like people leaving the Country, but the ones that they wouldn't mind leaving -- welfare leeches, bums, and general useless layabouts -- aren't going to turn loose of the Gummint free teat. The folks that actually make money, and thus get taxed to a fair-thee- well, Cali quickly figured out that they can't lose those folks and keep the free Government stuff flowing.

So. Me.

It's been long enough. I climb out of my rental car, amble (maybe even stroll) up to Fred's front door, and knock. Before my knuckles hit the wood for the third time, the door is snatched open, and Fred is standing there. Behind him, sitting on the sofa, a pretty woman, face drawn with stress, clutches two sub-teenage children to her sides.

I take off my hat, holding it at belt level -- coincidentally putting my right hand next to the .32 NAA semi-auto hidden in the hat -- and nod formally to the lady of the house, "Ma'am."

"Don't call me …" she stops the reflexive response, and smiles shakily at me.

"Kids. 'Morning, Fred. Shall we get this show on the road?"

He runs his hand over his mouth, and nods, "Yes."

I head back to the rental car, pull into Fred's driveway and on into the garage as Fred raises the door, and then I step back into the living room. "Let me have everyone's cell phones, please."

What the vast majority of people in Cali don't know, is that Cali geo-fences every phone in the country. It's a simple algorithm, based on the plain and simple fact that people are creatures of habit. It takes 60 to 90 days of carrying your phone around, and the algorithm plots where you're going to be most of the time. Take your cell-phone outside of your usual hang-outs -- how far outside, I don't know -- and your cell-account gets flagged.

Mostly, a travel flag doesn't get noticed or acted on -- however, I'm pretty sure that flags on the accounts of people who make money probably get a reaction. "Reaction" being a Latin word for "Things Are About To Suck For Your Humble Yet Dashing Hero", so no phones.

"Ma'am, did you call the children in as sick to their schools?"

Her mouth moves, without speech for a second, she swallows, and whispers, "Yes."

"Good. Do the children have phones?"

"No, we never … no."

I smile, hopefully reassuringly, "Good." I step into the kitchen, spot the 'fridge, hop up onto the counter, and toss her cell-phone into that stupid little cabinet everyone has mounted above the refrigerator. Why is that thing there? Can anyone actually reach it? I hop down, and put Fred's phone in my pocket.

"Ok, folks, let's go for a trip!"

We load into the rental car, buckle the kids into the idiot car seats, the family luggage into the trunk next to my backpack, and take off for the rail station. At the station, I look around the parking lot, and find a car with a parking sticker for one of the bigger Silicon Valley computer corporations. Little loop of duct tape, and the phone sticks nicely to the battery compartment of the vintage Toyota Pious. It'll stay there for a couple of hours, before bouncing loose. Hopefully, in a San Francisco or Marin county parking lot.

There is no way I'm going to pry the Missus from the kids, so I hand her three train tickets, "Second car from the end. Find a seat near the middle, please." I wave a finger gently in her face, "It's going to be okay." She tries to smile, takes a firm grip on the children's hands, and walks towards the tracks.

I put my hand up, as Fred involuntarily takes a step after his family, "Cameras, Fred. Trust me. This is why you're paying me a great deal of money." Rigid, he looks at me, nostrils flaring.

I hand a ticket to Fred, and we walk around the front of the train. As we walk, I recite the day's headlines from the paper, gesturing, to the four cameras I spot on the way, two men going about the day's business. On the other side, we step into the men's rest-room, and out of camera-shot.

"Fred, take a whiz. You need to, you just don't know it yet. Then go wash your meathooks, and go get on the train. Third car from the front, please."

The adrenaline is driving him so hard, he's practically dancing. I hope it just looks like a widdle dance, and he's out the door headed for the train. Sigh.

When I hear the whistle, I walk quickly, and hop into the train, holding the sliding door and winking at a little Latina, who gives me a slow up and down look and smiles. Even in post-Calexit Cali, women are proof that the gods love us and want us to be happy. There are no cameras on the train, but I'm not looking for cameras. Five minutes early, but expected, Fred comes hurrying down the aisle from the forward cars, and passes me, without even noticing me on the way back to his family.

We're up to full speed and around the first corner on the way to Modesto, when I get up, and stroll back to the restroom at the back of the car, pause, and pull gently on the door, knock on the door, shrug, and step through into the next car. Pasting a mildly confused look on my face, I go from car to car, finally stopping in the car occupied by Fred and his family.

Taking a seat at the front of the car, I look at my charges. They're sitting with the kids in-between them, stress clearly visible on their faces, holding hands so tightly I can see the white of their knuckles from here. It's good to see … a … doting …

Shit.

There's a Brownshirt on this car. And he's on the job. Shit. Shit. Shit.

He's a muscular bastard, bic-ink tattoos visible along his arms up to the Hawaiian shirt over a neutral t-shirt -- much like I'm wearing, come to think -- with an angular bulge on his right hip, scarred knuckles, and way-too- active eyes.

I take a newspaper out of my backpack, get up, sling the backpack and start walking back down the aisle, lost in the glories of whatever the celebrity du jour was up to. As I got level with the Brownshirt, I artfully stumbled against him, dropping the newspaper in his lap.

He grabs my shirt, lifting me off him, "Dude," I slur, "I'm … like… wow. Sorry, dude." I smile at him slowly, and get my balance back, he sneers at me, lifts the paper and smacks me in the chest with it. "Careful, *pinche*." He gives me a shove, "Lay off the *mota*, fool."

He's right handed. Thought so, but the pistol might have been set-up cross-draw. I slide into a seat in the back row, tip my hat over my eyes. There was no way he was going to miss Fred and his family, but I could hope. And he spots them.

Well, hell.

Twenty minutes out of Modesto, the Missus gets up with the kids, and walks up the aisle to the next car. In the next car, she and the kids will go into the restroom and shed their bright outer garments, go the second car along and take a seat next to the door. Brownshirt watches them go, and looks really hard at Fred. Oblivious, Fred is staring longingly in the direction his family went. Five minutes later, Fred gets up and goes to the restroom in this car, and steps inside to shuck his orange fishing shirt. Brownshirt watches him go, and when Fred comes out of restroom in an olive drab t-shirt, the Brownie's eyes go wide, and he gets up, moving quickly down the aisle but too late to stop Fred from getting into the next car.

Brownshirt stops at the restroom, and opens the door, not seeing me behind him. Things slow down as he spots the discarded shirt, he starts to turn, and I'm there, dagger point-down, my left hand sliding from behind to get a big handful of his right lapel, jerking it across his throat, cutting off his air. I hook the edge of my knife into the bend of his elbow, and rip back, severing arteries, tendons, pulling his suddenly-numb hand away from the grip of his pistol. As the knife comes free, I ice-pick into his subclavian artery, and shove the knife to lever him counter-clockwise, pulling firmly with his lapel in my left hand. The pivot slams us into the wall inside the restroom, and away from prying eyes. I jerk the blade free, hammer it into his lung, out, into the armpit for the axillary artery, out, and down into the femoral artery in his right leg, ripping out so hard I lift the dying man off the floor, and we fall sideways against the commode..

In less time than it takes for two slow breaths, I'm kneeling on a dead man, the old familiar stink filling the air. I reach back and push the door shut, turn the lock, take four deep breaths, stand-up -- ow -- and use my Hawaiian shirt and the sink to clear as much blood off of me as possible. A quick check of the mirror shows no blood, I drop my shirt on the dead guy's face, I slip out in my black t-shirt, using a coin to spin the lock on the restroom from the outside. Hopefully my little murder won't be found until the next time they clean the train car.

Two cars later, I take a seat. Four deep slow breaths, in through the nose, hold, out through the mouth, hold; and the adrenaline shakes start to level off. Once I'm in a state that I'm not liable to send Mrs Fred shrieking for the rafters, I move up to the car the family is in, and sit where they can see me. When the train pulls into Modesto, Mrs Fred gets off, holding the son. Fred and I move up a car, and get off on the same side, Fred holding the girl's left hand, me holding her right. We step off, I paste a smile on my face, and swing the little girl back-and- forth playfully, just another Inclusive Modern Couple with their kid.

I left a rental panel van in the far parking lot -- where the cameras probably weren't well maintained -- Fred lifting the daughter into the back, and we pull around to curbside pickup, where Mrs Fred puts the son in, then climbs into the front passenger seat.

We pull away from the train station, up onto Highway 108 towards Free America -- excuse me, Nevada -- and I set the cruise control at two miles an hour over the speed limit. Three hours later, we pull over at the 108/395 turn, I slip out, and open the back door. Inside the van is full of cases of bottled water. A very foo-foo bottled water, famous for foo-foo-ery in years past. Fred and I lift out the first four layers, revealing a padded cubicle with just enough space for a small family of four, they crawl in, and I replace the cases, bruises from my earlier dance with the Brownshirt screaming at me.

I get back behind the driver's seat, make sure the air conditioner is on full, blowing through a hose to the hidden spot, and head towards Topaz Lake, Nevada; this time with the speedo at five miles under the speed limit.

Half of a sweaty hour later, and I come into view of the Cali Customs Station just this side of the Cali/Nevada state line. There's nothing to show that anything's up. The concrete barriers to force you to slow down and zig-zag aren't blocked, the machine-gun muzzle in the guard tower is pointed skyward, and no-one comes out of the Customs shack for a moment as I come to a stop beside the mounted camera.

A moment, and the usual agent steps out of the shack. A rotund little guy, I always wonder what he did to wind up stuck out in the Great Back of Beyond, but my mama always told me not to look a gift horse in the mouth.

"Well, well, well. Mr Waterman! Starting to think your luck ran out and the Fascists caught you!"

I summon a grin, and hold my travel papers out the window. "Ah! You know, wife's mother got sick, had to go down south."

"Down south. You lucky fucker. How is civilization?"

"Not bad. Hot, though."

"Yeah, I'll bet. So, let's see it."

Behind him, the shack door opens again, and an unknown figure steps out. My heart sinks. I don't know this guy, but he has the stiff, pinched face, and fervent mien that usually belongs on the face of guys you see on the evening news after being caught with a basement full of young women and needles. I touch the butt of the pistol mounted under the dashboard for reassurance, but unless I'm very, very lucky, any dance started here will be ended by that machine-gun in the watch tower. I take a deep breath.

My Customs buddy turns, "Hey! This is the guy I told you about! The water-seller!"

Unknown guy steps up, regarding me with the sort of expression usually employed by scientists looking a particularly fertile petri dish. Crap. His voice is the dry rasp you would expect, "So. You expect me to believe you smuggle water to the Fascists?"

Behind him, Usual Guy smiles like there's a good joke in the offing. That creepy feeling is thundering up my spine with all the delicate grace of a rhino in combat boots.

"Yeah! Come on, come on! Let's see it!"

Moving slowly, I slide out of the driver's seat, praying that no kids start screaming, and stroll to the back of the van. "So, are you the new Supervisor here?"

He looks at me, but doesn't say anything.

I open the backdoor, and the regular guy beams like he's won the Christmas Lottery, "See? Water!"

New guy look at me, "Water?"

I try to look a little abashed, "The Fascists love Cali water. They'll pay five dollars a bottle for genuine Cali water."

He raises an eyebrow at me. I wave paperwork at him, "I've got manifests, and a contract. I pay half of the profit in tariffs. Right here, actually, I pay the tariffs." I try to look vaguely honest, with a touch of larceny.

Usual Guy grins, and smacks the spare tire housing on the right side of the inside of the van. A circular panel falls, off, revealing a distinct lack of a spare tire. Probably because of the rather large amount of oregano, stacked in neat bricks inside the compartment. "Ah!" says Usual Customs Guy, in the tone one would use at the height of a magic trick, reaches in, and grabs a roughly-wrapped partial bag.

We do this every time. One of these days, he's going to grab the wrong bundle, and find out that the partial bundle of *dispenseria*-supplied *mota* is the only non-oregano bundle in there, but all Customs people think everyone's dirty anyway, best to let him find some dope every now and then.

I look mildly offended, "I've got a 'scrip for that …"

New Guy fixes me with a gimlet eye. "Citizen, that's a bit more than 'personal use'. A lot more."

I look a bit discomfited. It's not hard just right now.

"But I really don't give a damn about what you sell to the Fascists. What I am concerned about is your obvious felony."

I blink at him.

He points to a corner of a magazine sticking out from the top of the pile of oregano bundles. "Objectifying women is a penal offense in California."

I look at the Playboy magazine. Out of the corner of my eye, I see Usual Guard slipping the four ounces of pot into the pocket of his jacket. Out here in the boonies, the closest *dispenseria* is hours away, and the poor little dears out here are sorrowfully deprived.

Other guy, though …

"So. I'm going to seize this unlawful pornography. Unless you have a problem…?"

"No, sir, I surely don't."

"All right, Citizen. On your way. Be sure to check in on your way back. And I expect an honest accounting for the tariff."

"Yes, sir."

"On your way, Citizen."

He hands me the travel documents back, and turns to go back into the Customs shack. I notice that the Playboy has been tucked gently under his arm.

Taking a deep breath, I get back behind the wheel, put it in 'D', and wave to the
Cali officials as I ferry Fred and his family into the American city of Topaz Lake.

Fifth Column

Kimball O'Hara

CALEXIT
D-45

Gary Simpson stood on the cracked concrete curb, behind a wall of blue clad police in riot gear and watched as his brother Tommy's head was pounded soft by a mob supporting Black Lives Matter placards. They'd been smashing and burning businesses on Ventura Boulevard for no reason beyond the fact that they were African-American. Their march was marked with a line of black smoke that stained the sky, pushed inland by an on-shore breeze.

The fact that Tommy Simpson was also black didn't enter into the equation because the blood lust was up and he decided to make a stand in front of the greasy spoon restaurant he managed for an owner who had taken out an insurance policy against just such an eventuality.

Tommy tried to stand in their way and speak to them, asking the mob to listen to reason. They didn't. The mob wanted to burn the whole world down. The police stood by and allowed them to. After Tommy fell and was stomped to death, the mob burned both his body and the diner.

The crush of numbers, the blood lust, the fire, the theft, the hysteria of the mob was lensed by Gary as a surreal act. He'd screamed and screamed, but no voice came out. He tore his hair, he ripped his clothes, and he clawed at the ground until his fingernails came off. It made no difference, but from that gaping wound in his psyche came a resolve as hard and pure as a diamond.

California's impending secession from the United States of America caused red, white and blue flight with many police officers and firemen taking their families east to Nevada, Arizona, Utah or even further east to Texas. Cities and counties tried to replace them, but it took years to train police officers, firefighters and paramedics. The police at the scene had been undermanned and Gary knew it. He bore the officers no malice. It wasn't only the cops. Doctors, nurses, and the best healthcare professionals all saw the handwriting on the wall.

CALEXIT
D+20

"I know what you're thinking so you can wipe that smug look from your face. I'm still here because I'm a drunk. An alcoholic has more dignity than a drunk because he's taken the time to *try* and fix the problem."

"It's just that you look like a derelict Mike and your breath smells precisely like dog shit pickled in cheap booze. Did you sleep in that uniform?"

Mike looked down at the gray militia uniform. Gone was the Sheriff's Department khaki shirt and green trousers. Gone was the star on the uniform, replaced by a round disk edged by stick people holding hands with the words, 'Cali Militia' in the center. "It's not much of a uniform is it?"

"You could have it tailored and it wouldn't sag so much. You're a major in the Cali People's Militia now, for heck sakes. You're a big shot."

"Yeah, Larry, you, me and thousands of untrained thugs and inner city people are in the militia now. When they opened the prisons and released people they called *political prisoners*, I knew things would turn out badly. When they replaced the criminals with political opponents, all of the guys with any integrity headed off for the states. Present company excepted."

"That's right," Larry told Mike, "and they walked away from their homes and their pensions. Yours is still intact."

Mike reached into his pocket and pulled out a wad of banknotes with the face of the late Governor Jerry Brown, a.k.a. Moonbeam, hero of CALEXIT, in the center. "We're being paid in script. The *People's Republic of Cali*," Mike amplified. "You got this bullshit?" He waved his hand around like a flipper.

Larry soothed him, "The militia conscripts are pretty raw, but they can keep order. At least I think that they can."

Mike Sanchez turned to go and then looked back at Larry Marcus. "Why'd you stay, Larry? You have a lot going for you. Army special forces with combat in Iraq and Afghanistan, a solid record here at the Sheriff's Department --- okay, now it's the Militia."

"I've got nowhere else to go. I figured that I'd stay and see how this all works out."

Mike grunted, and he kept on grunting as he walked. His reflection in the locker room mirror looked like twenty miles of bad road. He stopped at his own gray metal locker. His own image greeted him again as he opened the locker and peered into the mirror. Two days growth of beard, dark bags under his eyes and a swollen nose where Curtis James tagged him made him look more like a derelict than the sheriff's sergeant he once had been.

It took effort to remind himself that he wasn't a sheriff's sergeant. The title 'Sheriff' was judged to be a trigger word harkening back to America's colonial roots and it was no longer in use. Not anymore. Simply through attrition, Mike had become Militia Major and Station Commander. Having a Spanish surname boosted him over Larry Marcus, of mixed black and Vietnamese heritage, now a captain and Deputy Station Commander. Race had become everything in a society that rebelled against racism.

He pulled a safety razor and shaving soap from the shelf, took it to the sink and soaped up before dragging it over his hatchet jaw. He thought as he shaved. The National Militia absorbed him like a feeding amoeba. The old county of San Bernardino, which stretched from the outskirts of Los Angeles nearly all the way to

Las Vegas, Nevada had been renamed the Caesar Chavez State, of the newly minted National Republic of Cali. Law enforcement duties passed from the purview of cities and counties to the National Militia. They needed a Spanish surname for their new province militia chief, but he spoke no Spanish, and neither had his father or grandfather, for that matter.

Mike didn't have any mouthwash, so he took a bottle of Yukon Jack from his locker and sloshed two mouthfuls around before swallowing. Then he took a third. And then a fourth. He replaced the bottle in the locker, closed it and spun the lock.

He walked back to his office and wasn't the least bit surprised to find five-foot-four inch with lifts-in-his-shoes, *Colonel* Dorris Tyrone Johnson, the Provincial Commissioner, taking to Larry Marcus. Johnson's claim to fame was being a thirty-something community organizer, who had appointed his life partner, Luther Calder as his aide. He oversaw two states: Caesar Chavez and Eric Holder (had been Riverside County), and that made him Mike's boss.

"Those mother-fuckers are still burning their homes, Major Sanchez." Dorris never beat around the bush.

"They're burning their *mother-fucking* houses," Luther Calder echoed for effect. Calder stood two inches shorter than his mate and wore his hair in a man bun that didn't quite work with tight African-American curls doped down with Afro Sheen. The best thing about Calder was that you could smell him coming because of the volume of women's perfume that he wore. It was also the worst thing if you had to stand near him as Mike now did.

"I want militia troops dispatched to every cop's house in the city to arrest those disloyal bastards and their families and take them to work camps. The fires that they set spread to other homes 'cause there aren't any firemen. It's beginning to cause a problem." Dorris Johnson cleared his throat, indicating that he finished his rant.

Mike wanted to make the same argument to Colonel Johnson that he'd made to Larry a few minutes before. Paying the militia in script meant that they spent all of their time looting rather than enforcing the law.

By national order, the homes of police and firemen who fled the National Republic of Cali were subject to confiscation. Rather than let that happen, they'd begun setting them ablaze on their way out of town, heading for the border and the United States. Mike knew that Dorris and his cronies wanted the homes for themselves to dole out as favors for personal loyalty on the part of key supporters. So far, it hadn't worked out as planned.

Larry Marcus stepped in to save Mike, "We don't have any militia to send, Colonel. They're busy looting, or hunting down the disloyal and relieving them of their property. There's a very fine line between the two."

Dorris cleared his throat, signaling a pronouncement. "How many cops and their families have they brought to work camps?"

Larry smirked only slightly, "The militia is disorganized and the cops all have guns and know how to use them. Our people give them a bit of distance to keep from getting mowed down. We lost two entire squads out by the Barstow checkpoint three days ago. I sent two hundred more men out there, but I don't think that they'll last long either. We're going to need to recruit more militia. Only the new people will go to Barstow, where there's nothing left to salvage." Salvage had become the politically correct term for theft by looting.

"Well major, you need to get out there and lead them." Luther Calder chimed in, focusing back in on Mike. "What good is the militia if they can't capture the disloyal?"

Mike Sanchez said dryly, "None of them are trained. They were plucked off the street or out of county jail, handed truncheons and sent out to enforce vague regulations. A lot of those people that you pinned badges on can barely read. It might help to deal with training before you send them against police families, who are capable of defending themselves."

Luther Calder suggested to Colonel Dorris Johnson that an inspection of the militia would be a good idea since his was an official visit as the regional militia chieftain. Mike and Larry were able to round up a dozen men with a blend of official uniforms and gray clothes sporting a disk badge pinned over the heart. Grooming, uniformity and martial bearing were wanting, but they'd all been earning big since assuming the office of Militia Officer. The barter business out in the new nation was brisk.

CALEXIT
D+41

Captain Larry Marcus brushed down the street in the crowd and allowed the chalk in his hand to mark the stone on the side of the bank building. A squad of bodyguards flanked him while he stood off near a platoon of militia who were keeping the peace at an outlet mall as looters stripped the place bare. The chalk on the wall was not noticed and the militia moved on, disgruntled that Captain Marcus had not released them to beat away the looters and to scavenge for themselves.

Two hours later, Gary Simpson, drove past the bank building and noticed the chalk mark and then headed for the drop.

He'd never been the sort who volunteered, he mused, as he drove the old Ford pick- up down a narrow alley to the battered trashcan in the weeds behind a blackened skeleton that had once been a liquor store.

It had become all about Tommy. The something that snapped as he watched the mob kill his brother during the countdown to Cali's independence from the United States, lead to a calm understanding of what he needed to do.

Hysteria ran high in those days before CALEXIT and people tried to reason with his anger. Everyone he knew wanted him to transfer his hate to the mother country. Outwardly he'd played that game. Inwardly, however, it had been different and he went to the police and volunteered. There had been a shuffle as his handlers changed twice and he'd been thrust into a brief, intense, training course. At D-7, a week before the hand-off, they'd flown him to Luke Air Force Base in Arizona for more detailed training focused on what they wanted him to do.

"All I want to do is to pay back those people who killed my brother."

The grim and nameless men and women who served as his training cadre assured him that he would be given the opportunity to do just that. Not necessarily the mob itself, but the shot callers and community organizers.

His first pick-up was heavy, taped inside plastic wrap, surrounded by a greasy brown paper bag, and slid into a plastic bag from Target. There was a certain irony to that, and it was not lost on Gary. He put the package into his truck, behind the front bench seat and continued on to work.

CALEXIT
D+42

Gary had been an auto mechanic for the adult portion of his twenty-three years. He understood machines clearly and could tell when they were worn or out of tune. People posed a far more challenging problem. He quit his job after his brother died. When he returned to Cali after the grand secession from the United States, he'd been dropped by parachute. Since the U.S. military had destroyed their bases and had left Cali en-masse, there was no radar to detect the aircraft.

He'd been dropped into the desert and found the old Ford pick-up where they told him it would be.

He'd been instructed to apply at the Militia's motor pool in San Bernardino, east of Los Angeles.

Captain Larry Marcus, whose job included overseeing the vehicles that hauled members of the newly minted militia, interviewed him for the job, approved his hiring, and put him to work.

Captain Marcus had been cut from a different piece of cloth than the other former cops who ran the militia. He seemed organized, thoughtful and had a streak of kindness and thoughtfulness that appealed not only to Gary, but to the rest of the people who worked for him as well.

"Did billeting find you a place to live, Gary?"

"Yes Captain." He stood and wiped his greasy hands on a rag.

"How is it?" Captain Marcus had an easy way and Gary responded warmly.

"You know, Captain, things have changed. There hasn't been power there since Cali went on its own but I have running water."

"You're eating at the Militia's commissary, right?"

"Yes, Captain, and it's a lot better than most of the people out there have. I wanted to thank you for the job."

"Gary, you were qualified and we're fortunate to have you."

You wouldn't be if you knew what I'm going to do. "Thanks all the same."

"Don't you have work to get back to?"

Gary smiled and went back to patching the sheet metal on an armored car that had taken fire. Cleaning the blood out had been a grizzly task, but Gary did it with a chastened, holy, joy. Adding thin metal swatches to the clearly inadequate pierced metal skin did not strike him as odd in any way. The cops that left sabotaged the department's armored cars and the American military took theirs with them. That left the Calis with the job of putting together patchwork armor. Since none of them knew how to do that, there had been a lot of trial and error that led to a lot of militia personnel being shipped to the crematorium.

CALEXIT
D+43

When Major Sanchez drove up to the home that Larry Marcus lived in, he noted changes. Masonry buttresses had been constructed here and there. Shrubs, dug into the soil didn't do much to hide them. He opened the chain link gate and walked onto the property and it was only when he came up to the front door that he noticed that the concrete reinforced cinder blocks were backed by Claymore mines. Apparently Larry didn't want the back blast to rip the skin off his house. He sighed. It had come to this. He hadn't taken precautions, but he'd been drinking so much lately that often as not, he pissed the bed while he slept these days. The depression that closed in around him felt like a steel net. Southern Cali had fragmented and was coming apart before his eyes.

The stores had no food on the shelves, order broke down, and only the militia had a steady supply of gasoline. And the society that once believed that male and female were complementary rather than interchangeable had been labeled as misogynist. Owners of private property were tagged as being greedy. But they were now the victims of mobs and roving gangs, and the militia itself. There wasn't much private property anymore. It belonged to the people. As he knocked on Larry's front door, he couldn't help but wonder what would happen to Caesar Chavez State when the water pumping stations went off line the way that the power had. The state itself consisted mainly of land that could be classified as 'desert'.

Larry opened the door and ushered him in. There was a smell of bacon cooking in the kitchen, and, feeling a bit like Pavlov's dog, he began to salivate.

"Something smells amazing."

"It's the most important meal of the day, boss."

"Where did you find bacon?"

Larry smiled, "It's canned bacon. I have a few cans. I have chickens living upstairs since my wife left me and headed to the U.S., so we have eggs too. I also purloined some bread from the Militia commissary so we will have toast. I just don't have butter."

The milita captain cooked breakfast on a fuel-powered camp stove.

"This is great, Larry. Really great."

They sat down and Larry handed Mike a canned beer. "I thought this might be welcome before we headed into the office – hair of the dog and all that."

"Yes, that's great."

They ate in silence until Mike asked Larry the question that had been on his mind all morning. "What do we do when the water system fails?"

Larry smiled, "What do you mean?"

"You're not stupid, Captain Marcus. You know that the natural gas doesn't work and that we don't have electric power. Those are inconvenient, but when the water system fails, things will get ugly. No water to drink, no water for sanitation, and near as I can tell, only the militia will have water from the storage tanks."

Larry said, "I expect an outbreak of cholera. Hundreds of thousands will die in Caesar Chavez State alone, people will become desperate and it will get very bad. These are city people who are used to turning on a tap and flushing a toilet. When they can't do that, what will they do?"

Mike forked a huge wad of scrambled eggs into his mouth and washed it down with his beer. "No, what will we do?"

"What can we do?"

"It's our responsibility."

"I know that we have a water system, Mike, but I don't know how it works. Do you?"

"No, not really."

"We'll rely on the wisdom of the Cali National Assembly and that of President Newman to save the nation. The militia will keep order as best we can, but our salvage operation phase will come to an end and I can see us bunkering up inside the Sheriff's Offices."

"Militia compounds."

"You know what I mean."

CALEXIT
D+45

Gary Simpson understood that he was simply one of many when he placed each sock containing five pounds of C-4 plastic explosive where the diagram told him to place it and inserted the blasting caps at either end. The caps themselves had been crimped to det cord and led into a timing mechanism. His instructions had been specific, and he set the timer for midnight, one hour from now.

A water treatment plant is complex with its system of valves, pipes, pressure reduction and chemical treatment, but when you eliminate the input and the output with the proper explosive with the brisance; the hydraulic force will shatter the whole.

CALEXIT
D+46

With fifty-seven detonations at midnight, at the beginning of the 46th day of the Peoples Republic of Cali, the greater Los Angeles area became unlivable.

CALEXIT
D+48

By the 48th day of liberation from the United States, the dim bulb of bureaucratic thinking suddenly burned brightly and senior public servants, newly anointed by the new nation were invited to a meeting that was convened in the recently renovated Los Angeles Coliseum. Major Mike Sanchez and Captain Larry Marcus drove along nearly deserted freeways with Colonel Dorris Johnson and his aide, Luther Calder sitting in the back seats of the otherwise empty armored vehicle.

"I don't see why everyone is so hysterical," Colonel Johnson said, "it's just a little water."

"You've been busy. There's a lot on your plate. It was in the message traffic, sir. The U.S. blew the waterlines from the Colorado River and a saboteur took out the California aqueduct somewhere up in the San Joaquin Valley." Larry Marcus looked into the rear-view mirror that gave him a view of the passenger section of the Mine Resistant Armored Vehicle (MRAP) that he drove. Colonel Johnson still didn't get it and Luther Calder, his life partner did, but didn't seem inclined to help explain. "All of the water pumping stations in the Los Angeles, San Gabriel, and San Fernando Valleys and what used to be Orange County were sabotaged too. What few wells there are fed through pumping stations and from what the inspectors said, it will take months to repair them because they don't have all of the pipe and parts necessary. The U.S. isn't going to provide them and we'll need to source them from China or elsewhere."

"You mean no water at all?" Johnson seemed confused. "I had a long hot shower this morning."

"You're in the militia compound, Colonel. Everybody is on rationed water for drinking only except for you – and Luther, of course."

"Okay, then that's fine."

"But we will run out of water long before the pumping stations come back on line, whether you take long showers or not. I think that's the point. The emergency water tank was installed to provide a hedge in the event of an earthquake, not against a regional system that, from all accounts, was destroyed."

Mike Sanchez chimed in, "Things are going to get ugly. When the power went out, swimming pools were no longer filtered, so people are sucking what water there is out of those algae sumps, toilet bowls, and hot water tanks."

"What happens when all that water runs out?" Luther's question was rhetorical. "The desert reclaims the LA Basin?"

"We can't let that happen!" Johnson was suddenly feeling every bit the colonel and the military governor of Caesar Chavez State.

"Definitely not," Luther echoed. "What are you going to do about it, Major Sanchez?"

"I'm going to the same meeting as you are. But we need to start thinking about relieving some of the militia of their duties. They're sucking down the rationed water and once that's out, we're out of business altogether."

"Before the present system was in place there were two or three thousand people here. Now there are fifteen million in the affected area, less those who have been killed in the rioting and looting and those who took the big bounce and left Cali." Larry Marcus looked though his mirror. "It gets worse. We're down to under a thousand gallons of gasoline in our storage tank and there's none to be had outside of government rations. I called Sacramento and they said they hoped to have a truck to us within a month or two. They're dealing with widespread shortages since the port facilities were sabotaged and ships off-shore can't unload."

"Who do they think did the sabotage?"

"They know who. The Navy did it before sailing over the horizon to the U.S. They blew the facility and sank a civilian tanker to block access. We don't have the capacity to move the sunken ship and don't have spare parts to fix what they damaged. The Navy did it in full view and there wasn't anything that Cali could do about it."

"It was supposed to be our navy." Colonel Johnson muttered loudly and cast an eye at Luther. "You said that they would give us the ports and the ships, Luther."

"I thought that they would," Luther protested.

The meeting at the renovated coliseum took up a fraction of the seats. A man that none of them knew chaired the meeting, but President Newman presided and was clearly in charge. Given that the Los Angeles Basin was about to be unlivable, the militia would staff a redoubt at the Port of Los Angeles and would occupy the old Fort MacArthur area. Food, water and fuel would be brought in by ship to sustain them. Caesar Chavez State would relocate most of its personnel to Needles, Primm, Blythe and the California strip to the west of Yuma. Cali would try to supply them with necessities, but it was likely that the militia would have to live off the land for some time to come.

Mike whispered to Larry Marcus, "They'll all defect across the border to the U.S."

President Newman stood and walked to the lectern and looked at Major Mike Sanchez and Colonel Dorris Johnson, "You will shoot and kill anyone who is even suspected of planning to defect across the border. The U.S. is erecting a border wall as I speak across that portion of the Inland San Diego and Los Angeles area. We will build our own wall eventually. We must maintain order and must keep our people in Cali to rebuild what the U.S. is doing to us. Questions?"

"What about people in Southern Cali who have no water, food or power?" Colonel Johnson spoke for the group.

"I'm afraid that they're on their own. Up north we have Lake Tahoe to drain but since the mechanism to send water south has been destroyed, we have no way of supporting you except by ship. With the ports damaged or blocked, the only way we can do that is by off-loading big ships to small ships and landing them. We'll increase our capacity over time but right now things are stretched to just providing for the militia and special friends. We will make sure that the roads are open for anyone who wants to walk to Sacramento."

Dorris Johnson, showing an uncharacteristically sound grasp of the situation attempted to clarify what he heard. "But if they walk to Sacramento, they'll do it without food or water."

President Newman shuffled uneasily and said, "Yes, that's the situation, Colonel."

The remainder of questions put to the president were presented by panderers who tried to ingratiate themselves with the new leader of the nation and he warmed to them.

At the conclusion of the meeting, Larry and Mike waited by the MRAP for Dorris Johnson and Luther, who never strayed far from his man. General Brown, the militia commandant for Southern Cali and two captains walked up to them and informed them that Colonel Johnson had taken ill and that Mike was to drop Larry Marcus at the San Pedro depot to begin organizing the defenses there. "Larry, consider yourself breveted to major. We'll make it official within the week. The Fort MacArthur command is yours. We'll change the name to Fort Newman in honor of the president but for now, we just need to set that up and to make that the new beachhead for Los Angeles. Mike, we need you to pack up what you can, while you still have fuel, and get your militia to the border with the U.S. You'll be executive officer under Sheila Malik, the Colonel commanding that sector."

"So we're abandoning Los Angeles, General?" Mike Sanchez itched for a drink from the bottle in his bag in the truck and Larry saw him lick his lips thickly. All of it began to unravel and Mike read the tea leaves.

"Of course not. Major Marcus here is going to be holding down the fort, pardon the pun."

Mike slapped Larry on the back, "He's a good man, General!"

"Meanwhile, I'm moving my flag from Brentwood to Santa Barbara, where there are water wells that will keep the command supplied, and we can receive food shipments by sea." Brown had the pained expression of a man weighed down with the chains of command. "Oprah is making her home in Montecito available for our use. We'll make the regional headquarters there work as best we can."

"But Oprah's not visiting Cali?"

"Apparently there are no immediate plans for her to do so."

CALEXIT
D+60

Enterprising members of the militia were buying property for water. It worked like this. There were literally millions of empty homes and you could move into any one of them. By transferring the deed to your house to the Militia, which divided them up, and relinquishing legal ownership, and squatting in another house of your choice, you could receive water that the militia had control over, remain in the area and barter for food, again from the militia, which controlled all of it for distribution as they saw fit.

When Larry Marcus arrived at Fort MacArthur, he found that the militia was a going concern and that warehouses on the waterfront had been annexed by the officers for the scavenged loot that they'd been swapping for food.

He didn't stop the practice, but he drew the line at trading gasoline. It kept the militia loyal, if focused on personal gain, and determined to defend what they were continuing to accumulate.

The officers didn't object too strenuously when he walked the warehouses and selected his cut of the purloined goods.

The fortified boundary of the redoubt had expanded as militia members chose the most desirable homes for themselves and installed water tanks for a gravity feed on each of them, absent pumping capacity. Diesel generators provided light to the facility and to the residences. Labor, which lived outside of the wire, worked for food and water, which arrived as relief supplies from other nations and were stored specifically for the use of the militia.

A regional governor had been appointed but his entourage was ambushed on the freeway on the way to Fort MacArthur by persons unknown, who used anti-tank rockets to punch through the armored cars. Larry Marcus used the opportunity to reinforce the intelligence that well-armed roving gangs had taken over much of the city, and that the militia lacked the strength of numbers, vehicles, fuel and ammunition to sally forth and take them on. Another governor, dispatched by sea, also met his end before he could arrive. Pirates infested the sea lanes around the formerly prosperous and populated city. At D+54, there were no more trusted members of the inner circle who would volunteer to act as an administration in Los Angeles and there had been talk of elevating Larry Marcus to Colonel and increasing his legal authority to one of viceroy for the People's Republic in Los Angeles.

CALEXIT
D+62

Colonel Marcus pinned the new eagle devices on his collars and looked into the mirror. Then he depressed a hidden catch on the mirror and it slid silently on hinges to expose a satellite telephone cradled in a charger.

He called preset #1 and heard a voice on the line, "Green Tree". He replied, "Blue Hummingbird. The progressive cipher would change the next time that it needed to be used with the query and the response shifting.

"Good morning Larry."

"Good morning. We are keeping to plan but I need more watercraft and crews to control sea lines and approaches, looking and behaving sufficiently like pirates. They need to sink a few of the aid ships that are arriving to jack up insurance rates and turn others around. We're getting so much in here, even working glacially on unloading, that I am running out of room."

"Understand and will advise."

Larry Marcus ended the connection.

CALEXIT
D+120

The militia lined up at Huntington Beach, arms stacked, wearing their best uniforms, and greeted the gray ships disgorging Landing Craft Air Cushion and Marines in their amphibious armored fighting vehicles. The U.S. arrived to save Cali from itself.

What a difference four months, and several million lives had wrought. The place was a ghost town. The social experiment ended. Order would be restored, services restored and the flags of the People's Republic of Cali would become trophies of a sort to insanity that infected and destroyed a region.

The rest of the state followed closely on the heels of the capitulation of Los Angeles.

The Authors

JL Curtis-

JL Curtis was born in Louisiana in 1951 and was raised in the Ark-La-Tex area. He began his education with guns at age eight with a SAA and a Grandfather that had carried one for 'work'. He began competitive shooting in the 1970s, an interest he still pursues time permitting. He is a retired Naval Flight Officer, having spent 22 years serving his country, an NRA instructor, a retired engineer in the defense industry, and now a starving author. He lives in North Texas, He currently has two series in work. The Grey Man, a Texas based current fiction series revolving around LEOs and Marines. And the Rimworld Series, started with a short story that was an Amazon Best Seller for five days after its release. His Novella, <u>The Morning the Earth Shook</u> is the genesis for the anthology. His Amazon Author page is <u>HERE</u>.

Bob Poole-

Bob Poole is a U.S. Army Gulf War Veteran, former Ford Autoworker and presently working in the aviation field, you can find him at <u>www.mydailykona.blogspot.com</u>

Cedar Sanderson-

Cedar Sanderson was born an Air Force brat in Nebraska and spent her childhood enroute to new duty stations. Her formative years after her father left the Air Force were spent being home-schooled on the Alaskan frontier. She removed to the "more urban" climes of New Hampshire at the beginning of high school. She has had the usual eclectic range of jobs for Fantasy/ SF authors, ranging from balloon twister to apprentice shepherdess. She counts the latter as more useful in controlling her four children and First Reader. Her fascination with science dates to her early childhood spent with her grandmother on the Oregon coast studying the flora and fauna and learning to prepare a meal from what she could glean from a tidal pool. This lead to a lifelong interest in science, cooking, and wildcrafting. Her Amazon Author page is HERE. http://amzn.to/2yJEqcS

Tom Rogneby-

Tom Rogneby is a curmudgeonly husband and father who spends his time in the wilds of suburban Louisville, Kentucky. He lives with his wife, children, cats, dogs, fish, and various transient outdoors mammals, reptiles, and amphibians. His hobbies include reading, shooting, playing with a nine-year-old (It's great to finally have a companion at his level), and writing. He is a veteran, and has gone to many exciting places to do many boring things. He blogs at

DaddyBear's Den, http://daddybearsden.com. His
Amazon Author page is HERE.
http://amzn.to/2z8dCzc

Alma TC Boykin-

Alma T. C. Boykin is a historian, lapsed pilot, and
writer who lives on the High Plains, as far from floods
as it is possible to get and still find flat ground. She
discovered military science fiction in high school after
growing up reading military history, and has never
recovered. She is the author of over 40 novels and
short stories. Her Amazon Author page is HERE.
http://amzn.to/2kPotvJ

B Opperman-

Born in Illinois and raised in rural Indiana. An
electronics engineer by training, he left that field and
ran his own business for 20+ years before selling out
and retiring. He's currently an NRA instructor and a
fledgling pilot. This is his first published story. He
would like to dedicate this story to his parents, Molly
and Skip, and Stephanie.

LB Johnson-

A former airline Captain, L.B. Johnson grew up out
West where she later received a doctorate in a
Criminal Justice related major - the field she works in
after hanging up her professional wings. She lives in
Chicago with her husband and rescue dog Abby

Normal Johnson. Mrs. Johnson donates 100% of her writing proceeds to animal rescue and Search Dog Foundation.

L.B. is two times Reader's Favorite International Book Award Winner - 2015 SILVER for the Amazon #1 Best Seller "The Book of Barkley - Love and Life through the Eyes of a Labrador Retriever" and 2017 GOLD for Christian Fiction "Small Town Roads".

Her second book - "Saving Grace - A Story of Adoption" was also a #1 bestseller at Amazon. Her Amazon Author page is HERE. http://amzn.to/2giMzxp

Eaton Rapids Joe-

Born in Lansing, Michigan in 1959. He graduated from Michigan State University with an engineering degree in 1981. Three decades of experience in the automotive industry with areas of expertise in design, engineering and manufacturing. Special interest in improving throughput and quality. In his retirement Eaton Rapids Joe blogs, writes, and gardens.

D. Lawdog-

Born in Malta, he learned his miscreant ways at the feet of oil engineers in Africa, then returned to the states as a teenager. Finishing his 'education' in Texas, he embarked on a career in law enforcement, and has over 20 years with Bugscuffle County, Texas. The author of two books, one detailing his law enforcement career, and one his childhood in Africa. They can be found via his Amazon Author page, HERE. http://amzn.to/2ylcMjv He continues his trenchant observations on life from The Law Dog Files blog, HERE.

Kimball O'Hara-

Formerly employed by the State of California, he is now making his own Calexit to greener pastures while he still can.

We hope you enjoyed our foray into the fictional near future. Thank you for reading, and honest reviews are appreciated. Our authors have a wide selection of books available for your reading pleasure, and they are all highly recommended!

JL Curtis

Made in the USA
San Bernardino, CA
14 November 2019

59901885R00228